Name and Number

Anchor and the Moon, Volume 3

Maxx Victor

Published by Maxx Victor, 2025.

NAME AND NUMBER

First edition October 2025

Written by Maxx Victor

To Harvey and Alex, the first victims of my stories.

Prologue

Perched atop the cliffs, a grand house overlooked the coastal haven of Heathcote. Moonlight painted silver trails upon the sprawling lawns and glistened from the ornate ironwork and towering walls, cold and solid. The sleepy town below would soon rise with the morning sun, its occupants blissfully unaware of the events unfolding within the grandeur of the hilltop mansion that loomed over them. In the chilly darkness, a young child sought sanctuary in the claustrophobic confines of her wardrobe. Her heart raced with fear as the echoes of a terrifying confrontation resonated through the opulent halls.

The child, her eyes wide and brimming with innocence, clutched her weathered teddy bear close to her chest. The stuffed animal, her sole confidant in a world teetering on the brink. Her tiny frame trembled with trepidation as she peered through a hole in her wardrobe door, a silent observer to the conflict between two titans from realms beyond her comprehension. The air within the mansion crackled with tension as the giants engaged in a dance of ethereal power. Her father, his face twisted with anger and rage, lunged at his adversary. The unknown intruder, with eyes glowing like embers amidst the dim of the room, struck back with unimaginable speed and ferocity. Claws clashed and fangs pierced the air, the mansion echoing with the primal symphony of supernatural combat.

Ghostly light filtered through the ornate windows of the girl's bedroom, casting an otherworldly glow over the battle that approached its crescendo. Her father, propelled by an unyielding paternal instinct, seized the intruder in a grip fuelled by sheer determination. The struggle intensified, both combatants teetering precariously close to the vast windows that framed the panoramic view of the sleepy coastal town below. As the first halo of sunlight cleared the horizon, the girl caught its glint in her father's fierce, dark eyes.

'Cinder! Cinder, hear me, my daughter!' he yelled in a deep, resonating growl of a voice. Every muscle in his great body strained to hold on to the creature that tore at his flesh with clawed fingers. 'You are so loved. Never forget that you are so very loved and deserved to be loved; always!'

In a heart-stopping moment, Cinder watched as her father's skin pulsed, and his body grew. The tattered remains of his blood-soaked pyjamas ripped open as he took his full Lycan form. Bellowing and with a powerful thrust, he propelled both himself and the shrieking creature through the window into the embrace of the burgeoning dawn.

As they descended, the first rays of sunlight met them, transforming the adversaries into fiery silhouettes against the canvas of the early morning sky. A symphony of crackling flames and anguished roars filled the air as vampire and Lycan alike succumbed to the relentless touch of daylight. The mansion fell silent, the remnants of a clash lingering like wisps of a nightmare. As the flames consumed both combatants and the scent of burning flesh and fur filled the dawn air, Cinder's world crumbled. The innocence of her childhood shattered, replaced by the stark reality that she was now alone.

. . . .

In the sitting room of the grand house, Cinder's stepmother Louvelle watched as the red glow flickered on the large windowpane. The glow illuminated the sharp angles of her face and long auburn hair. A twitching vein in her temple, the only sign of emotion. She turned to watch as Cinder, still gripping her teddy, walked slowly towards what was now just a pile of smouldering ashes. Sensing something approaching, Louvelle turned. Someone stood in the hallway, their boyish face shadowed. They looked like a child, yet Louvelle knew better.

'Which one are you?' she asked. The intruder eyed her carefully, but grinned.

'I am the third of my father's sons.' He emerged from the shadows. 'It appears that my brother is dead,' he said, tilting his head towards the window behind Louvelle.

Louvelle turned again to observe Cinder crouching beside the charred remains of her father and his attacker.

'As is my husband,' she said, turning away from the window and sitting casually on the arm of a brown leather armchair.

'That does not upset you?' the boy asked.

'It annoys me.' Louvelle adjusted her night-shirt. 'But it does present some opportunities,' she continued in a business-like tone. 'I know why you seek the child. You wish to bring about the New Mother.'

'What do you know of the New Mother?'

'You will find I know a great deal about many things.' Louvelle smirked.

'Are you going to attempt to stop me then, Lady Gevaudan?' the boy asked, taking a seat in a matching armchair opposite Louvelle. He looked even more innocent in the oversized chair. The grandeur of the sitting room dwarfed his small body. Louvelle remained impassive but kept her eyes ever focused on the intruder.

'And end up as a burnt heap, like my late husband out there?' she said. 'No, thank you very much. I've just had my nails done.' Louvelle held out her hand and inspected her dark-red nails. 'In fact,' she continued, resting her hands on her lap, 'if you have some time to spare, I have a proposition for you.'

'I have all the time in the world,' the boy replied.

Chapter 1
Broken Wings

• • • •

'Get your dirty paws off me!' Angus yelled, his words slurred. His naginata, a long rod with hidden blades, swept out aggressively at the dark, hairy mass in front of him. Trembling, his right hand struggled to hold the unsteady naginata. His left fist clasped the neck of a wine bottle, the contents of which gurgled and splash against the legs of his black jeans. A cool breeze played across his warm face. He had the beginnings of a dark beard, and his black hair had grown longer than he had ever worn it. Thick locks of it flicked against his pale skin. Before Cinder, he'd have called the large wolf-creature a werewolf; however, he now understood it was a Lycan. Whatever it was called, werewolf or Lycan, it growled with annoyance at the weapon waving in its face.

Putrid spittle shot into the moonlit sky, as teeth bit into the naginata. Angus lurched forward with the force of the powerful jaws slamming shut. The wine bottle fell from his grip and smashed on a nearby tree stump. 'Now look what you did, you idiot!' Angus yelled, looking down at the dark liquid splashed across his boots. He sent an aggressive but uncoordinated kick toward the Lycan, connecting with its hairy groin. With a howl, the beast toppled forward, pinning Angus to the ground. He could feel the moist earth in his hair and ears and could taste the rich soil that stuck between his teeth.

'You are really starting to piss me off,' he said between breaths. Silvery moonlight filtered through the trees, illuminating the beast's glistening teeth and dark eyes. The full weight of the Lycan was pushing down the weapon straddled across Angus's chest. Moist breath blew his dark hair from his face. Instinctively, he pushed up hard. He knew the next thing he would feel would be sharp teeth. The veins at the sides of his neck pulsed thick and blue.

'Dom! Where the hell are you?' He grunted as the enormous jaws snapped at his reddening face.

'I've got my own problems.'

Perspiration pooled on Don's brow and chest. Stumbling backwards through thick undergrowth a few metres away, he moved his two tomahawks back and forth, frantically deflecting the attacks of a trio of assailants.

'Where are the others?' Angus growled through gritted teeth. 'Where are Duncan and Tor?'

'I told you before. They are on the other side of the ridge. These bastards are everywhere tonight.' Dom said, as he rolled out of the path of a Lycan that had just leaped in his direction.

With biceps bulging, Angus's elbows crept slowly down each side of his body. He could feel the Lycan's warm breath against his face again, and he could smell it too. Blood – the thing had fed tonight.

'Dom!' He yelled again. 'This thing's about to bite my face off. Get over here!'

The Lycan's jaws snapped shut, razor-sharp teeth slamming together just centimetres from Angus's left ear. A drop of frothy saliva dripped onto Angus's brow. He shut his eyes and tried to roll the Lycan off. Man and beast tumbled onto their sides. A spike of adrenaline shot through Angus in a moment of panic, as his weapon slipped from his grip. He watched the Lycan roll away from him as he searched the dark ground for his naginata. The beast rose on all fours, preparing to pounce, but before it could, two pairs of hands grabbed it and threw it against a tree.

As Dom turned to see who the new arrivals were, someone ran past him. They launched into the air, sending a flying kick into the head of the nearest Lycan and sending it howling and stumbling backwards. Upon landing, a swift turn and kick secured another hit on the Lycan's head. The appearance of the unknown person, with impressive fighting skills, startled the third Lycan, distracting it long enough for Dom to bring the side of his tomahawk down on its snout. Shaking its head and whimpering in pain, it dropped to all fours and ran away into the forest. Dom turned back to see a young woman with shoulder-length, dark, wavy hair and exposed muscular arms. Pulling on a pair of fingerless gloves, she jumped surprisingly high for her short stature. She took hold of a branch and kicked both remaining Lycans in their snouts.

'I've got this handled,' she said. 'Go help Black.' The stranger knew Angus's nickname.

'Okay then,' Dom said, tilting his head to one side to watch her drop to the ground.

'Go!' she said with a wink and a wave.

Not wanting to be told a third time, Dom turned to find Angus. Raising his hand to shadow his eyes from the glow of the full moon, he could see Angus using his weapon as a prop to help him up from the ground. Several meters away, two lanky men restrained a struggling Lycan against a tree. Although they had their red hair styled differently, the two young men were clearly twins. The same smile shone on their freckled, angular faces.

'Rory! Tavish!' Dom yelled, throwing his arms up in the air. They were his two younger cousins. He had not seen them since they had travelled north to be with their mother. 'Where did you two bastards come from?'

'Hey there, Dom,' the twins responded in unison. 'Uncle Gunn said you could do with some help.'

'No,' Dom said, waving away the suggestion like it was nonsense and making his way towards them. 'We had them right where we wanted them. Right, Black?' he patted Angus on his shoulder. Ignoring Dom and the twins, Angus lifted his naginata and brought the end down on the back of the Lycan's head with a crack. The beast went limp in Rory's and Tavish's hands.

'That's a bit harsh, mate,' Dom said, watching Angus as he walked away from the unconscious Lycan.

'Where did you two come from?' Angus asked without acknowledging Dom.

'Dad got a call from Gunn last week, so we decided to come back and help out for a bit,' Tavish said.

'No one told us about that,' Angus said in annoyance.

'We thought you'd be happy to see us. It looks like you have your hands full here,' Rory said.

'We're fine.' Angus said as he walked to the tree line, squinting to peer into the darkness.

'Don't worry about mister grumpy-pants,' Dom said, placing his hand on Rory's shoulder. 'We're happy to see you. And talking about happy to see you...' He watched as the mystery woman kicked the backside of a retreating Lycan. 'Who is that?'

'Down boy,' Tavish said. 'That's Alice.'

'Alice? Alice who?' Dom asked, running his eyes up and down the young woman as she walked towards them, smiling, and catching her breath.

'Alice Kinnard,' Rory said.

'As in, *your cousin Alice.*' Tavish added, and the twins laughed. Dom's shoulders dropped.

'Oh.'

Alice sat on a nearby tree stump and crossed her legs.

'Good evening boys,' she said. 'Remember me?'

'Of course,' Dom said, slipping his tomahawks into his belt. 'But you look... you look different.'

'Well, I should hope so.' Alice placed her hands on her hips. 'I was just a kid then.' She pushed her hair out of her face. 'What about you Black? Do you remember me?' she asked, giving her hair a ruffle.

'Sure, I do. Little Alice Kinnard. How did you get roped into coming here?' Angus asked.

'I wanted to come and see you.' Alice ran her eyes up his tall frame. 'You and my cousins. It's been too long.'

'Alice has been staying with us while her parents have been travelling.' Tavish said.

With only a muffled growl as a warning, the Lycan threw the twins off. Tavish crashed into the tree trunk, dislodging a shower of dry pine needles. The Lycan's attack sent Rory tumbling down a small embankment, and his left leg ended up sunk knee-deep in a boggy patch of ground he hadn't noticed until his boot squelched in the cold, damp mud.

'These are new boots!' he complained as the Lycan ran for freedom. The beast leapt the bog, forcing Rory to duck. A large hairy foot splashed down hard in the shallows on the opposite side. Mud and stagnant water splashed up Rory's left side and across his face.

'Are you serious?' he yelled, spitting the foul, earthy taste from his mouth. He wiped his face with his sleeve, but before he could remove the first layer of mud, a second volley of the undesirable substance erupted his way. Angus's large boot landed with a moist slap next to the print left by the fleeing Lycan. Rory threw his hands in the air, glowering at Angus's dark silhouette as it hurried down the hill towards Heathcote.

'Come on!' he called out after him.

With the dark shadows of the hilltop forest flashing past on his left and the twinkling lights of Heathcote far below to his right, Angus ran. His arms pumped ferociously, his weapon swinging back and forth, held tight in a white knuckled grip. Usually, he would have no hope of keeping pace with a Lycan in the open like this, but he could see it stumbling and falling on the uneven terrain, obviously still affected by being knocked unconscious moments before. Angus hoped it would turn back to the forest, where he would be the nimbler of the two. He knew he could weave in and out of the trees more successfully.

As though hearing his thoughts, the Lycan turned to the right and downhill towards the town. Angus cursed under his breath and leaped from the top of a large grey rock protruding from the hillside. As Heathcote and the dark ocean beyond loomed closer, the moon illuminated the slanting roofline of a large building. Shortly, Angus could see the gardens of the Heathcote Community Hospital below him, the place where he and Cinder had first kissed; that is if you didn't count her trying to give him mouth to mouth resuscitation.

Long weeds slapped against his shins and his feet slid and squeaked on the moist grass. It was difficult to keep his footing. At one point, he fell to one knee. Cursing at himself, he stumbled to his feet again and continued the pursuit. The Lycan ran on all fours along the top of a stone wall that formed the eastern boundary of the gardens. Pushing himself on, Angus came close enough to hear the raspy breaths and the tapping of the thick claws on the stones. He gripped his naginata in both hands and readied himself to strike.

With a yelp, the Lycan's right hind leg slipped from the wall, sending it flailing in a hairy mass down the three-metre drop. Angus skidded to a stop in the loose gravel atop the wall. A tall palm tree curved its way up from the manicured lawns of the gardens below. Large branches hung limply above Angus's head, blocking out the glow of the moon. Angus threw his weapon onto the grass. He gripped the trunk with his large hands, pushed his feet against the tree, and slid down into the gardens.

The Lycan stumbled on one of the gravel paths, sending a cloud of red dust and stones into the air. Seconds later, Angus's heavy leather boots crunched and pounded on the same path, his weapon once again held firm in his left hand. With the orange brick walls of the hospital behind them now, man and beast puffed and grunted their way through the beds of ferns, rhododendrons, and orchids. Trying to gain distance on the Lycan, Angus leaped over a low garden bed and ran at an intersecting angle with his prey.

There were two rules they lived by when hunting. One was 'No killing', and two, 'Never let the beasts make it to town'. At that moment, Angus felt inclined to break the first rule, but was damned sure he would not break the second. The snaking paths and wood-chipped gardens opened up to a large area of lawn. The moist grass glistened in the moonlight. Only a few metres of flat remained before the hill fell away sharply to the west and down to the town below. Angus could see the blue glow of the police station sign over the crest. He was getting close enough to the Lycan now to see that it was only running on three of its limbs, its left front paw held protectively against its large bony chest. It must have hurt itself when it fell. *Good*, Angus thought.

Within reaching distance for his weapon, Angus dared an attack. He swung his naginata in a wide arc, hoping to land it on the back of the Lycan's head. Halfway through the manoeuvre, his foot skidded on the wet, inclining grass. His naginata slipped from his grip and flew towards the beast. It struck the Lycan just behind its ear, hard enough to knock it off course, but not enough to stop it. Angus slipped and fell to one knee, a jarring numb sensation running up his thigh as he hit the ground. He rolled over on his right shoulder then back to his feet again. His leg, still numb, refused to take his weight, and he fell straight back to the ground, tumbling down the hillside that was now inclining steeply towards the buildings below. There was a second stone wall at the base of the hill. This wall, unlike the garden wall, was quite low. Angus tumbled over the ledge. Falling with a grunt to the stony gravel below.

To his surprise, the Lycan crashed to the ground a few metres ahead of him. Angus forced himself onto one leg and looked around frantically for his lost weapon. It sat in a tuft of grass just above the wall. Limping and angry, he pulled himself up against the wall and reached out desperately. The tips of his fingers just touching the end of the naginata. With another effort, he pinched the weapon with the tips of his thumb and index finger. Grunting, and with cold sweat pooling on his back, he dragged the weapon across the grass until he clasped it in his hand. Hobbling, he craned his neck, searching for the beast's path, then heard a crash followed by glass shattering. Willing his numb leg to cooperate, he ran towards the commotion.

A small, caged object that hummed and crackled, as it ended the lives of insects attracted by the light it emitted, hung from the eaves of a dark grey building. In the dull blue glow, Angus spotted a broken and bent door at the rear of the narrow wall. Colourful strips of plastic hung from the top of the now open doorway to the dusty floor. The strips flicked and clicked together in the breeze. Angus use the end of his naginata to push the strips to the side, trying to enter as quietly as possible. In the darkness, he could just make out rows of large bags, tins, and glass bottles lined up on metal shelves against one wall. A large metal basin, bathed in moonlight from a small window, sat in the far-right corner. A bucket and mop rested next to the basin, and a pair of disposable rubber gloves sat over the end of the mop handle. Ahead was another doorway that led into a darkened space. Angus peered into the next room then advanced cautiously. As he reached the darkened doorway, someone screamed, yelling in a language that he didn't understand. Angus ran forward into the darkness. An enormous shadow rose in front of him.

Without hesitating to determine if it was the Lycan or another entity, he thrust the blunt end of his naginata toward where he believed a Lycan's head might be. A hollow sounding thud followed by a pained and throaty growl confirmed he had hit his target. He sent another blow in the same direction. With the crash of tins and smashing of glass, the shadow fell to the ground. Hairy flesh slapped against the solid floor. The crushing of falling objects continued for a few seconds then ended with something unforeseen in the darkness that sounded like a large coin spinning on a tabletop before coming to rest. Behind Angus, a light switch clicked. Bright light filled the room as two sets of fluorescent lights flickered to life. Angus cringed away and covered his eyes with his arm.

'I knew they were real!' a voice said over by the light switch. 'Grandfather tried to tell all of you, but everyone thought he was crazy. I always believed him though.' When his eyes had adjusted to the light, Angus turned to see that the voice belonged to Ken Woo, the owner of the fish and chip shop.

Many years earlier, Ken's Grandfather – the original Mr Woo (or Wu before he westernised the spelling) – had claimed that he had cut the tip off the tail of a large beast that had been trying to attack his chickens. The locals had all thought Mr Wu was just a crazy old man. The rumours that had started from that were the reason Angus and his kin had come to live in Heathcote. Angus had never seen an expression like the one on Ken's face. It was somewhere between triumph and absolute horror. He stood with his back pushed up hard against the wall, one hand still trembling on the light switch and a large kitchen knife held firmly in the other.

'That's one of them, isn't it?' Ken said, looking down wide-eyed at the hairy mass, prostrate on the floor amongst broken sauce bottles and dented soda cans. The Lycan's blood-red tongue hung limply between its razor-sharp, canine-like teeth. Its large chest rose and fell in time with its shallow, raspy breaths. Angus didn't answer what he assumed was Ken's rhetorical question. Surely having a giant wolf-like creature crashing through your shop at 1am was confirmation enough. He stepped towards the Lycan with both hands gripped tightly around his weapon. Sliding one end of the naginata under one of the Lycan's arms, he lifted it then dropped it to the floor again. No reaction. He stepped back and relaxed. A knock on the glass front door sprung him back to attention.

'Mr Woo, are you alright?' came a call from outside. 'It's Detective Morgan. I heard a commotion.'

Angus looked at Ken, but Ken did not move from his position against the wall.

'Peter, it's me, Black,' Angus said, stepping carefully around the unconscious Lycan. Peter Morgan took a moment to reply.

'If you're in there, Mr MacAskill, then maybe I don't want to know.'

Angus had to take another long stride across the Lycan to get to the door. As he did, a growl rose from below him. One of the beast's dark eyes shot open. Angus twisted his hands on the staff of his naginata. A thin blade shot from the end. He lifted his weapon above the Lycan's neck and stabbed it down.

· · · ·

The sun dipped low on the horizon, casting a warm, golden glow over a large city harbour. Dark water shimmered like liquid diamonds, reflecting the hues of the setting sun. The iconic Sydney Opera House stood proudly against the skyline, its iconic curved roof capturing the last rays of daylight. As evening settled in, the city lights began to twinkle, painting the harbor in a magical dance of colours. The hum of urban life filled the air. Ferries criss-crossed the waters, leaving trails of gentle ripples in their wake. On the waterfront, people gathered at trendy cafes and waterfront promenades. Laughter floated over the harbour as friends shared stories, food, and coffee. Musicians strummed guitars, adding a melodious soundtrack to the vibrant scene. The scent of saltwater mingled with the tantalizing aroma of the many varied foods being prepared and consumed, creating a sensory tapestry.

As a backdrop, the Harbour Bridge stretched across the water like a giant steel ribbon. A sleek and elegant structure, its steel beams glinted in the red of the dying sunlight, a symbol of hope and progress, connecting the bustling city to the world beyond. It was a place of new beginnings, where people came to make their dreams a reality, or perhaps to escape their nightmares. As the sun set and the city lights ignited, the bridge became a magical wonderland. It was a place of romance, where couples came to share a first kiss or make plans for their future. It was a place of adventure, where thrill-seekers could walk or climb to the top and enjoy the breathtaking views.

For a lost child, however, the giant structure was a terrifying, looming thing.

The bright lights, a thing of beauty to others, only made it more frightening. The cold, hard metal creaked and rumbled as the traffic zoomed by. The water below looked black and deep, and they couldn't help but think about falling in. To a child, out alone, the bridge seemed to go on forever, and they didn't know where it led. The wind made ghoulish noises as it whistled through the metal struts.

In the shadow of the giant structure, one such child walked – a young boy, alone. His eyes darted nervously, wide with a mixture of fear and confusion. The vibrant energy of the city seemed to swallow him whole as he clutched a crumpled piece of paper in his trembling hands. His footsteps echoed against the pavement, a stark contrast to the laughter and music that surrounded him. He glanced up at the bridge, its grandeur casting a shadow over him. Hesitating at the edge of the promenade, he watched as couples shared tender moments and families revelled in the joy of the evening.

The lights that transformed the bridge into a wonderland only intensified the darkness that clung to the edges of his world. As he approached the bridge, its steel beams towered above him like a fortress. The city's symphony of life became a distant murmur, drowned out by the eerie sounds of the wind weaving through the metal struts. His slight frame seemed even smaller against the vastness of the structure. A train rumbled overhead. The boy turned his gaze upwards but dropped his eyes to the ground again as a bat, with a wingspan almost as wide as he was tall, glided overhead.

The boy clutched the crumpled paper tighter, glancing around as if expecting someone to appear and guide him through this urban maze. Each step he took was hesitant, as if the ground beneath him might give way. The water below, which shimmered so beautifully in the dying sunlight, now looked like an abyss that threatened to swallow him whole. The curved sail-like shapes of the iconic opera house loomed large and white behind him but cast ghostly shapes in the turbulent harbour. He turned away from the water, crossing at a zebra crossing like his father had taught him.

Dark buildings enclosed him on both sides and the street fell into shadow and grew quiet. A short distance further, he turned down a cobblestoned, single-lane street. Tall sandstone walls towered up on both sides. The wet ground glistened, turning from green to red under the streetlights and casting shimmering reflections on the cold walls. Two young men walking arm in arm and laughing passed him on the opposite side of the road. Turning to look at the boy, their laughter died down as they looked him over. It was uncommon to see a child this well dressed wondering the streets alone late at night, but the couple decided it was no concern of theirs and continued on. The young boy turned to watch them go, but continued forward. Coming to the end of the narrow street, he turned down a lane darker and more claustrophobic than the way he had come. A collection of large green bins lined one side of the laneway. Their overflowing contents, reeking of stale coffee and decomposing food, littered the moist ground.

As the boy went deeper in, the laneway inclined at a steep gradient. He had to stomp his feet to stop himself from running forward.

The traffic sounds died away to a low rumble, replace by the chatter of several voices. Another tall wall loomed up at the end of the laneway. The surface of the wall had once been a gun-metal grey but was now covered with an array of street-art and tags. A picture of a partially naked woman with a pig's head covered most of the dead-end wall. A second-floor balcony of rusted metal jutted out into the alley, providing shelter to a group of people below.

'Are you lost, kid?' came the voice of one of the people gathered in the shadows. The boy could make out about a dozen people of different shapes and sizes. Some of them were standing while others crammed onto a thread-bare and dirty sofa they had shoved into the dry corner of the alley. A small fire burned in the drum of an old washing machine, casting ghostly shadows that gave the appearance that the pig-lady might be moving. Black smoke rose from the drum and mixed with the smoke that was coming from the cigarettes and vapes that the members of the group were holding.

'I'm looking for my mother,' the boy said calmly. A figure rose from the sofa and came towards the boy. Her face was worn and lined, despite her youthful clothing and walk. She took a drag of her cigarette and blew the smoke out of the side of her mouth as she looked the boy up and down.

'No mummies here, kid,' she said, flicking her cigarette at his feet.

'He might be yours, Rach, you slut!' One of the others yelled. The young woman, Rach, smiled. Without turning to see who had called out to her, she raised her hand and stuck her middle finger up towards the group. Sniggers and wolf whistles echoed around the alley.

'Can you help me find her?' the boy asked, taking a step closer and pulling at the hem of his jacket.

'Piss off, kid!' a boy in a red cap standing by the fire yelled.

'No, no, it's okay kid,' Rach said, taking a cigarette lighter from her hip pocket and turning it over in her hands. 'We'll help you, but it's gonna cost you. You got any cash?'

'Money?' the boy asked. Rach laughed and looked back at the others.

'Yep, money. Got any?' she said, taking a step closer to him. The boy was still holding the crumbled paper against his chest. He pulled a colourful card from what Rach could now see was an envelope.

'It's my birthday today, and I got some money in a card. How much do you need?' the boy said, holding the card in a trembling hand.

'All of it,' Rach said, striking the lighter to life and moving the flame back and forth in front of her. The flame illuminated her thin face, her eyes deep-set in dark circles.

'No,' the boy said.

'No?'

'No! You can't have all my birthday money.' The boy started to slide the card back into the envelope, but Rach shot forward, snatching it from his hand. As Rach pulled the envelope into the air, the colourful card with a picture of a dog holding balloons slid out. The card fell to the ground quickly, but fluttering down after it were several green notes. The boy got down on his knees to pick up the money. When he took hold of the first note, Rach stood on his hand.

'Ow, you're hurting me!' he yelled. Rach ignored him and turned back to the others.

'There must be five hundred dollars here!' she called out. The others moved forward, but stopped as someone else entered the alleyway.

'Do you need some help, little boy?' a female voice asked. She wore all black and stood tall on heeled boots. A long jacket hung to her knees and a large hood shadowed her face. She walked in an arc behind the boy and stood on the smouldering cigarette that Rach had disposed of a few minutes earlier. She twisted the toe of her boot to snub it out.

'Do you need my help?' she asked again, moving her head from side to side. The sniggering rose again from the gang of youths.

'The only one that needs some help is you, lady,' the boy in the red cap said. Wordlessly, half of the group moved down the walls of the alley and behind the woman, blocking her exit.

'Get off me!' the boy said in a commanding tone. Rach dropped her head and took a step backwards. The boy, still on his hands and knees on the ground, grinned. Shortly his grin grew into a laugh, not a childish laugh but a triumphant, calculating, evil laugh.

'Yes, you can help me,' he said, turning his head to look at the woman in black. 'I'm hungry.'

'I don't have any food,' the lady said, pulling her gloved hands from her coat pockets and holding them out in front of her. Pale white skin appeared between the cuffs of her sleeves and her gloves. The boy eyed the blue veins just below the surface of her soft skin.

'Oh yes, you do,' he said, licking his lips. His chin dropped slowly and as it did, the canines on his top row of teeth grew long and pointed.

• • • •

Standing over the unconscious Lycan on the floor of Mr Woo's shop, Angus brought the blade of his weapon down towards the beast's exposed neck. Instead of finding flesh, the blade clanged down on something solid and metallic, ringing out like a blacksmith's hammer against their anvil. The blade veered off target, slashing the Lycan's shoulder.

'What the hell are you doing, Black?' It was Dom. He was lying, sweaty and breathless across the Lycan, his outstretched arm holding one of his tomahawks over its neck. The Lycan twitched under him as blood dripped from the wound and mixed with the debris on Ken's floor. Dom grabbed the Lycan's arm with his free hand.

'Put your blade away and get the door!' He barked up at Angus. Angus stepped towards the door but turned at the last moment and kicked the Lycan in the back of its head. Blood from its shoulder splattered across Dom's red face.

'Oh yeah, real nice!' he yelled as the Lycan went limp again under him.

With a flick of his wrists, Angus's blade retracted into the staff of the naginata. He propped it against the store window and opened the door. Detective Peter Morgan stood on the other side, his face, as usual, held stern and serious. His eyes, full of intensity and intelligence, shot around the room, analysing the situation before he entered. He held his Police-issued Glock 22 in both hands. 'Why is Mr Kinnard laying across the body of a werewolf in Mr Woo's shop in the early am?' he asked, stepping inside.

'You know me,' Dom said, getting to his feet. 'I'm into all kinds of kinky stuff.'

Angus and detective Morgan kept straight faces, but Ken gave a nervous laugh from behind him. Dom turned to look at Ken. 'Oh, hi Ken. I didn't realise you were here too,' he said.

'It looks like it's still breathing,' Detective Morgan said, assessing the situation.

'Yes, with no thanks to Black,' Dom said as the Lycan moved and let out a sound somewhere between a snore and a growl. Angus grabbed his weapon again.

'Move out of the way and I'll finish the job,' he said, stepping back towards Dom and the Lycan. Detective Morgan turned his weapon towards Angus.

'Everyone, just calm the hell down,' Dom said, raising his hand towards the others. 'No one's killing anything.'

'Since when do you care about them?' Angus asked, walking slowly past the beast.

'I don't care, but I do care about how you're going to feel about this tomorrow when you sober up.' Dom stood to face him.

'Just as well I don't intend to get sober.'

Angus retracted his blade and shouldered his way past Dom to the back room. The others could hear him fumbling around in the darkness. Shortly, he stuck his head back through the doorway.

'Can I have this, Ken?' he asked, holding up a half-full bottle of bourbon.

'Yes, please. It's yours.' Ken was still against the wall. He still held the knife, but now his arms hung limply at his sides.

'Can someone explain what's happening here?' Detective Morgan interrupted as he holstered his weapon.

'Black chased this one in here, like an idiot,' Dom said.

'It's not my fault it was too stupid to run back to the forest,' Angus said, taking a swig of the bourbon. 'And then it fell down the wall of the gardens,' he added, wiping his chin.

'You could have stopped chasing it.'

'And you can keep your opinions to yourself.' Angus raised the bottle in front of Dom's face. Dom pushed him away.

'Okay, okay.' Detective Morgan said. 'Let's work out what we're going to do about it now. Is it going to live?' he asked, looking at the puddle of blood next to the hairy body on the floor. Dom stepped over the Lycan and stood next to the detective.

'He'll heal up fine, but he's going to have a splitting headache in the morning. Can you cuff him and put him in a cell, out of the moonlight for the night?'

'Here,' Detective Morgan said, pulling handcuffs from his belt and handing them to Dom. 'You can cuff it. I'm not going anywhere near it.'

'I'm glad it was you and not O'Burket.' Dom said, kneeling next to the Lycan. 'This wouldn't be that easy to explain.'

'Do you know how to use those?' Detective Morgan asked, watching as Dom pulled the beast's limp arms behind its back. Dom sent him a mischievous grin.

'Oh yeah. Like I said before, kinky things.'

'I knew it! I knew they were real,' Ken said from the back of the store. 'Everyone thought my grandfather was crazy, but I always believed him.'

'Now, Ken,' Dom said, fitting the cuffs around the Lycan's large hairy wrists. 'You can't tell anyone about this.'

'Tell anyone,' Ken said. 'No way! It's taken twenty years for people to stop calling us the 'Crazy Woos'. I'm not telling anyone about this.'

'If we don't get them under control,' Detective Morgan said, nodding towards the Lycan on the floor. 'Then everyone will know about them anyway.' He opened the door and held it for Dom.

The waves crashed on the shoreline below, but it was otherwise a still and quiet night. Dom lifted the Lycan, carrying it like a child that had fallen asleep on a car ride – a seven-foot-tall child with a covering of thick brown hair.

'Marraine says they won't calm down without a queen,' he said as he squeezed the beast out through the door. Its head hit the door frame and its long tongue slid from its mouth. Dom paused as it growled, but did not regain consciousness.

'Speaking of that,' Detective Morgan said, as he stepped back and held the door open with the tips of his fingers. 'Has there been any news about Miss Delacourt?' he asked. Dom shook his head.

'No one has seen or heard from her since the fire. Marraine says she is trying to get access to her accounts to see if anyone is using them. She might be dead.'

'She's not dead!' Angus yelled from the back of the store. His voice booming in the quiet of the night. Dom and the Detective glowered at him then looked back at the Lycan in Dom's arms.

'Then, where is she?' Dom asked, in a whispered yell, watching as Angus marched out of the back door. He saw him take one more swig, the bottle glowing in the blue light of the insect killer. 'Are you going home?' Dom asked when Angus didn't answer his first question. Angus turned to look back at Dom and shrugged.

'I don't have a home,' he muttered to himself, then turned and walked away into the darkness.

• • • •

What moments before had been the laughter of a small child, now grew into a hyena-like cackle that reverberated around the walls of the alleyway. The woman in black watched as his smooth childish features changed to something animalistic and grotesque. Shadows from the firelight accentuated his angular cheekbones and prominent brow. The orange flames flickered in pupils that had grown large enough to fill his eyes with black. With the skill and speed of an experienced predator, the boy leaped at the woman. To his surprise, however, she moved faster still, side-stepping his attack. As he crashed into the wall behind where she had just been standing, the woman flew behind Rach and wrapped her arm around her neck. From near the fire, two youths ran to help; the woman countered with a swift kick to the groin and elbow to the face. Both youths fell to the ground, moaning in pain. Rach struggled in the woman's grip, yelling and cursing and calling her every horrible name under the sun. Cautiously, the rest of the youths closed in on the stranger.

'Tell them all to get back,' the woman said. 'I'm here for you. No one else needs to get hurt.'

'I don't know what you mean,' the boy said coyly, dusting off his clothes. 'This girl was going to hurt me. Why would they do anything I say?'

'You can cut the helpless little boy act,' the woman said, tightening her grip around Rach's neck. 'I know what you are and that these are your followers.' With her free hand, she pulled back the collar of Rach's shirt to reveal two small puncture marks surrounded by purple and yellow bruising. Like the flick of a switch, the boy's persona changed. He stood tall with his shoulders set back. He suddenly looked much older. Holding his hands behind his back, he strolled, slowly circling the woman. He gestured for the youths to step back. They complied; their heads dropped submissively.

'It appears you have me at a bit of a disadvantage,' he said, pausing to look into the flames that danced at the bottom of the drum. 'It would seem that you know what I am, but I don't know you.' He sniffed the air. 'Werewolf? Nephilim maybe? You certainly move like one of the Lycanthropes, but you have the air of arrogance of the Nephilim.' He continued to move around her until he was in front of her once more. 'So, what are you, girl?' he spat, running his eyes down her body. The woman leaned her head back, her mouth visible in the glow from the fire. As she did, a lock of red hair sprung from inside her hood. Opening her mouth, two sharp fangs appeared, white and glistening in the low light. The boy took a step backwards towards the mouth of the alley.

'Sister?' he asked, his eyes wide and his hands dropping to his side. The hooded woman hissed.

'No! I am not Sase,' she said, indignant.

'What then?' the boy's voice cracked. Rach had stopped struggling in the woman's arms. In fact, fear had frozen her to the spot. The woman released her and slid back her hood. Long red hair cascaded down her shoulders.

'There are some that call me Queen,' she said, walking towards the boy, pushing Rach forward. 'I have been a daughter, a friend, a lover. There is one that calls me Sweetie.' The boy backed away, looking over his shoulder.

'The mother!' he yelled.

'Oh yes, I am a mother now,' she paused to think. 'That is to say, the girl I once was, she was a mother. Her name escapes me at the moment.' Her eyes grew dark. She glared at the retreating boy. 'But you, vampire... You can call me *vengeance*.'

The vampire in the body of a small boy, pulled one of his followers in front of him and pushed them towards her.

'No step-mommy to help you now, little Miss Delacourt,' he said, for he knew who she was now; even if she couldn't remember herself.

She was Cinder, the mother of Annabelle.

Cinder, the Lycan Queen; the one who they had called The Queen of Hearts.

She was Cinder who had died protecting her daughter and been reborn as a vampire. Reborn into this new monstrous body that held her troubled mind captive. Trapped in her vengeance and self-loathing.

'You're a long way from home,' he continued, a vicious smile on his twisted face.

'I don't have a home.' Cinder said, grabbing the street kid and wrapping him in her powerful arms.

'Get her!' The boy-vampire commanded as he turned and fled into the darkness of the alley, tipping over one of the large bins as he flew past.

'I found you once, I'll find you again,' Cinder called after him, grinning as the gang of youths rushed in and over her, like ants to a fallen crumb of food. 'Tell your father I've come for him too. I'm coming for all of you.'

Chapter 2
Ashes and Wine.

The farmhouse smelled like cinnamon, cloves, and sweet orange peel. Alice leaned over the wide timber bench, her sleeves rolled to the elbows, pressing sticky handfuls of fruit and spice into a bowl while Uncle Gunn read aloud from a faded recipe card.

'Don't forget the whiskey, love. The cake won't keep wi'out it,' Gunn said, holding up the bottle like a sacred relic. Alice smirked, wiping her hands on a tea-towel.

'It'll keep just fine. You just want an excuse to open that bottle before dinner.'

Gunn chuckled, pouring a small splash into the mix and a larger one into a chipped mug for himself.

The kitchen door creaked open and Torry stepped in, her hair windblown and cheeks flushed, with Annabelle balanced on one hip and a baby bottle in the other.

'Here're my girls,' Gunn said, stepping forward to kiss Torry's cheek, then gently ruffling Annabelle's soft curls. 'How's my Little Red?'

Giggling, Annabelle reached for Gunn's spectacles.

Torry rolled her eyes and handed the baby to him. 'What are you drinking, dad?'

'I'm just checking the flavour,' he said, taking another drink. Torry moved next to Alice and dipped her finger in the batter.

'Hey cuz, I heard you were here,' she said, sticking her finger in her mouth. Alice smiled and looked up at Torry.

'Hey Torry. You're taller than me now.'

'It's been years since you were last here,' Torry said. 'I'm just glad there's another girl around. The testosterone levels in this house are getting dangerous.'

Alice laughed. 'Happy to bring some balance.' She reached to tickle Annabelle under the chin, and the baby squealed. 'So, why isn't Angus watching her today?'

There was a beat of silence. Torry's smile faded slightly. Gunn cleared his throat.

'He needed some space.'

'He's at The Big House again, isn't he?' Torry asked.

Gunn glanced at her, then nodded. 'Yeah. I reckon so.'

Alice looked down at the dough in front of her. 'He always goes there alone?'

Gunn sighed, adjusting Annabelle in his arms. 'That place still has a hold on him.'

· · · ·

The crumbled and scorched husk of the once-grand mansion loomed before Angus, a sombre reminder of the inferno that had consumed it. The fire left behind blackened walls and a crumbled roof, with only twisted metal remaining of the ornate balustrades. Although the smoke had cleared long ago, the air was still thick with its scent. This had been her home, the girl he loved, and the sight before him was a grim reminder of the tragedy that had taken place. With a swig from a half-empty wine bottle, Angus continued to stroll past the overgrown and unkempt gardens. He couldn't help but think about the life that had once been lived within these walls. Although she had wanted to escape this place, Angus still remembered good times shared with Cinder here. Being tied to a chair in her library as she yelled at him in anger would be preferable to the way things were now. But that chair and that library were gone; it was all gone, reduced to nothing but a shell of its former self. The fireplace that had serviced the grand sitting room and its accompanying chimney remained intact. Reaching to the sky like a red-bricked obelisk memorialising the once-noble building that stood there. Ironic, An-

gus thought, that the place that was built to contain the fire remained as all around it burnt to the ground.

The last rays of ochre light stretched their way across the hilltop
expanse where The Big House had sat proudly for over 150 years.
Long shadows like dark tendrils reached out over the devastation,
adding to the ethereal feeling. Something metallic flickered in the
dying sunlight. Angus sat the wine bottle down and walked carefully
across the ash and debris. He lifted a twisted and blackened piece of
a once-ornate balustrade out of the way. Ash dusted his face, making him blink. A silver fork from Louvelle's expensive dinner-set lay
amongst the rubble. Remarkably, it looked clean and ready to be set
on the table. Angus picked it up, marvelling that it had survived the
fire and the looters that had frequented the ruins in the months after
the police had concluded their investigation.

'What a mess.' A female voice spoke from behind him. Angus's
heart skipped a beat. For a moment he thought… hoped. He turned
to see a female figure walking towards him, silhouetted in the low
sun. No, not Cinder. Too short and too curvaceous. Angus raised his
hand to shadow his vision. Alice's round, smiling face came into focus. 'I never got to see this place up close.' She stood with her hands
on her hips, surveying the scene. 'It must have been something.'

'It was impressive,' Angus said, tapping the fork against his chin.
'Beautiful and a bit scary, actually.'

'Where is she?' Alice asked, taking a step closer.

'Where is who?' Angus slipped the fork into the back pocket of
his black jeans.

'The girl who lived here – Annabelle's mother.'

'How do you know this was her house?' Angus asked as he took
long, cautious strides out of the rubble. Alice walked forward to
meet him and stood close beside him, looking over the destruction.
After a moment, she turned to him.

'A picture paints a thousand words,' she said, waving her hand over him. 'So where is she?'

'No one knows,' Angus mumbled, kicking the heel of his boot against a charred section of wall. 'If you ask Dom, she's dead and her ashes are a part of this mess.'

'Do you think she's dead?'

Angus looked around the blackened remains of The Big House, then up to the moon that was just visible in the reddening-grey sky. He shook his head.

'The police did find some bodies when they went through the place. Too burnt to tell, but they were fairly sure they weren't female.'

'Hopefully they were some of the wolves,' Alice said.

'Lycan,' Angus corrected her.

'Same thing,' Alice said, whacking his chest with the back of her hand. Angus opened his mouth to correct her, but closed it again.

'So, you've met Annabelle?' he asked instead.

'Yep. Torry introduced her to me when I was helping Uncle Gunn this afternoon. She's very cute.'

'Yes, she is,' Angus smiled proudly to himself. 'Thank you for helping out too. You turned up just in time.'

'You would have been fine.' Alice said, placing her hand on Angus's shoulder. 'You've always been the strongest of us.' Her hand moved down to his ample biceps.

'I don't know. They had us on the ropes,' Angus said, taking a step back. Alice dropped her hand, holding her bottom lip between her teeth. She was much shorter than Angus; compact, but packed with a fullness that made her seem larger than life. Her eyes sparkled with a mischievous gleam, and her smile was large and bright. Rich chestnut hair cascaded down her back in soft waves. Other than a scar that cut her left eyebrow in two, her skin was as smooth as porcelain. A small patch of freckles dotted her nose and cheeks, giving her an air of innocence. She wore a casual outfit, a fitted tank top, and form-fitting shorts that strategically clung to her curves.

'I heard that one of them got you pretty bad a while ago,' she said.

'Yeah,' Angus rubbed the back of his neck. 'I've still got the scars to prove it.'

'Show me.' Alice stepped to him and pulled at the bottom of his shirt.

Angus could feel his cheeks warming as Alice gripped his shirt tighter. 'We've just met and you're already trying to get my clothes off,' he joked.

'Just met?' Alice dropped her head to the side. 'We've known each other since we were kids.'

'Yes, but I mean, I don't know you like this.'

'Like what?' Alice asked, moving closer and dropping her voice so it was almost a whisper. Angus swallowed.

'Like...' he looked Alice up and down. 'Like an adult.'

Alice's eyes gleamed as she looked at Angus. She took hold of the sleeve of his t-shirt.

'Take your shirt off,' she purred, her voice low and husky.

Angus hesitated, a flicker of uncertainty. Alice persisted. 'Come on, I'm just messing with you.' She let go of his sleeve. 'It's nothing I haven't seen before. We used to have baths together when we were kids,' she reminded him.

Angus slid his hands into the back pockets of his jeans, running his thumb over the silver fork.

'You're not a little kid anymore,' he said, his voice cracking.

'Show me your scars, Black. I won't bite.'

'Okay then,' Angus said, giving in.

Slowly, he slipped his shirt up and off, revealing the scars that crossed his muscular body. Alice's breath caught in her throat as she took in the sight of him, the sculpted lines of his chest and abs. She fought to conceal her excitement, but a wicked smile tugged at the corners of her lips.

'And you definitely aren't a little boy anymore,' she murmured, running her hand over his scars with a touch that was equal parts soothing and sensual. She circled him and ran both her soft hands across his back.

'Okay, you're making it weird now,' Angus said, making ready to pull his top back on.

'I'm just messing around. I'll behave, I promise. Let me have a proper look.' Alice placed her cool hands on Angus's hips and moved his back towards the setting sun.

'Wow. That must have hurt.'

'Yep, it hurt like hell.'

Alice studied the scars for a moment with her eyes only.

'You can see exactly where the claws went,' she said, spreading her fingers and placing one on each scar. She drifted them up the scars. As her fingertips reached his neck, Angus could feel her warm breath on his back. He knew he was walking a dangerous line, but in that moment, he didn't care. It was nice to have something to distract his thoughts. A cool breeze swept up from the ocean below. Alice felt the dozens of tiny bumps of his skin raise under her touch. She watched with interest as his exposed right nipple hardened.

The breeze danced and rustled through the gardens. The air filled with the scent of roses, lavender, and rhododendrons mixed with the ashes and wine at his feet. Thoughts of Cinder came flooding back in with every inhale. Angus sighed heavily, the weight of missing the woman he loved heavy on his heart.

'I can't stop thinking about her,' he said, gazing at the remains of the once grand house that now lay in ruins before him. 'It's been six months, and there's no trace of her.'

Alice moved around to face him but kept her hand on his neck, her eyes shining with a hint of flirtation. She knelt down and picked up the wine bottle from the ground, running her hand down his chest as she went.

'Perhaps a drink with me will help take your mind off things, even if only for a moment,' she suggested.

'I don't know,' he said, not wanting to be rude. 'I just can't seem to shake the thought of her.'

'That's alright,' Alice said with a smile. 'Maybe talking about her will help. What was she like?' A small smile touched Angus's lips as he remembered.

'She was... is... strong, smart, and has a quick wit. She loves the stars and the beach.' He looked out at the coastline that stretched out to the north towards Tallo's Bluff.

'She sounds great,' Alice said, taking a long drink from the bottle 'I hope you find her soon.' Her bare arm brushed against Angus's exposed skin.

'I do too,' he agreed, stepping away to get a better view of the coastline. The wind ruffled his thick, dark hair. Alice followed him and placed a hand on his back, offering him the bottle.

'I'm here for you, Black,' she said firmly. 'If you need someone to talk to, know that I am here.' Angus took the bottle and drank. They stood in silence for a moment, sipping the wine. Below them, sea birds circled, the ocean churned, and cars wound their way along the road that curved around the coast.

'She was everything to me, you know?' Angus said, beginning to slur his words. Alice nodded sympathetically.

'I understand.'

'And now she's gone,' Angus continued, his voice filling with emotion. 'I don't know if I'll ever find her.'

'Shh,' Alice soothed, rubbing his back. 'Don't think about that right now.' She turned to look down at the small town of Heathcote on the other side of the hill. 'This place hasn't changed a bit since we were kids. I always loved coming to visit Uncle Gunn in the holidays.

Do you remember the fun we used to have when we were all here together?'

'Hide and seek in the dunes?' Angus asked, turning to look at her.

'Yep, you would always find me.'

'I think you let me find you.'

'Maybe I did,' Alice said, looking up into his dark brown eyes. They watched each other until the silence between them felt thick and uncomfortable.

A cough behind them broke the silence. They turned to see Marraine strolling slowly along the grass next to the driveway, her fingers laced together in front of her.

'Good evening, Angus,' she said. 'I didn't mean to interrupt, whatever this is,' she added. 'It's just that Dom told me you might be here, and I thought I might come to see if you are okay. You appear to be well taken care of.' She ran a discerning eye over Alice. Alice crossed her arms over her chest. The corner of her lip twisted, and her eyes rolled at the sight of Marraine's designer heels and exposed long legs.

'This is Dom's cousin,' Angus said, sidestepping away from Alice. 'Her name's Alice,'

'Not your cousin, too?' Marraine asked.

'No, not my cousin.'

'Then it is most definitely interesting to meet you. Alice, was it?'

'Yep. And what do they call you?' Alice asked.

'I'm called many things. Some of them are quite unspeakable in polite conversation.' Marraine said, looking at Angus's bare chest.

'This is my good friend, Marraine.' Angus said. 'Can I put my shirt back on now?' he asked, feeling suddenly exposed.

'If you must,' both women said together.

Angus quickly slipped his shirt on under the gaze of both Marraine and Alice. Marraine, ever the composed figure, raised an eyebrow at the scene but remained unruffled.

'I hope I wasn't interrupting anything, Angus. Were you two doing a bit of forking?' she asked with a wry smile, noticing the silverware protruding from Angus's back pocket. Alice smirked.

'I was just helping Black finish a bottle of wine,' she said.

'Oh, really?' Marraine asked. 'I would think he would be quite capable of that himself. He has certainly had a great deal of practise of late.'

'Can we help you with something, Maryanne?' Alice asked.

'Only if you've finished helping yourself. And it's Marraine.'

'Sorry,' Alice said. 'I've just never heard that name before.'

'I wouldn't worry,' Marraine said with a polite smile. 'I'm sure you will get to know it soon enough.' Ignoring the banter, Angus stepped to Marraine.

'What brings you here, Marraine?' he asked.

'I've been looking into Cinder's financials,' she said in a more serious tone, 'and there's something you need to know.' Angus's eyebrows furrowed with concern.

'What is it?' he asked. Marraine hesitated for a moment before speaking.

'Someone has been using Cinder's bank accounts. I've tracked several transactions, but I can't pinpoint where the money is going. Her accounts are still active.'

'What do you mean, someone's using her accounts?' A spark of hope ignited inside Angus.

'I'm not sure,' Marraine admitted. 'I've been trying to trace them back, but it's proving difficult. We need to figure out who's doing this and why.'

'But it could be her,' Angus said. 'That's the most likely explanation. She's alive, and she's the one accessing the money.'

'Could it be someone else that has got access to her money, someone trying to take advantage of her disappearance?' Alice chimed in. Marraine nodded.

'That's a possibility. Part of me wonders if it could be some sick joke of Louvelle's that she has somehow orchestrated from beyond the grave.' Angus clenched his fists. He walked back and forth, shaking his head in frustration.

'I've been searching for her for months, and now this. It's got to be her. Or even if it's not, it might be someone who knows where she is.' He looked at Marraine with a painful longing in his eyes. Marraine walked to him and placed her hands on his shoulders. 'We'll find her, sweetie, and bring her home.'

'I hope so,' Angus said as he swept his concerned eyes over the burnt remains of The Big House. 'Who knows what trouble she might be in?'

A trickle of red liquid ran from the edge of Cinder's lip. Padding it away with a napkin, she looked around to see if anyone had noticed. She assured herself that the secluded corner she had sat herself in was too dark for anyone to see her face, even if they were looking her way, which it appeared no one was.

She had wandered listlessly amongst Sydney's pulsating nightlife, eventually drifting away from the harbour. Tucked away in a corner of an area the locals called The Cross, she found a bar that felt warm and inviting. A comforting orange glow radiated through the windows and calming, upbeat music filled the night. With a touch of bitter-sweet, it reminded her of Paddy's back home, a place that was special to her she knew, but her troubled mind was struggling to join those dots. The bar hummed with a symphony of joyful interactions of old friends and new, mingling with the heady fragrance of alcohol. The soft glow from pendant lights hung low over the grandiose mahogany counter, casts intricate shadows upon the walls. Bartenders, clad in attire reminiscent of a bygone era, moved with a graceful fluidity, their hands deftly crafting potions both potent and beguiling. Above, a canopy of fairy lights glimmered like stars. Sultry jazz drifted from hidden speakers. Although the ambience and company attracted Cinder, she contentedly observed the frivolity from her solitary corner.

She held a slender glass in her hand adorned with a celery stalk standing at attention. She had never had a Bloody Mary before, but it seemed an appropriate drink for the monster she now was. For she was a monster – a vampire. As much as she tried to ignore and deny it, that's what she was. Each sip held a subtle heat. Concentrating on the flavours helped her to filter the sounds and smells of the surrounding people. As a vampire, she experienced everything with heightened intensity. The colours, sounds, smells, and feelings were all at full volume all the time.

She was watching how the fairy lights flickered on her glass as she swirled the red liquid around when a shadow fell across her table. She moved her focus from her drink to a man that was standing by her booth. He wore a yellow polo-shirt tucked into dark blue jeans. His stomach hung over his jeans just enough to cover his belt. Pointed boots, well-polished with a short heel completed his ensemble.

'Hello there,' he said in a deep voice. Cinder raised her glass to him but said nothing.

There was a young woman at the bar telling a story with great animated moves of her arms. Her friends laughed as the telling got more involved and more parts of her body were required to convey it. Cinder smiled to herself. The young woman reminded her of Torry. Her memories of Torry were confused and scattered, like butterflies fluttering around an open field. Occasionally, one would land, and she could fully appreciate its beauty before it would take flight again. Cinder knew one thing for certain: She had no family left. No real family. The young girl that she called sister must be very important to her. When she caught hold of one of the memories of Torry, she felt deep love and trust.

'Would you like something else to drink?' the man standing by her booth asked. Cinder, drawn back from her swirling memories to the present, said nothing. For a moment, she watched the veins of the man's neck move just below the skin.

'Are you talking to me?' she asked, shaking her head as if she had just woken.

'Yes,' the man said with a smile that crinkled the corners of his eyes. 'I was asking if you would like something else to drink?'

'Why would you ask me that?' Cinder said. She could smell him now, smell that blood just beneath the flesh.

'It's just that you don't seem to be enjoying the one you have.' He gestured to Cinder's glass. Cinder wiped away the condensation with her thumb.

'I guess I'm just thirsty for something else,' she said. The man's eyes widened, and he moved closer to Cinder. She could hear his heartbeat over the music, pumping that tantalising fluid full of life through his veins.

'Maybe I could help you out with that,' he said.

'I don't think that is a good idea.' Cinder turned her head away, forcing back the desire for blood growing inside her. She held her lower lip between her teeth but didn't break the skin.

'It's okay,' he said as he sat in the booth next to Cinder and rested his arm behind her. 'I won't bite.'

'I might,' Cinder said to herself and closed her eyes.

'What's your name?' he asked as the tips of his fingers rested on Cinder's shoulder. Cinder opened her eyes and looked around. Two young people with colourful tattoos on their bared arms and legs shuttled back and forth behind the bar, moving in tandem. In turn, they leaned forward to hear orders over the music and chatter of the crowd, then busied themselves preparing orders and taking payments, cleaning their hands on their checkered aprons as they went. In the corner opposite Cinder, two middle-aged men yelled at a football game screening on a television hung from the exposed-brick wall.

'I'm Derick. What's your name?' the man asked again. Sometimes it was hard for Cinder to remember who she was before. Her name was always on the tip of her tongue, but right now, it evaded her.

'I'm Tribulation,' Cinder said, turning to look at him and sipping her drink. Her mouth filled with rich tomato, followed by the smooth embrace of vodka. She licked her lips. A lingering warmth from the spice ran over her tongue and down her throat.

'Your parents must have had a sick sense of humour,' the man, Derick, said with a laugh.

'Did I have parents?' Cinder asked, talking more to herself than to Derick.

'Everyone has parents.' Derick said, resting his hand on her shoulder. 'Unless you're an angel. Are you an angel, Tribulation?' He ran his eyes down Cinder's long legs. Cinder turned to look at his hand on her shoulder. She could feel the blood running through the veins in Derick's wrist pumping against her back and she could smell it. His life force, his memories flowing in the warm, salty fluid. It would be so easy to just have a taste. Who knows? Cinder thought to herself, he might be into it. Just a taste. I can stop after that.

'You need to go now, Derick,' she said without looking at him. Her teeth were tingling. She knew they would soon grow larger, elongating into sharp fangs.

'Only if you come with me,' Derick said. Cinder placed her drink down on the edge of the table, placing it strategically. When she took her hand away, the protruding celery stalk overbalanced the glass and sent the red liquid onto Derick's lap.

'Oh, shit!' Derick yelled as he jumped back. Cinder moved swiftly and silently. When Derick looked up from his wet and sticky crotch to reach for Cinder's napkin, she was already gone.

· · · ·

Torry sat on a mossy log studying a large toadstool that had recently pushed its way up through the blanket of pine needles on the forest floor. Its bell shape and bright red colour reminded her of a Christmas decoration. It was the kind of place a fairy might live in a children's story. It was late spring but still cold in the evenings, especially in the shaded valleys of the forest. Torry and Dom had lit themselves a fire to stay warm. They were in a small clearing, a place that they had been coming to since they were kids. Tall pines walled them in on three sides and the rocky wall of Vivien's Ridge was at their backs. They had fashioned a ring of upturned logs into seating, with a circle of rocks in the centre for the fire. Over the years, they had cleared the area of undergrowth, but the ground was green with grass and moss, and a sprinkling of pine needles.

'Is Black coming?' she said to the others around the fire, 'It will be dark soon.'

Dom stood by the fire, poking the red coals with a long stick, one eye closed against the smoke that was drifting his way. His two tomahawks hung from his belt.

'I haven't seen him all afternoon,' he said, trying to fan the smoke away from his stern face. 'I think he's done a runner again.'

'That's five nights in a row,' Torry said, looking around at the others that were sitting by the fire. Across from Dom, the twins Tavish and Rory were sharing a log as a seat. Duncan was leaning against one of the pines, looking out into the forest with his back to the fire, and Alice was laying back on a rock, looking up at the ridge.

'Does anyone know where Black has been going?' Rory asked, looking around. Dom shrugged. Duncan turned his head, shook it, and turned back to the forest.

'I might know.' Alice said, sitting up.

'Can you tell us then? Torry asked. 'It's the full moon tonight; we're going to need him.' Alice paused for a moment before answering.

'I'll go find him,' she said, standing up and coming to the fire.

'Just tell us and we'll all go get him.' Torry said.

'No, it's okay, we shouldn't all go,' Alice held her hands out to the warmth. 'You stay here. I'll just go.'

'If he's been drinking, just leave him where he is,' Dom said, stabbing at the coals and sending red sparks flying into the sky.

'Dom!' Torry said. 'We need him.'

'I know we need him,' Dom snapped the stick over his knee and tossed it in the fire. 'But we don't need this version of him.'

'Don't worry, I'll find him,' Alice said, stepping away from the fire and walking into the forest. Torry watched her go, then went to stand with Dom.

'What's she up to?' she asked, leaning in so only Dom could hear her.

'What do you mean?' Dom asked. The fire crackled and popped.

'I mean, I have a feeling about her,' Torry said.

'A feeling?' Dom asked loud enough for the others to hear. Tavish and Rory ignored him, but Duncan turned to look at Torry and smiled knowingly to himself.

'Yep,' Torry whispered.

'She seems fine to me,' Dom said, looking at the flames. Torry looked sideways at her brother. The sun had disappeared behind the hills and they were in the shadows now. The fire glowed red on Dom's face.

'You think anyone with a pretty smile is fine,' she said.

'And nice legs,' Dom added. 'A pretty smile and nice legs.'

'Nice legs or not, I don't trust her,' Torry said, placing another log on the fire.

'You don't know her,' Dom said.

'Well, I'll get to know her then,' Torry said and walked away.

Alice was already a long way ahead when Torry set off to follow her. Her *nice legs* as Dom had put it were only short, but that didn't stop her from hurrying through the trees. Torry had to jog to catch up to her. They were moving downhill, back towards the farmhouse. The lights of Heathcote flickered in the gaps between the trees to Torry's left. For someone unfamiliar with the terrain, it would be hazardous to move this quickly through the darkness, but Torry was a regular member of the nightly patrols now and knew the lay of the land just as well in the night as she did in the daytime.

She had had to leave school. She had one more year before she would graduate, but she didn't mind. School had been boring and annoying for years now, anyway. She had a couple of friends, but most of the kids she went to school with were immature idiots. School also meant catching an early bus to Tallo's Bluff because there was no high school in Heathcote. Did she miss sitting on a hot bus for an hour twice a day while pimply boys who smelled of body odour and rotten sandwiches, told her dirty jokes or tried to look up her school dress? No way. And that dress! Torry burnt it the day after she knew she didn't have to go back. Torry had always enjoyed spending time with older people more than she did people her own age. She always tried to tell herself that she shouldn't expect too much from other kids at her school, but no matter how low she put the bar, someone always seemed to slither under it. When Alice had arrived a few weeks ago, she was excited to have another girl around. Alice was three years older than her, but they had always had fun together when they were kids. But now, as she watched her big cousin weave her way through the trees, Torry had a gnawing, bad feeling that she couldn't quite put her finger on.

Alice disappeared from view. Torry caught her breath and waited to see where she would emerge. The forest south of Vivien's Ridge was thick and dark. The land fell away more steeply now, in a valley towards the river. Torry could smell the damp in the air and feel it on her warm skin. A chorus of frogs taking advantage of the many muddy pools at the bottom of the valley croaked their rhythmic songs. When she and Dom were younger, they would venture out here to catch tadpoles in nets.

Something moved in the moonlight. Torry watched as a shadow moved between the trees. There was a splashing noise followed by the unmistakable sound of Alice cursing. Torry smiled to herself, imagining Alice's foot slipping into one of the hidden puddles. *She should have let me go with her*, she thought to herself. Torry watched as Alice's dark silhouette turned east and moved along the top of the ridge that ran along the river, heading back towards the bridge. There was a shortcut and Torry knew she could catch her now. Torry turned back the way she had come. If she headed up the hill, there was a dirt-track that would take her straight to the old bridge. She had almost reached the track when she heard movement behind her. Something large was hurrying through the dark forest towards her.

• • • •

The music from the bar had fallen to a quiet rhythmic thud. Cinder walked alone down a dimly lit street, heading west back towards the harbour. She caught her reflection in the tinted windows of a red sedan parked close to the curve, turning away again quickly. She dropped her gaze to the footpath. Time had worn and cracked the concrete, spotting it with discarded gum, cigarette butts, and the occasional bird dropping. Advertising material plastered the brick wall beside her, the rear of the bar she had just left. Sun-faded sheets of paper with torn and missing corners flapped in the breeze. Cinder ran her tongue over her lips, tasting the last remnants of the drink she had sacrificed to the man's lap. What was his name? Derick. *It was a shame to waste my drink on Derick*, she thought. But that wasn't the red liquid you wanted anyway, was it? An accusatory voice asked from the dark corners of her mind. The thought of what she desired made her feel sick. She shook out her hands and swallowed the thought away. Someone called out from behind her, but she continued on with her head down and her arms crossed over her chest.

'Tribulation,' the voice called out again from behind her. She assumed it was Derick – Derick with the wet crotch – but she quickened her pace, not looking back. Not taking the hint, Derick ran after her, his heavy feet thudding on the concrete path. His heel caught on one of the cracks. He stumbled, but quickly regained his footing, and soon caught up to Cinder.

'Hey, Tribulation, I owe you a drink,' he said as he reached out and took hold of Cinder's shoulder. Cinder pulled away from his hand in a flash, turning on him, her eyes wide with rage.

'What are you doing?' she demanded. Derick swayed on the spot. Cinder hadn't noticed until now how inebriated he was.

'How about you come back to my place for that drink?' he said, running his unfocused eyes over Cinder. 'Then you can help me get out of these wet pants.' He rubbed his hand over the growing lump under the dark patch on his jeans. He reached out to touch Cinder again, but she took hold of his wrist, twisting his arm behind his back. Derick stumbled sideways and fell into the wall. Cinder forced his face against the wall, squishing his lip and right cheek toward his eye.

'What the hell, Tribulation? You're hurting me.' Derick's voice was muffled against the bricks.

'Shut up, you stupid man,' Cinder said. 'That's not my name.'

'Well, whatever your name is, can you let me go?' Derick asked as he struggled unsuccessfully to push himself away from the wall. Three young women were laughing and talking loudly as they exited the bar and headed towards Derick and Cinder. They fell quiet as they noticed Cinder holding Derick effortlessly against the wall with one hand. The first two women looked concerned and a little frightened. They gave Cinder a wide berth as they went past, stepping off the path onto the road. The final young woman smiled and nodded at Cinder as if to say *well done, sister*. Lost in thought, Cinder ignored them. Her true name was there again, just floating out of reach. She placed her finger on the tip of her tongue. No, no name there, just the saltiness of her fingers.

'I wonder,' she said, looking down at Derick's wrist in her hand.

'Wonder what?' Ow!' Derick called out. Cinder had pushed her thumbnail into his skin. A drop of blood trickled down her nail and onto her knuckle.

'Sweet, sour? Memories of loss or of power?' Cinder sung to herself as she circled her thumb in Derick's blood, smearing in on his wrist.

'Stop! Can you hear me?' Derick was yelling now, but Cinder heard another voice. A voice forcing itself through the dark clouds of her mind, searching her out from the past.

'Can you hear me?' it was a voice of so much fondness and warmth that tears filled Cinder's eyes and her breath caught in her throat. 'Cinder, Cinder, hear me, my daughter. You are so loved. Never forget that you are loved and deserve to be loved. Always.' It was her father's voice. The last words he had ever said to her. The last words, the most painful words and the most important.

'My name's Cinder,' she said as the recollection of her identity emerged through the fog of her troubled mind.

'Great, so your name's Cinder,' Derick yelled, kicking and pushing against the wall. 'Can you let me go?'

Cinder looked down at his blood smeared arm. Between her bloody fingers, she could see dark symbols tattooed on Derick's arm.

'What are these symbols?' she asked, pulling up his sleeve to get a better look.

'They're roman numerals. They're a date,' Derick said as he struggled unsuccessfully again to free his arm from Cinder's vice-like grip.

'What date?' Cinder asked.

'June 13th. It's my daughter's birthday; she's six.'

'Daughter!' Cinder said, loosening her grip on Derick's arm. 'What's her name?'

'Arabella, we call her Belle.' Cinder let go of his arm and stepped back. Memories of someone flinging themself from a rooftop to save a baby flashed through her mind.

'I'm sorry. You're not one of them,' she said, watching Derick push himself off the wall and compose himself as best he could.

'One of who?' he asked, glaring at her. 'And what's with this?' He held up his arm as a drop of blood fell from his wrist, splashing down on the concrete path.

'One of them... One of us... a vampire.' Cinder said.

'You're a crazy person. Look what you did,' Derick lurched his hand towards Cinder's face. Reflexively, she struck him on his chin. Derick's eyes rolled back in his head, and he swayed for a moment before collapsing in a heap on the dry grass that lined the verge between the road and footpath.

'Oh no,' Cinder said. She crouched down and tapped Derick's cheek. He was breathing, but she had knocked him out cold. Looking around to see that no one was watching, she picked him up. Derick's limbs flopped about. Other than their disproportionate sizes, it reminded Cinder of a parent lifting a sleeping child. She thought about Annabelle then. If her heart wasn't already so broken, she may have recognised the twinge of heartache that came along with those thoughts. Further along the road, away from the bar, Cinder spotted a tree growing out of the grassy verge. Leafy green branches hung low to the ground and roots had spread and cracked the concrete path. Cinder ducked under the limbs. Shadowed from the orange glow of the streetlights, she sat Derick down, propping his back against the trunk.

'I'm sorry,' she offered then ducked back under the branches and left him there. Cinder waited for a car to pass, then crossed the road and ran down a side alley.

A tall woman with long dark hair stepped aside as Cinder ran past, flattening herself against the wall of the alley. She watched as Cinder ducked under the branch of an overhanging tree, leaped up a flight of concrete steps and disappeared amongst the shadows. The tall woman pushed herself off the wall and retrieved her phone from the inside pocket of her knee length jacket. The screen light illuminated her thin face, sending shadows up from her prominent cheekbones. She tucked one side of her long, dark hair behind her ear and held her phone close to her cheek.

'Yes, sir,' she said when someone answered. 'It's her. Yes. Cinder Delacourt.'

• • • •

The crashing sound moving towards Torry grew louder. She prepared herself for the worst. A second later, Duncan emerged, moving fast on his long legs.

'Good, it's you,' he said as he ran past Torry, his giant boots crushing the sticks and leaves of the forest floor. 'Follow me.'

'But I'm following Alice,' Torry said.

'She'll have to look after herself. We've got an entire pack heading towards the house.'

'What?' Torry said in concern. 'How did they get around here without us seeing them?' she asked. Duncan shrugged as he continued to run.

'The bastards seem determined to get to town,' he grumbled. Torry hesitated, watching Alice move further away. Deciding that it was more important to protect the farm, she turned and ran after Duncan.

Chapter 4

Beasts at the Door

Gunn sat watching as Annabelle slept in her crib. Her little chest rising and falling under a blanket as her precious little pink lips twitched. She wasn't his grandchild, but he loved her like she was all the same. He was already in his fifties when he had his own children and thought that he might not live to see babies in his home again.

'Get a hold of yourself, man,' he said to himself as he removed his spectacles and dried his moist eyes. He cleaned his lenses on his shirt and bent down, kissing Annabelle's soft cheek. Outside, a sound like someone kicking over a metal bucket rang out in the stillness of the night. Annabelle stirred but didn't wake.

'What's all this then?' Gunn grumbled to himself. 'I've just got her off to sleep. If they wake you up, there'll be hell to pay,' he said to Annabelle. There was another crashing sound, louder and closer. Gunn cursed under his breath and left the room, marching down the hall towards the back of the house. He swept through the laundry that led to the rear exit. Flinging open the solid timber door, he put his hand on the handle of the fly-wire screen. Something flashed past a few hundred metres away. Gunn froze and watched, squinting and moving his head from side to side to see through the screen. He saw the eyes first, glistening in the moonlight, like two points of light floating in the shadows beside the woodshed.

The moon hung low in the sky, casting a dim silver glow over the yard. Crickets chirped their symphony over the distant rhythm of the ocean. The scent of earth and pine mingled with the faint aroma of livestock nearby. The shadowed creature shifted. Sinewy muscles rippled beneath its fur as it slowly emerged, nostrils flared as it caught wind of the people in the farmhouse. It crept forward, step by cautious step, the soft soil beneath its paws betraying its presence with each silent tread. Moonbeams danced and rippled through its fur, illuminating the beast in a ghostly glow as it approached the house. It paused in front of the woodshed, a small structure of weathered planks and rusty corrugated iron.

Gunn retraced his steps away from the back door, quickly but quietly. He closed the door to Annabelle's room, keeping his eye ever on the hallway behind him. Hurrying into his own darkened bedroom with as much pace as he could muster from his ageing legs, he crouched beside his bed. Flicking up his bedspread as his joints cricked and complained, he slid a large metal chest from under the bed. Chipped dark green paint and black spray-painted numbers gave the box a military appearance. Gunn shot his eyes back towards the doorway as he gripped a chain around his neck. He pulled the chain over his head and unlocked the chest with a key that hung from it. Stiff metal hinges squealed as he lifted the lid. Gunn pulled his old friend from inside and held it up to the light coming in from the hall. The light glinted off the sharp edge of a long Bowie knife. Gunn gripped the time-worn wooden handle firmly in his fist as he pushed himself up from the floor, pushing down on the bed with his spare hand.

As Gunn rose to his feet, his grip tightening around the familiar weight of the Bowie knife, a sense of determination settled over him. One way or another, there was no way he was letting that beast get in here, not with Annabelle. The crashing sound rang out again nearer, sending shivers down Gunn's spine. Chances were there were more of them out there besides the one he had just seen in the yard. He knew he couldn't let any of them inside. With each step toward the door, his resolve solidified. As he reached again for the knob of the back door, a blood freezing howl filled the night. Gunn flung open the door. The moonlight illuminated the yard, casting elongated shadows across the ground. Standing just a few paces away was the Lycan, its form looming large against the darkness. It tilted its head from side to side, watching Gunn with its dark eyes. Gunn took a step forward, his grip on the Bowie knife unwavering.

'I'm not backing down,' he declared, his voice ringing out with defiance. The wolf growled, its eyes narrowing as it assessed the man before it. But Gunn stood his ground, his resolve unyielding. With a sudden lunge, the wolf charged, teeth bared and claws extended. But Gunn was ready, his blade flashing in the moonlight as he met the creature head-on. The clash of metal against claw filled the night as Gunn engaged in a deadly dance with the relentless beast.

• • • •

Torry ran after Duncan, a blur of dark shadow as his giant frame crashed through the overhanging branches of the forest. The wide grassy paddocks of the farm opened up in front of them, inclining down towards the house. Torry could see the thin cracks of light from the windows and moonlit wisp of smoke from the chimney. She heard her father before she saw him, crying out in agony.

'Dad!' she cried out, quickening her pace.

'There! By the woodshed,' Duncan called. Four large figures moved in the lowlight between the farmhouse and the woodshed. Torry and Duncan vaulted a wire fence and ran, slipping and stumbling on the moist grass down towards the house. Gunn called out again, cursing into the night. One of the Lycan howled, drowning out his cries.

'We're coming dad,' Torry yelled between fast breaths. Duncan's long legs propelled him forward in front of her, his heavy boots pounding the ground. Torry struggled to keep up. She watched as he pulled a large knife from a sheath at his hip and leaped over the wire gate on the path that led to the house. Torry followed soon after. Her foot clipped the top of the gate, rattling it on its rusty hinges. She fell to her side and rolled in the dirt.

• • • •

Gunn lay on the ground near the back door of the farmhouse. One of the Lycan ran forward and took hold of his legs in its powerful jaws, and tossed him aside. Fresh blood dripping from its teeth, the beast turned towards the house and made to run for the door. Gunn took hold of its tail and held it back. The Lycan howled angrily and turned back towards the old man. A large boot collided with its face. The Lycan yelped and fell to the ground, shaking its head. A second kick came straight after. Duncan's size 20 combat boot crashing into its ribs. The startled and injured beast ran for the cover of darkness.

'You'd best run beastie, or I'll have ya head,' Duncan yelled. Torry ran past him and fell to her knees next to her father. Gunn had several scratches on his arms and hands, but Torry was most concerned about the puncture wounds in his leg.

'We need to get you out of here, Dad.; you're bleeding everywhere,' she said.

'I'm fine,' Gunn reassured her. 'I'm just angry that I've wrecked my good jeans.'

'We need to get you to the hospital.'

'I'm fine. You need to check on Annabelle.' Gunn said, trying to stand.

'Just stay down 'til I can wrap your leg a bit,' Torry said as she sent an exasperated look towards Duncan. Duncan nodded and headed for the back door.

'I'll go check on bub,' he said, and ran inside the house.

Torry wrapped her arms around her father to keep him warm.

'I'm alright, love,' he said, patting her hand.

'You're not,' Torry spat back at him, looking at the wound on his leg.

Something rustled in the shadowy darkness just beyond the woodshed. With a growl, a silvery grey Lycan padded slowly into the low light.

'Piss off!' Torry yelled, tightening her grip around her father. The Lycan stopped. A long tongue flopped from its mouth and it stood panting for a moment. Torry and Gun shuffled back towards the house. 'You heard me,' Torry yelled at the beast again. 'Get outta here.' Retracting its tongue, the Lycan inclined its head to one side and stared at Torry. Torry glowered back. The silver-haired beast sniffed the air, turned slowly away, and trotted back into the shadows.

Chapter 5
Everywhere is Lost if You Have No Home

Through these streets, I'll drift and roam
Everywhere is lost without my home.

• • • •

'Excuse me, Ms Delacourt, but you have something on your chin,' a young man with very white teeth in his slightly off-centre smile said. He wore a cream-coloured shirt under a navy suit and stood behind the counter of the Sir Stamford Hotel. With one hand behind his back, he motioned with the other towards a spot on his own left cheek. It took a moment for Cinder to register that she was Ms Delacourt and that the young man was talking to her. She ran her thumb along her chin. When the dry substance did not come away, she licked her thumb and tried again. It came away with a smear of dark-red.

'Oh, it's just some blood,' she said, wiping the remaining blood with her sleeve.

'Do you need some assistance?' the young man asked with concern.

'It's alright. It's not my blood,' Cinder reassured him. The young man thought about this for a moment then returned to viewing the screen in front of him. *I wonder what his blood tastes like?* The thought had crept into her mind like a spider that was climbing up her neck. Like one would with a real spider, Cinder chased the thought away with a shudder.

'That's all done,' he said with one more click of his keyboard. 'I've booked your room for two extra nights.'

'Would you like me to pay for the first part of my stay now or later?' Cinder asked.

'That's all been taken care of, Ms Delacourt. Your friend finalised your bill this morning.'

'None of my friends know I'm here... Unless. Marraine? Did they leave a name?'

'No name,' he said, running his eyes over the information on his monitor. 'But there is a note here for me to pass on a business card.' He crouched, and retrieved something from a set of hidden shelves under his desk. He removed a yellow sticky note with Delacourt written across it in neat handwriting and handed Cinder a card. Cinder read the front of the card before turning it over.

'Do you know where this is?' She showed the young man the address printed on the back.

'Yes, I do,' the young man said, his brow raised. 'But I wouldn't recommend going there alone, Ms Delacourt. It's not somewhere we would usually recommend to visitors.'

'Thank you for your concern,' Cinder said, turning the card over between her fingers. 'I'll be fine. I can look after myself.'

'I see.' The young man glanced at the bloodstain on Cinder's sleeve. 'Would you like me to organise a car for you, Ms Delacourt?'

'No, thank you. I would prefer to walk. I've been enjoying wandering the streets of the city. Is it far?'

'I would say it could take the best part of an hour to walk to that part of the city,' the young man said.

'That's fine,' Cinder replied with a smile. 'I need something to fill in my day. If you could just point me in the right direction, I'll find my way there.' The young man turned his monitor so that Cinder could see. When Cinder was confident that she could remember his directions, she thanked him and slid the mysterious card into her pocket.

'Very well then,' the young man said, 'Thank you again for staying with us. Please feel free to call us if you get lost.'

Everywhere is lost if you have no home, Cinder thought to herself.

• • • •

Angus sat in the shade of an oak tree, his head in his hands. He had employed an empty oil tin as a make-shift stool. The great, green branches of the old tree twisted up above him into a clear blue morning sky. A cool breeze blew across the open green fields and rustled its way through the long, dry grass along the fence line. The cold was soothing to his sore and troubled head. He had positioned himself at the west end of the milking yard, near a small wooden building with a single door and two dusty windows. His eyes were closed as he listened to a soothing mechanical hum coming from the building that was no larger than a child's playhouse. The morning milking was already over for today. The cows had once again returned to grazing. It was Angus's turn to help today, but after a big night, he had made his way back to his room to get some more sleep. The stiffness in his neck and a pounding at the back of his skull had other ideas. What he really needed, he thought to himself, was another drink. Some hair-of-the-dog would set him right. As yet though, he had found no alcohol in the usual places. Someone had even moved Uncle Gunn's moonshine from the little wooden building.

Hearing the footsteps of someone approaching, he lifted his head slowly from his hands. His eyes were blurry and took a moment to adjust to the light. With a few blinks, he recognised the figure coming towards him as Torry. Torry held an old cap in her hand. She used the cap to swat away a fly before she slipped it onto her head.

'They told me that you didn't turn up for milking again today,' she said as she sat down cross-legged in front of Angus. Angus nodded but did not answer. 'I thought you might have wanted to help with Annabelle's bath last night, too,' Torry continued. She put her hands down on the ground behind her and looked up at the branches of the tree moving gently in the breeze. 'She's getting strong now. We could use your help. It takes both me and dad to stop her wriggling around. Dad complains every time that he is too old to bend over a kid's bath, but he has a smile on his face the whole time. I'm sure Annabelle would love to have her daddy there.'

'Her mum too,' Angus mumbled.

'At least one parent would be good,' Torry replied. As she did, Dom strolled around the corner of the milking shed and walk to the small wooden building. Angus and Torry watched in silence as he unlocked and opened the door, ducked his way into the darkness inside and emerged moments later carrying two glass bottles of thick, red liquid. He sat the two bottles on the deck of the small building as he locked the door. Collecting the bottles, he opened one and took a sip as he walked over to the others. When he came level with Torry, he pushed one of her elbows with his foot so that her arm buckled and she fell over to one side. Torry laughed and, after sitting herself up straight, she punched Dom's thigh. Dom took a step back and laughed, too.

'How you feeling today, Black?' he asked. Angus lifted one hand and pointed his thumb towards the ground. 'Have one of these. It'll make you feel better.' Dom held a bottle towards Angus. The liquid in the bottles contained vitamins and minerals and an age-old formula that increased their strength, energy, and healing abilities. It was true, a drink of what Dom was offering would make him feel better, but Angus also knew that a large proportion of the liquid was blood taken from their dairy cows. The thought of forcing some of that thick liquid down his throat this morning turned his stomach. He waved the offer away.

'No thanks,' he said in a gravelly voice. Dom took a large mouthful from the open bottle and swallowed it with an audible gulp and exaggerated smacking of his lips.

'Mmm,' he said. 'Are you sure? It's extra lumpy today.'

'Piss off,' Angus said, the colour draining from his already pale face. He smiled, but that created a throbbing pain between his eyes. He put his face back in his hands.

'I think he's going to pop,' Dom said to Torry.

'You're not helping,' she said as she got to her feet and placed her hands on Angus's shoulders. Dom ignored her disapproving glare and took another swig. Tipping his head back, he gargled the liquid before swallowing it. Some of the dark-red substance dribbled out on to his chin as he began to laugh at his own immature behaviour.

'You're a great mate,' Angus mumbled through his hands without looking up.

'Come on, Black,' Dom said. 'A little cow juice is a sure-fire hangover cure. It might help you remember where you left your responsibilities last night, too.'

Angus lifted his head and squinted at Dom, his throbbing head making it hard to focus.

'When you start lecturing me about responsibilities, then things must really be getting bad?' he said as he stood up slowly. He walked to Dom, keeping one eye closed against the bright sunlight when he exited the shade of the tree. Torry chuckled, enjoying the exchange but sensing an underlying tension.

'I can't believe I'm saying this, but Dom's right,' she said. 'You can't keep disappearing. The girls need milking, and Annabelle needs a dad.' She sat down on the oil drum that Angus had just vacated. Angus sighed and took the unopened bottle from Dom.

'Yeah, yeah, I get it. I messed up last night, but it's not like the cows can file a complaint. And Annabelle won't remember if I was there or not,' he said. Torry's expression turned serious.

'It's not just about the cows or Annabelle, Black. It's about being part of this family, about being there when we need you. Dad's getting old, and I can't handle everything on my own. I love Annabelle, but she's not my daughter.' The three of them waited in an awkward silence, the morning breeze rustling the leaves overhead. Angus, deep in thought, finally mumbled,

'I'll help with the milking tomorrow. And Annabelle's bath tonight. Just give me a day to get my head straight.' Torry smiled, relieved.

'That's all I'm asking for, Black.'

'It's not all I'm asking,' Dom added. Torry glared at him. 'What?' he asked.

'And what else can I do for you, Dom?' Angus asked,

'You can get your head out of your arse and help us keep the wolves under control. One of them made it to town. What if one of them does that during tourist season? It will be a bloodbath.' Dom said. Angus shrugged, but noticed Torry and Dom exchange a look.

'What?' he asked. 'Did something happen?'

'It's fine,' Torry said.

'The hell it is,' Dom rebuffed. 'A pack of them came here last night. Dad ended up needing stitches.'

'What?' Angus asked, alarmed. 'Why didn't anyone tell me?'

'Because, dumb arse, no one knew where you were,' Dom growled. 'No one ever knows where you are.'

'Maybe you should have let me kill that one the other night, then,' Angus said.

'Right,' Dom said. 'Let's just start leaving dead bodies all over Heathcote.'

'Wait,' Torry interrupted, getting to her feet. 'You tried to kill one of them?'

'Hell yeah,' Dom said. 'I got there just as he was about to put a blade through its skull. Right there on the floor of Ken Woo's shop. He's either doing nothing or making stupid decisions that are putting us all in danger.'

'What's wrong with you, Black?' Torry asked.

'There's nothing wrong,' Angus raised his voice, his cheeks and neck flashed red. 'Other than my splitting headache, I'm fine.'

'The hell you are,' Dom said, stepping towards Angus. Torry put her hand on his chest to stop him. Angus dropped his head to one side and glared at Dom.

'We're worried about you, Black,' Torry said. Angus rubbed his neck.

'Can you be worried about me more quietly?' he said, closing his eyes. Dom pushed past Torry and leaned in close to Angus's ear.

'WE WILL STOP WHEN YOU GET YOUR SHIT TO-GETHER!' he yelled. Angus pulled his head away and shoved Dom in the chest. 'Come-on,' Dom said as he threw his arms open and stumbled backwards. Angus pushed his messy hair away from his face, spat at Dom's feet, turned, and walked away.

'That's right. Weak as piss. Just walk away again,' Dom called after him.

'Black!' Torry called to him, but he ignored her and kept walking.

'Just leave him,' Dom said.

'You two are just as bad as each other,' Torry said as she started walking back to the farmhouse.

'What did I do?' Dom asked, following her.

· · · ·

Cinder weaved through the bustling streets of Sydney, alive with the hum of midday activity. The city thrived in the daylight, a tapestry of colours and sounds, where the rhythm of footsteps blended with the chatter of pedestrians and the distant honking of car horns in a ceaseless discord. Sunlight played upon the towering buildings, casting a warm glow on the vibrant urban canvas. For every street, there seemed to be a dozen side streets or hidden stairways that led up to some hidden vantage point of the harbour. Cinder stopped in the shade of a clothing boutique's portico. Leaning against the window, she slid her hand into her hip pocket and pulled out the mysterious business card that she had received from the hotel clerk. She studied it for a moment, then stepped away from the window into the busy flow of pedestrian traffic.

'Excuse me,' she said to a young man in thick framed black spectacles. 'Could you tell me where this is?' She held the card out to him. The young man stepped aside, looked at Cinder as if she had asked him to give over all his worldly belongings instead of some simple directions, then continued on without a word. Cinder dropped her shoulders. 'Okay then,' she said to herself. Two men in navy suits and brown shoes walked past her, speaking in a very serious tone. She addressed them, however, they proceeded resolutely. A white delivery van came to a stop opposite her, the driver revving the engine impatiently against a stall in the flow of traffic. A teen in black clothes, carrying a large pack on their back, stepped out from behind the van and pushed past. Large headphones covered their ears. *Not even worth trying*, Cinder thought. The delivery van moved on and Cinder watched it go.

Across the road, sitting in the alcove of a glass fronted building, a woman sat on the ground holding a cardboard sign. It was hard to tell her age. Her hair was tucked under a woollen hat, and she wore many layers of clothes. Her face was gritty and worn from sunlight and exposure. Cinder looked both ways and crossed the street towards her. She halted, dodging a cyclist, then jogged onward, anticipating more traffic. Cinder approached the woman with a friendly smile. In thick black marker, she had written "MONEY FOR FOOD" in large letters on her sign. Cinder could see a sleeping bag behind her and a plastic garbage bag full of what might be all her worldly possessions.

'Hello,' Cinder said, stepping into the shadow of the alcove. The woman looked up at her and smiled. She was missing one, maybe two teeth from her bottom row.

'Hello there, love,' she said, straightening.

Cinder, aware of how she was towering above her, crouched in front of the woman. With her enhanced sense of smell, it was difficult for Cinder to ignore the odour. The woman and her clothes clearly hadn't been washed in some time. Cinder attempted to breathe through her mouth, not her nose.

'Hi, I'm Cinder,' she said.

'I'm Lucy,' the woman replied. 'But everyone calls me Lulu.' The tone of her voice made Cinder think she was likely younger than she looked.

'Nice to meet you, Lulu. Do you know where this place is?' she asked, showing Lulu the business card.

'Sure do. A bunch of weirdos they are,' Lulu said.

'Weirdos?' Cinder asked.

'Yep, they sell all kinds of strange fings,' Lulu squeezed her sign with dirty fingernails.

'What kind of things Lulu?' Cinder asked, stretching out one leg so that she could slide the card back into her pocket. Lulu leaned in closer and looked from side to side before replying.

'I've never been in myself right, but as I hears it, they got knifes and swords and the like,' she glanced over Cinder's shoulder and went on in a whisper. 'They say they have all kinds of old books, you know, with spells and witchy stuff. And..' she leaned in closer still and Cinder inclined towards her. 'Then there's the body parts.'

'Body parts!' Cinder exclaimed. Lulu shushed her with a finger at her lips.

'Yeah, yeah. That's what I hears,' Lulu went on. 'Like old ones, dug up from graves and stuff. But it's the people that go in there that are the real weirdos. You know all the freakies in dark clothes that only come out at night. You know the type I mean?'

'I know the type.'

'You're not one of them, are you?' Lulu asked, looking Cinder up and down. 'Coz it's okay with me if you are.'

'Oh no, I'm not one of them. I'm something far worse,' Cinder said and winked at Lulu. Lulu laughed and flashed the gaps in her lower teeth. 'You know what Lulu?' Cinder said, standing up. You've got me intrigued now. I'm going to have to go see this place for myself. Can you tell me how to get there?'

'You can walk there from here.' Lulu said, laying her sign to the side. 'If you buy me lunch, I can take you there.' Cinder looked around the busy street.

'You know what, Lulu? I could do with some food. Let's get some lunch, have a few drinks, and then you can take me there. After that, we will get some dinner too. How does that sound?'

'Perfic,' Lulu said, folding her sign and sliding it into her garbage bag with her other belongings. 'You know someone's following you, right?' she said, bundling up her sleeping bag.

'What?' Cinder said, looking around.

'Yep. I was watching them watch you, and they followed you for the last block. Not sure where they gone now,' Lulu shrugged and pushed the sleeping bag in next to her sign.

Cinder swivelled her head from side to side in concern, but could not see who Lulu was referring to.

Chapter 6
A New-Path

A ngus stormed through the bushland, his footsteps heavy, fuelled by anger. The heated argument with Dom echoed in his mind, each word a reminder of the tension that lingered between them. He held the bottle of red liquid in his hand; its contents diminishing with every swig. The stone path beneath his feet guided him out of the open fields of the farm into the wilderness. Each step took him deeper into the rugged beauty of untamed nature until the only sign of civilisation was the foot-worn path. Rows of ancient trees stretched their limbs towards the sky. Their leaves rustled in the breeze, releasing a medley of familiar scents. Lining the meandering path, a carpet of wildflowers bloomed amongst the long grass, creating a colourful mosaic on the forest floor. As he walked, Angus occasionally caught the scent of their subtle perfume. The distant murmur of flowing water hinted at the proximity of a hidden stream. The sunlight filtered through the leaves, casting dappled shadows on the ground. It was difficult to hold on to his anger amongst such serenity, but Angus was determined to ride his feelings out.

Eventually, the path twisted downhill toward the ocean. The track worn into the landscape by decades of foot traffic led him through an area scarred by a fire that had ravaged the countryside three years earlier. The blackened trunks of trees stood as solemn witnesses to the destructive force that had swept through. A lingering scent of burnt wood still hung in the air. Angus navigated through the twisted, skeletal forms of the trees, their branches reaching out like accusing fingers. The anger that fuelled him seemed to resonate with the desolation of the landscape. He stopped and looked out at the blue-green waters that were now visible through the blackened trunks. In his frustration, he kicked at a burnt stump. When the stump refused to yield, he kicked again, over and over until the stump came free of the sandy soil. He bent over with a hand on his knees, puffing. Having caught his breath, he kicked at the stump once more for good measure. His rear foot slipped on the rocky path and his toe slammed into a solid knot of exposed root. Pain shot through the outside of his foot and up his leg. Angus yelled in pain, cursing and gritting his teeth.

'ARE YOU SERIOUS!?' he yelled. He hobbled to the stump, lifted it above his head with his free hand, and threw it deep into the forest. As the stump crashed through the undergrowth, he heard what sounded like a female voice laughing.

'Hello,' he said, looking around. 'Is anyone there?' When there was no reply, he turned and continued on.

As he limped along the path, memories of the teenagers who had sparked the fire surfaced in his mind. Foolish actions, reckless choices that had left an indelible mark on the land. They had snuck away from a school camp and were smoking cigarettes in the bush. Thankfully, no one was injured, but firefighters only controlled the fire after it had burned several hectares of bush. The fire destroyed a shed on a neighbouring farm and damaged several thousand dollars' worth of equipment. The fire had moved away from Heathcote towards the river, but the smoke and the fear had sent many of the tourists packing.

'Stupid kids,' he said to himself. Their actions had caused all this destruction, and a stupid choice had placed people in danger. As he said it, Angus realised Dom had just said the same thing to him about his own actions.

Taking another swig from the bottle, Angus found a fallen log to sit on. Out of the blackness that remained, fresh growth had emerged. The forest floor was awash with green shoots. Grasses and flowers that now had renewed access to the sunlight bloomed and flourished. Many of the damaged trees had sprouted new limbs. The thin green branches hung heavy with leaves bobbing in the breeze. He stared into the distance, lost in thought. His anger waned, replaced by a sense of weariness. The bottle in his hand felt lighter. The thick liquid inside was hard to swallow but was providing a temporary reprieve from both the physical and emotional pain. With the relief, also came clarity. Although he hated to admit that Dom was right, he couldn't help thinking about Uncle Gunn. Since losing his parents, Gunn had become like his father. He could have been killed. *If he died while you were off drinking somewhere instead of helping the others, could you ever forgive yourself?* he thought. With a final swig from the bottle, he rose from the fallen log, leaving behind the remnants of the fire-ravaged past, and continued on his journey through the bushland, seeking solitude amidst the tangled undergrowth.

As Angus approached the river, the soft murmur of flowing water became more pronounced, a soothing melody that accompanied his steps. The sun was high in the sky now, casting short shadows that danced on the stone path. Despite the picturesque scene, an uneasy feeling gnawed at Angus. He couldn't shake the sensation that someone or something was trailing him. He quickened his pace, glancing over his shoulder at irregular intervals. Every rustle of leaves seemed to whisper secrets of unseen observers. With every step, the unease intensified. He slowed the rhythmic cadence of his footsteps, his ears listening keenly for anything out of place. Finally, he reached the riverbank. The water flowed gently over smooth rocks. The tranquillity of the scene clashed with the disquiet in Angus's mind. He scanned the surroundings, eyes darting between the shadows beneath the trees. A sudden snap of a twig behind him jolted Angus, and he spun around, his senses heightened. The forest stood silent, as if holding its breath, and yet, Angus couldn't see anyone.

'Who's there?' he called out, his voice cutting through the stillness. The only response was the whisper of the wind through the leaves and the gurgle of the river. He knelt by the water's edge, dipping his fingers into the cool stream. His reflection in the water showed tense lines across his brow. A rustle to his left made him whirl around again, but as before, there was nothing there. The forest seemed to play tricks on him, shadows morphing into phantoms and the gentle breeze carrying echoes of imaginary footsteps. Determined to dispel his unease, Angus continued along the riverbank. He soon found a patch of smooth dry grass next to a pool of slowly flowing water. Steep banks and overhanging trees shielded him from the breeze and prying eyes on both sides. Before he sat, he lifted his shirt and pulled something from the back of his jeans. The sun warmed his face, and the grass was soft as he sat. He lay the empty bottle beside him and held the object that he had retrieved in both hands. He ran his hand over the object, a black covered notebook just larger than one of his hands. A thin red ribbon that acted as a bookmark, attached to the cover at one end, sat between the pages. Angus flicked to the marked page and read the words there. As a single tear rolled down his flushed cheek, he held the notebook to his face and breathed in its scent.

'I hope you're alright,' he said, as he sat the notebook on his lap and rested his troubled head on his fist.

• • • •

To the west of where Angus sat, the river rose to a steep bank of dark sandy soil and exposed roots. Atop the bank, grey barked trees stood sentinel along the edge, holding the bank from toppling into the running water below. Green tendrils of ivy twisted their way up the trunks and fell from the branches like a natural curtain. Behind the curtain, a large grey rock, polished smooth by wind and running water, protruded from the dark earth. Alice sat cross-legged on the rock, running her index finger over a stone she held in her palm. A cool breeze blew through the ivy. The vines swayed and the leaves pitter-patted together. Between the gaps, Alice could see Angus hunched over the book in his hands.

'Don't worry, Black,' she said. 'I'm going to make it all better.'

• • • •

Cinder stood in a wide industrial street. Lulu stood next to her. Directly in front of them, blocking the mid-afternoon sun from their eyes, were three identical red-brick buildings. Each building had a row of bared windows and a single door. Above the windows, several rows of bricks rose towards the skyline, forming a large rectangular area. On the building closest to them, a sign had been hung in this blank area, taking up most of the space. Cinder and Lulu had their heads tilted back to see the sign in full. In black swirling text identical to the writing on the business card that Cinder was holding were the words "Inkerman's Inquiétant Ipermercato."

'They're back,' Lulu said, leaning towards Cinder.

'I know.'

Cinder looked down at the business card. She could not see the person who had been following her since she left her hotel. They were hidden away in the alleyway that she and Lulu had walked down a few moments ago. Whoever or whatever they were, they were very skilful at avoiding being seen. But since her change, Cinder's eyesight was not all that had improved. All of her five senses were super-charged, sometimes to the point of being nauseating. She may not have seen her pursuer but here, away from the noise of the city centre, she could hear them breathing and hear the low and rhythmic pumping of their heart as it cycled blood around their body. Cinder closed her eyes and turned her head towards the alley. Now she could smell that blood, or taste it – she wasn't sure which. A breeze drifted down the wide street. It ruffled Lulu's garbage bag of belongings and flicked at the end of Cinder's hair. All that Cinder could smell then was Lulu.

'Have you got somewhere to stay tonight, Lulu?' Cinder asked, turning away from her towards the alley.

'I got a spot out the way. People leave me alone there mostly and it keeps dry,' Lulu said, hitching her belongings up on her shoulder. Cinder looked up at the sign on the building again. As on the business card, the three I's at the beginning of each word were written in large capitals, like Roman numerals. She slid the card back into her pocket and took a step towards the alley and her hidden pursuer.

'You can come out now,' she called out in a commanding voice. She could hear the shuffling of feet and an odd clicking noise, but they remained concealed. Cinder took another two steps towards the alley. As she took her third step, the door of Inkerman's Inquiétant Ipermercato swung open and a woman with long, dark hair stepped out. It was difficult to determine her age under the large dark glasses that covered most of the top of her face.

'Hello, Miss Delacourt. We've been expecting you,' she said. She was very slim and wore a grey woollen jacket that reached down below her knees. She appeared serious and businesslike in her fitted suit that was a shade darker than her jacket. Her stiletto heels added a few inches to her height, but she was still shorter than Cinder –most women were.

'Who's "we"?' Cinder asked, stepping back next to Lulu. Lulu looked the slim woman up and down.

'I work for a man named Inkerman. The owner of this business, among other things,' she said. Her hands were in the pockets of her jacket. She inclined her head towards the brick building she had just emerged from.

'Is that one with youse?' Lulu asked, pointing to the alley. The slim lady turned her face to Lulu but said nothing in reply.

'Someone has been following me since I left my hotel this morning,' Cinder said. The slim woman smiled. She had a small gap between her front teeth at the top, otherwise her teeth were perfect.

'We just needed to ensure you made it here safely,' she said.

'Why? She not gonna be safe?' Lulu asked. This time, the slim lady ignored her altogether.

'Please come inside, Miss Delacourt,' she said, opening the door and stepping back for Cinder to enter.

'Not me,' Lulu said, taking a step back. 'They got weird shit in there.'

'Just wait for me out here,' Cinder said. *I don't think you were invited anyway*, she thought to herself. She, too, was reluctant to enter the strange building owned by the person who had paid her accommodation bill and had her followed all day. Cinder stepped inside and the slim woman followed her in, closing the door behind them. It was much darker inside than it had been out on the street. It took a moment for Cinder's eyes to adjust. As everything came into focus, she looked around in amazement. She had seen nothing like it.

Dim light filtered through the dusty windows, casting eerie shadows on the shelves and curiosities that crowded the space. The air inside was thick with a musty scent – a blend of old leather, ancient paper, and metal. Dark, weathered wooden shelves overflowed with oddities. Antique dolls with glassy eyes stared out from dusty corners, the webs of micro-cracks on their porcelain faces bearing the weight of forgotten playtimes. A grandfather clock ticked away rhythmically; each tick muffled by the many strange objects that filled the room. In the back corner, an ancient typewriter sat on a cluttered desk, its keys stained with the ink of countless unwritten tales. A tarnished silver mirror reflected distorted images, warped and elongated in a haunting dance of reality and illusion. Rows of dusty books lined the shelves, their cracked spines revealing titles that hinted at forgotten lore and forbidden knowledge. A mysterious man, who could have been older still than many of the antiques, stood behind a worn counter, his eyes hidden beneath the brim of a faded, green-grey fedora. He raised his eyes as the two women entered, then returned his gaze to a newspaper he had laid out on the counter.

'Is that him?' Cinder asked in a hushed voice, leaning in towards the dark-haired woman. 'Is that the one that left me the card?'

'Oh, no,' the woman said with a scoffing laugh. 'That most certainly is not Mr Inkerman.' The man behind the counter mumbled something to himself, licked his thumb and index finger, and flicked a page. 'Mr Inkerman is away on business today,' the woman continued. 'He would like you to meet him here tomorrow.'

'What does this Mr Inkerman want with me?' Cinder asked, continuing to look around, trying to take everything in.

'He is looking for some help,' the woman said as she studied her own reflection in the old mirror.

'Help with what?'

'With this.' The woman swept her arm around in front of her.

'He's offering me a job?' Cinder asked. The woman laughed and raised her eyebrows.

'Don't get ahead of yourself, Miss Delacourt. He's offering to meet you, nothing more. Mr Inkerman will meet with you here at 3pm. And I would make sure you are on time. He doesn't like to be kept waiting.' She looked Cinder up and down. 'We can assist you with some wardrobe options if you would like,' she said, with poorly masked disdain. Cinder slid her blood-stained sleeve into her pocket and smoothed down her wind-blown hair with her free hand.

'I'm sure that's not necessary,' she said. 'I'll find something appropriate.'

'Very well then,' the woman said, raising an eyebrow and running her eyes over Cinder again, clearly unconvinced.

Chapter 7
New Wave

A ngus sat on the sand; his surfboard lay across his knees. His face was resting on the smooth, cold fibreglass surface. Closing his tired eyes, he listened to the rhythmic lullaby of the crashing waves. A gentle breeze swirled around him, repeatedly lifting and dropping his hair on to his face. Aware of the presence of someone approaching, he opened one eye. Alice sat down cross-legged beside him. Just like Angus, she was wearing a wetsuit. A surfboard that she had borrowed from Torry sat face down on the sand next to her.

'Good evening,' she said, noticing the glint of Angus's one open eye in the moonlight.

'Alice,' he said, moving his head in greeting and closing his eye again. Alice watched him for a moment. His large chest rising and falling with his breaths.

'You seem very calm tonight.'

'I am.' Angus's eyes remained closed.

'The moon will be out soon,' Alice said, looking up at the clouds that were rolling slowly across from the hills behind her and drifting out to the ocean. 'It's full tonight. Doesn't that worry you?'

'Nope,' Angus said, opening an eye again. 'It's going to rain soon.' He pointed to the sky. 'The wolfies don't like the rain.'

'I can't see any rain,' Alice said, turning to look back at the clouds above the hills behind Heathcote. Angus slid his board from his knees and stood.

'I can smell it,' he said, taking hold of a strap that hung behind him. He passed the strap over his shoulder, pulling it up to zip up the back of his wetsuit. Alice ran her eyes up his large frame.

'I don't smell anything but ocean and your B.S.' she said, writing her name in the wet sand with her foot.

'It's just the other side of the hills,' Angus said. As if on cue, light-ning flashed and lit up the clouds and formed a momentary halo on the hilltops. One corner of Alice's mouth pulled up into a half smile.

'I'm impressed,' she admitted. 'Should we stay out of the water?'

'It's still a way off,' Angus said, picking up his board as thunder rumbled over them. 'We should have time for a few sets before the storm. Besides, a little lightning never hurt anyone.' He walked to-wards the ocean. Alice picked up her board and followed him. She had to jog through the soft sand to keep up with Angus's long strides.

'I admit that you were right about the rain but I'm 100% sure lightning has hurt plenty of people. Killed a few, even,' she added. Angus shrugged and kept walking.

'There're worse ways to die, I guess.'

'Better ways too,' Alice said, clenching her teeth against the cold water that had just touched her toes. Angus paused to let a wave in the shallows crash against his thighs.

'Can you surf?' he asked as he wiped a splash of salty water from his chin. Alice propped the end of Torry's surfboard in the wet sand and fitted the velcro of the ankle strap tightly in place.

'Yes!' she said indignantly. 'Can you?'

'Yes!' Angus matched her indignation.

'That's not what Dom tells me.'

'Is that right?'

'Two left feet, apparently. And you're too precious to get your hair wet,' Alice said, splashing water up at him. 'That's just what he told me.'

Dom was still at the top of the dunes, sitting on the hood of their late friend Blair's Volkswagen. Angus could just make out his figure in the lights of Heathcote.

'Oi, Kinnard!' Angus called out in his direction. When Dom turned his way, Angus stuck the middle fingers of both hands aggres-sively in the air.

'Love you too!' Dom called back to him with his hands cupped around his mouth.

'Are you two okay?' Alice asked. 'I heard that you were fighting.'

'Fighting?' Angus said with a smile. 'That's just how we talk to each other.'

'Well, I'm glad you came out here tonight,' Alice said, resting her head on his shoulder. 'I thought you might go off by yourself again.' She looked up into his sad eyes. Angus shrugged.

'I need to get back into life sometime,' he said, as another clap of thunder rumble down from the mountains. Alice was reluctant to turn the conversation to Cinder, but she felt she needed to ask.

'Has there been any news?'

'No,' Angus said, swishing his leg through the cold water. 'Marraine is still following up leads, but she hasn't found anything...yet.'

'Are we surfing, or what?' Alice asked, to change the subject. She bent down and picked up her board. Angus laughed.

'I love your enthusiasm,' he said. 'But the moon isn't out yet. We won't be able to see a thing.'

'What should we do in the dark while we wait then?' Alice asked.

'We could talk. Get to know each other,' Angus suggested.

'That's one idea, I suppose.' Alice shrugged and pulled her bottom lip between her teeth.

'Do you have something else you would like to do?' Angus asked. Alice smiled to herself.

'No, talking is fine,' she said after a pause. 'What do you want to talk about?'

'I'd like to know more about you,' Angus said. He turned to see that Dom was still sitting on the car. 'I mean, I knew you as a kid, but I don't know much about you now.'

They walked back from the water's edge, and Alice sat back down in the sand. She shifted her board to rest against her side, wrapping her arms around her knees as she gazed out at the dark horizon.

'Where to start?' she mused, a hint of melancholy in her voice. 'I suppose you could say I've been a bit of a wanderer for the past few years. After high school, I left *the family business,*' she said, forming quotation marks in the air with her fingers. 'I drifted from place to place, trying to find where I fit in.' She clasped her hands tightly in front of her legs. Angus nodded, his eyes reflecting the flickering light from the distant lightning.

'I can understand why you wanted something different,' he said. Alice smiled softly, her eyes far away.

'Yeah, I guess so. I tried my hand at a few things. Waitressing, retail, even had a stint teaching suburban housewives self-defence.'

'Self-defence?' Angus said as he sat next to her.

'Yeah,' Alice said with a laugh. 'But nothing felt right. It was like I was always on the outside looking in, watching everyone else live their lives.' She ran her hands through her hair. Angus listened intently.

'How did you end up back with your cousins?' he asked. Alice sighed, drawing a pattern in the sand with her finger.

'I think I needed to confront who I was, who we are. We aren't like normal people. Most people don't know anything about our world.' She reflected. 'You know, coming back here feels like I might find some closure of some things. Plus, I missed the ocean. There's something about the waves, the salt in the air, that makes me feel at home. And something about being here with you, all of you, just feels right.'

Angus glanced at the rolling waves, nodding in understanding. 'The ocean has a way of calling you back, doesn't it?'

'Yeah,' Alice agreed. 'And the family you have here. You don't know how lucky you are. I know Gunn isn't your dad, but he's a better parent than my mother and father combined.'

'You don't get along with your parents?'

'My father never speaks to me because he wanted a boy, and my mother never stops talking at me because she expects perfection.' Alice's voice was rising to a yell. Angus moved uncomfortably in the sand. Alice looked at him, her eyes searching his face in the glow that was just appearing on the horizon. He was smiling, but she could see the sadness in his eyes. 'I'm sorry I'm complaining about my parents; that's insensitive of me.' Alice reached out, placing a comforting hand on Angus's arm. 'You know you're not alone, right? We're all here for you,' she said. Angus gave her a grateful look.

'I know.'

They sat in companionable silence for a moment, the sound of the waves crashing around them. Alice broke the quiet, her voice gentle.

'You know, Black, it's okay to lean on others. You don't have to carry all that weight by yourself.'

Angus nodded, her words settling on him. 'I know. I guess...' He trailed off as they heard Dom descending the timber steps that led down through the dunes. Alice gave Angus a reassuring smile.

'One step at a time. We'll get through this together,' she said as they watch Dom jump down the last few steps and jog across the sand towards them.

'You feeling better tonight, Black?' he asked as he kicked some sand up Angus's back. Angus dusted the sand away.

'I'm doing okay. Alice has been helping me out.'

'Nice!' Dom said, over emphasising the 'i'. 'I wondered what you two were doing down here in the dark.'

'We were just talking,' Angus explained. Dom sat his surfboard in the sand.

'Hey, no judgment from me,' Dom said. 'You two can do whatever you want as long as it stops you from being a tool.'

'So, I'm a tool now, am I?' Angus said as he got to his feet. Dom tapped a beat with his knuckles on the bottom of his board.

'Not just now,' he said. 'It's been going on for some time.' He flicked his messy hair out of his face. Angus got to his feet and took a step towards him, but Alice stood up between them.

'Can we play nice boys?' she pleaded, holding a hand up to each of their chests. She looked at Dom. 'Can we stop calling Black a tool, please?'

Dom nodded in agreement. 'What about, Angus Grinder?'

'No,' Alice said.

'Angus Mac Kita?'

'No.'

'Black and Dicker?' This time Alice laughed. 'I'm sorry, Black, but that one was pretty funny,' she said, rubbing her hand over Angus's chest. Angus tried to keep the angry look on his face, but the other two could clearly see a smile in his eyes.

The clouds parted slightly, allowing the first beams of moonlight to spill over the ocean. They all looked out to the water, seeing the waves illuminated by the soft, silvery light.

'The moon's out,' Alice said excitedly. 'Shall we?' Dom was the first to run out into the ocean, leaving the other two standing on the beach. Alice's hand was still resting on Angus. He took it in his.

'Are you coming in?' he asked.

'You go. I'll follow you.' Alice said, waving him away.

Angus let go of her hand, slid his surfboard under his arm, and trudged into the water. When the water was splashing against his torso, he hopped over the next wave and slid onto his board. Alice followed close behind and they paddled out to Dom together. As they paddled into the rolling waves, the moonlit sea stretched before them, a vast canvas of liquid silver. The salt-scented air mingled with the anticipation of the approaching storm, lending an electrifying energy to the atmosphere. Dom, perched on his surfboard beyond the break, couldn't help but notice the dynamic unfolding between his friends. Alice's laughter, punctuated by occasional splashes of seawater and distant thunder, drifted on the breeze as she paddled beside Angus.

'Having fun there, Black?' Dom called out, a mischievous grin playing on his wet face.

Angus shot him a quick glance, a half-smile playing on his lips.

'Always, mate. Just enjoying the waves,' he said as he drifted up to Dom. Alice splashed water towards Angus, her eyes glinting with a mix of mischief and flirtation.

'He's just trying not to drown,' she teased. Dom ran his eyes along the shoreline and the lights of Heathcote beyond. He folded his arms across his chest against the cold and listened as the waves rolled and crashed onto the sand. As the water receded back to the ocean, it left a line of foamy bubbles. Silver in the moonlight, the foamy band slowly dissipated, only to be replaced by the next tumbling wash.

'Do you ever wonder what it would be like to ride some different waves?' he asked.

'You have ridden some different waves,' Angus said with confusion. 'You told me that you surfed all over Europe while you were missing.'

'I didn't mean me,' Dom said. 'I've ridden all sorts. I was talking about you. I think it would be good for you to try something new.' He ran his eyes over Alice as she paddled up, her board bumping into Angus's. Angus placed his hand on Alice's back to steady her.

'I love it out here, though.' Angus said, looking up at the twinkling lights of Heathcote. Dom paddled closer to him and sat himself back up on his board.

'Me too. But even if you enjoy something, sometimes it's fun to give something else a go, something new. Isn't that right, Alice?' he asked. Alice nodded and took hold of Angus's hand to push herself away from him, holding it longer than necessary. 'I get that you get used to something and so that feels right,' Dom continued, 'but what if you're missing out on something new? And what if the surf just stopped here one day and didn't come back? What would you do then?'

'What do you mean, if it stopped?' Angus asked.

'What if one day the ocean just went flat here, and the waves never came back?' Dom asked. 'Wouldn't it be good to know that you had a back-up ride?'

'Firstly,' Angus said, laying back down on his board. 'Oceans and tides don't work like that. And secondly, do you have a back-up ride?'

'I've always got a back-up ride or two.' Dom said. 'And I know how the ocean works. I'm talking metaphorically.'

'Metaphorically!' Angus repeated. 'Have you been learning your big-boy words, Dom?' he teased. Alice returned, paddling up beside them. She sat up and ran her hands through her wet hair.

'What are you two talking about?' she asked.

'I'm trying to convince Black to try some new things,' Dom said. 'Do you think that sounds like a good idea?'

'Definitely,' Alice said. 'Live a little, Black.' She splashed him. A crease formed between Angus's eyebrows, but he smiled.

'I'm not sure what's going on, but I think you two are ganging up on me,' he said, splashing water back at Alice. Alice giggled and held her hand to her chest.

'I don't know what you mean,' she said, batting her wet eyelashes innocently.

The sky lit up. For the briefest moment it was almost like daylight had returned. Seconds later, thunder boomed and rumbled down from the mountains. Dom cursed. Angus could feel the thunder's vibrations in the board beneath him. He looked to the sky behind the town. Thick, dark clouds were rolling in over the hills.

'I'm not sure we're going to be able to stay out here much longer,' Angus said, as the first drops of rain slashed down in the surrounding water. 'That rain is moving in faster than I thought it was going to.'

'Let's not sit around here anymore then,' Dom said, turning and paddling to catch the next break.

'You can go next,' Angus said, motioning to Alice with his head. 'I'll follow you in.'

Dom surged forward, paddling hard to catch the incoming wave. It rose majestically behind him, and with a swift movement, he stood, riding its crest with an ease born of countless hours spent on the water. The wave carried him forward, and he could feel the raw power of the ocean beneath his feet, the board slicing through the moonlit water. Alice watched, mesmerized, as Dom expertly navigated the wave, carving graceful arcs on its surface. The storm continued to build, and the wind picked up, sending sprays of salty water into the air.

As Dom reached the shore, he hopped off his board, looking back at his friends with a wide grin. 'Come on, Black! Your turn!' he called out, his voice barely audible over the increasing roar of the waves. Alice took a deep breath, adjusting her position on her board. She looked at Angus, who gave him an encouraging nod.

'Not this one,' Angus said, watching the waves forming in the deep. 'The third one from now.'

'How do you know?' Alice asked, looking over her shoulder at the dark waters rising and falling. 'I can't tell the difference.'

'It's more of a feeling than anything,' Angus said as the second wave rolled under them, lifting them towards the sky. 'Okay, this one.' He pushed Alice away from him.

'Alright, here goes nothing,' she muttered to herself, paddling with determination as the next wave swelled up behind her. Angus followed closely behind. The wind was growing in strength, making the waves larger and more unpredictable, the storm's energy adding a sense of urgency to their actions. Alice felt the swell beneath her and, with a burst of energy, pushed herself up, shakily finding her balance as the wave lifted her. For a moment, everything seemed to fall into place. She felt a rush of exhilaration as she rode the wave, the wind whipping through her hair and the water spraying up around her. She could hear Angus cheering behind her, his voice a mix of joy and admiration. As she glided towards the shore, the wave grew more tumultuous. Alice struggled to maintain her balance. The storm's intensity was making the ocean unpredictable, and she could feel the wave's power threatening to overtake her. With a sudden jolt, she lost her footing and tumbled into the churning water.

Concerned, Angus caught the next wave with relaxed skill. He rode it smoothly, his movements fluid and confident. Alice surfaced, coughing and laughing, as she watched Angus glide effortlessly towards her. 'Show-off,' she muttered with a grin. Angus turned and glided over the back of his wave so that he came to a stop next to Alice.

'Are you all good?' he asked. Alice pulled wet strands of hair from her face and nodded.

'Yes, I'm fine, thanks.' Her surfboard was bobbing on the waves in front of her. She pulled on the ankle strap and retrieved it.

As Alice and Angus headed to join Dom on the beach, Dom paddled out past them with a look of determination on his face.

'What are you doing?' Angus called out after him.

'I just want to catch one more,' Dom said.

'The storm is almost overhead now, you idiot,' Angus said, shaking his head. Dom ignored him.

The rain was now coming down harder, each drop creating ripples in the water. Lightning flickered in the distance, illuminating the storm clouds that had now rolled in fully over Heathcote.

Angus turned and continued to the shore. Alice joined him, wrapping her arms around herself to ward off the chill of the rain.

'That was amazing. I don't know how you two do it,' she said, her eyes sparkling despite the weather. 'Shouldn't we head back before this storm really hits?' she asked. Angus nodded, glancing at the darkening sky.

'Yeah, I don't fancy getting struck by lightning tonight.'

A bolt of white lightning branched its way across the sky like a momentary crack in the atmosphere. A crackling boom followed immediately after.

'Hurry up, Dom!' Angus yelled, as the rumble echoed along the coastline. 'Come on,' he said, turning away from the churning ocean. 'Let's head back to the car.'

'You're not going to wait for him?' Alice asked, watching Dom catch the next wave. As he got to his feet, he threw his head back and screamed at the turbulent sky in defiance.

'Do you think he would wait for me?' Angus asked. Alice shrugged. 'He wouldn't,' Angus added and tucked his board under his arm. Alice lifted her board out of the water but grimaced as she started to walk. 'What's wrong?' Angus asked, noticing her limping.

'I think I twisted my ankle when I came off,' she said, lifting her left foot off the sand. The rain was now falling in steady cold drops, dotting the sand with thousands of tiny impressions. 'Give me your board,' Angus said, pushing his wet hair back from his face. He took Alice's surfboard, slid his under one arm and hers under the other. 'I'll take these to the car and then come back and help you.' He turned and trudged up the beach.

The clouds had grown thick and drifted down from the hills. A translucent curtain of grey shrouded the moon. Angus utilise the distant glow from the streetlights to see as he secured the two surfboards to the roof-racks of the Volkswagen. The rain beat down, rumbling against the surfboards and pinging off the hood of the car. Squeaky hinges complained as Angus opened the rear door to collect two towels. Dom arrived and pushed past him. Angus looked around.

'Where's Alice?' he asked.

'Down on the beach where you left her,' Dom said, lifting his board on to the roof.

'Did you just leave her there to hobble up on her own?'

'You still have much to learn, Grasshopper.' Dom said, pulling a strap across the three surfboards.

'What's that supposed to mean?' Angus asked.

'She wants to be carried up here.'

'So why didn't you carry her up here, then?' Angus asked, slamming the door closed. Dom checked the surfboards were secure, then snatched a towel from Angus.

'She didn't want me to carry her,' he said, drying his hair and unzipping his wet suit.

'Did you even ask her?' Angus asked, opening the door again and collecting another towel. Dom smiled and peeled himself out of his suit.

'I didn't need to,' he said. He wrapped the towel around his waist, pushed past Angus again, tossed his wetsuit into the back of the car, climbed into the back seat and closed the door.

'I'll go get Alice then, will I?' Angus asked. Dom pointed to his ear, pretending that he couldn't hear Angus over the sound of the rain on the roof.

When Angus returned, Alice was limping her way up the sand. He wrapped a towel around her shoulders and lifted her into his arms.

'Oh, I'm getting the full service,' she said, draping her arm over his shoulder.

'Are you okay?' Angus asked. Alice dried her face with the corner of the towel.

'I am now,' she said. 'But I can't wait to get out of these wet clothes and get dry and warm.' She looked into Angus's eyes. The rain was running down his face. Alice pulled the towel free from between them and pushed the wet hair back from his brow.

'I'm sorry that Dom just left you down here,' he said.

'Oh, that's okay. I didn't want him to help me, anyway.' Alice grimaced as she turned her ankle from side to side. Angus laughed.

'That's what Dom said,' he said as they climbed the steps to the carpark. The swirling winds blew over the dunes. The green shrubs with their twisted branches bobbed back and forth and the tufts of long grass thrashed wildly in the moist air. Alice pulled the towel over her head, grinned smugly to herself, and rested her head against Angus's warm chest.

Chapter 8
Sydney's Night-life Sucks

Cinder whistled as she walked. As far as her jumbled mind could remember, she had never been a whistler before...before she changed. Whistling, she imagined, wasn't something that was a vampire trait. Perhaps she retained it from the parts of Angus or Marraine that she absorbed with their blood when they betrayed her. Now that she had time to come to terms with her new life – after-life –she was beginning to understand that they had done what they had out of love. She was still not prepared to forgive them. Maybe she never would. Maybe now that they had prolonged her life, she would carry around that anger for centuries.

Her whistling echoed off dark walls and the smooth blackness of windows to her right. On her left, across a quiet street, a grassy embankment rose gently to a row of trees that bordered parkland beyond. Cinder's eyesight had always been sharper that an average human. Now with vampire eyes she could pick up even the most minute sway of the branches and rustle of leaves in the still night air. The moon was yet to rise, so even with the eyesight of a monster, it was difficult to make out anything in the darkness beyond the tree line. She walked on, whistling the same tune she always did now. She didn't know its name but recognised it like one would an old friend. Sliding her hands into the pockets of her long black coat, she turned sharply. Skipping the gutter, she jogged across the street. She made her way up a flight of concrete steps that cut their way up the rise into the park, taking three steps at a time. As the blanket of the shadows covered her in darkness, she paused and ceased whistling.

The constant hum of city traffic rumbled away behind her. Unseen tiny creatures climbed, crawled, and scurried around in the darkness. Leaves rustled, and the gravel moved under her feet, but with the ears of a predator, Cinder listened for something else. It was there, a sound that she had made into her pillow herself many times over the past few months. It was quiet and distant, the breathy rumble of a muffled scream. Cinder turned her head slowly from side to side to pinpoint the direction of the sound. It was moving – moving quickly. She walked further into the darkness, slowly at first, but picking up speed as she went. She soon lost the sound under the stomping of her own feet, but now there was something else to follow. The unmistakable scent of blood permeated the air. Cinder's head shot to the right and her nostrils flared. Her running turned into a sprint. Soon she was flying through the darkness like a shadow, her long coat and hair flicking behind her like flames in a gale.

The muffled screaming came again. Cinder pinned it down to a section of low bushes at the far end of the darkened park. In the shadows, she could make out the shape of two people wrapped together. If one didn't know better, they could have been mistaken for a couple sharing a moment of passion. As Cinder came closer and her vampire eyes became accustomed to the darkness, she could see a young woman struggling, her feet kicking into the dirt around the dark bushes. A small male child had one hand gripped around her chest and the other covering her mouth. The boy had his face buried in the woman's neck. The woman pulled desperately at the boy's hair, to no avail. Cinder slowed, then came to a stop by a tree a few paces away from the disturbing scene.

'Let her go,' she ordered. The boy lifted his head slowly. In the glow of Sydney's distant lights, Cinder could just make out the glistening white of two long fangs. His eyes were shut, and his face wore a look of exhilaration. Blood lingered on his smiling mouth. His tongue moved slowly across his teeth and over his lips. His eyes fell open lazily.

'You again,' he said in a distant, uninterested tone, almost like someone just waking from a dream.

'Let her go,' Cinder repeated as the woman's struggling intensified with renewed hope.

'But I haven't finished with her yet,' the boy vampire spat, wiping the remaining blood from his chin with his shoulder.

'You've finished.' Cinder growled, her own fangs growing larger. The boy laughed.

'I'm happy to share,' he said, moving the woman's neck into the light. 'You don't mind my sloppy seconds?'

Cinder turned her face away.

'You disgust me.'

'Mutual,' the boy said as he stood and dragged his captive along the ground. The woman kicked at the dirt again and scratched at the boy vampire's arms. Deep scratches opened up in his flesh, but almost as quickly as they appeared, they healed themselves.

'Drop her,' Cinder said, taking a step towards them.

'Now, now,' the boy said, holding up a finger. 'I'll snap her neck.'

'If you do, then your neck is next.'

'Oh, you're fun.' He took another few steps back, licking the puncture wounds on the woman's neck as he went. Cinder moved quickly to circle around behind him, but as she did, he threw the woman forward into Cinder's arms.

'I'm done now. Your turn,' he yelled, darting behind the bushes. Cinder sat the woman down carefully and followed him. A sharp pain exploded in her head as something metallic slammed into her face. The blow that may have killed her if she was human sent flashes of light across her vision. Before she could regain her focus, a second object crashed into the back of her knees and sent her falling backwards.

Cinder rolled to her side to see Rach, the girl she had met in the alley earlier that week, looking down on her. Rach's face still showed the evidence of their last encounter. A purple and yellow hallo around her left eye, and a cracked and swollen lip. Rach lifted a length of iron-bar above her and made to bring it down on Cinder's head. More out of reflex than conscious thought, Cinder kicked out hard at Rach. The iron bar dropped to the ground with a ping, narrowly missing Cinder's head. With a shriek, Rach flew into the low bushes. A second bar came swinging down towards Cinder. She swatted it away, but not soon enough. The pole scraped down her cheek, opening a large cut. She grabbed hold of the bar and shoved it hard back up towards the young man holding it. The man groaned in agony, doubling over and fell to the ground. Cinder rolled over onto her knees, but as she tried to get to her feet, another metal pole slammed into the back of her head. She fell to the ground with a thud. She could taste the moist soil in her teeth and her ears were ringing. Three more of the youths appeared in front of her now, holding poles of various lengths. She could sense an unknown number of them behind her, one of them that had obviously just connected with her head. And even more were running in from the sides. Cinder launched herself onto her feet. Now, her fangs were at full extension. Her face twisted and animal-like. Long, sharp claws sat in place of her fingernails.

'Enough,' she yelled, stepping forward and snatching one of the metal poles from the vampire's gang of youths. The weapon-less boy retreated but the rest of the group ran forward, swinging their weapons wildly. Cinder was fast enough to duck and weave her way past many of the attackers, but several blows connected with her already painful head. A blow hit her just above her left eye, and blood splattered from a cut across her face. Struggling to control her rage, she took hold of the attacker's arms, yanking it towards her. The arm came towards her more freely than she had expected and from the sickening sound that accompanied it, Cinder realised with a shock that the arm had detached from the youth's body. She could hear the young man screaming in pain, but there was nothing she could do for him in that moment. The barrage of pipes continued.

'Leave our Lord Gemminae alone,' one youth called out. *So, that's his name – Gemminae,* Cinder thought as she slammed two of his follower's heads together. Over the yelling of her attackers and the ringing in her ears, Cinder could hear the boy vampire, Gemminae, laughing maniacally. She felt something heavy crash into her back. Small arms wrapped around her head and chest. Gemminae's voice was right there in her ear, his blood-wreaking breath, cold and moist down her neck.

'Did you come here to kill me? Was that your plan?'

'It still is,' Cinder growled through gritted teeth. Gemminae laughed.

'Well, you have made my night more fun,' he said, groping at Cinder's breast. 'I wonder what a vampire woman tastes like?' He ran his tongue up her neck.

'I hate you,' Cinder said, reaching up and grabbing his hair. 'I hate all of you.'

'Dear pet,' he said, taking hold of her arm and holding on tighter around her neck. 'You are one of us.'

'I'm nothing like you,' she yelled, trying to pull herself free of his grip.

'Are you hungry?' Gemminae whispered in her ear. 'You are, aren't you? Look around.' He pulled Cinder's head back. 'You can drink from any of my followers. With just a word from me, they would open a vein to you. What do you like? Boy? Girl? Young? Old? I've got them all. Nothing as sweet as sexy Nephilim, of course, but delicious all the same.'

'I am going to kill you!' Cinder whispered back.

'You think you can take me?' Gemminae taunted. 'I can tell you haven't eaten because it weakens you. Don't be fooled by my appearance. I may look like a child, but I have the power of centuries behind me.'

'I don't care how old you are,' Cinder replied, her voice cold and steady. 'You're still a monster, and I'm going to stop you.' With those words, she lunged backwards, her claws extended, fangs bared. Gemminae was caught off guard. He lost his grip as he crashed against a tree trunk. Quickly regaining his footing, he fought back with his own claws and fangs, but Cinder slipped from his arms. Cinder turned on Gemminae. The two vampires clashed in a fierce battle, their claws and fangs tearing at each other's flesh as they fought for dominance. Gemminae was cunning and ruthless, but Cinder was strong and skilled, blocking his attacks and striking back with precision. Gemminae's followers backed away in fear of being caught up in the rage. As the fight raged on, Gemminae tired, while Cinder seemed to gain the upper hand. Sensing this, Gemminae launched himself into the branches of a tree.

'Get her!' he yelled to his followers. The youths rushed at Cinder again, but froze as she turned on them. Her face was twisted and animal-like, fangs bared, unmistakably vampire. Many of the youth still carried the wounds from their last encounter with this red-haired monster. One of them rushed forward, but Cinder grabbed him and held him in front of her like a human shield. From up in the tree, Gemminae laughed.

'Have a taste, Miss Delacourt!' he called from his perch. 'Feed on them.' The youth in Cinder's arms pulled up his sleeve, revealing a trail of puncture marks old and new up his arm.

'No!' Cinder growled, turning to look up into the tree. 'I'm not like you. I'm nothing like one of...' but before Cinder could finish, one of Gemminae's followers hit her legs out from under her.

'Kneel before the almighty Gemminae,' the youth called out. The other young man slipped from Cinder's grip and scurried free. Gemminae dropped onto Cinder's chest and pinned her arms to the ground.

'Yes, beg for mercy and I might keep you as my little pet,' Gemminae whispered in Cinder's ear. 'I'll break you in and then offer you to my fath..'

Gemminae's eyes shot wide as the pointed end of a wooden stake exploded out of his shoulder. The woman that was Gemminae's victim held the stake in two shaky hands. With an exhausted grunt, she pushed the stake deeper, pulling open Gemminae's flesh and tearing through his tendons. Gemminae yelped in pain and Cinder felt his grip on her loosen. She pulled her hands free. Taking hold of the protruding end of the stake in one hand, she gripped the boy vampire's injured arm in the other. Gritting her teeth, she forced her hands apart. Flesh tore, bone and cartilage cracked and popped. Gemminae screamed and watched in horror and disbelief as his arm came free of his body. Cinder threw the arm away in disgust, kicked the stunned Gemminae away and crawled free.

Screaming like a petulant child and cursing in a multitude of languages, Gemminae lashed out at Cinder with his remaining arm.

'We will kill you, bitch!' he screamed. Cinder dodged his flaying arm, got to her feet, took a step back and kicked him hard in the face. Gemminae toppled backwards and fell to the ground. Screaming again, Gemminae struggled to get to his knees. Cinder ran forward and kicked him in the chest. There was the audible cracking of ribs as he flew several feet before flopping to the ground like a one-armed rag-doll. Before the stunned onlookers could react, Cinder darted at one of the youths and snatched a metal bar from his hand. Gemminae turned his blood-smeared and dirty face towards her. His dark eyes glared at her in disbelief. He stumbled to his feet, turned, and ran. The sound of iron pipes falling to the ground echoed through the air, accompanied by the pounding of feet. Gemminae's followers scurried away into the darkness like rats. All except Rach.

'You! You did this, you bitch!' she screamed as she charged at the woman who had stabbed Gemminae with the stick. Cinder whirled around and caught Rach by the neck, hoisting her off the ground. Rach kicked and spat in Cinder's face.

'You're dead now, bitch. When his father finds out what you've done, he'll come for you,' she said with a throttled voice. Cinder calmly wiped the spittle from her face with her spare hand.

'I look forward to it,' she replied, tossing Rach backwards. Rach stumbled and fell onto her backside. Cinder could sense that she was contemplating launching another attack. She stepped closer, her head shaking in warning. 'Go home. Find something better to do with your life.' Rach got up, dusting herself off as she walked backwards, glaring at Cinder and the woman. Before she disappeared into the shadowy trees at the edge of the park, she raised both middle fingers and hurled a stream of obscenities.

Cinder turned back to the woman, who was still clutching the stake tightly and staring down at Gemminae's severed arm.

'Thank you,' Cinder said. 'I think you just saved my life.'

'You saved me.' The woman said. She looked down at the stake in her hand. 'I found this in the garden bed. Should I have stabbed him in the heart?'

'You did brilliantly,' Cinder said, placing a reassuring hand on the woman's shaking shoulder. She had leaves and twigs in her long blond hair and blood stains on her t-shirt. 'What's your name?' Cinder asked.

'Phoebe. Phoebe Hartill.'

'Do you live close by, Phoebe?'

'No, I'm not from here. I was walking back to my hotel and... he... I thought he needed my help.'

'That's what he does. He's a predator, praying on people's goodwill.'

'It was a vampire, right? A real-life vampire.' Phoebe asked.

'Yes, yes, he was.' Cinder said.

'Should I tell someone, the police?' Phoebe asked, placing her shaky hand on the puncture marks on her neck. 'Should I go to the hospital?'

'What would you tell them?' Cinder asked. 'Do you think they will believe you?'

'I'm not sure I believe it,' Phoebe said. Cinder put an arm around her and turned her towards the city.

'I'll walk you to your hotel. You should have a warm shower and a glass of wine.'

'I think I need a whole bottle.' Phoebe said, trying to laugh.

'We'll stop by the bottle shop on the way, my shout.' Cinder said, and they walked towards the city lights. Cinder touched the scratches on her cheek. 'I hope they didn't mess my face up too much. I think I have a job interview tomorrow.'

Chapter 9

Inkerman.

Mr Inkerman was not what Cinder had expected. She had pictured someone older, but Joseph Inkerman, the owner of Inkerman's Inquiétant Ipermercato, still had a full head of blond hair that sat in tight curls against his scalp. His eyes appeared bright, knowledgeable and full of life experience, but his wrinkle-free skin told another story. He was perhaps in his late 30s, Cinder thought. His light-coloured eyebrows were almost indistinguishable from his pale skin, giving his eyes a strange, bird-like look. He stood slightly pigeon-toed, which added to his overall avian appearance. He was not attractive in the traditional sense – far from it – but he emanated the confident appeal of a man that knew he was in charge. Despite his crooked smile, his teeth were straight and white. What he lacked in looks, he more than made up for in arrogance. Cinder recognised this from her step-mother, the way the rich and powerful move through their world, like a cruise ship on the ocean crashing through the waters and creating its own waves.

The slim woman with the long black hair had been there to meet Cinder when she arrived with five minutes to spare. From the twist of her lips when she consulted her watch, the woman didn't consider five minutes to spare as early as Cinder did.

'Follow me. He's waiting,' were the only words she offered Cinder as she led her through the shelves of oddities. The elderly man with the fedora was at the counter again. He grunted in Cinder's direction when she offered him a 'Good afternoon.' They weaved their way behind the counter and through a narrow archway. The mysterious Mr Inkerman was standing in a small room with his hands in the pockets of a knee length grey coat. The room was dark, save for a few shafts of light sneaking their way through drawn shutters on a small window set high in one wall. Mr Inkerman stood next to a table which was too small to be a dining table but too tall for a coffee table. A collection of old books and empty boxes sat at one end. At the other end, a stack of papers held his attention.

'Miss Delacourt is here to see you,' the slim woman said. Mr Inkerman slid a hand from his pocket. Without looking up from the papers, he dismissed the slim woman with a wave.

'Good afternoon, Miss Delacourt,' he said, picking up one of the sheets of paper.

'Hello,' Cinder replied, wondering what was so interesting on the papers that was keeping him from looking up. She twisted her fingers together behind her back as a few beats of uncomfortable silence hung in the claustrophobic room. Finally, Mr Inkerman placed the paper down and turned his bird-like eyes towards Cinder.

'Please, will you come this way?' He directed with his hand for Cinder to walk into a narrow, darkened hallway. Along the walls reaching from the floor to a low ceiling, dozens of dusty boxes sat on rows of deep shelves. The boxes reminded Cinder of shoeboxes, but they were narrower and longer. Under the layers of dust, the boxes appeared to be made from black cardboard with silver-coloured lids. Handwritten labels adorned the front of each box. Hesitantly, Cinder entered the narrow hallway. Logically, she knew it was unwise to enter an unknown place with a strange man that she'd just met, but then again, she was the monster in this scenario. Maybe it was Mr Inkerman who shouldn't be inviting her in. He followed her into the narrow space as they made their way past row after row of the boxes. Cinder tried to read the labels, but the decorative writing was hard to make out and she didn't recognise many of the words, anyway.

Halfway down the narrow passageway, Mr Inkerman reached up and pulled a white string hanging from the ceiling. With a click. A light bulb flickered on, illuminating the second half of the hallway. A set of steps with worn carpet led downwards. The strange boxes on their shelves continued down one side of the narrow staircase. On the other side, chrome fixtures secured a thin wooden handrail to a brick wall. The air grew cooler and there was a distinct smell of mould and dust. Shortly, the narrow passageway opened into a large, low-ceilinged room. Timber rafters ran along the ceiling. Fluorescent lights hung two to a rafter, humming away and flooding the room with a yellowish glow. Apart from the dust and the occasional cobweb in the corner of the room, Cinder noticed that the space was well organised. There were more of the strange little shoe-like boxes along one wall and then another wall with similar boxes but much larger. A desk sat in one corner. A chrome and green-glass lamp sat on the desk next to an old computer. In the centre of the room sat a large wooden table. Several large black binder books covered the surface. One of them was open, showing the plastic pockets inside. Cinder stepped into the room and turned back to watch Mr Inkerman come down the last few steps behind her.

'Please take a look around,' he said with another gesture of his hand. Cinder took a slow lap around the room, her heels tapping loudly on the stone floor. She placed a hand on one of the black folders. With an approving nod from Mr Inkerman, she opened the cover. The pockets made a peeling noise as she pulled the plastic apart. A collection of old newspaper articles had been neatly placed in the pockets. Cinder flick through the time yellowed pages. They were from a variety of different newspapers, but all dated within a few days of each other. As she continued to flick through, the headings at the top of the articles grew smaller and smaller. Although they were all different, they told the same story. A wealthy family had all been brutally slain in some kind of sick, ritualistic murder. Their bodies all drained of blood. The police had no suspects and no leads. The only family member remaining alive was a small boy. Cinder could see his face in some of the accompanying photos. Pale skin, eyes bloodshot, and his face grubby with tears. She could see the large house in the background of many of the photos. Memories of the house she had grown up in suddenly surfaced in her mind. *Was there a fire?* She thought to herself. She shook off the memories and continued to flick through the pages. A rich family dead, and the only one left to inherit a substantial fortune was this boy. He's just like Batman, she thought, but decided that this might be inappropriate to say out loud. There was also a parallel to her own life. She, at least, had been left with a stepmother for all that was worth. This poor boy had no one. She turned over the next page and this time she noticed the boy's name. "Joseph Inkerman Inherits it All" the headline said. And there was little Joseph Inkerman; the tears had dried up, but the same vacant stare was there and then she could see his eyes, the same eyes that were looking at her now from across the room.

'This is you?' Cinder asked what she already knew. Mr Inkerman watched her face intently for a moment before he answered.

'Yes, I was the talk of the town for many weeks, as you can see. There was so much interest in where the money was going that people soon forgot to keep asking why. Or more importantly, who?'

'I'm so sorry,' Cinder offered, 'I know something of how this feels.'

'Indeed, you do, Miss Delacourt. I feel it's quite possible that you know far better than many. Which is why I invited you here. That is to say, just one of the reasons why I invited you here.'

'And the other?' Cinder asked, closing the book and moving so that the table was between her and Mr Inkerman.

'I'm offering you a job, Miss Delacourt,' he said.

'And what makes you think I would like a job?' Cinder asked. Mr Inkerman smiled. His teeth a testament to the dental work that good money could buy.

'As much as we would all like to live without money, it's just a necessary evil, I'm afraid,' he said, moving closer to Cinder.

'This is true, but I have my own money, thank you,' she said, watching him cautiously. Mr Inkerman laughed.

'Now, Miss Delacourt, for this relationship to work, it will need to be built on honesty.'

'Are you calling me a liar, Mr Inkerman?' Cinder asked.

'Miss Delacourt, when I am deciding to enter into business with somebody, I make a point of doing my research. I know just as well as you do that your accounts are all frozen. It appears that you have been the victim of one last act of control from your late stepmother.'

'That woman!' Cinder said. 'Even from beyond the grave, she is still a thorn in my side.' She turned away from Mr Inkerman and strolled around the room looking at the shelves of boxes. Mr Inkerman leaned against the table with one leg crossed over the other.

'Never mind, Miss Delacourt. I am quite happy to help you out with that situation but in the meantime, I would like you to come work for me,' he said, sliding his hands back into his pockets. Cinder stopped in front of a box. A jolt of surprise rushed over her when she recognised the word Nephilim. She tried to mask the recognition and keep her face neutral.

'It does appear that I am in need of a job,' she said, turning back to Mr Inkerman. 'But you have to forgive me for not jumping at the chance. To be completely honest with you, this is all a bit strange and mysterious.'

Mr Inkerman stood and turned to another of the folders. 'Yes, I'm sorry about all the secrecy, but I needed to know that I could trust you before we met face to face,' he said, opening the folder.

'So can you trust me?' Cinder asked, looking over his shoulder at the news articles. Unlike the ones she had already seen, these articles didn't feature Joseph Inkerman. These articles were all about murders and strange disappearances. Mr Inkerman paused for a moment before answering.

'I have heard much about you, Miss Delacourt. You have been asking the same questions that many do, going to the places that most would usually avoid. This happens from time to time, people with romanticised ideas. Some of those people have ended up in these pages,' he said as he ran his hand over the plastic pockets. 'I needed to read your reaction to these photos. I needed to know how you felt about them.' He closed the folder with a thud and turned to look at Cinder 'And now I can see that you hate them too.'

'Hate who?' Cinder asked, puzzled.

'Vampires, of course.' Mr Inkerman said, looking into her eyes. 'You hate the vampires just as much as I do. I can see it in your face. That's why you want to find them and that's why I'm going to help you.'

Chapter 10
Unloading

Angus pulled his knife from its sheath at his hip. He ran his finger lightly along the blade to confirm its sharpness. Dom stood a few metres ahead of him, his back turned, resting his gloved hands against the tray of a flat-bed truck. The truck had a white cab with large front grille and dual headlights on either side. It had a used, industrial but robust appearance. The extended flatbed platform sat on dual rear axles and had a dark, weathered wooden surface. This truck had carried many things over the years, but today it was transporting several large hay bales.

As Angus approached, Dom slipped off the gloves and sat them on top of one of the truck's large wheels. Angus tightened his grip on the handle. Dom wiped some sweat from his brow with the hem of his t-shirt, then removed it, pulling it over his head. His thistle tattoo glistened in the sheen of perspiration on his muscular back. The truck sat atop a hill near the north-west boundary of their property. Dom looked out over his home. The farm stretched out before him, overlooking the ocean. Mid-afternoon sun had just broken through a gap in the wisps of white clouds, warm and bright. The air was thick with the scent of the fresh hay, blooming wildflowers, ocean, and a heady combination that hinted at both earth and livestock. A tapestry of emerald-green fields swayed gently in the breeze and below that, lining the coast, sat Heathcote. With a pang of jealousy, Dom could see surfers braving the cool spring waters. Their distant black dots gliding over the glittering aqua surface that stretched out to the horizon.

Unnoticed, Angus moved closer. He lunged silently forward with his knife. Dom jumped aside in surprise. The knife sunk easily into a large bale of hay. Angus pulled the blade back out through the nylon ties that held the bale together.

'What did that poor hay ever do to you?' Dom asked, seeing the satisfaction on Angus's face.

'It had it coming,' Angus said, stabbing his blade in a second time. Dom sat his t-shirt on the tray of the truck and collected his gloves.

'It's good to see you enjoying your work,' he said as he slipped the gloves back on and vaulted up onto the truck bed. 'It's good to see you actually doing some work,' he added. Angus gave him the middle finger.

'I can leave you to do this yourself if you want.'

'No thanks,' Dom said, lifting a bale onto his shoulder. The truck's suspension creaked with the movement of the weight.

'We're supposed to roll those off the tray,' Angus warned, as he watched Dom struggle with the massive roll of hay on his back. Dom let out a long breath.

'This way I get a workout too,' he said.

'What if someone sees you?' Angus asked. 'Those things weigh half a tonne when they're dry.'

'They will probably be too turned on to think about the weight,' said a female voice from the opposite side of the truck. Marraine strolled around the end of the tray. 'Torry told me you two were out here working, but it looks more like you're setting up for a calendar photoshoot. You've got Mr July up here with his shirt off,' she said as she rested her elbows on the tray and looked up at Dom. The already flexed muscles in Dom's torso tightened. He stared out into the middle distance. Taking one hand carefully off the hay, he wiped his brow slowly with a gloved hand. Marraine rested her head in her hands and raised her eyebrows.

'Just put it down.' Angus said, sliding his knife into its sheath. Marraine turned to him and dropped her bottom lip.

'Maybe he needs some help,' she said. 'Why don't you get your shirt off and get up there and join him?'

'It's always good to see you, Marraine,' Angus said, grinning to himself and shaking his head. Dom took hold of the bale again in both hands and took a step towards Marraine. Beads of sweat trickled down his torso, glistening in the mid-spring sunshine.

'Why don't you come up and help me, wolf-girl?' he said. Marraine licked her lips.

'I'm not exactly dressed for manual labour, sweetie,' she said, looking down at her dress pants and the mud on the soles of her heels.

'That's fine, clothes are optional,' Dom said.

'Okay!' Angus interrupted. 'Can we get on with this? I don't want to be here all day.'

'I'm sorry, Black. We're being very naughty,' Marraine said and pushed herself away from the tray. 'As much as I'd like to stay around for the show, I came here to talk to you about some things I've found out.'

She circled her way around the bale that Angus was undoing and came to stand next to him. She took hold of his arm and kissed his cheek.

'How are you doing, sweetie?' she asked.

'I'm doing okay,' Angus said, resting his hands on his hips. 'Have you got some news?' he asked hopefully.

With a grunt, Dom dropped the bale from the tray. It hit the ground with a thud, rolling half a turn before coming to rest. Dom jumped from the tray and came to join them.

'I have some good news and some bad news,' Marraine said as she watched Dom's chest rise and fall from the corner of her eye.

'I'd like the bad news first, I think,' Angus said. 'Get that out of the way.'

'We are getting closer to finding her, sweetie,' Marraine prefaced. 'But I don't know where she is now.'

'What do you mean now?' Angus asked.

'That's the good news,' Marraine said. 'The money trail I was following panned out. I tracked her to a hotel in Sydney.'

'But you just said you don't know where she is,' Dom said, crossing his arms and leaning back on the hay bale.

'Is she there or not Marraine?' Angus asked. Marraine looked out at the horizon quickly, then down at the ground. She held her palms towards Angus.

'She was there; we know that much. But she's not there now.'

'Then we need to go there. Ask questions.' Angus said as he paced back and forth between Marraine and the truck, like a caged dog. Marraine followed him with concerned eyes.

'I had a friend of mine called Carmichael go and check it out.'

'And what did this Carmichael find?' Angus spat, sensing another dead-end.

'He found a homeless woman named Lulu living there. She confirmed that Cinder had been there only a week or so ago, but she doesn't know where she is now.'

'Doesn't know or won't tell?' Angus asked, stopping to grip the edge of the truck bed. 'We need to go there and get it out of her.'

'Get it out of her *how*, sweetie?' Marraine asked. Angus took a step back and dropped his head between his outstretched arms.

'Anyway we can,' he said darkly. Marraine crossed her arms and dropped her head to one side.

'Are you suggesting torture?' she asked. 'Because I've done a lot of questionable things in my time, but I will never be party to torturing innocent people.'

'Yeah, mate, you're starting to sound a bit crazy now,' Dom added. Angus lifted his head and slammed his palm into the side of the truck bed. The truck rattled and the remaining hay bales wobbled.

'I know,' Angus said, dropping his head again and kicking the dirt with his boot heel. Dom moved to stand next to Marraine.

'This is good news,' he said. 'We know she's alive and we're getting close. Just let Marraine keep doing her thing. You'll have Cinder back in no time. That's right isn't it, Marraine?' He looked at Marraine, but saw something unexpected in her expression. He sent her back a questioning look, but she gave her head the smallest of shakes.

'Yes, that's right,' Marraine said, but the exchange between her and Dom hadn't gone unnoticed.

'Marraine, is there something else?' Angus asked, turning to look at her.

'Just leave it, mate,' Dom said. 'Thanks for letting us know, Marraine. Now we need to get back to work.' Dom turned, took two long strides and leaped back on to the truck bed.

'Marraine, is there something else?' Angus asked again, more forcibly. Marraine sighed.

'The woman, Lulu, told Carmichael that she didn't know where Cinder was, but she knew who she was with,' she said.

'Who is she with, Marraine?' Angus asked.

'Lulu said she didn't know his name, but that he was, in her words, "Some creepy rich dude". She might be living with him, apparently.'

Angus turned back to the truck. He pressed both palms into the bottom of the tray and pushed. A deep, throaty yell rose from his chest and out through his clenched teeth. His face turned red as the veins in his neck expanded and pulsed. Shoulder and arm muscles tensed, pulling his shirt tight across his back. Slowly, the left side of the truck inched off the ground. Angus threw his head back, opened his mouth, and roared at the sky. As impossible as it seemed that he would be able to actually flip the truck over, Dom didn't want to take that chance. He leaped from the tray and rolled clear. Angus dropped the truck back to the ground with a thud. It wobbled and rattled from side to side as he walked away.

'I think he took that well,' Dom said as he came to stand with Marraine. They watched Angus walk away. When he disappeared around the corner of an old shed, Marraine turned to Dom.

'I need to find her Dominic; that's all there is to it.'

'You're getting close. That's good,' Dom said, then turned to look at the truck. 'I guess I'm doing this by myself now, then.'

'Will you be putting your shirt back on?' Marraine asked.

'Probably not. It's hot work.'

'I suppose I could give you some help, then.' Marraine said with a wink.

Chapter 11
A Real Job

Cinder sneezed. She was carrying a stack of small black boxes. The dust from boxes untouched for some time was getting up her nose. She sneezed again and the contents of the boxes rattled. She steadied herself not to drop any of them. For all she knew, they could house priceless, one-of-a-kind relics. Mr Inkerman's store, she was discovering, held all kinds of trash and treasure. From mass produced plastic vampires with wobbling heads that said, "I vant to suck your blooood," when you flicked them, to large swords that came with certificates of authentication. And these were just the things that were available to the public. There was an entire sub-basement, filled with one-of-a-kind items in glass cabinets. Only the most exclusive clientele could make an appointment to view these items, and only when Mr Inkerman was available to show them personally.

Cinder sat the boxes down on a glass-topped display counter. The dust rose into the air and Cinder could see the fine particles dancing in shafts of morning light that were coming through the high storefront windows. Aside from the ticking of the grandfather clock, the store was empty and quiet. But in the stillness, it vibrated a haunting energy, as if the spirits of the past lingered among the trinkets and treasures. Cinder imagined the ghostly figure of a Victorian-era lady browsing through the faded books or a spectral child reaching out to play with the wind-up toys. The dim light played tricks on her eyes, casting odd-shaped shadows along the walls. Despite the apparent disorder of the store, there was an underlying sense of organisation. A method to the madness, Cinder thought. Each item, no matter how obscure, had its place in the symphony of antiquity. The store seemed like a living, breathing entity, carefully curating its own history within the confines of its cluttered walls.

The doors opened to the public at midday. Mr Inkerman had explained that his clientele were not morning people. There were many who called themselves vampires. Mr Inkerman referred to them as *Vamposers*. They dressed in black gothic clothing and painted their faces white. Mr Inkerman had explained that some of them even went as far as sleeping in coffins and drinking each other's blood. These customers, of course, only came out after dark. Cinder had met two of them the previous night, a young man and a young woman. Their clothes were very beautiful. The young man wore a top hat and a long black coat over a vest and cravat. But Cinder was most taken with the woman's floor length dress that was corseted at the waist and frilled out in a bell shape at the bottom. Black lace gloves ran all the way to her elbows and a matching parasol hung by the handle from her arm. After her initial distaste at someone wanting to call them self a vampire when they weren't, Cinder actually found the two young people in their impressive outfits to be perfectly friendly and polite. She spoke with the young woman for some time about one of the antique books, and the three of them laughed about how the young man's hat kept bumping into a dream catcher hanging from the ceiling. Cinder found that having her mind occupied with a purpose other than hunting down vampires was calming. This was her life now, and it helped her feel grounded. It was also easier to remember her own name when it was on a nametag pinned to her shirt.

Mr Inkerman's other customers were collectors. The people who could afford to buy the artefacts from Mr Inkerman's collection could afford to sleep in. There was also, of course, the benefit of carrying out some of the less-legal business dealings under the cover of darkness. So even though the doors did not open until midday, Cinder had come in early to make a start on some of the organising that Mr Inkerman had assigned for her. She was excited to have a "real job" as she had been telling herself. It was quiet and peaceful in the store in the mornings. Mr Inkerman had shown her how to connect her phone to the shop's speaker system. She had lost her phone in the fire when The Big House burnt down. Not so much lost as deliberately left on her bed to burn. Mr Inkerman had given her a month's advance on her wages, so she had plenty of money to get herself some things.

'I need clothes and a phone. For work!' she had said excitedly to a middle-aged woman named Flo behind the counter at Myer. Flo didn't appear to have the same enthusiasm as Cinder did about her "real job".

Now in her new shirt and tailored pants, Cinder chose a playlist on her new phone and pressed play. She listened as the music played through the store's speakers. She sang along as she went to work. A sneeze erupted as she opened a dusty box. She sat the lid on the counter. The box had a lining of dark red felt. Sitting snugly in three indentations, were three long fang-like teeth. They had been polished to a bright white and glistened as Cinder moved them through the sunlight. A handwritten card that was pasted into the lid claimed they were the teeth of a vampire named Trei. The card was folded in half. Cinder opened the card to find a short story about the fangs. The story spoke of how the vampire Trei had lost his fangs in a bet with a Lycan Alpha. Three weeks later, when his fangs had fully grown back, Trei used his new fangs to drain the alpha's mate of all her blood. The box had originally had a full set of four fangs, but one was lost years ago. At the bottom of the card was a five-digit code. Two capital letters and three numbers. Cinder slid over a large black folder that she had sat on the display cabinet earlier. She flicked through the many pages until she came to the one she was looking for. She slid her index finger about two-thirds of the way down the page and stopped. Thin red lines crisscrossed the yellowing white pages. Atop the line where Cinder's finger now hovered was the code AO426, the same code that was written on the card with Trei's fangs. Cinder filed notes: good condition, fangs for sale.

The page showed a shadow, followed by a dark figure at the shop's entrance. Assuming it was a potential customer who was not aware of their opening hours, Cinder watched to see if they would read the sign on the window or try unsuccessfully to open the door. The door rattled and Cinder assumed they had taken the second option. She sat her pen down and stepped out from behind the cabinet. She stopped when she heard a key sliding into the lock. A small metal bell hung strategically above the door rang as the dark, hooded figure entered the shop.

'Buna dimineata,' the new arrival said as they removed a pair of black leather gloves. They pulled back the hood of their knee length dark grey coat. 'How is my favourite employee this fine morning?' It was Mr Inkerman, beaming.

'I'm well, thank you,' Cinder said, returning to her place behind the display cabinet. 'I'm sure you tell all your employees they are your favourite.'

'This is not true,' Mr Inkerman said, placing his gloves in one hand and holding up a finger. 'I have many employees. You are just the only one I trust with this important work.'

'Well, I'm glad you trust me, but I'm not sure how important cataloguing these things is. Don't get me wrong, I'm enjoying it, but couldn't this be done more efficiently with barcodes and digital scanners?' Cinder asked, placing the lid back on the box of fangs.

'Yes, indeed, there are always the quicker ways, but I am a patient man. I could have sent anyone in here to mindlessly bleep-bleep away for the day. They would come in mindless and leave mindless. What would they learn?' He sat his gloves down next to the boxes Cinder was cataloguing. 'Tell me, Miss Delacourt, what have you learned today?'

'I've learned that vampire's teeth can grow back. I didn't know that before.' Cinder said, holding up the box of fangs.

'And do you know how long they take to grow back?'

'Three weeks or less,' Cinder said, lifting the box. Mr Inkerman smiled.

'Excellent. A digital scanner wouldn't have told you any of that, would it?' He picked up one of the dusty boxes and inspected it. 'Anything else?'

Cinder thought for a moment.

'I found out that there are alpha-male Lycans. I never knew that.'

Mr Inkerman opened the box. 'Do you know of the Lycan-thrope?' he asked, removing a tightly wrapped parcel of red silk.

'No, not much at all, really.' Which was true, she thought to herself. 'I'd like to know more,' she added. Also, the truth. Mr Inkerman unwrapped the silk parcel to reveal a small golden pendant.

'Good,' he said without looking up at Cinder. 'I am happy that you have an inquisitive mind, like my own.' His eyes were such a light shade that they almost faded into the whites.

Cinder had her hair pulled up into a ponytail, but her hair was long enough to be hanging over her left shoulder. The morning light was now bright through the shop windows and a shaft of light was shining through her ponytail.

'You have very red hair, Miss Delacourt.' Mr Inkerman said, holding the silk ribbon up next to her hair.

'Yes, I got it from my mother.'

'It reminds me of my sister.'

'Oh, I thought you didn't have any other family. The papers said you were left with the family fortune,'

'She's my mother's daughter,' Mr Inkerman said with a scowl.

'Oh, I see. Are you two close?' Cinder asked.

'No. I hate my sister. I like to stay as far away from her as possible. What about you, Miss Delacourt? Do you have any siblings?'

'I have a little sister.' Cinder said, inspecting the box of fangs one last time.

'Then you have my condolences,' he said, placing his hand on Cinder's shoulder. Cinder laughed.

'I love my sister,' she said as she shuffled past Mr Inkerman.

'Does she hate them too, your sister? Does she hate the vampires?' he asked as he carefully re-wrapped the gold pendant. Cinder had just placed the box on a high shelf. She pulled her hands to her chest and clenched her fist in front of her, where Mr Inkerman could not see.

'I've tried to keep my loved ones away from them,' she said, releasing her hands and turning back to Mr Inkerman with a smile.

'Yes, that's very wise, Miss Delacourt. Very wise.' He placed the pendant back in the box and slipped on the lid. 'Talking of loved ones, do you have a special someone? Boyfriend? Girlfriend? Anything like that?'

Cinder shuffled back past Mr Inkerman and picked up another of the small boxes.

'No. No one special.'

Chapter 12
In the Shadows

Angus sat with his feet dangling over the edge of the old bridge that led to the small inland town of Brookesmarsh. They had erected a modern concrete and iron replacement structure 4km upstream. Any traffic was now diverted to the new bridge, but the old one remained. A towering timber structure that spanned the river. Twenty-two pairs of giant supports fashioned from the straight timber of ancient forests, stretched up from the marshy ground below. Each beam, weathered and grey by countless seasons. They showed the scars of age but were just as imposing and solid as the day they had been hoisted into place by man and beast. The bridge itself was only ever wide enough to support one lane of traffic and spanned a 42-metre gap over the valley. Angus sat almost dead centre, directly over the running water some 30 metres below. An intricate lattice of wooden beams and planks stretching across the darkening sky. Rusting but holding firm, handcrafted bolts as thick as a man's arm, held the crisscrossing beams in place. Golden grasses swayed gently in the breeze beneath the bridge, their tips brushing against the sturdy wooden supports. On either side of the valley, hillsides dotted with trees and shrubs rose gently to meet each end of the bridge. The sun cast sharp shadows through the gaps in the beams, creating a mesmerizing dance of light and dark on the ground and water below. It was a marvel of engineering, a wooden wonder that connected not just two points of land, but the past with the present.

Whistling a tune his father had taught him, Angus got to his feet, holding on to the handrail to steady himself. The sudden change of position made his head spin. He leaned with his arms against the handrail. Originally, the rails had been white but now they were just as grey is the supports below save for a few flakes of paint that's still stuck under the rusty bolts. Angus kicked his right foot backwards and forward as he watched the river far below snake its way through rocks and reeds. The water rippled hypnotically in the retreating daylight. Angus reached down to a collection of bottles at his feet. After fumbling for a moment, he lifted one to his mouth. Finding only dregs left, he held out his tongue and tapped the bottom of the bottle to force out the last drop. Sure that the bottle was empty, he cursed and dropped the bottle into the running water far below. The air whistled in the narrow opening as it fell, then the bottle hit the water with a plop. Lifting one of his long legs, Angus threw it over the handrail and sat straddled with one leg dangling off the side of the bridge. He watched the breeze blow through the valley, swaying the long grass, and soon his body was swaying in time. He pulled his other leg over. Gripping the rail behind him, he leaned out over the water. The river lapped against the bases of the large wooden supports.

Angus felt the vibrations of footsteps through the bridge before he heard them. He leaned forward to look through his legs. From this angle, he could only spy a pair of female legs through the gaps in the handrail.

'Everyone is looking for you.' It was Alice. 'They need you,' she said, making her way over to lean on the rail next to him.

'Well, everyone should be doing their jobs and not looking for me. If they all just did what they should, then they wouldn't need me,' Angus said, pulling himself back upright. With some effort because of her short legs, Alice climbed up and sat on the handrail next to him.

'They want you. They need your direction,' she said.

'I'm not exactly in the right headspace to give directions at the moment, if you know what I mean,' Angus said, turning around and bending over the handrail. 'My decision making may be impeded.' He picked up one of the empty bottles and squinted at the label. 'I also shouldn't operate machinery, drive a vehicle or get pregnant,' he said. Alice could see the remainder of a six-pack scattered around the bridge. She took the bottle from Angus and inspected the warning.

'It's only a problem if you're already pregnant. You aren't pregnant, are you?' she asked.

'I haven't done a test or anything, but I'm fairly sure I'm not,' Angus said.

'If you're just trying, this isn't a problem, then,' Alice said. 'In fact, I think beer has been a contributing factor in more than one conception. Am I right?'

'Do you want some?' Angus asked.

'What pregnancies?'

'No, do you want a beer?'

'I would have liked one, yes,' Alice said, putting her hand on Angus's back as he swayed again, 'but it looks like you have finished them all.' She sat the bottle on the ground with the others.

'No,' Angus said in a slurred voice. He climbed and stumbled back over the handrail onto the bridge. Glass rattled and clinked together as he fumbled with the bottles. One of them rolled off the shoulder where they were standing and onto the road. Angus stood up straight and crossed his arms. 'Someone drank all my beers,' he said.

Alice climbed back over the handrail and bent down to retrieve the bottle that had rolled away. As she did, her t-shirt slid up to expose her stomach. Angus's attention lingering on her exposed skin. Alice noticed him looking and smiled.

'Why are you out here, anyway?' she asked, stepping close to him and placing the bottle with the others.

'I come here to get away sometimes. To be by myself. How did you find me?'

'I um...' Alice blushed. 'I've followed you a couple of times.'

'You've followed me?'

'Yep.'

'Why?'

'I... I'm a stalker. You have a stalker now.'

'Well, that's new. I don't think I've ever had a stalker before,' Angus said, rubbing his stubbled chin.

'It's not new,' Alice said, chewing her lip.

'What?' Angus asked.

'Don't you remember me following you around as a little kid?' Alice said, running a lock of her hair through her hands. 'I used to love visiting all of you. I remember you lived by that lake.'

'Lake Beramura?'

'Yes. I always wanted to see you. You've had a stalker since we were kids.'

'I have great memories of you visiting, too.' Angus looked over his shoulder. A golden halo above the distant dark hills was the only remaining evidence of the sun. The waxing moon was now the prevailing light in the sky. A smile spread across Angus's shadowed face as he watched its beams play on the grey surface of the river. 'Things were simpler when we were kids,' he said. Alice placed her hand on his shoulder and turned him so that she could look into his dark, bloodshot and blurry eyes.

'Tell me what you're doing out here, drinking by yourself,' she said in a hushed tone.

'I'm not drinking now, am I?' Angus said, kicking one of the empty bottles and sending it spinning over the side of the bridge.

'Black!' Alice said seriously, taking his hand. 'You weren't going to jump, were you?'

Angus looked down at their hands wrapped together. He ran his thumb across her small fingers.

'No, of course not,' he said. 'I think I'd survive that fall, anyway. Probably just break my leg or something.' He let go of Alice's hand, turned and gripped the handrail. 'Sometimes I just need some time to myself. I have everyone depending on me and… it gets hard some-times… doing it by myself.' He looked down at the valley.

'Good for you,' Alice said, sidling up next to him and resting her head on his shoulder.

'What?' Angus asked. It wasn't the response he was expecting.

'I said, good for you.'

'I thought you were coming to take me back,' Angus said. Alice slid her hand up to his ear. She needed to stand on tiptoes.

'I'm here to do what's best for you, no one else,' she whispered in his ear. 'Come on. I want to take a closer look at the water.' She took hold of Angus's arm. Unsteadily, Angus stepped back from the handrail. He put his arm over Alice's shoulder, and she led him away.

A few metres from the end of the bridge, a rough track snaked its way through long grass and shrubs down the side of the valley. Alice led Angus down. He slipped a few times on the loose soil and tripped over an exposed tree root. Alice held firmly to his hand, but he was much bigger than her and he fell to the ground several times. Each fall was funnier than the last. By the time they made it to the bottom of the valley, they were both covered in dirt and their cheeks were wet with hysterical tears. Alice held her ribs, trying unsuccessfully to stop the laughter by taking deep breaths. Angus stumbled past her to the water's edge.

The moon hung large and luminous in the clear night sky, casting a soft, otherworldly glow over the tranquil river. The water, calm and clear, reflected the moon's brilliance, creating a path of shimmering light that seemed to lead into the heart of the wilderness. Smooth stones and patches of moss dotted the riverbank, their outlines soft-ened by the moonlight. Along the shadowy edges long reeds swayed gently in the breeze. The air was crisp and filled with the earthy scent of the valley, mingling with the sweet aroma of wildflowers that peeked out from the tall grasses. Somewhere in the distance, a night bird called out, its song a haunting melody that echoed through the stillness. Angus turned his head towards the sound and slipped in the mud. He cursed as his foot slid into the water. His arm shot out to Alice to steady himself, but Alice fell on top of him. They lay in a twisted pile in the long grass. Roaring with laughter, their chests vibrated against each other, which only added to the hilarity of the situation. Alice rolled off and lay down next to Angus. She held her ribs again as she caught her breath. Angus sat up and rubbed his eyes with the heel of his palm.

A family of ducks that had been startled by the new arrivals paddled quickly across the river, leaving V-shaped ripples in their wake. Two large rocks, white and pale green with lichen, jutted out from the opposite bank, reaching down to unknown deaths below the dark, mirrorlike surface. The rocks created a natural dam to the flow of the river, forming a wide pool. Angus and Alice lay on a muddy bank, lined with tall reeds and trees whose branches reached out to the water like twisted fingers. The water lapped gently against the mighty pylons of the old bridge that now towered up beside them. Alice sat up and started untying the laces on her boots.

'What are you doing?' Angus asked as she pulled off her boot and threw it up the bank behind them.

'I'm going for a swim,' she said, sending the second boot flying to join the first.

'Isn't it a bit cold for a night swim?' Angus asked, sitting up next to her. Alice shrugged, then lifted her shirt up over her head. Angus turned away, surprised and embarrassed by the sudden appearance of so much exposed flesh. Alice stood up, her navel level with the top of Angus's head. He turned and looked up at her, but shot his eyes away again as she unbuttoned her jeans and pulled them down over her hips. She pulled her legs free and threw her t-shirt and jeans next to her boots. Folding her arms over her chest, she stepped cautiously down the muddy bank. She paused for a moment at the river's edge, then waded hurriedly into the reedy waters. The riverbank inclined sharply. Her legs quickly disappeared under the dark, glistening surface. When the waterline reached her stomach, she let out a squeak.

'Are you alright?' Angus asked. He was still having trouble looking at her directly. She was more covered than many of the bikini-clad women on the beach, but something about seeing Alice in her lace-frilled black underwear felt much more intimate.

'I'm fine,' Alice said, unconvincingly.

'Aren't you cold? It's not a warm night.' Angus stood and stepped closer to the edge. Alice bobbed her entire body under the water. She shot back up, breathing heavily with exhilaration and laughing.

'If you're worried about me, them come in and warm me up,' she said, her teeth rattling together. 'You're not afraid of a little cold, are you? Are all the stories of the great Nephilim warrior Black all made up?'

'Are you serious?' Angus asked.

'Yes, come on. It's not that bad once you're in.' Alice slid back under the water so that just her head was above the surface.

As Alice watched Angus undress, she soon forgot about the coldness of the water. Her heart raced as she took in the sight of him. Tall and muscular, his shirtless chest glistening in the moonlight.

'You're so beautiful,' she whispered, unable to tear her eyes away from him.

Angus placed his clothes in a pile next to Alice's and stood on the bank in his underwear.

'Are you sure it's not too cold?' he asked.

'Warming up by the second,' Alice called back. 'Now get in here, you big baby.'

Angus took a deep breath, steeling himself against the chill, and waded into the river. The cold hit him like an electric shock, but he pressed on, gritting his teeth. When the water reached his waist, he dove in, surfacing again beside Alice. She laughed, the sound light and joyous, echoing across the water.

'See? Not so bad,' she said, wrapping her arms around his neck. Angus shivered but smiled, the warmth of her embrace chasing away the cold.

'You're right,' he said. 'This isn't so bad at all.'

Alice was still cold, but the shivering had subsided. She looked at Angus, her eyes sparkling with mischief.

'You know,' she said, her voice teasing, 'for a big, tough warrior, you sure took your time getting in here.' She ruffled his wet hair. Angus grinned, splashing the cold water up at Alice.

'I was just savouring the moment,' he said. Alice giggled, pushing herself away and ducking under the water to avoid another splash. She resurfaced a few feet away, her hair dripping and her laughter infectious.

'That's good. You should have some moments for yourself. Let yourself have some fun.' She reached her hands up over her head and let herself fall back into the water with a splash. Angus swam closer, his movements smooth and deliberate.

'Alright, Miss Fun,' he said. 'What do you have in mind?'

'How about a race?' Alice challenged, her eyes twinkling. 'First one to touch the bridge wins.'

'You're on,' Angus said, his competitive spirit ignited.

They lined up, side by side, ready to race across the moonlit water.

'On three,' Alice said. 'One, two...' Alice leaped forward. 'Three!' She dove into the water. Angus growled and took off after her, his strokes powerful and determined. Alice pulled ahead at first, her laughter mingling with the sound of their splashing. But Angus quickly caught up, the gap between them narrowing. Alice reached the bridge pylons first, turning swiftly to head back. Angus was right behind her, his laughter mingling with hers as they swam neck and neck. As they approached their starting point, Alice gave one last burst of speed, her competitive streak shining through. She touched the bank just moments before Angus, her victory cry filling the night air.

'I win!' she declared.

'You're faster than you look,' Angus said, puffing and trudging up the bank.

'Hey, just because my legs are short doesn't mean they're not powerful.' Alice lifted her left leg and held it out in front of her. She eyed Angus and traced the length of her thigh seductively with her fingers. A lump grew in Angus's throat.

'It's cold out here now,' he said as water dripped from his hair and ran down his body. Staring into his eyes, Alice reached her hand behind her back and unclasped her bra. Angus turned away.

'What are you doing?' he asked, blushing.

'I don't want to walk all the way back to the farm in wet underwear.' Alice said, throwing her bra at his feet. Her underpants followed shortly after.

'Are you getting out now?' Angus asked, still facing away.

'No, I think I'll stay in for a bit longer,' Alice said.

Giving into temptation, Angus turned back to look. Alice had moved deeper in. Only her head and shoulders were above the waterline.

'Come back in with me, Black,' she said.

• • • •

In the deep, late hours of the night, Cinder prowled the rooftops of Sydney's towering buildings, the city below bathed in a golden glow from the streetlights and the soft, ambient light reflecting off glass and steel. The historic façade of a nearby building stood in stark contrast to the sleek, modern towers surrounding it. Intricate stonework and arched windows reveal a past valuing craftsmanship and beauty over haste and frugality. Cinder paused on the rooftop of the historical building, her boots barely making a sound on the edge as she surveyed the cityscape beneath her. From her vantage point, Cinder watched the coming and goings of people in Hyde Park, unaware of the predator watching from above. Around her, skyscrapers loomed like silent sentinels, and the neon reflections glimmered off their glass surfaces, their mirrored windows making the city feel like an endless labyrinth of light and shadow.

With feline grace, she leaped across the gap between buildings, a black blur against the bright night sky, her dark form moving effortlessly, as if weightless. Her heightened senses allowed her vampiric eyes to discern even the faintest details, even from that height. The pulse of life below, the sound of heartbeats, the scent of fresh blood, the electric hum of the city – it was intoxicating. As she moved along the rooftops, her pale skin glimmered faintly under the city lights. She was a phantom, her footsteps soundless, her movements fluid as water. With a grinding of unseen gears, a clock on a nearby building clicked over to 3am, a fitting hour for a creature like her to be lurking in the darkness. Her eyes flickered as she spotted movement in the park below. Overcome with carnal desires and desperate for privacy, a couple left their park bench and moved together into the shadows of the towering trees. Memories of Angus's body entwined with hers swam in Cinder's mind. She paused, trying to hold the memory, but it drifted away into the cloudy darkness. Turning back to the park below, she searched for the couple, but even her vampire eyes could not find them.

Turning away from the lights of the park and into the shadows of the towering buildings, Cinder climbed a sloping roof to the peak of the old building. The Sydney Tower loomed beside her, like a giant hypodermic needle piercing the night sky. As she lifted her head, the unmistakable scent of blood overwhelmed Cinder's senses, a sickly, familiar sweetness interwoven with the metallic tang of iron. But more than that, layered beneath it, was something darker – a familiar but unwelcome scent. Gemminae was nearby. Cinder pivoted sharply, her focus narrowing as she honed in on the scent, the city falling away as her heightened senses led her toward it. Down below, through the labyrinth of alleyways and forgotten corners of the city, she followed the trail, leaping gracefully from rooftop to rooftop until she found herself above a dark, desolate alley. The tantalising reek of blood hung thick in the air. Cinder crouched low, blending into the shadows of the rooftop as she peered into the alley below. Her eyes quickly adjusted to the darkness, picking out two crumpled figures on the cold sandstones of the alley floor.

A tall man, his black hair matted with blood, lay sprawled against the brick wall. His eyes were glazed, empty, his body disturbingly still save for the faint rise and fall of his chest. He was barely clinging to life. Beside him, a woman with fiery red hair slumped against a bin, her face ghostly pale in the dim light. Cinder dropped to the ground. She hurried towards the injured man and woman but froze when she noticed something she hadn't when looking down on them. Both victims were missing an arm, their stumps still bleeding sluggishly, the dark liquid pooling beneath them. An unmistakable message for Cinder: Gemminae's twisted signature.

Cinder's fury flared. This was not Gemminae feeding to survive; this was mutilation, an act of cruelty for no purpose other than his own sadistic pleasure. She knelt next to the woman. Her lips moved, her voice faint, a broken whisper that barely reached Cinder's ears. She was still alive, but just barely. The man, too, clung to the fragile edge of life, his heartbeat erratic, fluttering like a dying bird.

'Hang on,' Cinder whispered, her voice surprisingly gentle despite the storm of fury inside her. 'You're not dead yet.'

Cinder removed her jacket, ripping it in half from hem to collar. As she held the bundled fabric to the woman's wound, her eyes flicked toward the darkness beyond. She could feel Gemminae's presence lingering in the night air, his scent still fresh. Probably, he was watching, waiting to see if she would come after him. He wanted her to see this. He was taunting her.

Placing her arms under the woman's legs and supporting her back, Cinder manoeuvred her so that she was leaning with the torn jacket wedge between her and the wall of the alley. Blood covered Cinder's hands and clothes. Conflicting feelings of desire and repulsion muddled her thoughts. She stood to assist the man, but the woman said something again. Cinder knelt in close, and the woman whispered the two last words to pass her lips. Cinder stumbled backwards. Her legs gave out and crumpled to the ground. She sat looking at the scene in front of her.

'It can't be,' she said. The woman slumped forward, leaving a trail of blood along the wall, then fell motionless to the ground. Cinder stared past her at the bundle of bloodied-material next to her. It looked simply like a pile of rags. Maybe the man and woman had used it to soak up some of the blood. But it was moving when Cinder first dropped in from the rooftops. She had paid it no attention then, but she remembered now that it was moving. Cinder crawled towards it. There was no movement now, only a bundle of blood-soaked yellow material. Cinder hoped she had misheard the woman but as she opened the bundle, when she saw where Gemminae had removed a third arm Cinder confirmed that the now dead woman had said, "my baby."

Chapter 13
Night Swimming

Biting her lip, Alice beckoned for Angus to join her again in the river. As she did, Angus noticed the curves of her chest as it rose above the waterline. His mind raced. Surely the best option, the right option, would be to walk away. His mind was saying one thing, but his body was screaming another. Why should he always need to be the one to make the sensible decisions, anyway? He ambled back into the water. The insects and other nocturnal creatures of the valley chirped and called and the water splashed against the bridge, but the sound of Angus's heart pounding in his head drowned these sounds out. He stopped just out of Alice's arm's reach. She ducked her head under the water and popped back up right in front of him. He could feel her hands on the waistband of his boxer-shorts.

'What are you doing?' he asked, raising his eyebrows.

'Shhh,' Alice said, holding her finger up to her lips. 'I'm just helping you out. You don't want to walk back in wet underwear either.' She submerged once more and when she returned to the surface, she was holding Angus's shorts over her chest. She watched his eyes navigate her body, then threw his shorts onto the bank with her underwear. Angus went to say something, but she pushed her lips against his. Angus relaxed into the kiss. Alice's hands ran up the tight muscles of his torso, her breath was warm on his neck. Angus took hold of her cold, wet shoulders, her skin smooth to his touch – electrifying. They moved as one, deeper into the river. As the dark water lapped at his chest, Angus moved his lips to Alice's neck. She dug her fingers into his back, as he kissed slowly towards her ear. He drew back and looked into her eyes.

'Why did you stop? – Oh,' she gasped as he took hold of her waist and lifted her up, pulling her in close again. She wrapped her legs around his hips, bringing them face to face. Alice moved her hands over the scars on his back. Under the water, Angus's powerful hands gripped her thighs. Alice's desperate fingers gripped the thick, wet mass of his dark hair as she pushed her lips to his once more. Angus pulled her in tight, their bodies locking together as one. Warm flesh against warm flesh in the cool of the water.

Far above, the clouds were forming in the star-filled sky. The laughter of the two young people frolicking in the water filled the night. Behind them, framed by the large, timber supports of the bridge, the moon sat large and bright, like an ever-watchful eye.

• • • •

Cinder stumbled back from the blood-soaked bundle, her chest heaving as she struggled to process the grotesque reality before her. The alley felt colder, the walls of the city narrowing in around her. Her vampire senses heightened every detail. The tang of iron thick in her nostrils, the faint sound of distant sirens, the rustling of rats in the shadows. But nothing cut deeper than the sight of the lifeless child cradled in the bloody rags. With trembling hands, Cinder closed the rags over the child's face, muttering a quiet apology.

'I'm sorry, little one.' She rose to her feet, her eyes burning with unshed tears that she wouldn't allow to fall. There was no time for crying now; there would be time for that later. Turning to the injured man, she knelt beside him. His heartbeat was faint, faltering, but he was alive. She worked quickly, tearing strips of fabric from her shirt to bind the oozing stump of his arm. He groaned faintly, his glazed eyes briefly flickering open.

'Stay with me,' Cinder urged, her voice steady despite the storm within her. 'Help is coming.'

She knew she couldn't stay there any longer. Sirens wailed in the distance, drawing closer. Cinder spared one last glance at the woman's lifeless body and the bundle next to her before retreating into the night. The darkness swallowed her form as she climbed back to the rooftop.

By the time she reached her hotel, the city was waking up. The first tendrils of dawn were stretching across the sky, painting the horizon in soft shades of pink and gold. Cinder entered her room quietly, closing the door behind her with a soft click. Lulu lay sprawled on the bed, using her patched coat as a makeshift blanket. She stirred at the sound, her wild hair framing her face as she squinted at Cinder.

'Late night?' Lulu asked, her voice scratchy but warm.

'Sorry, I didn't mean to wake you.' Cinder said, avoiding the older woman's sharp gaze as she tried to conceal her blood-stained hands. She wiped a spot of blood from the door handle with her sleeve, hoping Lulu wouldn't notice. But Lulu noticed everything. Her gaze narrowed.

'What happened?'

'Nothing,' Cinder lied smoothly, heading to the bathroom. 'Just work stuff.'

'Uh-huh,' Lulu muttered, clearly unconvinced. She stretched, then sat up, watching Cinder through narrowed eyes. 'By the way, some guy was asking about you.' Cinder paused, one hand gripping the edge of the sink.

What guy?

'Black fella. Tall, good-looking, dressed like he just stepped off a magazine cover. Said his name was Carmichael.' Lulu's lips twitched into a sly smile. 'He ya boyfriend?'

'No.' Cinder said, coming back into the room. 'And you shouldn't say "Black fella"; he was a First Nations man.'

'No.' Lulu said, scratching her chin. 'He wasn't from here. He was a yank. Gorgeous voice he had too. Got my juices flow'n, he did.'

'A yank? Do you mean he was an American?' Cinder asked, trying not to think about Lulu's last comment. 'What did he want?'

'Asked a lot of questions. Wanted to know who you work for, where you've been. I told him you're not much for talking about yourself.'

'And?' Cinder pressed.

'Didn't tell him much,' Lulu said, shrugging. 'Just that you've got a boss, and that you're working for someone important. Didn't tell him where, though. Figured you wouldn't want me to.'

'Good. Thank you.' Cinder relaxed and returned to the bathroom. Lulu watched her go, then shrugged again.

'Your business is your business. Just thought you should know he's looking for you.'

Cinder nodded as she washed the blood from her hands. She stared at her reflection in the mirror. For a moment, she thought she saw Gemminae's face behind her, his cruel smile twisted in mockery. She spun around, but the bathroom was empty. She steadied her breath and said

'You can stay here as long as you need Lulu, but I think I need to find somewhere else to stay.'

Chapter 14

A Generous Benefactor

'Thank you. Come again,' Cinder said as the bell on the door of Mr Inkerman's store rang and a customer exited. She picked up a silver chain from the counter. She watched as the pentagram pendent hanging from it twirled one way then the other. As she turned to replace it, Mr Inkerman appeared from the back. He stood close to her and looked her up and down.

'Come,' he said. He stepped back and motioned for Cinder to walk down the passage. They walked past the small cardboard boxes that lined the walls. Cinder knew more now about the contents, but many of them were still a mystery. They entered the room at the rear of the store and Mr Inkerman positioned himself beside a bright green suitcase tucked away in the room's corner. He crossed his arms and leaned back against the wall. 'What is this?' he asked, motioning sideways with his head. Despite being shorter than Cinder, he always seemed to look down on her.

'That's my bag,' Cinder said. 'I can move it if it's in the way.' She took a step towards the bag, but Mr Inkerman raised his hand to stop her. He dropped his hand then lifted it again, rubbing his chin.

'Are you sleeping here, Miss Delacourt?' he asked.

'Only the last two nights,' Cinder said, blushing. 'My living arrangements at the moment are um...' She paused. 'Not appropriate for my needs. I was just sleeping here until I can make other arrangements.'

'This won't do, Miss Delacourt,' Mr Inkerman said, shaking his head. 'I can't have someone living here.'

'I'm sorry.' Cinder moved for her bag again, but Mr Inkerman sat his hand on top of it.

'No, no. Leave it. Ms Chase will take care of it.'

Ms Chase, Cinder had discovered, was Mr Inkerman's PA. She was the slim woman that Cinder had the displeasure of meeting the first time she came to the store.

'What will Ms Chase take care of?' Cinder asked.

'You will be staying with me from now on, Miss Delacourt. My guest house has just become available. Ms Chase will have your things taken there for you.'

'You don't have to do that,' Cinder said. 'You have already been so generous.'

'Nonsense,' Mr Inkerman said, waving away her protest. 'Your training will be easier if you are close by, anyway.'

'Training?'

'Yes. We will start your training this weekend. Which reminds me...' Mr Inkerman moved away from the bag and stepped to the top of the stairs that led down to the basement. 'I have a gift for you down here. Come, come.'

Cinder crossed the room and descended the stairs.

'How are you feeling about your new clothes?' Mr Inkerman asked, following her down.

'I'm happy with them.' Cinder said, unsure how to respond. 'Thank you again for organising the payment for them.'

'If my staff look good, I look good,' Mr Inkerman said as they stepped from the last step into the basement. 'Perhaps we could ask Ms Chase to assist you with some more choices.' He looked Cinder up and down once again. Cinder looked at herself to see if there might be a stain on her white shirt or a hole in her tailored pants.

'Is there something wrong with my clothes?' she asked.

'They are perfectly adequate.' Mr Inkerman said with an unconvincing smile. 'But Ms Chase knows how to add a bit of style and a bit of sex appeal to things, don't you think?'

'Are you asking me to show more skin?'

'Of course not.' Mr Inkerman assured her. 'I can completely un-derstand why you would like to keep all those freckles covered up,' Mr Inkerman said. Cinder pulled self-consciously at the collar of her shirt. 'No, not less clothing, Miss Delacourt,' Mr Inkerman contin-ued. 'Maybe just smaller sizes.' He held his cupped hands out in front and moved them slowly towards each other. Cinder read the gesture as showing something shrinking.

'These clothes are my size and I'm comfortable in them.' Cinder said, pulling at her jacket.

'Hmmm,' Mr Inkerman said, appraising her, 'Never mind. Per-haps it's not the clothes. Anyway, your gift is here.' He moved next to her, close enough for Cinder to be overcome with his expensive cologne.

He placed his arm over her shoulder and moved her towards the bench in the centre of the room.

'Um, okay,' she said, still trying to process what he had just said about her clothes and about her.

'This is for you,' Mr Inkerman said, drawing her attention back to the bench. On one side was a stack of paperwork next to two opened storage boxes. On the other side sat a long slim box made from glossy white cardboard. Cinder estimated it was about one and a half me-tres long. A blood-red ribbon spiralled down the box, tied with a bow at the centre.

'You have already been so generous. I really don't need any more gifts,' Cinder said. Mr Inkerman waved away her protest.

'This is important,' he said and collected the gift box. 'If we are going to work together to eliminate our nocturnal friends, you will need this.' He passed the box to Cinder. Cinder untied the bow and slipped off the ribbon. Sitting the box on the bench, she removed the lid to find a long, black cylindrical item.

'Is this a sword?' she asked, lifting the item from the box. It was heavier than she expected.

'No, not a sword,' Mr Inkerman said, shaking his head. 'This is a katana. A hand-forged Japanese weapon made from Tamahagane steel. It is too elegant a weapon to simply be called a sword.'

Cinder looked down at the weapon in her hands. Black silk, crisscrossing in a meticulous pattern that provided both grip and elegance, wrapped around its hilt. Beneath the silk, textured leather made from ray-skin peeked through, adding a subtle contrast to the dark wrapping. The tsuba, or guard, was a simple yet graceful oval, etched with swirling clouds and coiling dragons.

'Thank you,' was all that Cinder could manage to say, taken aback by the beauty of her gift.

'Draw it.' Mr Inkerman instructed. Cinder wrapped her fingers around the hilt and gently pulled the blade free of the scabbard. The long, slender blade shimmering under the glow of the fluorescent light. The steel gleamed with a silvery, almost ethereal quality; the edge so sharp it seemed to slice the very air around it. An intricate wave pattern ran along the blade. Cinder sat the scabbard on the bench and held the blade up-right. This was no mere weapon. It was a work of art, a masterpiece of balance and precision.

'It's beautiful,' she said, watching the light play along the edges of the blade as she twisted it from side to side.

'Yes, it is,' Mr Inkerman said, watching her. 'But do not be fooled, it is also very dangerous. Much like you, I think, Miss Delacourt. This is not just a gift; I'd like you to learn how to use it. I've organised for you to have lessons.'

'I still don't understand,' Cinder said.

'If you have attracted my attention, then you will most definitely have attracted the attention of the vampire. And now, the two of us together...I'll put it this way. We are making a lot of noise. I want to make sure you can take care of yourself.' Mr Inkerman said.

If he only knew how well I can look after myself, Cinder thought.

Chapter 15

Beasts and Bourbon

A cool breeze whistled through the grassy dunes. The waves crashed against the rocks at the far end of the surf beach, sending sprays of water high into the air. Thick green branches of the trees at the edge of the forest that ran down to the coast moved violently back and forth as the wind picked up. The silver of the full moon, set high in the night sky, reflected in the misty plumes of the crashing water. A dark shadow moved briskly through the trees. The rumble of the breeze and turbulent ocean barely masked the sound of crushing leaves and breaking twigs. An enormous creature emerged from the shadows and leapt over the stony dunes, its large hairy feet sinking deep into the moist sand. The moon reflected off its large dark eyes as it backed away from the waves rushing up the sand towards it. Its ears twitched, and it stuck its long snout into the air, sniffing inquisitively at the smells on the breeze.

Two young men huddled together under a blanket, their backs leaning against the front window of Bartlett's surf shop. As they sat with their fingers intertwined, they looked out over the glistening ocean. They shared a bottle of cheap bourbon, passing it back and forth. The shorter of the two rested his head on his companion's shoulder as they continued to talk in whispers and giggles. The taller kissed the top of the other's head and tucked the blanket under his backside to shield it from the cold concrete.

The creature on the beach sniffed the air once more and turned its head towards the lights of the town. Dropping on to all four limbs, it let out a low, rumbling howl. Five more dark figures emerged from the shadows of the forest and dropped to the sand. A large rolling wave crashed against the rocks, showering them with spray and sending them running along the beach. Jets of warm, moist air rushed from their mouths and snouts, turning to blood-scented mist on the chilly night air. Clumps of sand clung to their large, hairy feet and flicked into the air. Their sharp claws sunk deep and propelled them forward.

'What was that?' one of the young men said, lifting his head from the other's shoulder.

'What was what?' The second young man asked, taking a drink from their bottle.

'The howl. Didn't you hear it?' The shorter of the young men stood and listened to the night.

'It might be The Heathcote Beast.' The other said, sitting the bottle on the ground. He held his hands claw-like and waved them in a slashing motion.

'What if it is?' the shorter man said, looking around.

'Jake, you don't believe that rubbish, do you? You know it's just rumours the locals made up to keep the tourist numbers down.'

'If you must know, Brandon, it is true. My cousin Izzy saw one last year when we were here. Her dad nearly hit it with their car. He thought it was just a deer, but Izzy saw it in the taillights standing by the side of the road.'

'What do you mean, standing?' Brandon asked, his voice cracking.

'Standing on its back legs, like this.' Jake ran his hands up and down his body. Brandon laughed and picked up the bottle.

'It's not true. Your cousin Izzy was probably high or dreaming.' As he raised the bottle to his lips, a second howl echoed through the night. Brandon had to hold the bottle with both hands to stop it from shaking.

'You must have heard it that time!' Jake exclaimed, taking a step back towards the shadows of the surf shop.

'It was probably just a dog or a sea-bird or something.' Brandon didn't sound convinced.

'I think I want to go now,' Jake said, sitting and pulling the blanket back around his shoulder. Brandon nodded in agreement, but remained silent. Jake made ready to stand, but Brandon took hold of his shirt front and pushed him back. Jake's head hit Bartlett's shopfront window, making a sound like a muffled gong and vibrating the glass.

'Hey!' Jake protested, but Brandon shushed him.

'Look,' Brandon whispered, bringing his face close to Jake's ear and pointing towards the beach.

A group of shadowy figures frolicked along the beach. As the first moved into the moonlight, Brandon thought they were a pack of dogs that had escaped from their yard, but as they came closer to town, it became frighteningly obvious that they were too big and too fast to be someone's absconded furry little friends. Jake's eyes widened as he watched the approaching figures. Brandon tightened his grip on Jake's shirt, his own eyes fixated on the creatures as they turned towards the dunes.

'Dude, what the hell are those?' Jake muttered, his breath catching in his throat. Brandon's mind raced, searching for a logical explanation, but the eerie howls echoed again, drowning out any attempt at denial. When the creatures disappeared amongst the long grass and shadows of the dunes. Brandon leaped to his feet.

'Run!' he shouted, pulling Jake up from the cold concrete.

They stumbled down the esplanade, desperately trying to put distance between themselves and the approaching shadows. As they reached the mouth of an alleyway that led uphill beside the shops, something in the shadows collided with a skip bin, sending it crashing to the ground. Shivers shot down their spines.

A Lycan, hidden in the shadows, emerged with a predatory growl. Its fur bristled, and moonlight gleamed off its sharp claws. A terrifying screech of metal on concrete sent the two men reeling into the road. Jake's foot twisted on the gutter and he fell. Brandon tried to avoid him but he tumbled over him and they both rolled across the street, grazing their hands and knees on the asphalt. The Lycan lunged from the alley, aiming for Jake. Jake barely avoided the beast with a jump. The creature's claws scraped against the road, leaving deep gouges in the surface. The Lycan scratched at the asphalt and turned on Jake once more. Its large eyes, dark and menacing, fixed on the terrified young man. Jake shuffled backwards on all-fours, like a frightened crab scurrying across the beach. Hungry jaws snapped at him, and he kicked out in desperation. Brandon tried to pull Jake away, but the monstrous creature took hold of Jake's leg in its powerful jaws. Jake screamed in agony as the razor-sharp teeth punctured flesh and scraped bone. Brandon jumped at the Lycan, wrapping his arms around its thick, muscular neck. The Lycan reared up onto its hind legs, dragging Jake from the road and leaving him hanging from its mouth. The powerful beast shook itself free of Brandon's grip, and he fell to the road once more. With a flick of its mighty neck, Jake flew from the Lycan's mouth, crashing into the window of one of the Esplanade shops. The impact against the glass knocked the breath from his lungs. Dozens of cracks spider-webbed their way across the window as Jake fell to the ground with a whimper. Brandon made to run to Jake, but a second figure emerged from the alleyway.

At first, Brandon thought it was more of the terrifying creatures. His heart that was pounding and racing felt like it might actually beat its way into his throat. With some relief, he saw that the new arrival was a man; a giant of a man with a beard and a bald head that shone in the moonlight. The mountain of a man ran straight past Brandon, ignoring him completely, and swung something large and metallic at the Lycan. The surprised creature howled with pain as his weapon sliced through its hairy shoulder.

'There's more coming, kid. Get your friend out of here,' the man said in a booming voice.

Brandon ran to Jake, whom now had a pool of blood forming around his lower leg. As he bent down to pick up his injured boyfriend, he saw the Lycan crouching, ready to lunge.

'Look out!' he yelled as the Lycan leaped.

The giant man took hold of the Lycan's neck and spun it around in the air like an athlete taking part in the hammer-throw. Brandon threw himself over Jake as the hairy beast smashed through the window beside them. Most of the glass fell and scattered across the inside of the store, but a few pieces sprinkled down on the two boys, like sharp-edged hail stones. Scratches and bleeding marred Brandon's exposed skin on his face and hands, but he was more concerned about Jake. Jake was conscious, but he was shaking with shock and fear. Brandon lifted him to a sitting position and tried to get him to stand. Jake's leg gave way, and they both stumbled to the ground again. Brandon felt something on his shoulder. He yelled with fear and rage and swung his fist at whatever the thing was behind him.

A girl about the same age as him caught his fist in her hand. She looked at him with serious but kind eyes.

'I'm Torry,' she said. 'And this is Duncan.' she pointed towards the large man who was now bending over to pick up a sword that he had dropped on the road.

'What are you?' Brandon asked.

'That doesn't matter, but we're here to help,' Torry said, helping him lift Jake off the ground. 'You need to get your friend to the hospital.' she put Jake's arm around Brandon's shoulder and as she did, Jake vomited in the gutter. Jake almost stumbled into the gutter after his vomit, but Brandon held on to him. Duncan took two long strides towards the shop front. With one mighty kick with his long legs and combat boots, he broke down the door and entered the dark store. Wide-eyed, Brandon looked to see where the monster had gone.

'Is that...' he asked, but Torry cut him off.

'Just go,' Torry yelled as she shielded her eyes and tried to peer into the dark store. As the two young men limped away, Torry could just make out shadows moving within the darkness. The ping of something metal drew her eyes towards a shadow in the far corner. A moment later, something heavy fell to the floor with a thud.

'Are you OK Duncan?'

'All good,' Duncan's voice called out from the darkness. 'Are the rest of them here yet?' he asked, crunching over broken glass. He stood in the moonlight at the front of the store, looking out onto the street. Torry looked along the Esplanade towards Paddy's. A handful of large shadowy figures moved quickly but erratically along the street. She couldn't be sure, but they appeared to be moving in their direction. Duncan could see the moonlight glistening on their moist noses and dark eyes.

'I think they'll be here soon,' he said regretfully.

The streets lit up with a flash of blue light and a single burst of a siren rang out, echoing off the hills in the quiet of the night.

'Oh no,' Torry said, 'the O'Burkets are here.' The Heathcote police wagon turned from a side street into the esplanade. Its blue light reflected from the store windows and the ocean below. A second stab of the siren pierced the quiet. A single howl joined the wail, followed shortly by a second, then two more. Soon the entire pack had joined in a mournful discord.

'They need to shut that sound off!' Duncan growled. 'It's stirring them up.' He ran forward to meet the wagon, waving his giant arms. He stepped out onto the road to wave them down.

The wagon pulled up at an angle to the curve. Henry Burket stepped from the driver's seat. He turned the engine off but left the blue lights flashing and the headlights glaring in Duncan's face. Henry stood, keeping the open car door between him and Duncan. The flashing blue reflected from a pair of aviator-style sunglasses he was wearing. Duncan stopped approaching and held his hand out in front to shield his eyes from the headlights.

'Firstly, you need to stop making all that noise and turn those blasted lights off,' he called to Henry. 'Secondly, you need to get out of here.' He swapped hands to try to get a better look at Henry's face, then added. 'Thirdly, why in the hell are y'wearing sunglasses at night?' Henry swiped the glasses from his face and tossed them onto the driver's seat. 'There was a report of a disturbance and a possible break-in.' he said, reaching and flicking off the flashing lights. 'If you'd be so kind as to move from the road, Mr Craig, I need to investigate what looks like a broken store window up there.' He motioned with his head towards the store that Duncan had just left.

Torry ran up beside Duncan.

'I lost track of them,' she said to him from the side of her mouth. 'Hey Henry!' she called out. 'You need to get out of here now.'

'I need to do my job, Miss Kinnard,' Henry called back, taking a step away from his vehicle and resting his hand on his holstered weapon.

'Watch out, Henry!' Duncan yelled, but too late. A Lycan with thick black hair pounced from the rear of the police wagon. The Lycan slammed Henry against the open door before he could turn. His shriek of surprise and pain accompanied the door hinges, squawking as they bent beyond their design. The Lycan continued on towards Duncan and Torry. Henry slumped to the ground. The door of the wagon hung at an angle, bent towards the front of the vehicle. Duncan side-stepped the beast as it ran at him. He swung one of his hefty fists and collected the Lycan behind its left ear. It stumbled for a few steps, then collapsed on the road, wheezing with its tongue hanging limply from between its jaws. Torry watched to see that it had stopped moving, then ran to help Henry. Blood was running from a cut above Henry's left eye. He was laying in the gutter with one of his arms pinned under his chest. As Torry approached, she could hear him moaning. *At least he's alive,* she thought.

Chapter 16
Two Good Hands

Cinder held her nose with one hand as she dropped a garbage bag into a large green metal bin with the other. The streetlights had just flickered on outside of Mr Inkerman's store. Cinder swatted away some flies buzzing around her head as she walked back up the laneway to the front door. Opening the door, she turned a plastic sign so that it showed closed to the outside; it rattled against the glass a few times before coming to rest. Closing the door behind her, Cinder set the deadlock in place with a loud metallic click. She pulled a key from her hip pocket and tended to the lock as a secondary precaution. Long beaded-metal chains hung at the corners of the blinds. She pulled the first chain, a clunk of protest let Cinder know she had pulled the chain in the wrong direction; he blind simply flipped over in place. She took hold of the other side of the cord and pulled it gently. The blind made slow progress down the windows. As it did, it cast darkness over the contents of the store. Many of the bizarre objects in Mr Inkerman's store looked quite strange in the daylight, but now in the darkness, some of them looked truly terrifying. Cinder pulled down the blind on the second window. Other than the pale light coming from the hallway behind the counter, the shop was now in darkness.

'Miss Delacourt,' a voice called from the hallway. Shortly after, the silhouetted figure of Mr Inkerman was blocking out the remaining light. 'This way,' he said.

Navigating the near-dark shelves proved difficult. Cinder moved behind the counter and followed Mr Inkerman into the passageway. At the top of the basement stairs, the external wall featured a large grey door made of solid timber. Mr Inkerman opened it and motioned for Cinder to walk through. An orange streetlight hummed above her, illuminating a narrow laneway. Dark grey stonework ran down their side of the laneway. A brown brick building, three storeys high, occupied the other side, dwarfing Mr. Inkerman's store. Sandstone paving, worn smooth by time and traffic, lined the laneway floor. Afternoon rain had left wet pavers; Cinder stepped down carefully to avoid slipping in her heeled boots. Mr Inkerman followed, closing the door behind him, and locking it with a key from his hip pocket.

'Down towards the back please Miss Delacourt,' he said and motioned for her to go ahead of him. Years of walking had created a central channel in the lane. Puddles formed where the surface showed most wear. Cinder stepped around the puddles, not wanting to get her new work boots wet. The laneway went on for several metres, opening onto a delivery area. There were several buildings that backed onto this area and a narrow roadway exiting to the north side. Cinder noted that each building had their own security cameras mounted high on the walls. Mr Inkerman had three that she could see. There was a large blue skip-bin in the yard, overloaded with packaging materials and fast-food containers. A cyclone wire fence and gate blocked off a similar narrow laneway beside one of the other buildings. The thick ivy, winding around the gate and up the building's wall, showed the gate's long disuse. As Cinder stopped and looked around, Mr Inkerman continued across the yard to another grey-stone building. This building looked similar to his, the same grey stones and pointed metal roof, but it was much smaller and windowless. Mr Inkerman removed one of his black leather gloves. He opened a panel next to the single door in the centre of the smaller building. Surveying his surroundings, he tapped a code into a hidden screen. From across the yard, Cinder could hear the metallic clicking noise inside the door. The door popped open slightly. Mr Inkerman took a hold of the edge of the door with the tips of his fingers and pulled. The door had no handle. Pulling the door open, Mr Inkerman motioned for Cinder to follow him.

'Come, come,' he said as he slid his hand back into the leather glove. Cinder followed him into the building. As she entered the door, Mr Inkerman clicked on a set of lights. Cinder had been expecting something more impressive. The small building was, in fact, mostly empty. There was a shelf in the corner, housing some dusty books. Resting against another wall were some antique-looking gardening tools. Behind the door they had just entered were a few buckets and mops and chemicals used for cleaning. Mr Inkerman grinned when he saw her expression.

'Not what you were expecting?' he asked.

'Honestly, no,' Cinder admitted, looking around. Mr Inkerman laughed and placed his gloved hand on the small of her back, guiding her further into the building.

'We have some visitors arriving shortly,' he said. 'When they arrive, then you'll understand.'

Cinder looked at him inquisitively, but he offered no more information.

'Okay then,' she said. She turned and walked to the dusty bookshelf. A cloud of dust filled the air as she picked up one of the books. She turned her face to the side to avoid getting dust up her nose. She carefully opened up the pages but couldn't read the words. The book was in a language she didn't know. Russian or perhaps German, she wasn't sure. As she continued to flick through the pages, she heard a car pulling up outside. She turned back to the door. Mr Inkerman was watching her.

'One of my favourites.'

'What's it called?' Cinder asked.

'Rumpelstilzchhen, the little rattle stilt. You probably know it as Rumpelstiltskin,' Mr Inkerman said, then turned and exited the building.

A few moments later, he returned with a tall man with white hair and a large, round stomach. The man had an odd orange tone to his skin. He was talking loudly and making animated gestures with his hands as he spoke.

'Hello, who do we have here?' he said when he noticed Cinder.

'This is my new assistant, Miss Delacourt,' Mr Inkerman said, walking to the far corner of the building. 'And this, Miss Delacourt, is Mr Duncan – one of my most valued customers.'

'Please, please, no. Call me Arthur,' the man said, extending one of his large hands in Cinder's direction. 'And what's this *one-of-my-most-valued-customers* rubbish? Like your mother said to me on her wedding night, "I'm the best you ever had".'

Cinder closed the book, returned it gently to the shelf, and shook Arthur's hand. His hand was warm and sweaty, and he held onto her hand longer than what she was comfortable with. His eyes also rested on her body in a way she didn't like.

'Your assistant, hey?' he said, turning back to Mr Inkerman, still holding Cinder's hand. 'And what exactly does she assist you with?'

Mr Inkerman bent down and slid a large mat across the floor. 'I assure you Miss Delacourt and I have a strictly business relationship.' He came over and stood next to Cinder. 'Please excuse me,' he said. Cinder moved out of his way, finally able to free her hand from Arthur Duncan. Mr Inkerman removed another book from the shelf and reached his hand inside the gap.

'She's a beautiful woman, Joe Joe, my boy. It's hard to mix business and beautiful women. Your father taught me that,' Arthur said.

'Miss Delacourt is proving to be very good at her job. As for her being beautiful, I will have to take your word for that. She reminds me very much of my sister. And you know how I feel about her, don't you?' Mr Inkerman said, giving Cinder a wink. As he did, something clicked inside the bookcase. Cinder wasn't sure how she felt about being compared to Mr Inkerman's despised sister, but she was sure that she didn't like Arthur Duncan. She smiled politely but could feel him still ogling her.

Mr Inkerman walked back to the corner where he had removed the mat moments ago. He knelt and pushed firmly on a join that ran along the floorboards. With another click and a creaking of timber, the floorboards rose until they were sitting at a 45-degree angle. Mr Inkerman reached inside the hole and flicked a switch. Light flooded up from an opening below the floorboards

'Oh!' Cinder exclaimed.

'Is this your first time, love?' Arthur asked.

'Yes.'

She walked forward and peered down the opening. Mr Inkerman offered her his hand. Cinder could see a set of timber steps with a hand railing. She took Mr Inkerman's hand and stepped onto the first step. As she made her way down, she needed to duck to fit under the floorboard hatch. At the bottom of the steps, a large space opened up. It reminded her of the wine cellar in The Big House that had become her gym. A momentary shiver of anxiety washed over her.

'I wasn't sure about this the first time he brought me down here either,' Arthur said, as he came down the steps behind her. 'I thought he might have been luring me down here to rob me or some other kinky business.'

Like Cinder's gym at The Big House, large stones formed the floors and walls. Timber support beams ran across the ceiling. This room, unlike The Big House, contained no exercise equipment. Four rows of glass display cabinets stretched out along the space. Other than the one light globe at the stairs, the room seemed to have no other lighting. Cinder soon saw why. When Mr Inkerman reached the bottom of the stairs, he flicked another switch. Each of the display cabinets sprung to life with white light. Cinder blinked at first to adjust to the intensity of it.

'I hope you can deliver the goods,' Arthur said, looking into the nearest cabinet. 'I used to do business with your father. He was a right arsehole. Are you an arsehole, Joe, my boy?'

'I am most definitely an arsehole of the worst kind,' Mr Inkerman said. 'But I'm the arsehole with the best stuff, so what ya gonna do?' He held his hands at his sides, palms up, and shrugged. 'Come. It's down here.' He motioned for Arthur and Cinder to follow him.

In the far corner of the room sat a cabinet. Unlike the others, it was not lit up by the bright white down-lights. There was a single item on the shelf. A wooden box, similar in size and dimensions to a large shoebox. It sat in darkness in the centre of a glass shelf. It was a dark mahogany colour, with intricate carvings on the four sides. The curved lid had a polished finish and embossed copper symbol. Mr Inkerman knelt next to the cabinet and unlocked it. He slid the key back into his pocket and retrieved a pair of white silk gloves. He slipped off his leather gloves and exchanged them for the silk ones. Rubber seals around the edge of the glass door gave a kissing sound as he pulled it open.

'Does the girl know what's in here, Joe Joe?' Arthur asked.

'No,' Mr Inkerman said, lifting the box and moving it closer to the edge.

'You're in for a surprise, missy.' Arthur elbowed Cinder's arm. Cinder forced another smile as images of sinking her teeth into Arthur's neck flashed in her mind.

Mr Inkerman lifted off the lid and sat it down with great care next to the box. Dark brown fur lined the interior of the box. An object sat in the centre, wrapped in black material. Pinching a corner of the material between his gloved fingers, Mr Inkerman slowly pulled it to one side. Cinder saw what looked like a thin sliver of old, grey, polished wood. When Mr Inkerman peeled back the second layer, she gave a start and stepped back. Arthur laughed, his large stomach bobbing up and down. What Cinder had thought was a slither of wood was, in fact, a long fingernail. There were four more of these nails, all attached to grotesquely withered fingers. An entire mummified hand sat in the box. Grey-brown skin, like leather, clung to the bones of the palm and twisted fingers. For a moment Cinder thought it might be a practical joke that they were playing on the new employee, but Mr Inkerman was not laughing, and Arthur had stopped laughing too. His eyes had grown wide and in the quiet of the basement room Cinder could hear his heartbeat quicken.

'Beautiful, isn't it?' he said, rubbing his sweaty hands together. Warily, Cinder leaned towards the cabinet for a closer look.

'Beautiful is not the first word that comes to mind,' she said. This time, Mr Inkerman laughed.

'This is the hand of Sarah Good. A witch hung in the Salem witch-trials,' he said. 'Legend has it that it comes to life on a blood moon and goes in search of her relatives to bring them good luck. It's known as the "Good Hand".'

'This is going to be a gift for my first wife. Her mother was a Good.' Arthur said, circling the display cabinet.

'You want your ex-wife to have good luck?' Cinder asked.

'Yep, if she gets lucky then maybe our deadbeat kid won't need to keep leeching off me.'

• • • •

A cold-white glow illuminated one side of Angus's stern face. He sat on a concrete retaining-wall on the edge of a cigarette-littered garden bed. From his vantage point, he looked down on the stillness of Heathcote. The small town he called home had once again fallen dark and quiet after the commotion a few hours earlier. Noone walked the paths, and no vehicles moved along the streets. The streetlights glowing orange in the mist of the early morning, the only sign of life. It was too early even for the birds to be awake. All was still and silent save for the ever-present background pulsing of the crashing waves, now obscured by the darkness and mist.

The worst was over when Dom and Angus had made it to the town. They had been chasing off a stray Lycan that they had spotted in the forest in the hills above the surf beach. When they heard Henry's siren, they had run, but only made it as far as Paddy's when they heard Henry's distressed cry.

After helping run the remaining Lycan out of town, Dom pulled the bent door from the hinges of the police wagon while Angus lay Henry on the back seat. Angus now sat outside of the Heathcote hospital waiting for news. Turning, he looked into the darkened gardens. The glow that flooded from the glass sliding doors of the front entrance extended for a few metres. He could not make out anything beyond that. He knew that just beyond the halo of light was the place that Cinder had waited for Torry to recover after being attacked by Louvelle, the place of their first kiss. Pain stabbed at Angus's chest, but the door next to him slid slowly open with a hiss – his sorrow would need to take a back seat for the moment.

'Any news?' he asked as Dom emerged, silhouetted by the brightness behind him.

'They said he has a few broken ribs and a concussion, but he should be okay,' he said, sitting his foot up on the wall next to Angus. Angus glanced out into the darkness of the gardens again.

'Does Henry know what attacked him?' he asked nervously.

'Yep, sure does,' Dom said, leaning forward and flicking a cigarette butt into the garden bed. 'He's been telling the whole hospital.'

'Oh shit.' Angus's shoulders dropped. Dom stretched and yawned.

'Yep,' he said again. 'A gang of vandals got the drop on him. A whole bunch of them, that's what he's saying.'

Angus grinned to himself. 'Good old Henry.'

'Good old Henry,' Dom agreed sombrely. They were silent for a moment, both watching the mist grow thicker around the streetlights of the esplanade.

'What about the two kids?' Angus asked. Dom didn't answer. His jaw moved stiffly, as if he was chewing on something hard. 'What about the kids, Dom?' Angus asked again. Dom pulled a stick from the garden and dug at the dirt.

'He lost too much blood,' he said, pushing a cigarette butt into the hole he had made.

'What do you mean, too much blood?' Angus asked.

'You know, the kid that got bit. He bled out. They didn't get him here in time.'

'Time for what?'

'To save him.' Dom flicked the stick away.

'Are you saying he's dead?' Angus asked, his eyes wide. Dom nodded as he let out a long breath.

'They had been drinking and smoking the wacky-weed,' he said, sitting down next to Angus. 'We might be able to convince their families that someone attacked them, too. Maybe they had a dog with them and the kid just imagined the rest. But the hospital staff have seen this too many times now to keep believing our bullshit.'

'So much bullshit,' Angus said, resting his face in his hands.

'We need to do something about them,' Dom said. 'They've never come further than the ridge but now there here in town.'

'They've killed before and we've found a way to cover it up.'

'This is different, Black, and you know it,' Dom said. 'The others have been out in the bush in the dark. This was under streetlights in the middle of town. There was a witness right there when it happened. Hell, there'll probably be security videos of it.'

'Cinder will be able to control them,' Angus said, lifting his head and studying the lines of his palms. 'When she gets back... *if* she comes back,' he amended, seeing the look on Dom's face. Dom sat his hand on Angus's shoulder.

'You need to forget about Cinder.'

'Forget about Cinder!' Angus dropped his hands and glared at Dom. 'Forget about the mother of my child? Forget about the woman I...' He trailed off.

'Okay look,' Dom said, interlocking his fingers and resting his hands on his head. 'I know I've been giving you a hard time, but at least you're here, mate. At least you're showing up. Where's she? Annabelle has a father and a mother.'

'So what? I'm supposed to just go on without her like she never existed? Is that what you mean?' Angus asked.

'I mean, we need to start making plans without her being the answer,' Dom said. 'Cinder might not be coming home. Hey, who knows, mate? She's a vampire now, she's probably off living some fancy life and forgotten all about us.'

. . . .

Cinder stood next to the skip-bin in the alleyway, trying to ignore the notes of stale coffee and rotting fruit. Mr Inkerman stood beside her, watching as Arthur's car pulled out of the yard. He turned to her.

'Now, Miss Delacourt, it has come to my attention that you have been leaving the guest house each evening and not returning until the early morning? You are free to come and go as you please, obviously, but I wonder, is there something wrong with your accommodation?'

'No, not at all,' Cinder said. 'Your guest house is amazing, and it's far more than I deserve. I just don't sleep very well. I need to go out and clear my thoughts, that's all.'

'Then where do you go?' Mr Inkerman asked, walking back towards the windowless grey-stone building. Cinder followed him.

'Nowhere.'

'Nowhere?' Mr Inkerman asked and re-entered the little building. 'What do you mean?'

Cinder stood in the doorway and leaned on the frame. 'I've spent the last few nights exploring the city.'

'Wandering the streets by yourself at night,' Mr Inkerman said, his brow wrinkled with concern. 'No, no, we can't have that.'

'I'm fine. I can look after myself, and Sydney is so beautiful at night. Have you seen the view from Observatory Hill? The lights of the bridge and Luna Park reflected in the water?' Cinder asked. Mr Inkerman replaced the mat over the trapdoor, straightening it before answering.

'Yes, and I have seen the view. I also know that is definitely not a place for a young woman to be frequenting at night by themselves.'

'It's fine,' Cinder reassured him. Mr Inkerman placed his hand on her arm.

'You're too important, Miss Delacourt, and you'd make a delightful meal for a vampire.' He squeezed Cinder's arm, like testing the ripeness of a tomato. 'If you want to explore the city, I'll show you the city. I'll show you my Sydney.'

Chapter 17
A Little Party

The grandeur of Mr. Inkerman's home unfolded like a chapter from an ancient tome. Each room echoed centuries of historical tales. Tapestries adorned the walls, depicting scenes from forgotten legends, their colours muted by time. Mr Inkerman's collection of antiques and art filled every available surface. Rare artefacts, mysterious curiosities, and priceless paintings were carefully arranged in a symphony of history and culture. The dining hall resembled a banquet chamber from a fairy-tale. A long wooden table adorned with silver candelabras and fine china. An impressive chandelier, a cascade of crystal, hung from the ceiling, casting a warm glow over the room. Wandering through the corridors felt like navigating the labyrinthine passages of a castle, each turn revealing a new marvel. Stained glass windows filtered the light, casting vibrant hues across stone floors. In the library, shelves upon shelves housed an extensive collection of leather-bound books, their spines worn with time and handling. A magnificent fireplace, made of richly veined marble, dominated one wall. Above the mantle, a masterfully framed oil painting portrayed a scene of colonial Sydney, capturing the bustling harbor with its iconic ships and distinctive architecture. Throughout the mansion, hand-made antique furniture filled every room.

The training room was a stark contrast to the opulence that surrounded it. Gleaming hardwood floors reflected the light from six simple down lights and a single tapestry hung from the clean white, windowless walls. In the centre of the room, Mr Inkerman adjusted his grip on his own sword, a finely crafted katana that gleamed under the lights.

'Miss Delacourt,' he began, his voice calm but authoritative, 'the key to mastering the samurai sword lies in understanding its balance and respecting its power. It's not just about strength, but precision and control.' He looked to Cinder for her understanding. Cinder nodded, her grip tightening on the hilt.

'I understand. I'm ready.'

Mr Inkerman stepped back, positioning himself into a fighting stance, his movements fluid and practised.

'Watch closely,' he instructed. With a swift, precise motion, he demonstrated a series of basic strikes and blocks. The blade cut through the air with a sharp, satisfying sound. Cinder watched intently, mimicking his stance and movements. Her first attempts were clumsy, her strikes lacking the finesse of her teacher's. Mr Inkerman approached, correcting her posture with gentle, but precise, adjustments.

'Relax your shoulders, Miss Delacourt. Let the sword become an extension of your arm.'

Cinder took a deep breath, relaxing her muscles as she tried again. This time, her movements were smoother, more controlled. Mr Inkerman nodded approvingly.

'Better. Remember, it's not about forcing the sword to move; it's about guiding it.'

They continued the training, moving through various techniques and forms. Mr Inkerman's patience was unwavering, his instructions clear and precise. Cinder's confidence grew, but she knew she needed to restrain herself. It would be dangerous for her to show her true speed and strength to her new teacher. They practiced into the late-hours of the evening. Finally, Mr Inkerman called for a pause, sheathing his katana with a satisfied nod.

'You've made good progress today. But remember, mastery comes with time and practice. Respect the sword, and it will serve you well.'

'Thank you,' Cinder said, looking at her reflection in the blade of her weapon. 'But wouldn't some guns be better?' she asked, collecting her saya from the corner of the room to stow the blade for her next training session. Mr Inkerman shook his head.

'For one thing, it is far easier for me to import items like that.' He pointed to Cinder's katana 'It's not so easy to get hold of firearms in this country, not without drawing a lot of attention. As a collector of antiques, I have a legitimate reason to import these weapons.' He sat his hand on the hilt of his own sword. 'But most importantly,' he said, pulling his weapon from its sheath, 'while a gun is an effective weapon for killing humans, it is not so effective a weapon for taking down a vampire.' He rested the blade on his arm, like he was nursing an infant. 'I have seen men empty dozens of rounds into a vampire and it has still kept coming. Then what?' he raised a questioning brow towards Cinder. 'A vampire can move fast enough to snap your neck in the time it will take to re-load. No re-loading with this.' He ran his fingers lovingly along the glimmering blade. 'But in the right hands, this can take a vampire's head off with one swipe and they don't come back from that.'

'You've seen this?' Cinder asked, sliding her blade into the saya.

'Yes, I have,' Mr Inkerman said thoughtfully. 'It is something that sticks in your memory.' He re-sheathed his own weapon.

'Are there vampires here in Sydney?' Cinder asked, looking at the Japanese style symbols on the wall tapestry.

'Now, come Miss Delacourt, you know very well that if you're here, then there is at least one vampire in Sydney.' Mr Inkerman said as moved swiftly and swung his sheathed weapon at her. Cinder blocked the attack and stepped to the side.

'What do you mean?' she asked. If her heart still beat normally, it may have skipped a beat. What was he implying?

'You have impeccable reflexes, Miss Delacourt.'

'I've trained most of my life.'

'Good, good.' Mr Inkerman swung at her again and she sidestepped away. *Was it too fast? Be careful here, Cinder.*

'What did you mean? Why would I know there are vampires here?' she asked.

'Why else would you have come to Sydney? Why would you leave your friends and come all this way, if not to track down a vampire? Just like me, you have followed the rumours and analysed the evidence.'

Relieved, Cinder asked. 'Why Sydney? I mean, I always pictured vampires in the grand old cities of Europe.'

'Ah, yes, the enigmatic and seductive count living in his dark castle,' Mr Inkerman said, lowering his weapon and bowing to Cinder. 'People here are more trusting and less superstitious than Europe. More than that, Sydney is a truly multicultural city. Why travel from country to country when every flavour of blood is here for the picking? It's like a smorgasbord.'

'That's horrible,' Cinder said. Mr Inkerman shrugged.

'Not everyone thinks so.'

'What do you mean?' Cinder asked. Mr Inkerman sat his sword across his shoulders and smiled.

'That's the main reason a vampire would be here. People come here looking to find something, find their place in the world. There are many here freely willing to give what a vampire needs just to feel part of something, to feel needed. That's not so different to you and I is it, Miss Delacourt?'

'It's very different to me,' Cinder said, turning for the door. 'Thank you for the lessons and thank you again for my gift.' She held up her sword. 'I look forward to putting it to good use soon.'

'Speaking of that,' Mr Inkerman said, as Cinder started walking, 'I have another gift for you.'

Cinder stopped and looked back over her shoulder.

'More gifts?'

'Yes,' Mr Inkerman said, following her and draping his arm over her shoulder.

'I really don't need anything else,' Cinder protested as he led her from the room. 'You have been far too generous.'

They walked together down a hallway lined with more tapestries. At the end of a hall was a floor to ceiling glass door that opened onto the gardens. 'This gift is just as much for me as it is for you,' Mr Inkerman said as he pushed open the glass door. 'So, you can stop now about my generosity.'

Outside, it was a clear night. A waning moon sat high in the sky. It was difficult to make out many stars against the glow from the city. Cinder missed the stars. They turned and climbed a set of limestone steps. Cinder was not staying in the main house. She had lodgings in a guesthouse that looked out onto a pool and the gardens. They turned and headed that way.

'Is it another weapon?' Cinder asked excitedly at the top of the steps. Mr Inkerman thought about this before he replied.

'There are some who would say it is.'

'And what does that mean?' Cinder asked.

'You'll see Miss Delacourt. It's in your room.'

The moon's reflecting shimmered in the dark surface of the pool. Steam rose from the water and Cinder could feel its moist heat on her skin as they passed. Although Mr Inkerman owned the guest house, it was Cinder's space. It felt right for her to lead the way now. She slid open the glass entrance door. From the outside, the guest house, which had once been the servant quarters, still displayed the old-world charm from when it had been constructed by Sydney's early settlers. Inside, however, the guest house was modern and sleek. This was also where Mr Inkerman kept any artwork that was too new to fit the aesthetic of the main house. Other than the ensuite, the guest house was one open plan room containing a bed, a sitting area, and a kitchenette. Cinder switched on the light and could see that someone had made her bed. Sitting propped against the pillows was a large flat box made of glossy black cardboard, wrapped in a blood-red bow.

'Open it,' Mr Inkerman directed. Cinder sat on the bed, removed the ribbon and slipped open the box. The crisp sound of tissue paper filled the quiet room as she peeled back the layer that hid the contents. Beneath the delicate wrapping lay a dress, its deep black fabric as smooth and lustrous as polished obsidian. She hesitated for a moment, as though touching it might disturb its perfection, then slid her fingers under the gown, lifting it gently from the box.

As the dress unfolded, it revealed its full splendour: the plunging neckline formed a soft, elegant v, full length sleeves, a narrow, tapered waist and a flowing skirt that shimmered faintly in the light. Cinder's deep green eyes sparkled as she took in every detail; the way the fabric caught the golden glow of her bedroom lamp, the elegance of its tailored cut. She ran her fingers along the hem, feeling the cool silkiness of the material. Even the faint scent of lavender from the box seemed like an intentional flourish, designed to evoke a sense of mystery and allure. Memories of getting ready to go out to Paddy's with Marraine flooded Cinder's mind. The joy and anticipation. The excitement of meeting Angus and his friends for the first time. It was hard to know which of the memories were her own, but they all moved her.

'I have no idea about women's clothing,' Mr Inkerman said, appraising her. 'I had my tailor stalk you in the store to get your measurements.'

'Is that who the lady in the green dress and red shoes is?' Cinder asked, carefully folding the dress and placing it back in the box. 'She's in the store every second day. I thought she was just a crazy lady that never buys anything.'

'Oh, no. That's Ms Deopopolus. She is a crazy old lady. I think she steals some of the brass fixtures from time-to-time.'

'Why haven't you got rid of her?'

'Get rid of Ms Deopopolus? Heavens no,' Mr Inkerman said, holding his hand to his chest. 'Every Impermercato needs its own crazy lady. The place wouldn't be the same without her.' He grinned and Cinder laughed.

'It's a beautiful dress,' she said, running her hand over the fabric, 'but I'm not sure it's appropriate for work. Why are you giving me this?'

'It is still work related,' Mr Inkerman said, scratching the end of his nose with his thumb. 'I would like you to attend a function with me this Friday. There will be some very influential people there and it's important that you make an impression on them.'

Cinder placed the lid back on the box.

'Now I'm nervous. I'm not sure I know how to make an impression on important people.'

'You've made an impression on me, Miss Delacourt. You will just need to be yourself.' Mr Inkerman placed his hand on Cinder's shoulder. *I'm not sure I know how to be myself anymore, she thought.*

'What kind of function will we be attending?' she asked. Mr Inkerman squeezed her shoulder.

'Just a little party.'

• • • •

Angus stood at the door to the room that, until recently, had been Torry's. The door stood slightly ajar, and through the crack, Angus could see his daughter Annabelle's smiling face. Torry was talking to her as she bounced her on her hip. Annabelle giggled as Torry pulled a face. The sound of his daughter laughing sent a wash of warmth and love through Angus. He paused to watch a moment longer. Annabelle's round rosy cheeks trembled. The corners of her eyes crinkled as they opened and shut. Knocking gently, Angus pushed open the door and entered. Torry glanced in his direction then looked back at Annabelle.

'It's Daddy,' she said. 'He doesn't need to knock because this is supposed to be his room. Who's a silly daddy?' Annabelle giggled again at the funny voice that Torry was using. Angus stepped into the room. It smelled of fresh linen and talc, evoking a sense of calm and cleanliness. A soft, plush cream-coloured rug covered most of the polished wooden floor. The metal crib that Gunn had fashioned stood in one corner, its slatted sides adorned with a mobile of pastel-coloured stars and moons that twirled gently. The crib's bedding was a mix of soft pinks and whites, with a quilted blanket featuring tiny, embroidered animals folded neatly over the side. Next to the crib was a bed that was meant for Angus, but he had hardly used it since the room had been set up for him and Annabelle six months ago. A changing table with neatly organised supplies was situated against one wall. On its shelves were stacks of neatly folded clothes, wipes, and baby lotions. Next to it, a comfortable rocking chair with a plush cushion waited, its armrests worn smooth from countless soothing sessions. A soft, golden light filtered through sheer white curtains that fluttered slightly with the breeze from an open window. The gentle rustling of the curtains and the distant sound of the ocean added to the tranquil ambiance of the room.

'You're just in time,' Torry said, and handed Annabelle to Angus. 'I've just fed her and it smells like she needs to be changed before we put her down for her afternoon nap.'

'Oh! I think I can hear your dad calling me,' Angus joked and started backing back out of the door.

'Oh no you don't,' Torry said, manoeuvring herself between Angus and the door. She took hold of his shoulders and guided him over to a low shelf that held Annabelle's clothes. Annabelle reached a tiny hand up to her father's face and talked to him in indecipherable baby babble.

'Is that right?' Angus asked, looking down into his daughter's face. Her eyes were a lighter shade of brown, but were remarkably similar to his own. Annabelle's other features were dominantly Cinder's.

'So how do I do this?' he asked, turning to Torry. Torry rolled her eyes. 'What was that for?' Angus asked.

'Just because I have a vagina doesn't mean I know how to do everything for a baby,' Torry spat.

'I just meant that you have been doing this stuff,' Angus tried to clarify. 'It's not because you're a girl.'

'I love Annabelle and I would do anything for her, but I'm not her mother.' Torry grumbled.

'Yeah, her mother's not here. She ran away and left her.'

'I know that, Black. Trust me, I know that. Do you think you're the only one that misses her?'

'I'm the only one that loved her,' Angus said, lifting Annabelle up and holding her close to his face.

'That's some BS and you know it,' Torry said. 'We all love her, and we all want her back. The only difference is that the rest of us are getting on with life until she comes back.'

'You think she's coming back?'

'I have to think she is.' Torry knelt to rummage through Annabelle's clothes.

'I hope so. Annabelle needs her mother,' Angus said.

'Annabelle needs a parent, not a mother. She'd have a father if you could pull your head out of your arse.' Torry stood, holding a set of tiny clothes.

'I don't know how to be her father,' Angus said, watching his daughter reach out to touch his face again.

'You're not meant to know,' Torry said, taking hold of his spare hand and depositing Annabelle's clothes in it. 'You're meant to learn.' Torry gave Annabelle a kiss, patted Angus on the shoulder and left the room.

Angus sat Annabelle down on the bed, the bed that was meant to be his but that he wasn't using.

'Now, how do I do this?' he said, sitting the clothes down on the bed next to his daughter. Annabelle giggled and cooed at him as he pulled open a set of press-studs on the back of her top. Sensing someone behind him, Angus turned to see Gunn entering the room. Gunn stood in the doorway, rubbing the grey stubble of his chin with his large leathery hand.

'Better to do that on the changing table, boy,' he said, grinning at Annabelle. 'Y' don't want baby poo on ya blankets, believe me. That stuff sticks like tar and you won't never get the smell out.'

'The change table?' Angus asked. Gunn thumbed towards a waist-high white bench behind the door next to him.'

Angus carried Annabelle to the changing table and lay her on her back. Gunn leaned against the wall next to the table; his arms crossed over his chest. With Gunn's instructions, Angus attempted to change Annabelle into fresh clothes. Gunn laughed out loud at the expression on Angus's face when he was confronted with some of the sights and smells.

'Smells like the bowels of hell themselves have opened up, don't it?' Gunn teased as Angus lifted the collar of his t-shirt over his nose. Annabelle wriggled and squirmed and Angus struggled to keep her from launching herself off the table.

'She's so strong!' he said, scratching an itch on the end of his nose with his shoulder and keeping both hands on Annabelle.

'Aha,' Gunn agreed, laughing again.

Eventually, Angus wrangled his baby girl back into her clothes. He carried her back to the bed and lay her down. Gunn limped across the room and sat pillows either side of her to stop her from rolling off.

'I'm sorry I've been useless.' Angus said, looking down at Gunn's leg. Gunn's jeans were covering the bandaged area where one of the

Lycan had bitten him. The old man would never be one to let anyone know he was in pain, but Angus was sure it must be still hurting.

'You haven't made things easy, that's for sure,' Gunn said, lowering himself onto the bed next to Annabelle. Annabelle reached a tiny hand to him, and he offered one of his large fingers for her to squeeze.

'I let my feelings get the better of me. I'm sorry,' Angus said, looking down at the floor and interlacing his fingers behind his head. Gunn looked up at him.

'You're allowed to be upset, boy, and angry. In fact, you should be. No one's telling ya not to have the feel'ns – ya should.'

'Dom is,' Angus said, looking at Annabelle and smiling. She stared back at him with her dark brown eyes. Gunn rubbed the grey and black stubble of his chin.

'You know that boy's words are always ten steps-head of his brain. If yer listening to him for advice, then I know you've truly lost yer marbles.'

'I feel like he is just saying what everyone else is thinking,' Angus said.

'It's more what he's not saying, lad.' Gunn got up from the bed and placed his hand on Angus's shoulder, his palm resting on the scars under Angus's shirt. 'Like I said, it's normal for ya to be feel'n what yer feel'n, but those feelings don't need to control ya. When the bloody cancer took my Emily, I thought my world had ended, but it hadn't. I still had you kids rely'n on me, a farm to run, and a town to protect. The world was still turn'n, fast as it ever had. I just had'ta take hold and keep riding that bastard 'til the end.'

'What if I can't? What if I'm not as strong as you?' Angus asked.

'Then you look into those big brown eyes,' Gunn said, bending down and pinching Annabelle's chubby chin. 'Tell her that you can't do it for her, cause she's the one ya need be strong for.'

'That's not fair,' Angus said, looking from his daughter to the grin on Gunn's face.

'Who said anything about be'n fair?' Gunn said, giving him a sideways glance. 'This is love m'boy, nothin' fair 'bout it.' Annabelle giggled. 'Your daddy thinks love should be fair,' Gunn said in a high-pitched voice. 'Isn't your daddy a dilly-duffer?' He took a breath, set his shoulders back and looked at Angus, serious. 'The truth of it, boy, is that no one is strong enough by themselves. That's what family's for. We're all here to help, lad, but you got to get moving first. A ship on the shore never got nowhere, no matter how strong the breeze.'

Angus wrapped an arm around Gunn's shoulders and kissed the top of the old-man's head. 'Thanks,' he said. 'Thanks for everything you've done for this family.' Gunn patted Angus on the back.

''Tis been a privilege and an honour,' he said. 'And while I'm handing out the good advice, here be another three-pence worth,' he continued in a whispered tone. 'I'd tread carefully with that girl.' He motioned with his head towards the door.

'Who? Torry?' Angus asked. Gunn put his finger to his lips.

'No, me niece.'

'Alice?' Angus asked.

'Yep,' Gunn answered in a whisper. 'Now don't get me wrong, I love all my family, I do. Including all in-laws and out-laws. But that one reminds me too much of her mother.'

'What's wrong with Alice's mother?' Angus asked, as Annabelle got restless and rub at her eyes with her tiny hands.

'Well, nothin' at all. She's a strong, intelligent, hard-working woman, and quite easy to get along with when things are going her way.'

'And what if things aren't going her way?' Angus asked, lifting Annabelle from the bed. Gunn took a step closer to him and looked out through the doorway to see that no one was outside the room.

'Then she's as slippery as a snake,' he said. 'She'll manipulate things' 'til they is goin' her way. She's the reason I don't see me brother anymore. She didn't agree with the way Dand and I wanted to run things and she twisted all his thoughts.'

'I'm sure Alice isn't like that,' Angus said, rocking Annabelle as she started to grizzle.

'Just be careful, that's all I'm sayin.' Gunn squeezed Angus's shoulder, lent down and kissed Annabelle. She was fighting a losing battle with her heavy eyelids. Angus watched as they closed and shot back open again. He lent down and kissed her too.

'I'm back now, angel,' he said. 'I'm going to do better. I promise.'

'Here, give her to me,' Gunn said, reaching out for Annabelle. 'I'll put her down for her nap. You oughtta get ready.'

'Ready for what?'

'The surf club fundraiser's tonight.' Gunn said, laying Annabelle in her crib.

'I forgot all about that.' Angus said. Gunn laughed.

'I think yer silly daddy's forgettin' a lot of things,' he said to Annabelle as she lost the fight with her eyelids and drifted off to sleep.

Chapter 18

Charity

Dom and Angus walked along the Heathcote esplanade. The last of the afternoon sun glowed over the hills above them, adding a pink hue to the dimming light. They both wore black pants and black shirts – their "going out" clothes. Now that Angus's hair had grown longer, they looked more similar than ever. Angus's hair was darker, of course, the reason for his nickname. They walked, tall, confident and dark, past the ice-cream shop as it closed its doors for the day. Dom's shirt had short sleeves; 'All the better for showing off the gun show,' he had said before they left home. Angus's shirt had full-length sleeves, but he had them rolled up to just below his elbows. He caught the reflection of his anchor tattoo in one of the shop windows, but quickly turned away.

'Mmm, smell that,' Dom said, sniffing the air like a hungry dog. The smell of onions and sausages cooking filled the air. 'I'm going to eat fifteen.'

'Fifteen!' Angus said as they looked both ways and crossed the road towards the foreshore. 'What's your record?'

'I did twelve three years ago.'

The surf club's fund-raising barbeque was an annual event. For the past few years, Dom had given himself a personal challenge to eat as many sausages as he could before they finished cooking. The surf club was a white, flat-roofed building that sat on a grassy area above the sand dunes. To the south, it looked out over the rocks. The surf-beach stretched out to the north. Dom and Angus were still some way off, but they could hear music and excited chatter over the crashing of the waves below.

'Does it count if they come back up?' Angus asked.

'If one comes up, I'll shove it back down.' Dom put two fingers in his mouth and moved them in a shoving motion. Angus felt his stomach churn. He put his hands over it.

'I'd rather not see that, thanks very much. I don't even want to think about it,' Angus said. Suddenly, the smell of the barbeque didn't smell as inviting as it had.

'Hey, what's up with you tonight?' Dom asked, looking at the smile on Angus's face.

'What do you mean?'

'I mean, you seem normal. Almost happy.'

'I am happy,' Angus said. 'It's the Surf Club Barbecue. Everyone's happy at the Surf Club Barbecue.'

Colourful festoon lights hung from the balcony of the surf club. Leaning against the handrail, three men with greying beards watched the ocean. They raised their schooners of beer to welcome Dom and Angus. Dom and Angus waved back and made a beeline to the barbeque. Two teenagers, a boy and a girl wearing red aprons and white latex gloves, greeted them. They both had their long sun-bleached hair tied back in ponytails and when they smiled, they revealed matching sets of braces.

'How many would you like?' the girl asked, clicking a pair of metal tongs in her hand.

'I'll take five to start with,' Dom said, eyeing the shiny brown sausages as they sizzled on the hotplate. 'How about you?' he turned to Angus.

'Just the one,' Angus said, holding up a finger.

'One?' Dom asked, looking almost offended. 'Weak!'

They paid for their sausages and made their way inside the club. Even with his large hands, it was a balancing act for Dom to hold his first round of food for the evening. He held three sausages in one hand; each sausage nestled in a napkin-wrapped slice of white bread, topped with onions and barbecue sauce. The other hand held the remaining two, one of which he had already begun to eat while they walked.

'Can't you wait?' Angus asked. Dom shook his head and swallowed a mouthful.

'I'm going to need a drink to get this down,' he said, taking another large bite.

They climbed a set of metal stairs that led up to the main area of the club rooms. Faded photographs of young men and women with surfboards or standing in groups next to long boats, hung in frames on the walls. An old fishing net with orange buoys hung over the handrail. When he got to the top, Angus looked back at Dom. Dom smeared sauce from his face with the back of his hand but only cleaned away a small part of the mess. Angus shook his head and continued into the room without him.

The upstairs of the club had a large, open room. At one end, floor to ceiling windows looked out onto a deck and the ocean beyond. On the opposite end of the room was a small bar and kitchen and a unisex bathroom. There was a pool table and a dartboard in the front corner and a half a dozen tall round-topped tables scattered throughout the space. A portable DJ booth had been set up on the deck. Local DJ Hank the Crank was blasting out some 90s rock. The banner that hung from his lighting rig claimed he was the best DJ in town. This was, in fact, true because Hank the Crank was the only DJ in town. The room was already beginning to fill with people; many of them were familiar to Dom and Angus. The annual barbeque was an important social event on the local calendar, and most of the town would be there.

Heathcote's finest, Rebecca O'Bearn and her partner, Henry Burket, stood next to the bar. The duo, known as "O'Burket", were still in their police uniforms, their hats hanging from hooks at the top of the stairs. Henry's movements were slow and deliberate, and he held one hand over his broken ribs. The reddening in his cheeks alluded to the fact that the drink in his free hand was not his first.

'Good evening, Officers O'Bearn and Burket,' Angus said as he and Dom approached the bar.

'Hey. It's just Beccy,' Rebecca said. Her hair was in a tight bun at the back of her head. She pulled it loose and ruffled her hands through her shoulder length hair. 'Can I buy you a drink?' she asked, looking past Angus at Dom.

'Sure,' Dom mumbled through a mouthful of food.'

'Just a couple of pots, thanks,' Angus added.

'Pints,' Dom mumbled, pointing up with his hand that was now free of the first two sausages. Beccy turned to the bar, but Henry stepped forward.

'I'll get this one,' he said with his hand on Beccy's shoulder. In the bright down lights above the bar, Angus could see his bald scalp through his combed over wispy blond hair.

'You two not working tonight?' Angus asked.

'Nope,' Beccy said. 'I mean, we're still on duty but we wanted to come to this, so Peter is holding down the fort.'

'You mean Detective Morgan?' Henry said, handing Angus a cold glass. 'He hates when Beccy calls him Peter.'

'Oh yeah,' Beccy said, finishing her drink and sitting her glass on the bar. 'Looks like you've got yourself all loaded up there,' she said, looking at Dom's handful of sausages.

'This is just round one,' Dom said, taking his drink from Henry.

'I love a good sausage,' Beccy said. Dom gave her a questioning, sideways look.

'Really?'

'Yes. Why do you ask?' Beccy said.

'I just thought. Well, you know,' Dom pulled at the collar of his shirt. 'I thought you were a no-sausage kind of girl.'

'I like meat just fine. But I do like vegetables as well.'

'Beccy eats from both sides of the plate,' Henry added, handing Beccy her drink.

'That's good to know,' Dom said, holding his glass up to Beccy. With a wink, Beccy tapped her glass to Dom's and then to Angus's

'Cheers,' Angus said. Over Dom's shoulder, he spotted Torry and Alice coming up the stairs. Like Angus and Dom, the two girls wore all black. Torry wore skinny jeans and a singlet. Alice was sporting a little black dress. Angus raised his glass to them as they approached. Alice's face lit up when she saw him and she skipped over to him with her hands in the air.

'We're here now! The part-A can start-A!' she yelled and bumped Angus with her hip. Angus put his arm around her and dragged her into a side-ways hug. She was wearing heeled boots that added a few inches to her height, but she still needed to stand on her toes so that she could whisper in Angus's ear.

'Can we talk?' she asked, just loud enough for him to hear over the music.

'Yep, sure,' he said, looking down into her expectant eyes.

Alice took Angus by the hand. They weaved their way through the growing crowd and out through a sliding glass door onto the deck. Torry, now standing next to Dom at the bar, watched them as they went; her arms crossed and her brow creased.

'What's she up to?' she asked, elbowing Dom in the ribs.

'Ha?' Dom replied. 'Who?'

'Alice,' Torry said, jutting her head in Alice's direction. 'What's she up to?' she asked again. Dom could just see Angus and Alice through the crowd. Their faces were dimly lit by the colourful glow coming from DJ Crank's light show. He watched them for a moment and shrugged.

'I don't know. Maybe she just wanted to talk to Black.'

'What does she need to talk to Black about that she can't say here?' Torry asked, stepping from side to side to keep an eye on them.

'Maybe she wants to complain about her annoying little cousin,' Dom said, shoving another sausage in his mouth.

'I'm serious,' Torry said, glowering at her brother. Dom swallowed.

'I'm serious too. You're little and annoying,' Dom said, patting the top of Torry's head with the hand that was now free of food. Torry elbowed him in the ribs. 'Ease up,' he said. 'You'll damage the merchandise.'

'Something's up and I don't like it,' Torry huffed.

'Good,' Dom said, lifting his drink off the bar.

'Good?' Torry exclaimed. Dom took a drink and sat his drink down again.

'Black's happier than he's been in months. So, whatever they're doing, I hope they do more of it,' he said, lifting the next sausage to his mouth. Before taking a bite, he said. 'Actually, I hope they find a dark corner somewhere here and do it right now.'

'Sometimes I'm sure I'm adopted,' Torry said and turn to the bar to get a drink.

Out on the deck, DJ Crank was just launching into some classic Guns and Roses.

'Welcome tooooo the jungle!' he bellowed through a crackling microphone. The three old men below, who were still watching people arrive, cheered in agreement. Alice was leaning with her back to the balustrade. She held a lock of her dark hair in one hand to stop it from flicking around her face in the ocean breeze. Her other hand still held Angus's.

'You look nice,' she said, letting go of her stray hair and pulling at the hem of his shirt.

'You too,' Angus said, letting go of her hand. 'Are we okay? After the other night at the river?'

'What night was that?' Alice teased, stepping closer to him. Angus blushed and rubbed the back of his neck.

'I just hope it was okay. I mean, I'd been drinking and...'

'Are you worried you took advantage of me, Black?' Alice said, looking up into his eyes. 'That's very noble of you, but you don't have to worry. I had fun. I hope you did too.'

'Yes, it was fun,' Angus said with an embarrassed grin. 'It's just that I was drunk, and you were naked... I.'

'It's fine Black. If you're worried that I wasn't into it, I think you are remembering it differently to me. I was definitely into it. I was into it more than once, if you recall. And like you said, you were the drunk one. If anyone took advantage, it was me.'

'So, we're okay then?'

'We're more than okay. We're great. We're both grownups and we had some fun. You are allowed to have some fun sometimes, Black,' Alice said, leaning forward and kissing Angus's cheek. Behind them, someone coughed. They both turned to see Marraine standing a few metres from them with her arms crossed over her chest.

'Oh, hey Marraine,' Angus said, stepping back from Alice. 'I didn't know you were here. You snuck up on us.'

'Oh really, sweetie? I didn't mean to surprise you,' Marraine said, batting her eyelids. 'Hello again,' she turned to Alice. 'April, was it?' she asked.

'It's Alice,' she said, looking Marraine up and down. Marraine was wearing something similar to Torry, slim black jeans and a singlet top. The coloured light glistened off her dark skin.

'You look nice,' Alice said unconvincingly. Marraine smiled and inclined her head.

'You don't mind if I steal Angus away for a moment, do you, Alice?' Marraine said. Without waiting for Alice to respond, she took hold of Angus's elbow and led him back inside. 'Let's get a drink, sweetie. I have some news about Cinder.'

Marraine and Angus leaned against the wall of a darkened corner of the surf club. Marraine was trying her best to enjoy the glass of what she had been told was a Riesling; she had her doubts. Angus was halfway through his third pint. The room was continuing to swell with happy punters, and the air buzzed with laughter and excited chatter. The beats from DJ Crank pumped along in the background. Marraine leaned in to talk to Angus over the noise.

'I think we should go to Sydney. If Cinder's there, I want to find her,' he said.

'It's a big place, sweetie. We don't know where to look.'

'Then we look everywhere. We start with this Lulu woman and we go from there.'

'You just say the word,' Marraine said, placing her hand on his stubbled face. 'I always have a bag packed ready to go.'

Angus finished his drink and looked around the room. The surf club was near capacity now. Groups huddled around the tables or by the bar. Three young women who he recognised as employees of the ice-cream shop, were dancing in DJ Crank's flashing lights on the deck. Torry was still near the bar with the two police officers, but Dom wasn't with them. Probably getting more sausages, Angus thought. He took Marraine's hand from his face. Holding it, he said,

'I'm just going to let Dom know what's happening and then I'll come back and we'll make plans to leave.'

He turned and headed for the stairs. A blond-haired boy ran across in front of him.

'Lachlan Taylor!' a woman who appeared to be the boy's mother called after him.

'What?' the boy asked.

'Sorry,' the woman said as she stepped past Angus. 'How many sausages have you had now?' she asked, looking at the boy, who was holding a sausage in each hand.

'This is only my fifth and sixth one,' he said, holding up his hands. There was barbecue sauce smeared across his chin and running between his fingers. Angus smiled and step past the woman. Dom might have a challenger for the championship, he thought to himself. He waded through the sizeable crowd gathered near the bar, winking at Torry as he went past. At the top of the stairs, he felt a hand on his elbow. He turned and found Alice standing close behind, looking up at him.

'Where are you going, big man?' she asked, continuing to hold on to his elbow. Angus bent down to talk to her over the sound of the crowd.

'Marraine had some news about Cinder. We're going to go find her. I was just trying to find Dom.' He said excitedly. Alice dropped her eyes to the ground. She placed her other hand on Angus's chest and pulled her face up to his ear. Her breath was warm on his neck and smelled of wine.

'That's great news,' she said. 'Can we finish talking first?'

'Of course,' Angus said.

Taking his hand in both of hers, Alice led him back out onto the deck. The young women dancing watched them with interest and they giggled and whispered to each other as Angus and Alice retreated to a shadowed corner. The sun had dropped behind the hills and the night was cooling. Alice wrapped her arms over her chest and leaned against the handrail, looking out to the reflection of the Heathcote lights playing on the dark surface of the ocean.

'When are you going?' she asked without looking at Angus. Angus sat his hands on the rail and stood next to her.

'As soon as we can organise a flight, I guess.' The scent from the barbeque below them wafted on the breeze. Angus looked down to see if he could spot Dom. He spotted his mop of dark hair as he retreated into the surf club, both hands loaded with fresh sausages. Angus turned back to find Alice standing close to him, looking up into his face.

'Do you really think you should go?' she asked. A breeze from the ocean rolled over her, flicking her hair and threatening to blow up her skirt. She held her skirt down to her thighs and turned her face into the breeze. Her bare arms thrilled with the cold. Seeing her shiver, Angus wrapped his arm around her and rubbed the skin of her shoulder.

'I need to find her,' he said, his eyes flicking to the top of the hill at the far end of the beach. 'I should have left weeks ago.'

'We need you, Black,' Alice said in a voice somewhere between a plead and a demand.

'You don't need me. You'll all get by fine.'

'But they are coming closer to town every time. Someone's going to die. We need you here.'

'I haven't been here for months, not really. If anything, I've just been making things worse.' Angus dropped his hand from Alice's shoulder and placed both hands back on the rail. 'It's time for me to go,' he said and turned his head to look back into the clubroom.

'I need you,' Alice said, too quietly for him to hear.

'What was that?' Angus asked, turning back to her.

'I have something for you. I've been trying to decide when I should give it to you, but if you're leaving, I think you should have it now,' Alice said, pushing his hips with hers and reaching down the front of her dress. 'I just don't have any pockets in the dress,' she said, seeing the confused look on Angus's face. She took hold of his hand. 'Here,' she said, placing something hard and smooth in his palm. 'I want you to have this.'

'It's warm,' Angus said, looking down at the dark grey object in his hand.

'Of course it's warm. It's been in my bra. Like I said, no pockets,' Alice did a twirl. Angus flipped the object over in his hand. On the underside there were angular symbols carved into the polished surface.

'Is it a rock?' Angus asked. Alice smiled and shook her head.

'It's more than that. It's a talisman.'

'A talisman? What for?'

'For you, Black. You're hurting and this is to heal you.' She ran her hand up Angus's arm.

'And what do these symbols mean?' he asked. Alice glanced over his shoulder back into the room where Torry and Dom were looking at them. She moved Angus to block out their prying eyes.

'It's an incantation,' she said.

'What does it say?' Angus asked, holding up the talisman so that the coloured DJ light illuminated it. Alice lowered his hand and wrapped his fingers around the stone.

'It says Oblivisci.'

'And what does that mean?'

'I forget.'

'You forget?' Angus asked, looking up from his hands.

'No, I forget,' Alice said.

'Ha?' Angus asked. Alice checked to see if Torry was still looking at them. Torry was talking to O'Burket. Alice pulled Angus's face towards hers and pushed her lips to his. She kissed him firmly for a few seconds, then rested her cheek against his, whispering something in his ear.

'Cinder,' Angus repeated absentmindedly. Alice left him there and strolled back into the clubrooms. Angus stood looking out to the ocean with the talisman clasped firmly in his fist.

Back inside the clubrooms, Marraine had found Torry. They were huddled together near the top of the stairs, leaning against the balustrade.

'What is she up to?' Marraine asked, craning her neck to see through the crowd.

'That's what I want to know,' Torry agreed. Dom arrived at the top of the stairs, his cheeks bulging with a mouthful of food.

'What do you want to know?' he asked after swallowing half the contents of his mouth.

'We want to know what that one's up to,' Marraine said, motioning towards Alice and Angus. Dom lent against the balustrade. He watched as Alice walked away from Angus, turning and smiling in his direction as she entered the clubroom. Dom then turned to look at Angus, laughing at the goofy look on his face.

'Just a bit of flirty fun, I reckon,' Dom said, starting on his next sausage.

'Why's he doing that?' Torry demanded, her cheeks reddening.

'Because it's fun,' Dom mumbled. 'Something to take his mind off things.'

'His mind off things? What things? Things like Cinder?' Torry tried not to look at the masticated food in her brother's mouth as he smiled.

'Yep. Have at it. That's what I say,' he said, licking sauce from his fingers.

'Have at it?' Marraine asked, raising an eyebrow.

'Yeah, have at it!' Dom said again, wiping his hand on the back of his jeans.

'Are we talking about a human female here? Or a piece of cake?' Marraine asked, stepping closer to Dom. Dom looked past her. Alice was swaying to the music.

'She's rich dark chocolate cake,' Dom said, watching Alice's hips move.

'Dude!' Torry said, walking away. 'That's our cousin you're talking about.'

'You do have a way with words, don't you, Dominic?' Marraine said, stopping in front of Dom. She took hold of his head, licked her finger, and wiped away the sauce at the side of his mouth. Dom raised his eyebrows.

'What are you, my mother?' he asked, cleaning his face with the empty balled-up napkins. Marraine ran her eyes up and down his body. When her eyes met his, she slipped her finger into her mouth slowly, then opened it so Dom could see her massaging the tip with her tongue.

'Do I still remind you of your mother?' she asked.

'Yes, Mummy dear,' Dom grinned. Marraine slapped his shoulder and turned away.

'Sicko,' she said as she walked away, following Torry.

'Have I been naughty, Mummy?' Dom called out. 'Do I need a spanking?'

Torry walked to the far end of the room to intercept Alice.'Dance with me,' she ordered, hip-checking her older cousin.

'Oh yeah,' Alice said, draping her arm over Torry's shoulder and swinging her hips to the beat. Marraine came to stand with them but stood a short distance away, watching Angus. Dom arrived a short time later, holding two drinks. He smiled as he handed one of the drinks to Alice and ignored Torry's look of disappointment that the second didn't come her way.

'Looking hot tonight, cuz,' he said.

'Thanks,' Alice replied with a wink. 'You're not looking too shabby yourself,' she said, running an appraising eye over Dom's outfit. Dom flexed his chest muscles and adjusted his collar.

'I do alright I guess.' He winked back.

The music pumped, and Dom joined in dancing with his sister and cousin. He was careful not to spill the contents of the glass in his hand. Angus returned from the deck and stood against the wall behind them. Alice raised her arms over her head and turned slowly, swaying her hips. The hem of her skirt brushed over Angus's hands.

'You're fighting a losing battle there, you know?' Dom said, leaning in so only Alice could hear.

'What do you mean?' Alice asked.

'Trying to get Black to dance,' Dom replied as he also handed Angus a drink. 'He doesn't dance,'

Alice dropped her bottom lip.

'His loss,' she said, turning to face Angus and walking her fingers up his chest. 'What do you think of this dress?' She asked, turning back to Dom. 'It's sexy, isn't it?' she said, loud enough for Angus to hear.

'Very sexy,' Dom agreed.

'It's Torry's,' Alice said with a mischievous grin.

'What?!'

'It's my dress,' Torry said from behind him. She pushed her brother's shoulder and laughed. 'Not so sexy now, ha?'

Dom looked as though he had just unexpectedly eaten something sour. 'You have sexy clothes?' he asked.

'Yes.' Torry said, continuing to sway with the music, moving towards Alice.

'Why?' Dom asked.

'Because I like sexy clothes.'

'But you never wear them.'

'Who says I need to wear them?' Torry spun, flicking her ponytail through the air. Dom stood on the spot, looking perplexed.

'Then why do you have them?' he asked.

'I told you,' Torry said. 'Because I like them.'

Marraine pushed past Dom, sauntering around the two girls dancing and squeezing her way in next to Angus, still leaning on the wall.

'How are you doing, sweetie?' she asked, placing a hand on his chest.

'I'm good,' he said, looking her up and down. 'Better now that you're here.'

'So, when do you want to get out of here?' Marraine asked, taking Angus by the hand and leading him away from the group. Angus followed her, turning to give Dom a smile and a wink as he went. Dom did not return his smile. He continued to look confused. Marraine led Angus back out on to the deck and leaned against the railings, looking up towards the hill where the burnt remains of Cinder's house sat in the darkness. The movement of the clouds and the swaying of the treetops gave the illusion that the hill was slowly creeping towards them, like some Godzilla-esque creature stalking the twinkling lights of Heathcote, readying to devour the little town. Angus stood next to Marraine and rested his arms on the rail. He looked out to the ocean. Heathcote's lights danced on the ripples of the dark, mirror-like surface.

'It's a beautiful night,' he said, turning to look back at Marraine.

'Yes, it is. Although it's a bit cold for my liking,' she said, rubbing her hands up and down her exposed arms. Angus wrapped a warm arm around her shoulder. 'Why, thank you kindly, sir.' she said, resting her head on his shoulder.

'My pleasure.'

The smell of alcohol hung heavy on Angus's breath and Marraine noticed his words starting to slur together.

Back inside the clubroom, Alice was using her best "yeps" and "aha rights" to try to slither away from Torry. Torry, however, had asked Alice if she knew anything about roller derby. When Alice had responded with a distracted 'um, no, not really,' Torry had taken that as an invitation to offer her a very excited explanation of the rules and game play. She was now into the third minute of giving Alice a blow-by-blow description of the Surf Coast Banshee's last game.

'I'm number 7, Gopher Kinnard. Get it? Go fark'n 'ard,' she said enthusiastically.

'Ha, ha. Yes, I get it,' Alice said, shooting sideways looks in Angus and Marraine's direction. 'Sorry, Torry, I just need to tell Angus something. Excuse me for a second.' She started to move across the clubroom, pushing her way through the growing throng. She was halfway across the room when a tall middle-aged man in a red flannelette shirt stood in her path. Alice smiled at him politely and tried to move past him, but he moved in front of her again.

'Hi,' he said. 'You're not from around here, are you?'

'No, I'm visiting family,' Alice said, trying again to move past him.

'I knew it. I'd remember you if I'd seen you before,' he said, nodding and taking a triumphant drink of his beer. Alice glared at him. Without a word, she pointed past the man.

'Oh, yeah. Sorry,' he said and stepped aside. As he did, Alice could see Angus and Marraine on the deck. Angus had his hand on Marraine's waist, and their mouths were pushed together in a kiss.

Chapter 19
Inkerman's World

Sydney's backstreets at night were a labyrinth of shadows. Graffiti adorned the walls like the chaotic whispers of a forgotten underworld. The paint, weathered and worn, told stories of rebellion, despair, and the twisted yearnings of society. The colours clashed violently, forming a mosaic of urban decay. Images of grotesque creatures, half-formed and nightmarish, leered from the brick canvases. Their twisted limbs and hollow eyes seemed to follow you, as if the very essence of the city had been captured and imprisoned within the layers of spray paint. Occasional streaks of blood-red paint slashed across the walls, resembling wounds inflicted upon the city itself. The graffiti spoke of an underworld, a subterranean realm where the forgotten and the forsaken found solace in the darkness.

As Cinder walked through those back streets, the oppressive weight of the night hung heavy in the air. The graffiti whispered stories of urban legends and unseen horrors lurking just beyond the edge of perception. In the dim glow of the few streetlights, the walls seemed to come alive. She walked a few paces behind Mr Inkerman, and a few paces behind her, was David – Mr Inkerman's head of security. David had thick arms, thick eyebrows, and, as Cinder had discovered, little interest in conversation.

They turned a corner and found another wall covered in street art. Vibrant blues, reds, and greens. To Cinder's eyes, the painted objects seemed to loom out of the wall. David pulled a small object from his pocket. With a click, a blueish tinge appeared at the end. Ultraviolet light illuminated the images on the walls. A set of arrows glowed brightly in David's beam. When his light flicked away, the arrows were still visible to Cinder, but from David's action of checking and double checking, she assumed he could only see them under the ultraviolet light.

'There they are, sir,' he said, pointing to an arrow at the top of the wall. Cinder could see a collection of them running along the top of the wall, coming from both directions, pointing to a small gap in the wall.

'What are we looking for?' she asked, pretending that she could not see the arrows.

'There,' Mr Inkerman said, laying one arm over her shoulder and pointing to the illuminated symbols with the other hand. Cinder's first instinct was to pull away, but she didn't. The last man to touch her with affection was Angus. In fact, other than her father, Angus was the only man that had touched her.

'Yes, I see the arrow,' she said as she placed her hand over Mr Inkerman's hand on her shoulder. David moved the light. The next arrow angled down towards the base of the wall. He followed the direction with the beam. On the bottom corner of the wall, just before it ended at the intersection of the narrow gap, the beam illuminated a different symbol. Cinder would have been able to see it without the ultraviolet light, but it wasn't until the beam fell on the symbol that she could see that it was not part of the other artwork around it. The symbol looked like an eye, formed from eight straight lines and one circle. The four longer lines formed a diamond that lay horizontally, the four smaller lines also formed a diamond, but the smaller diamond sat vertically, with the circle at its centre.

'What does it mean?' Cinder asked.

'In means,' Mr Inkerman took his hand from her shoulder and walked towards the gap. 'We need to go down here.' He motioned for Cinder to step forward and see. The narrow gap between the walls was very dark, even for Cinder's eyes.

Cinder squinted to peer into the darkness. To the left, as far as she could make out, the wall rose flat and solid. Above her head, perhaps ten feet from the ground, a row of barred and darkened windows ran the length of the building. Cinder assumed the windows, which may have once illuminated the building's interior before the construction of the building to the right, were now useless. The brick-wall on the right was windowless, probably because they would have been as useless as the windows across the gap. The right side did, however, contain three doors, evenly spaced along the wall. At the end of the gap was an impenetrable darkness that Cinder took to be a dead end.

'Go,' Mr Inkerman said, and David moved into the gap, his broad shoulders almost touching the walls of the confined space. 'After you,' Mr Inkerman said, motioning for Cinder to follow next.

Cinder hesitated for a moment, fully aware that this was a dangerous position for a young woman to put herself in, entering a dark alley with only one way out with two men. *What are you afraid of?* she thought to herself. They are in more danger here than you. She stepped forward into the gap. Once inside, the darkness was more intense than Cinder had predicted. The only light was the dull purple glow from David's ultraviolet torch. The narrow area was clear of rubbish and debris, very clear, in fact, as if it had recently been cleaned. It smelled damp, musty, and old, like soil and rust. And there was something else, a noise or perhaps just the feeling of a rumbling vibration. Cinder could feel it through the balls of her feet. Something below them was pulsing like some giant machine or underground river. She stretched her arms out and pushed her palms flat against the cold walls.

'Can you feel that?' she asked, turning to look back at Mr Inkerman as he followed her in. He stood close behind her and placed his hands next to hers.

'I feel the cold, that's all,' he said. Cinder turned her head from side to side and closed her eyes.

'No, there's something else, a rumble. I'm not sure if I'm hearing it or just feeling it.'

'I must be getting old,' Mr Inkerman said, taking his hands from the walls. 'All I can hear is my own stomach rumbling. Have you found it yet?'

'Yes, sir,' David said. Cinder opened her eyes. The ultraviolet beam was illuminating another of the eye symbols. It was far smaller but glowed bright orange in the top corner of the door farthest down the gap.

'Now what?' Cinder asked. Mr Inkerman took hold of her waist and slid himself past her. Their bodies sliding against each other in the narrow space.

'Now, we knock,' he said.

Mr Inkerman approached the door. The three doors were identical in size and shape and spaced evenly along the wall. They were a faded rusty brown colour but looked black in the lowlight. As Mr Inkerman stood next to the last door, Cinder inspected the door closest to her. The middle of the three. It appeared to be constructed of some kind of flat metal, with rivets running around the border. There were no handles on the outside of the doors, just a circular keyhole. Mr Inkerman knocked twice. He paused, knocked twice again, paused a second time, then pounded four slow blows with the side of his fist.

Cinder heard something click inside the door and the door opened, creaking loudly on rusted hinges. There was only just enough room for the door to open in the narrow gap between the two buildings. For a moment, the door blocked her view of the others, stopping before it continued to swing out against the wall. A dull light filled the space.

A large, bald man dressed in a dark suit stepped out of the doorway. Saying nothing, he inspected the arrivals one at a time, Cinder last. Apparently satisfied with what he saw, he motioned for them to follow him in. Mr Inkerman waited at the door for Cinder. He put his hand on the small of her back and leaned close to talk to her.

'Are you having fun, Miss Delacourt?' he asked. Cinder turned to answer him, but the sound of voices behind her interrupted her. A moment later, three people holding their own ultraviolet light rounded the corner. Cinder could see that they were all around thirty years of age. Two thin men and a large woman dressed in designer clothes. They fell silent when they saw Cinder and her companions. The large man who had opened the door stuck his bald head around the corner of the doorway. He raised a large hand towards the new arrivals, telling them to stop, then waved Cinder and Mr Inkerman inside. They stepped through the doorway. Cinder turned, expecting David to follow. David took a step back and folded his hands in front. The large man in black closed the door behind Mr Inkerman, leaving David outside.

The vast space inside the building they had just entered was lit by a single, bare bulb. It sat at the end of a verdigrised copper pipe protruding from the wall, glowing a dirty yellow. They stood on a small pressed-metal landing. The sound of Cinder's heeled boots rang out in the vast empty space as she moved to accommodate all three people on the small landing. Roughly cut pieces of one-inch box steel welded to the landing acted as a makeshift handrail. Cinder leaned cautiously against the rail and looked out into the space. There was a cracked and rubble-strewn concrete floor about ten feet below them. Brick pillars, evenly spaced, ran in three lines along the length of the building. Cinder guessed they had once supported a floor that would have been at street level and that she was looking down on what had once been a basement. There were no remnants of the floor now. If anyone had the misfortune of trying to enter through either of the other two doors, they would have fallen the ten feet down to the hard floor. Cinder could see the other two doors-to-nowhere, sitting high on the brick wall, looking more like two framed artworks than doors. A staircase constructed of the same pressed metal as the landing, led down to the basement floor below.

'Come, Miss Delacourt,' Mr Inkerman said, taking her hand and leading her down Cinder lifted the hem of her dress with her free hand, to not trip on it on the way down. It was cold at the bottom of the steps, cold and still. The single light above was casting eerie shadows on the peeling paint, crumbling bricks and the remnants of rusted machinery. The air was thick with the scent of industrial lubricants, mould, and dust. As she moved into the space, the pulsing rumble she had heard earlier grew louder. Cinder stopped to listen, but jumped when a loud bang came from above.

'It's okay,' Mr Inkerman assured her. 'It's just the others arriving at the door.' More banging followed and Cinder recognised it as the same pattern of knocks that they had employed.

'I'm not imagining it,' Cinder said as she watched the bald man in black open the door for the others. 'I can hear something.' She turned back to Mr Inkerman. He smiled but said nothing.

There was some movement at the far end of the building, Cinder could just make it out in the darkness. She moved her head to one side to see around the brick pillars. Someone in all white had entered from an archway in the far wall, most likely a woman in heels from the way they were walking. Mr Inkerman walked forward to meet them and Cinder followed, careful to not trip on the cracked and broken floor. When the person in white came further into the light, Cinder could see that it was a woman. She was a short woman in a tailored three-piece suit. Her black hair was short and combed flat against her scalp. She had dark skin, white teeth, and fingernails painted orange.

'Welcome,' she said in a voice deeper than Cinder would have expected. 'Please follow me and I will take you the rest of the way.' They followed, and for a time none of them spoke. Cinder's heels clicked against the hard floor and reverberated around the vast, empty space. Anticipation grew with each step, but anticipation of what? This night became more mysterious with each passing moment. They passed through the archway that the woman in white had entered from. The floor changed from concrete to large cobblestones. Once again, they were in a narrow walkway. Above their heads, at what would be the street level, ran dirty and rusted metal bars. Through the small gaps between each bar, Cinder could see the clouds of the night sky. They drifted by slowly, glowing a murky grey in the lights of the city. The rumbling noise was louder still in this cramped space, vibrating and pulsing through the floor and the claustrophobically close walls.

'Where are you taking me?' Cinder asked.

'You will see very soon,' Mr Inkerman said. The woman turned to look back at Cinder and smiled.

'It's just up here,' she said. Cinder looked past her and could see the walkway continuing on for a few more metres. Up ahead was another door, similar to the three doors in the narrow alley.

When they got closer, Cinder could see the symbol of the eye again, but this one was large enough to take up most of the door and was visible without the use of the ultraviolet light. There was no door handle on this door again, and no lock that Cinder could see. The woman in white removed a card from the inside of her jacket and slid it into a small slit in the wall. In the darkness, you would not see the slit unless you knew where to look. A moment later, the card sprung back out with a click. The door fell ajar, a strip of light around three sides. Cinder realised then that the sound she had been hearing was music. The woman in white slipped the card back into her pocket and opened the door. The music grew even louder, accompanied by the sound of people talking excitedly. Light of many colours filled the narrow walkway. The woman in white stood back against the wall for them to walk past. Mr Inkerman took Cinder's hand and led her through the doorway.

'Enjoy your evening,' the woman said before closing the door behind them.

Cinder looked around in awe. They were standing in a huge subterranean warehouse. A curved ceiling far above was lit by slowly moving lights of green and blue. Their shimmering beams evoked a feeling of being underwater. Cinder's immediate reaction was to hold her breath. Below the flowing ceiling was a grand dining hall unlike anything Cinder had ever seen. Long banquet tables stretched across the vast space, draped in deep blue cloth that shimmered under the moving lights. Glass domes held flickering candles on each table, their flames bending and shifting as if responding to the currents of an invisible tide. The silverware gleamed, reflecting the glow of the lights drifting lazily above the guests.

The people seated at the tables were dressed in an array of elegant and eccentric outfits. The air hummed with conversation and laughter, voices rising and falling like waves, blending seamlessly with the music that filled the cavernous space. Along the edges of the room, waiters in crisp black uniforms wove effortlessly between guests, carrying trays laden with food that looked almost too beautiful to eat. The scent of roasted spices and something sweet lingered in the air.

Mr Inkerman released Cinder's hand and took a step forward, surveying the room with the ease of someone who had been here before. Cinder, however, remained rooted to the spot, overwhelmed by the sheer grandeur of it all. A woman dressed in midnight blue approached them with a welcoming smile. Her eyes, bright and sharp, flicked over Cinder with interest.

'Welcome,' she said smoothly. 'You must be our newest guest.' She turned gracefully, beckoning Cinder to follow. Her movements were fluid, almost hypnotic, and as she led Cinder through the hall, the sounds of music and laughter swelled around them. Mr Inkerman had already slipped away, moving between groups of people. The woman stopped at a long, dark wooden table surrounded by a raucous group of guests. A man with a wild mop of silver-streaked hair laughed loudly, slamming his hand down on the table in delight. His velvet coat was half-unbuttoned, his tie forgotten somewhere, and his face was flushed from drink. Beside him, a woman with bright red lipstick leaned heavily against another guest, her fingers lazily tracing patterns on the rim of her glass. The group barely noticed Cinder's arrival until the woman in blue cleared her throat.

'A fresh face for the evening,' she announced with a smile. 'Play nice,' she added as she walked away. The silver-haired man looked up, his sharp eyes flicking over Cinder before he grinned.

'Well now, aren't you a curious one?' he said.

'Look at those eyes!' the woman with the red lips said. She gestured at the empty seat beside her. 'Sit, sit!' she said. 'You look like you could use a drink.' Cinder lowered herself into the chair. Immediately, a glass of champagne was shoved into her hands.

'To new friends!' a wide-faced man across the table cheered. The others raised their glasses with a chorus of agreement. Cinder smiled and took a sip from her glass. She cast a glance across the hall, spotting Mr Inkerman in conversation with a group near the dancefloor. He didn't look back.

The bubbles fizzed against Cinder's lips as she took another sip. Around her, the table erupted in laughter as the silver-haired man finished his scandalous tale, slapping the table once again for emphasis. A few drops of wine splashed from a nearby glass, but no one seemed to care. Cinder sat quietly, watching. The people sitting around her were loud and uninhibited. They leaned into one another, gesturing wildly as they spoke, their voices rising above the music in bursts of excitement. The woman with the red lips had begun absentmindedly braiding a lock of her seatmate's hair while a broad-shouldered man on Cinder's other side was trying, unsuccessfully, to stack empty glasses into a precarious tower. Cinder cast another glance around the room. Mr Inkerman moved like a shadow, slipping between clusters of guests with an effortless grace. His presence was magnetic. People turned toward him, drawn into his orbit. He leaned in close as he spoke, his voice too soft for Cinder to hear, but his listeners nodded eagerly, some laughing, some very serious. She watched as he took the hand of a woman in a gold-threaded gown and kissed her knuckles with an effortless charm before moving on. Another group intercepted him, and he welcomed them as if they were old friends. There was something rehearsed about it, something deliberate. Cinder's fingers tightened slightly around her glass.

'He won't stay in one place for long,' the silver-haired man mused, following her gaze. He swirled the dark liquid in his glass lazily. 'Inkerman never does.' Cinder turned back to the table, forcing a smile.

'He seems to know everyone.' The man laughed, a deep, rich sound.

'Oh, darling, everyone knows him. Or at least, they think they do,' he said, taking a long sip, his sharp eyes gleaming over the rim of his glass. 'And yet, no one really knows a damn thing,' he added.

Before Cinder could respond, a waiter materialised beside her, silent and swift. He replaced her glass, the liquid glistening under the candlelight.

'I didn't order this,' Cinder said. The waiter merely inclined his head.

'A gift,' he said before slipping away into the crowd. Moving the drink next to her other half-full glass, Cinder looked up to see Mr Inkerman returning, his expression unreadable as he pulled out the chair beside her and sat down.

'I trust you're enjoying yourself?' he asked smoothly.

'She's barely touched her drink,' the red-lipped woman teased, giving Cinder a playful nudge. Cinder ignored her, turning to Mr Inkerman.

'What have you been doing?' she asked.

'Taking care of things.' He glanced at the glass in front of her and gave a small nod. 'Good. Our food should be arriving any moment now.'

As if summoned by his words, a waiter glided toward them, carrying two finely presented plates of food. With careful precision, the waiter placed the plates. Sizzling meats drenched in thick sauces, golden pastries filled with unseen delights, small crystal bowls of something that shimmered like captured moonlight. The scent was warm and intoxicating. The moment the waiter's hand left Mr Inkerman's plate, he stabbed the meat with his knife. He pulled the meat open with his fork, then slammed his knife down on the table, rattling Cinder's glass.

'Boy!' he yelled at the waiter. When the waiter turned back, Mr Inkerman slid his plate to the side. 'This is not rare,' he protested.

'Sorry sir,' the waiter said as he quickly swept up Mr Inkerman's plate and hurried away.

'How's yours?' Mr Inkerman asked, turning back to Cinder. She had just taken her first bite. She swallowed before answering.

'Mine's fine,' she said.

'Fine?'

'Yes, fine' Cinder repeated. Mr Inkerman spun around to find the waiter again.

'I didn't pay for fine. They need to take yours back, too.'

'No, I mean it's good,' Cinder said, not wanting to trouble the poor young man. 'It's delicious,' she added.

'Inkerman likes his steak rare,' said the man with the grey streaks. 'I think he'd be happy if it was still mooing.' He laughed at himself and the others around the table joined in.

'It's true,' Mr Inkerman said, grinning.

A moment later, a waiter returned with a new plate of food for him. Cinder watched as he cut into the stake. He appeared pleased with the red liquid that drained out onto his plate. Even amongst the other delicious aromas, Cinder could smell the raw flesh. Her stomach churned as she watched Mr Inkerman lift the pink meat to his lips. He sucked the remaining juices between his teeth before sliding the morsel into his mouth. Cinder turned back to her plate and continued eating.

'This is very good,' she said, patting the edge of her mouth with a napkin. 'Are you happy with yours now?'

'Good enough,' Mr Inkerman said, but he appeared distracted. Cinder noticed his gaze flicking from his food to something over her shoulder.

'Is something wrong?' she asked. Mr Inkerman looked back to Cinder and gave her a charming smile, but there was a hint of arrogance in his eyes.

'Not at all, my dear. I was just admiring the view,' he said, his eyes flicking back beyond Cinder again.

She turned and followed his line of sight to a woman standing near the wall, swaying to the music. Slim and pale, with black hair that fell in glossy waves around her shoulders, she moved sensually in her floor-length, strapless dress. Every movement was graceful and controlled, as she sipped her drink with the air of someone who was used to getting exactly what they wanted. Her eyes were dark and piercing, and they were watching Mr Inkerman too. It was clear that she was aware of the effect she was having on him. Cinder turned back to Mr Inkerman. She could see the hunger in his eyes. He watched, captivated, as the dark-haired woman moved with a confident stride towards the dancefloor her hips swaying with each step.

'Will you excuse me?' he said.

Without looking at Cinder or waiting for a reply, he stood and left the table. Cinder watched him go. He paused a few times to say hello to some of the other guests, but Cinder knew where he was heading.

The dark-haired woman was standing at the edge of the dance floor. She placed her empty glass on a table and raised her arms above her head, twirling slowly to the beat. She was very thin. Her dress, although very small, still hung from her body. Cinder turned away and looked down at her plate of food, suddenly feeling a loss of appetite. She pushed her fork through an unknown green paste on the edge of her plate, wondering if she still needed to eat human food at all. She decided then to give up eating.

As she looked around at the strangers sitting around the table with her, she became aware of another feeling, homesickness. Sydney was amazing, but something about the city felt off and throbbed at the back of her mind. At first, she thought it was the constant flow and hum of people. In her old life, she would regularly sit in her room reading and writing her poetry and not see another person for days at a time. But it wasn't the people and Cinder knew that. Sydney was truly a melting pot of different cultures and Cinder loved being surrounded by the different fashions, languages, and ethnicities. No, it wasn't the people that were making Cinder miss her home. It was the smell. Sydney was essentially a beach town like home, only a thousand times larger and a thousand times busier. There were places she could go to feel the salty breeze on her face and take in the scent of the ocean and the sand, but there was always the industrialised and mechanised odour of urbanisation. The bouquet of concrete, plastic, petroleum, and garbage clung to her hair and clothes. Worst of all was the smell of the people. There was the homeless, of course, with no access to clean clothes or shower. But even the wealthy, with their designer clothes and more bathrooms than the number of occupants in their giant beach front properties, even they smelt of stress and business.

Cinder looked at the woman who now had her hand on Mr Inkerman's arm. Her long, black hair framed her impossibly slim face. Each lock hung glossy and perfectly formed, as if carved from obsidian. The woman's skeletal fingers crept their way up Mr Inkerman's arm. She let out a laugh like a hungry hyena and pushed her bony hips against his. Cinder let her fork drop to her plate. She picked up her napkin, squeezing it in both hands, then dropped it over her uneaten food. The others around the table continued to fill themselves with food, drink, and superficial conversations. Cinder reached across the table and collected Mr Inkerman's steak knife. She cleaned it with the edge of the tablecloth and slid it handle-first into the sleeve of her dress.

Mr Inkerman and the slim woman drifted together away from the dancefloor towards the shadows. The colourful lights flashed across their faces as their bodies writhed as one to the beat of the pulsing music. Cinder kicked her chair back and rose from the table. She almost knocked over a waiter as she marched towards the dance floor. The waiter struggled to keep the tray of champaign he was holding from tipping over. He swore, thinking that Cinder could not hear him over the music. Cinder turned to glare at him, her pupils, large dark slits in a pool of emerald-green. The waiter turned and almost fell over the table Cinder had just vacated.

Cinder continued forward through the crowd of perspiring and throbbing bodies. A young woman wearing a fur-coat that reached almost to the floor, fell against Cinder as she pushed past. Her dark-skin and bald head glowed in the multi-coloured lights, as she embraced Cinder. Cinder pulled herself free and set the woman back on her feet before she continued.

'I love your hair,' the woman said, letting her fingers trail through Cinder's hair. Ignoring her, Cinder moved on, weaving and pushing her way towards Mr Inkerman and the slim woman, still glued to each other. The music grew louder as she moved further towards the front of the dance floor. The lights flashed in her eyes, making it hard to keep track of where she was going. A grey-haired man with broad shoulders forced himself in front of her. He slid a warm, sweaty hand around her waist. Cinder took hold of his wrist and flicked his arm like a whip. Agony and surprise flashed across the man's face as his arm fell limp beside him. Cinder continued on. Blinking against the lights, she spotted Mr Inkerman against the far wall. He had one hand in the woman's dark hair, holding it back to kiss her long neck. His other hand was on her backside. '*Ha*,' Cinder thought, '*there's nothing there to squeeze.*'

The woman's head fell back as she looked up at the flashing lights. Cinder quickened her pace. Mr Inkerman looked up and smiled at her. Cinder stopped. Mr Inkerman held eye contact with her, but continued to kiss the woman's neck. Cinder slid the knife from her sleeve, squeezing it in her fist. Then she ran.

Chapter 20

Clubroom Blitz

Marraine pulled her face away from Angus and placed her hands on his chest. Angus stood for a moment with his lips pursed and eyes closed. Feeling her moving away, he opened one eye.

'Thank you, sweetie. But also no, thank you,' Marraine said when he looked at her. Angus took a step back.

'No?' he asked. 'Are you sure?' Marraine could feel the swell of his large chest through his shirt.

'Oh, believe me, sweetie, under different circumstances I would be all for that.' She placed a cool hand on his warm cheek. 'But, no. Definitely no,' she traced the line of his cheekbone with her thumb.

A disturbance erupted from inside the surf club. A woman gave a startled scream and many other voices of concern and surprise joined hers. Glass smashed on the floor. The crowd parted as a tall man in the red flannelette shirt stumbled and fell to the floor with a thud. Alice stood over him with her fists clenched. The man on the floor propped himself up on one elbow. His face had turned pale and clammy except for the red mark that glowed on his left cheek. He looked at the smashed glass and shiny liquid on the floor that was beer he had just been drinking moments ago. Holding his hand over the growing redness on his cheek, he glowered up at Alice. Alice swivelled her head around to glare at Marraine, who was still holding Angus's face in her hand. Alice turned back to the man on the floor. She pulled her foot back, readying to kick the injured man in the stomach. Torry tackled her to the ground before her foot could make contact. Her boot flew into the air and fell with a splash in the beer puddle on the floor. The two members of O'Burket rushed forward. Henry held out a hand to help the man off the floor, and Becky went to help Torry with Alice.

'Get off me, you bitches!' Alice yelled as she thrashed around in Torry's bear hug. 'This is your fault. You and that blue-eyed cougar.' She glared at Marraine.

'Okay, just calm down.' Beccy said, taking her by her shoulders. Alice wriggled free of Torry's grip and head-butted Beccy in the nose. A cheer rose from a group of young men that had now gathered close to the action.

'Leave her alone, copper,' one of them shouted. 'She was just standing up for herself.'

'Mind your business,' a large man with greying hair from behind them said.

'Are you going to make me, pops?' the young man said. The older man stepped forward and took hold of his shirt. Officer Burket had just pulled the man from the floor. He hurried to get between the two men.

Dom stopped Angus and Marraine at the surf club door as they tried to re-enter.

'What the hell?' he yelled and shoved Angus in the chest.

'What?' Angus said, swatting his hands away. 'You're the one that said I should have some fun.'

'I didn't mean this, dickhead. What are you thinking?'

'It's okay Dominic,' Marraine said, placing her hand on his arm.

'Get your hands off me,' he said, pulling away.

Behind him, Alice wrestled herself free of Beccy and Torry's grip and collided with another young woman. The woman's glass tipped onto a couple that were standing next to her. The argument that sprung up soon turned to pushing and more drinks being spilt. Angry murmurs grew into a cacophony of yelling and curse words. A man with short, spiked blond hair was yelling something in Dom's direction, but Dom couldn't make out what he was saying over the noise. The man was red faced and agitated. He was pointing aggressively at Dom and pushing his way towards him. A tall, thin woman in front of him, trying unsuccessfully to calm him down. The angry man pushed the woman aside. As he did, he knocked a glass from a table; adding a second smashed glass to the floor. Alice stormed towards Angus and Marraine, who were still trying to get back into the club.

'Get out of my way!' she yelled as Dom moved to intercept her. Torry and Beccy caught up with Alice again and pulled her back.

'You okay?' Torry asked Beccy, who had a stream of blood running from her nose.

'I've had worse,' Becky said with a smile as she tried to wipe away some of the blood with her shoulder.

'Get off me!' Alice yelled as they pulled her away.

'See what you've done,' Dom said to Marraine and Angus. When he turned back to watch Alice, the red-faced man was in front of him. He was much shorter than Dom and appeared to be in his mid-thirties. He jabbed a stubby finger into Dom's chest.

'Where you going, pretty boy?' he said, jutting his chin up towards Dom's face. Dom knew he should just ignore the man, but this guy was asking for it.

'Back to your mum's place,' he said, stepping past the man. The man swung at him, a slow lumbering haymaker. Dom moved out of its path easily and slapped the man's hand as it went past. Dom's second slap landed firmly on the man's left cheek. The slap was loud enough to turn heads, even over the din of the room. The man stumbled back, holding his face. He looked around the room like someone who has just woken from sleep and found themselves somewhere unfamiliar. Sniggers and some applause arose amongst the yelling and shouting. Metallica's Enter sandman was playing in the background but stopped suddenly, replaced by an ear-ringing squeal of feedback. Amid moans and holding of ears, the arguments ceased. Detective Peter Morgan was standing by the DJ booth, holding the microphone into one of the speakers. He lifted the microphone to his mouth and waited for the feedback to stop.

'Alright everyone, party's over,' he said. 'Anyone who is still here in ten minutes will be spending the night in the lock-up.' The two members of O'Burket positioned themselves at the top of the stairs. Ignoring the complaints and snide remarks, they directed the crowd out of the club. With an imprint of Dom's hand on his cheek. The blond man said nothing as he followed the other's out, but he checked several times to see that he wasn't bleeding. The man Alice had knocked to the floor came to complain to Detective Morgan.

'Look at what she did,' he said, lifting his hand from his jaw to show the mark that was now turning from red to purple. Detective Morgan handed the microphone back to DJ Hank the Crank and turned to the injured man.

'Nine minutes,' he said.

'What? But I want to press charges. She attacked me,' the man said, pointing towards Alice who was now sitting on a stool near the bar with her arms crossed. Torry stood next to her. Detective Morgan shot a look from Alice to Torry then to Dom and slid his hands in to his pockets.

'Come and see us tomorrow,' he said.

'But,'

'Tomorrow,' Detective Morgan said. Then added. 'Eight minutes.'

The man shook his head and walked away, glaring at Alice as he went. Seeing him looking, Alice screwed up her face and gave him the finger.

'What about all these others?' the man asked as he got to the top of the stairs.

'Seven minutes,' Detective Morgan called out, pulling his hands from his pockets and holding up seven fingers. The man gave a few more complaints under his breath and descended the stairs. Detective Morgan motioned for Torry to come over to him. Torry came towards him but kept her eye on Alice. Alice got up from the stool and Torry stopped.

'I'm just getting my boot. Is that alright with you?' she asked with her hands on her hips and her head inclined to one side. Torry said nothing but continued over to Detective Morgan. Alice limped over to where her boot was lying on the floor. The heel of the boot she was still wearing clomped loudly on the timber floor of the now empty room.

'Hey Torry,' Detective Morgan said when she stood next to him.

'Hey Peter. How's things?'

'Same as always, unfortunately it would seem,' he said, looking around the room. 'So, can we sort this all out?'

'I think the worst of it is over now.'

'Good. Do you think you can help me get everyone out of here?' Detective Morgan asked.

'Sure thing, Detective,' Torry said, patting him on the back.

'Thank you,' Detective Morgan said, pulling his notebook from his pocket. 'Mr Kinnard, could I have a moment?' He motioned for Dom to join him, and they walked together to the far wall.

Alice walked back to the bar stool, letting her heel clomp loudly again as she went. The legs of the stool squawked on the timber floor as she slumped down aggressively. She forced her foot into the boot and scowled at Angus and Marraine, who were now being ushered towards the stairs by Torry.

'I'm sorry,' Angus said. 'I don't know why everyone is acting like this.'

'You don't?' Marraine asked. Torry and she both looked at Angus with the same incredulous look. Dom came to join them. He had his hands shoved deep in his pockets and he was looking at the floor avoiding eye contact.

'Some night, hey?' he said to no one in particular.

'I think you should take Angus home and let him sleep tonight off,' Marraine said.

'Sounds good,' Dom replied, still avoiding Marraine's eyeline.

'Is everything okay, Dominic?' she asked, reaching out for him. Dom turned away before she could make contact.

'I'll call you tomorrow. There's something we need to talk about,' he said, taking hold of Angus's arm.

'We're out of here.' He motioned for Angus to go ahead of him.

'I'm sorry we ruined the night.' Angus offered as he passed officer Beccy O'Bearn and her blood-stained shirt. Beccy leaned in close and whispered.

'Best surf club fundraiser ever.' She winked and slapped Angus's butt. 'Don't tell the detective I said that.'

'Come on idiot, let's get out of here.' Dom took hold of Angus's arm. 'Hopefully there are a few sausages they need me to clean up for them.'

Chapter 21
Arm-less

Cinder sat with her back against a large green bin, holding her hand over her mouth and nose to block out the stench of rotting meat and vegetables. A rat, the size of a domestic cat, sat a few metres in front of her chewing the remains of God-knows-what. Its beady eyes glared at her as if to say *"Just try to take this from me lady and see what happens."*

'You don't have to worry about me,' Cinder whispered to the rat. 'I Just came from a three-course gourmet meal, prepared by international chefs with all the trimmings and I hardly touched any of it. I think your rotting scraps are safe.' She still had the knife tucked up her sleeve. She pulled it into her hand and held it up towards the rat, hissing. The rat sniffed the air twice, then took its prize in its mouth and ran away into the shadows. A predator scurrying around in the shadows. *Just like me*, Cinder thought. At least you have found your prey.

Cinder had left the party – scurried away – leaving Mr Inkerman in the slithering arms of the slim woman with the dark hair. She was out for blood, in more ways than one, and painfully aware of how conflicted that made her feel. Mr Inkerman, she assumed, would not have noticed her absence. He was too wrapped up in the thin woman, literally.

Closing her eyes, Cinder listened to the movements of the city around her. The rat had not gone far. She could hear it scratching around in the hollow areas behind the bins and she could hear its tiny heart beating in its furry little body. In the distance, the traffic revved and hummed, tyres rumbling along the streets. The breeze rustled leaves and discarded takeaway containers and whistled through cracks in grey buildings. There were voices too, and busy shuffling feet, thousands of them skittering about the city. But the busy people were far from here, away in the well-lit part of town. Cinder thought of her step-mother's reprimands about her poor listening skills.

'I can hear everything now, bitch,' she said to herself as she stood and looked up.

It was an unfamiliar part of the city. Dirty walls rose on all sides and a labyrinth of alleyways ran up and down in all directions. A drainpipe painted green ran down the wall to her right, dripping dirty water from its rusted and slimy end. She studied the walls for a moment, then looked down at her dress and shoes. She slipped off her shoes and picked one up. Taking hold of her dress where the slit ran up her thigh, she stabbed her heel into the material near the top of the split and tore a hole large enough to squeeze her fingers through. Then she ripped and continued to rip until she had torn all the way around the skirt of her dress. The seams on either side of the split gave some resistance, but she pulled the fabric free and dropped the lower section of her dress to the ground. It was a shame to destroy such a beautiful thing, and she didn't know how she was going to dispose of the rest of the dress without Mr Inkerman seeing. Unfortunately, as beautiful as it was, that dress was just going to hamper her movements.

After checking that no one was watching, she vaulted on top of the bins and scurried up the wall, leaping from hand-hold to hand-hold, her powerful arms and legs pushing her up towards the sky. Reaching the top of the wall, she pulled herself up and crouched on the edge. The cool night air whipped about her, flicking stray hairs across her face. The twinkling lights of the great city stretched out in all directions around her, their combined glow illuminating the clouds far above.

Far off in the distance, bats circled around the tops of the giant trees of Hyde Park. Beyond that, the Sydney Tower rose up like a great beacon in the dark sky. Cinder had tracked down Gemminae's scent there once before, so it seemed like a good place to start.

She ran along the rooftops, leaping from building to building, clinging to walls and climbing like a giant spider when required. She could see what Mr Inkerman was saying about Sydney being a great hunting ground. There were unsuspecting people walking everywhere and a labyrinth of twisting and turning alleyways for someone to get lost in. Someone walked alone along the shadowed paths of Hyde Park. *"I wonder what they taste like?"* The thought filled Cinder's mind. She chased it away and closed her eyes. Up here, she could not only hear the city, she could smell it, and feel it. Her senses filled with the city's movements and its emotions. Overcome, her head fell backwards, and she almost toppled over and back down the wall again. Her eyes shot open. She steadied herself, then whipped her head around. Gemminae was close. She could sense him.

Crashing in from above, Gemminae's child-like body slammed down on Cinder's head. She yelled and almost stumbled over the edge of the building once again. Steadying herself, she swivelled around to confront Gemminae. Her eyes darted from shadow to shadow, but he was gone. Cinder sniffed the air. He was still close, but just like the rat in the alleyway, he had scampered away into some dark hiding hole.

Moving away from the edge, Cinder crept cautiously into the shadows. She heard something move. Ahead of her was a small and narrow rectangular structure constructed of grey bricks. The structure rose from the otherwise flat surface of the building's roof. There was a green fire-door at one end and a row of vents along the south side. The rush of air from the vents grew louder as she approached. She checked the door but found it locked. As her hand dropped from the handle, she was struck from above again.

Cinder slammed against the door, but managed to take hold of Gemminae's arm. She pulled the boy-vampire over her shoulder. Gemminae crashed into the door. This time, the lock smashed, and the door flew open, banging against the brick wall. Directly inside the door was a small landing. A set of concrete steps led down away from the landing into darkness. Gemminae tumbled down the steps. Cinder jumped into the darkness to pursue him, but was struck from behind once again. She slipped and fell. Behind her, she thought she glimpsed Gemminae at the door, but it couldn't be him, not even a vampire could move that quick. *Could he?* She searched the darkness below for movement, but behind her the door slammed shut.

Since her re-birth, Cinder had the eyesight of a nocturnal predator, but even vampire eyes needed time to adjust to the sudden change in light. She saw the fist too late. The small but powerful hand shot out of the darkness, striking her mouth. Blood from a split lip slid across her tongue. Cinder fell backwards against the steps. She still could not see Gemminae, but she could hear his footsteps padding down the stairs. 'I hope you liked my gift,' he called out. His youthful voice, full of malicious laughter, echoed around the narrow space.

'You disgust me!' Cinder called out behind him, pushing herself up.

'Just a little fun between friends,' Gemminae called back, 'an arm-less little joke.'

'You're an arm-less little joke,' Cinder shot back, running downwards after him. Gemminae's laughter grew into a cackle.

'Oh, my, she's a feisty one!' he yelled.

From somewhere below, Cinder heard a door open then slam shut again. Soon after, she came to another landing. The door she had heard was on her left. It opened far easier than she expected. She sent it swinging wide and thudding against the wall. Through the doorway she found herself in an open office space, illuminated by the dim light filtering in from windows along three sides. Several rows of pod-like desks ran across the room. On the opposite side of the room, standing on top of a desk near the windows, Gemminae was holding a stack of papers.

'Now Daryl, did this really need to be printed out? Surely this could have been sent in an email,' he said, before shoving the pages in his mouth and picking up a staple machine from the desk. Fumbling with his one hand, he squeezed a staple into the stack of pages. 'No one thinks of the environment!' he mumbled.

Cinder ran at him. Gemminae squealed and laughed. He threw the staple machine at her, but she rolled across the desks to avoid his missile. Enraged, Gemminae pulled the papers from his mouth and threw them. The papers fluttered in the air for a moment, then flopped down on the next desk. Cinder came closer. Gemminae jumped from desk to desk. Cinder vaulted over one row then the next, closing in on her quarry.

Gemminae was running out of desks and approaching another wall. In desperation, he took hold of a chair and hurled it at the window ahead of him. The window smashed in a shower of glass and the chair continued out and down to the street below. On the wind that whistled through the opening, Cinder could hear yelling and confusion. She hoped that no one on the street was hurt. Gemminae leaped onto the window frame and slipped out into the night. Cinder vaulted the last row of desks and followed him. She needed to kick out some of the remaining glass to fit through the gap. Below, a small group had gathered. They looked up, pointing and yelling as Cinder climbed out on to a narrow ledge that ran along the side of the building.

'It's just a boy!' someone below yelled. Cinder looked to where they were pointing. Gemminae was shimmying along the ledge with his back to the wall, the streetlights glinting in his mischievous eyes. Cinder pushed herself against the wall and ran after him, glad that she had disposed of her heels. She was faster and more agile than the boy vampire and was soon within reaching distance. She grabbed at his arm, but Gemminae pulled away and pushed himself off the wall. One of the spectators screamed. 'He's going to fall!' another yelled.

But Gemminae didn't fall. He flew gracefully across the street below and landed safely on a balcony of the building opposite. Cinder leaped after him, but he had already dropped the few remaining storeys to the footpath and darted into a narrow side street. Murmurs of shock and confusion rose from the growing crowd on the street. Cinder didn't like the idea of exposing her supernatural abilities to the public, but she was determined to make Gemminae pay for his mutilation of the couple and their baby. She landed in a crouch with both feet on the flat metal handrail of the balcony. Checking that no one was below her, she flipped backwards, landing on the street just seconds behind Gemminae. Cinder's feet slapped against the pavement as she tore after Gemminae, her rage fuelling each step. The boy-vampire darted through the narrow alley, weaving between piles of rubbish. Gemminae's small body moved quickly through the tight spaces, but Cinder was faster. She closed in, reaching out just as Gemminae skidded around a corner into an even darker passageway. Cinder followed without hesitation. The moment she turned, the world erupted in pain.

Something hard and metallic crashed against the back of her skull. Cinder staggered, her vision lurching as another blow struck her ribs. A sharp crack resounded through her chest, and she knew something had fractured. More strikes rained down. The blunt force of sticks and metal bars hammering against her body. She dropped to one knee, hissing, her fangs bared. Around her, shadows moved. Feral things with gaunt faces, their eyes alight with the glee of cruelty – Gemminae's gang.

'Not so quick now, are you?' Gemminae's voice slithered through the assault. He crouched on top of a wall grinning down at her. A pipe crashed against Cinder's shoulder, sending a shudder through her bones. She twisted, glimpsing her attackers. Ragged, half-starved street kids wielding scavenged weapons with vicious efficiency. There were at least two dozen of them, circling like wolves around a wounded stag. Cinder spat blood.

'Face me yourself!' she yelled. 'And lose another arm, or a leg? No, thank you.' Gemminae snapped his fingers.

The next barrage came all at once. A bar slammed against Cinder's thigh, knocking her off balance. At the same time, a wooden club struck the side of her head, leaving her ears ringing. A chain wrapped around her wrist, pulling her off-balance, as a boot drove into her stomach, sending her sprawling onto the grimy pavement. The kids shrieked and howled, a symphony of madness echoing off the alley walls. Cinder rolled onto her back, gasping, her muscles protesting. Her body couldn't heal fast enough. Another blow was coming. She caught the blur of a pipe descending toward her skull. She moved. With a sudden burst of speed, she caught the weapon midswing, twisting the wielder's arm. The kid yelped, bones snapping as she wrenched him aside. She rolled to her feet, spinning, catching another attacker by the throat. Gemminae's laughter cut through the chaos.

'Now, now, Miss Delacourt. Play nice,' he said, crawling along the top of the wall like an inquisitive cat. Cinder flung the street kid into the wall. Another came at her, a jagged piece of rebar in hand. She ducked, twisted, and drove an elbow into his sternum. He crumpled with a wheezing gasp. They came at her once more. She got to her feet, but the chain-wielder lashed out, snaring her ankle and returning her to the ground. The barrage of make-shift weapons started again, smashing into her head, spine and legs. Cinder pulled the knife from her sleeve and threw it at the chain-wielder. Yelling in surprise and horror, the kid with the chain fell against the wall. They dropped the chain and took hold of the knife handle protruding from their abdomen. Instinctively, they pulled the knife out and threw it to the ground. Blood flowed from the wound. Cinder pulled herself free from the chain. With an anguished scream, she launched herself into the air, flipped over and landed in a crouch. She wiped the blood from her mouth, green eyes glowing in the dark. The boy-vampire's grin faltered.

'Well,' he mused, leaping down from his perch, 'that was unexpected.' He drifted amongst his followers, eyeing Cinder. He slipped behind one of the street kids and seemed to disappear.

Before Cinder realised what was happening, someone grabbed her from behind. A small but powerful arm wrapped around her neck – Gemminae's arm. Somehow, he had circled behind her.

Cinder grabbed at his arm, but a boy ran forward and slammed a metal rod into her elbow.

Pain shot along her arm and her fingers went numb. Gemminae ripped his arm free and pulled her head towards the sky.

Cinder could feel the spaces between her vertebrae widening. Her ears were ringing as an immense pressure filled her skull. She grappled at his arm again, but dozens of hands pulled her arms down and pinned them against her side. As her vision went dark, she heard running footsteps. Oh no, she thought, there's more of them.

'Were you expecting me?' a man's voice said from the darkness behind her.

Chapter 22
Alliances

Two well-dressed figures emerged from the shadows. Mr Inkerman, with the slim dark-haired woman from the party on his arm. His face was calm, unreadable, his pale eyes gleaming under the dim alley lights. Under his other arm, he held a long, lacquered wooden case. Cinder felt the pressure around her neck lessen, but Gemminae's arm remained.

'Look how nicely your friends have dressed for your execution,' he whispered in her ear. Wordlessly, Mr Inkerman slid his arm from around the dark-haired woman, and opened the lid of the case. Nestled inside was a gleaming samurai sword, its curved blade reflecting the light with an eerie shimmer. Gemminae's grip tightened again. Cinder's feet thumped against the ground, fingers twitching uselessly against the swarm of hands pinning her. Her vision warped, blotches of black pushing in from the edges. Mr Inkerman lifted the katana from the case.

'Catch,' he said simply, and threw. The sword spun end over end, glinting like a falling star. The street kids, startled by the flash of metal, instinctively loosened their grip. That was all Cinder needed.

With a strangled cry, she wrenched one arm free and twisted toward the incoming blade. Her fingers found the hilt in mid-air. The moment her hand closed around it, she drove the handle backward, smashing it into Gemminae's eye socket. He hissed and staggered, releasing her completely. The kids flinched and fell back as he reeled, clutching his face. Cinder rolled to her feet, katana flashing up defensively

Mr Inkerman stepped up beside her. David stepped forward and handed him his own sword. Behind them, a group of imposing figures emerged. Mr Inkerman's bodyguards. Silent, disciplined, their suits crisp and clean – a stark contrast to the filth of the alley. They moved into position without hesitation, forming a defensive line between Cinder and Gemminae's gang. The dark-haired woman turned and strolled back in to the darkness. Gemminae let out a low whistle.

'Well, this is a surprise. Everyone's here tonight,' he said.

'You've had your fun, boy,' Mr Inkerman said, his voice a measured threat. 'Now it ends.'

One of the street kids lunged. A bodyguard intercepted, landing a punch to their chest with brutal efficiency. Then, the alley erupted, fists flying, weapons clashing. Cinder moved like liquid fire, the sword slicing through the air, deflecting blows, forcing the gang back. She felt her strength return with every swing. Gemminae's confident smirk cracked. He stumbled back, glancing at his scattered, struggling followers. Cinder pushed through the mass of bodies to get to him, but when she found her way to where he had been standing, he was gone. She looked up at the top of the wall, but he wasn't there. Realising that the yelling and crashing of metal and wood had stopped, she turned back to see Mr Inkerman standing in the dull light with his bodyguards. The street kids had all slipped away into the darkness. As quickly as they had come upon her, they were gone again. A few patches of blood and a discarded rebar were the only evidence that they had been there.

'Shit,' Cinder said, handing her sword back to Mr Inkerman, 'we'll get him next time.' Mr Inkerman brushed off his sleeves and adjusted his jacket.

'I'll see you back at the house, Miss Delacourt,' he said. Without looking at Cinder, he turned and walked away. His bodyguards followed him.

Chapter 23

Stoned?

Uncle Gunn sat in his armchair. His pipe in his hand had gone out several minutes earlier. His chest rose and fell in deep, sleepful breaths as he mumbled to himself. As the front door opened, his sleepy eyes shot open, and he adjusted his position in his seat. His pipe fell to the floor. The room was dark except for the low burning fire still giving off some warmth. Angus entered the sitting room and slumped down on the seat next to Gunn.

'Did you have a good evening, boy?' Gunn asked him.

'I had a great evening,' Angus said, grinning widely, 'but everybody else appears to have had a terrible night.'

'We were having a good night until you went and put your dirty lips all over Marraine,' Dom said, as he entered the room and stood by the fireplace

'What? What were you thinking, boy?' Gunn said to Angus as he bent down and picked up his pipe from the floor.

'I was thinking I wanted to have some fun, like Dom told me I should.'

'I didn't mean with her, idiot,' Dom said as he turned to warm the front of his body.'

'I didn't know you liked her,' Angus said, leaning back with his hand behind his head. Dom shot him an indignant look over his shoulder.

'I don't like her. And that's got nothing to do with it, anyway,' he said, throwing his arms in the air. Angus crossed his arms.

'Then what's the problem?' he asked. Dom turned to his father. Gunn rubbed his chin and tried to contain the grin that was tugging at the corners of his mouth.

'He's your problem now. I'm going to bed,' Dom said, turning and heading out of the room. He saluted Angus as he passed. 'Good night, dickhead.'

Gunn watched Dom turn down the hallway. When the slamming of a door announced Dom had exited the house, he turned to Angus.

'It seems like you all had an eventful night, then,' Gunn said. Angus yawned and stretched, then shrugged.

'I had a good night,' he said. Gunn let out a sound that started as a cough but ended in a laugh.

'I bet you did, kiddo.' Gunn pulled his spectacles from his chest pocket and cleaned them on the hem of his shirt. He slid his spectacles on and leaned closer to Angus. 'It's good to have some fun, but you just be careful, lad,' he said, reaching and placing a hand on Angus's shoulder.

'I don't know why everyone got so upset,' Angus said, slipping his hand in his pocket and running his thumb over the carvings on the stone that Alice had given him. Gunn squeezed his shoulder affectionately.

'I think the old noggin's a bit messed up tonight, ain't it?' he said and ruffled Angus's hair with his other hand. Angus grinned and pushed his hand away.

'The cogs might be turning a little slowly,' he said, getting unsteadily to his feet. Gunn squinted and adjusted his spectacles.

'You feeling okay, boy?' he asked, looking up into Angus's eyes. One after the other.

'I feel great. Why?' Angus asked as Gunn stood up next to him.

'Did you drink anything funny tonight, boy? Accept any drinks from strangers?' Gunn asked, circling Angus.

'Just beers. Dom and I were buying.'

'Eat anything?' Gunn asked, stopping in front of Angus and looking into his eyes again.

'Just a sausage.'

'Didn't smoke any of the happy weed?' Gunn asked, holding two fingers up to his lips. Angus laughed.

'No! What's going on?'

'Probably nothing,' Gunn said, waving away Angus's concerns. 'We all need a good night's sleep, is all. We'll all feel better in the light o'day.'

Angus yawned again.

'Well, I'm heading to bed now, so I hope you're right,' he said, stretching and yawning more enthusiastically. 'What about you, old timer? Are you turning in?'

'Soon,' Gunn said, sliding off his spectacles and folding them back into his pocket. 'I just need to call an old friend first.'

'Now? But it's the middle of the night.'

'Ti's fine; she'll be up.'

'She?' Angus asked, raising an eyebrow.

'Night lad,' Gunn said dismissively.

'Good night,' Angus said, moving into the hallway. He kept one hand on the wall to steady himself as he went.

'Annabelle was fine, if ya care,' Gunn said as Angus opened the front door to let himself out. Angus thought for a moment.

'Annabelle's a nice name,' he said, then exited.

Chapter 24

Intersection

Cinder stood in Mr Inkerman's office. Mr Inkerman was at his desk making some notes on important looking documents, handing them in turn to Ms Chase, who stood attentively beside his desk.

'You've dyed your hair, Miss Delacourt,' Ms Chase said, inspecting her.

'Yes, Ms Chase, how observant of you.' Cinder replied. Ms Chase rolled her eyes and busied herself with the stack of papers already in her hands. Cinder had indeed dyed her hair. She had caught an early morning ferry to Manly to spend the day at the beach, avoiding seeing Mr Inkerman. She spent most of the morning sitting on the sand running the events of the party and the following pursuit of Gemminae through her mind. As the tide slowly crept closer to her, the idea of dyeing her hair had popped into her head. She had found an expensive looking but friendly salon on The Corso, that fortunately had just had a cancelation for that afternoon and said they could fit her in.

Mr Inkerman handed Ms Chase the final document and motioned for her to leave. Cinder noticed her pull her shirt collar up to conceal an area of yellowing marks on her slim neck. Mr Inkerman's handy work, she guessed. Ms Chase looked Cinder over once more as she walked past and exited the room. Cinder didn't know if her look was one of approval or distaste. Ms Chase's expressions were all the same.

'I'm not sure if she likes my hair,' Cinder said when she was out of earshot. Mr Inkerman grinned his crooked grin. He got up from his desk and walked to Cinder.

'Never mind Ms Chase; she plays her cards close to her chest.' He stopped in front of Cinder, crossing his arms and appraising her new look. 'As for me,' he said, reaching one hand forward. 'I think it is most definitely an improvement.' He took a lock of Cinder's now deep-black, silky hair between his fingers. Cinder looked past his shoulder at a vase that was locked behind a glass panel recessed into the office wall.

'Is that something special?' she asked to change the subject. 'Why is it locked away by itself?'

Mr Inkerman dropped his hand from her hair onto her shoulder. He guided her over closer to the vase. With a wave of his hand, a light lit inside the display cabinet. Cinder could see her reflection in the glass. The vase was about the same size and dimensions as her torso, she noted. Possibly it was originally white but was now yellowed with age. A small section had chipped away from the rim, showing the brown clay underneath. Strange black symbols and writing ran down the sides in six distinct columns. Mr Inkerman pushed against the wood panelling next to the display cabinet and a door popped open. Inside were two glasses and a small array of expensive looking alcoholic beverages.

'Would you like a drink, Miss Delacourt?' he asked, lifting the two glasses.

'Yes, thank you,' Cinder said as she took a glass from his hand. The tips of her fingers brushed against Mr Inkerman's. 'And I think you can call me Cinder now.'

'Very well then,' Mr Inkerman said, sitting his glass down and filling it with brown liquid from one of his bottles. 'And you should call me Joseph.' He filled Cinder's glass.

'Thank you... Joseph,' she said. Joseph Inkerman sat the bottle down, and they tapped their glasses together. Cinder took her first sip. Her face flashed with surprise.

'This is very good,' she said.

'Only the very best for my new friend, Miss... I mean, Cinder.' He placed his free hand on the small of her back. 'It is not a particularly expensive item,' he said, turning back to the vase. 'But it is the first item of antiquity that I procured, so as you could understand, it holds great sentimental value for me.'

Cinder leaned forward for a better look at the writing. Joseph's hand dropped lower on her back.

'What does it say?' she asked, feeling Joseph's chilly hand slip from her back. He stood tall and slipped his hands into his pockets.

'It's the tale of Humbaba.'

'Humbaba?' Cinder asked, turning to look into his eyes. Mr Inkerman turned away to look at the writing on his valued possession.

'Humbaba, the fearsome guardian of the Cedar Forest. His legend is told throughout the ancient Mesopotamian lands and strikes fear into the hearts of all who hear it. You see, Humbaba was no ordinary creature. He was a giant with a face so terrifying it would make the bravest warrior quiver in fear. The writing speaks of him having a lion's mane, and his voice was like a thunderstorm rumbling in the distance. It was said that no mortal man could defeat him, and he was feared by all.'

Joseph slid open a narrow draw below the display cabinet to reveal an illuminated pin pad. He typed in three numbers and the locked cabinet clicked open. Folded neatly beside the screen was a pair of white gloves. He slid them on and gently rotated the vase before continuing.

'One day, two brave warriors, Gilgamesh and Enkidu,' he pointed to two painted characters, 'set out to prove their bravery and defeat Humbaba. When they found him, he was asleep, and they considered killing him in his slumber. Enkidu convinced Gilgamesh to face him in an honourable battle instead.' Joseph paused and motioned for Cinder to refill her empty glass. Cinder stepped past him and poured herself another drink.

'Would you like me to refill yours?' she asked.

'Yes, thank you, Miss Delacourt.' Joseph said. He watched Cinder fill his glass, then continued his story.

'Humbaba awoke to find the two warriors standing before him, weapons drawn. He was furious at their attempt to kill him and attacked them with all his might. They fought a great battle. Humbaba appeared to be too strong for them, but Gilgamesh and Enkidu fought with all their strength. Finally, the two warriors emerged victorious.' Joseph rotated the vase once more to show the opposite side.

'After their victory, Gilgamesh and Enkidu cut down the Cedar Forest and returned to their city as heroes. But their actions angered the gods, who punished them by causing Enkidu's death. Gilgamesh was left to ponder the consequences of his actions.' Joseph returned the vase to its starting position, closed and locked the cabinet with a click then removed the gloves and lay them neatly next to the pin pad.

'What do think of that story of Gilgamesh, Miss Delacourt?' he asked as he slid the draw closed.

'I don't think anyone who kills a poor animal and then cuts down a forest should be considered a hero,' she said, frowning and handing Joseph his glass.

'No, not very heroic at all,' Mr Inkerman said, grinning again. He waved his hand in front of the cabinet and the light went out.

'So, tell me, Joseph,' Cinder said as he took the glass from her. 'What are your thoughts on the story of Humbaba?' Joseph drank before answering.

'If we're already damned by the gods, why should we bother being honourable? I would have killed the beast while it slept.' Cinder frowned and took another sip.

'Did anyone think to just ask poor Humbaba if they could share the forest?' she asked, turning back to the vase. 'Does it say that anywhere in the story?'

'Humbaba was a monster,' Joseph said, finishing his drink and pouring another. 'Would you try to reason with a monster or just destroy it?' Cinder finished her glass and held it out for a refill. 'I'm not sure it's that black and white,' she said as Joseph filled her glass. 'It's difficult to tell who the actual monsters are sometimes.'

'Very true,' Joseph said, his crooked grin returning. Cinder eyed him for a moment.

'So, is this it? Your most prized possession?' she asked. Joseph looked towards the door of his office, thoughtful.

'Bring the bottle,' he said. He slid his free hand into his pocket and strolled for the door. 'Come on,' he said when Cinder hadn't moved. Cinder collected the bottle and followed him as he disappeared around the corner of the doorway.

When she caught up with him, Joseph was standing at a doorway to a room that Cinder had never been into before. Up close, Cinder could see that there were intricate details etched into the surface of the dark mahogany. Swirling clouds and raging waves on a turbulent ocean. A Japanese-style dragon rose from the ocean. Its large eyes glared out at Cinder. Joseph entered a code into a touchpad next to the door. With a muffled click from inside, the door opened an inch. Joseph pushed it forward to reveal a darkened room beyond. He stepped back and gestured for Cinder to enter. In the low light from the hallway, she could see a four-poster bed, similar to the one she slept in as a teenager, only much larger. What did Marraine call it? Bedroom diplomacy?

'Is this your bedroom, Joseph?' she asked. Joseph answered with a nod. 'Now, now, Mr Inkerman. I thought our relationship was strictly professional.'

'Have no fear Miss Delacourt, we are not here for the bed.' Joseph said as he moved past her into the room. It was a large space, and it took him several steps to cross the distance. When he came to the foot of the bed, he knelt. Cinder heard a metallic click, followed shortly by a second identical sound. The base of Joseph's bed appeared to move out towards him. He moved back with it and a moment later, a bright light that seemed to rise from the floor illuminated his smiling face. He stood, drank the last of his drink and turned back to Cinder.

'Come, come.' He beckoned her forward. 'I have another Humbaba vase locked away in storage. It's not as nice as that one but, like I told you, it's always good to have a spare. But this...' He threw his empty glass onto the bed. 'This is one-of-a-kind. There is no other.' Cinder walked forward and looked down into a large draw that Joseph had slid open from beneath his bed. It took a moment for her eyes to adjust to the glow from a strip of lights that ran around the top edge of the draw. Inside, resting on a white-silk pillow, was a sword.

From memories passed onto her from Angus, Cinder knew something about weapons, but even someone who knew nothing could see that this was a thing of beauty. The blade gleamed with an otherworldly luminescence. Its surface shimmered with a subtle, rippling pattern. The razor-sharp edge flicker in the light. Intricate engravings of swirling clouds and mythical beasts adorned the tsuba, or guard. The hilt was wrapped in midnight-blue ray-skin and silk etched with silver dragon scales. A single crimson tassel, the colour of blood, hung from its pommel. Next to the sword lay the scabbard, crafted from lacquered wood, polished to a mirror-like sheen.

As Cinder looked at down at the sword, she couldn't help but feel that there was more to it than just a beautifully crafted weapon. It radiated a quiet, commanding energy that seemed to hum faintly.

'What is it?' she whispered.

'The Honjo Masamune,' Joseph replied, also in a hushed tone. 'It is not just a weapon but a masterpiece of artistry and engineering, representing the height of Japanese sword-making. It was believed missing after World War Two, but I found it here in Australia.' Cinder handed Joseph the bottle and her empty glass, then knelt for a closer look.

'How much is it worth?' she asked, almost afraid to find out.

'As far as the rest of the world is concerned, it is still lost. It is truly priceless.' Joseph's face glowed with pride, almost like a parent looking at their child. Cinder looked up into his wide eyes. The way Joseph moved through his world and among the things he had collected, usually spoke of wealth and arrogance, but now as Cinder watched him, she could see the little boy in the newspapers who had lost his family. Maybe these valuable things were a way of compensating for what he had lost.

'I guess we won't be training with this one,' she said, holding her hands clasped behind her to fight the urge to lift the sword from its bed.

'No, we most definitely will not,' Joseph said. Cinder stood and retrieved her glass from him.

'How did you get it?'

'I think perhaps that is a story for another time,' Joseph said, pushing the draw closed with his foot. When the draw front was again level with the foot of the bed, it clicked and locked in place. Other than the light from the hall, the room was dark again. Joseph looked into Cinder's eyes. His own pale eyes unblinking.

'I don't have a replacement for you,' he said before he turned away. 'Do I need to lock you away too?' He sat on the end of the bed and Cinder sat next to him. Alcohol worked differently for Cinder now. At first, it would appear to have no effect, but then it would hit her all at once. Just as she had sat down on the bed, a rush of dizzying relaxation flooded through her. Her lips and the ends of her toes and fingers tingled.

'Thank you for coming to rescue me last night,' she said. Joseph filled her glass once more and sat the bottle on the floor.

'I understand your need for revenge, but you need to trust that I'm here to help.' He reached and took a few strands of her hair between his fingers. 'It does look much better this colour.' His wrist pushed against Cinder's ear, and she could hear the blood pumping through his veins. She licked her lips, lent forward, and rested her lips against Joseph's neck.

'This doesn't seem very professional,' he said, but leaned his head to the side to receive her. Cinder's canine teeth grew in her mouth, pushing against the inside of her lips. She pulled her head away. Joseph stroked her ear with his thumb. Cinder took hold of his face in both her hands. She could feel the blood pumping through the veins at the top of his neck. She pulled his head towards her and kissed him.

• • • •

Dom leaned in close to Angus and sniffed near his mouth. Angus pulled back from him and gave him a quizzical look.

'What are you doing?' he asked, pushing Dom's shoulder.

'I was just wondering if you had been drinking today,' Dom said, slapping Angus's hand away.

'Why would I be drinking? We're on patrol tonight.' Angus sat on a bench at the intersection of the esplanade and Jenkins Street. Jenkins Street ran up the centre of Heathcote, uphill past the hospital. The glow from the hospital lights could just be seen over the dark rise of the community gardens. Dom watched Angus for a while to see if he was joking, then took a seat next to him.

'It's good to have you back,' he said, elbowing Angus annoyingly in the ribs. Angus ignored him and looked down the esplanade towards the hill where The Big House had once stood.

'That's weird,' he said.

'What is?' Dom asked

'There are no lights on. Usually on a clear night like this, you can see it lit up like a Christmas tree.'

'No lights?' Dom asked, following Angus's gaze. He could see the lights along the esplanade and the flashing lights of the fish and chip shop. The Jenkins Street intersection boasted the only set of traffic lights in the town. They turned from red to green. 'What are you talking about? It all looks normal to me.'

'Up on the hill. The Big House,' Angus said, pointing. Dom studied his face; still no sign that he was being funny.

'Did you hit your head, mate?'

'If you two have finished jacking each other off, we should go make sure the furries aren't heading towards home,' Duncan called out to them.

'Come on,' Angus said, standing and pulling Dom up by his shirt-front.

Chapter 25
Who is Cinder?

Cinder awoke with a start. She felt a flicker of awareness, a gradual return to consciousness as unsettling images retreated to the dark parts of her mind. Hidden, set to make an unwelcome return on some other night. She opened her eyes to find herself in what seemed like the familiar sanctuary of her bedroom. The soft glow of moonlight filtered through the curtains, casting a gentle luminance on the walls adorned with chalk pictures and poetry. The room appeared just as it had before the fire, before the chaos. Had Marraine done this? Or had her room somehow escaped the flames? Relief washed over Cinder as she sat up, the sheets clinging to her skin. The air felt stifling, and beads of sweat adorned her forehead. *It was just my nightmares*, she thought. The only thing from her old life that she knew was hers. As she attempted to swing her legs out of bed, an icy shiver ran down her spine. The cool touch of the hardwood floor seemed odd. She glanced down to see a dark liquid pooling beneath her, staining the wood. With growing horror, she realised that what she thought was sweat, the liquid that made the sheets cling to her and the liquid that now made her feet slip across the floor, was blood.

Panic surged within Cinder, her hands frantically checking her body for the source of the bleeding. A chilling realisation set in. The blood was coming from everywhere, out of her very pours. Her sweat was blood. Horror tightened its grip on her heart. An ominous figure, a silhouette in the dimly lit room, emerged from the shadows. She wore an expression of both concern and delight, a twisted dance of emotions that sent renewed shivers down Cinder's spine.

'Look at this mess!' the figure said, followed by a disapproving click of their tongue. 'Why are you sweating blood, my dear?' Louvelle's voice echoed, a macabre melody in the unsettling atmosphere.

'I... I don't know. Wait, how are you here? I saw you die,' Cinder stammered, her voice barely a whisper.

'And everyone saw you die, my dear. They all stood back and watched as you threw yourself from the roof like some kind of mindless idiot. Yet here you are. So why shouldn't I be here?' Louvelle asked, crossing her arms. Cinder tried to stand, but her feet slipped once more in the growing puddle. She fell back onto the bed.

'Did you do this to me?' she demanded.

'Moi?' Louvelle said, holding a hand to her chest. 'Why do you always insist on blaming me for all your mistakes, my dear?' She leaned in, her eyes glinting with an otherworldly knowledge.

'You're changing, Cinder. Becoming something else. Embrace it.'

As Cinder tried to comprehend Louvelle's cryptic words, Angus appeared in the doorway, his eyes cold and distant. He moved towards her with an unnatural grace, his touch chilling against Cinder's skin as he pinned her down on the bed.

'Black, what's happening?' Cinder pleaded, but his response was silence. The weight of his presence bore down on her, an oppressive force that left her breathless. Outside, the sun rose. A warm orange glow slowly replaced the moonlight. Cinder struggled under Angus's grip but could not get herself free. Seconds later, blinding sunlight filled the room. Cinder and Angus writhed in pain on the bed as the sun's rays pierced through the window, scorching their skin. The air filled with the sickening scent of burning flesh.

'Black!' Cinder screamed. 'Black! What's happening?'

'Stop struggling. Freci meta,' Angus said.

'You've made the transition now, Miss Delacourt.' It was Joseph, standing where Louvelle stood moments before. 'All your Lycan blood has gone. Now you will burn like all the others.'

Cinder's eyes shot open. She rolled away to avoid the sun's burning power, but she soon realised the nightmare was over. The sunlight was warm, comforting, and safe. Her heavy eyelids fell shut, and she snuggled into the soft sheets and quilt around her. Cinder's eyes shot open once more. The surprise of her unfamiliar surroundings roused her to consciousness. She was not in her bedroom in The Big House as she had been dreaming, nor was she in the bed in Joseph's guest house. Cinder looked around. Her clothes from last night hung neatly over the back of a chair at the end of the bed. Sitting up, she could see her shoes sitting next to the chair. She pulled back the sheets. With relief, she saw she was still wearing her underwear. As she turned, the room seamed to spin slowly around her. She climbed out of the bed and walked towards a room she guessed was Joseph's wardrobe. She guessed correctly; Joseph's wardrobe was larger than most people's bedroom, larger even than some people's homes. Lines of clothes, colour-coded and neatly pressed, hung along both sides. An island bench ran down the centre of the room. At the far end of the wardrobe, was a floor-to-ceiling mirror. Cinder pulled a black shirt from a hanger and walked towards her reflection.

Cinder examined her reflection in the mirror. The old myth that vampires had no reflection was not true. But in that moment, Cinder wished it was. She turned away and returned to the bedroom. She sat on the edge, one leg folded under her, the other hanging down to the floor. Her head throbbed. She pulled open Joseph's bedside drawer, maybe he would have some painkillers in there. There was nothing in the drawer on that side except a single paper clip. Cinder flopped down on the bed with a huff. She pushed the heels of her hands against her eyes then stretched to the opposite side of the bed. Something rattled in the draw as she pulled it open. Cinder got to her knees and shuffled across the bed; her leg caught in the sheet. She moaned and pulled herself free.

'Oh' she said, looking at the object in the drawer. Knowing what she did about Joseph and about vampires, she wasn't surprised that Joseph owned one of these items. However, she was surprised that Joseph would leave something so valuable in his bedside drawer.

Maybe it was a fake. Cinder picked it up. It sent an invisible flicker of energy down her arm. Not a fake, she thought. She held it up, the moon pendant, just like her own, but this one had a blue stone, not a red stone. This was one of the seven that originally belonged to the heads of the seven Nephilim families. There were footsteps outside in the hall. Cinder quickly placed the pendant back, closed the drawer and slid under the covers. A moment later, Joseph was in the doorway. He knocked on the open door before entering.

'I have coffee,' he said, holding up the mug in his hand. Cinder stretched her arms above her head.

'Thank the lord,' she said. 'Do you have any painkillers around here?' she asked, looking around. Joseph held up his index finger and placed the mug on his bedside table. He reached into his chest pocket and pulled out two white pills. 'Thank you,' Cinder said, picking up the pills and the mug. Joseph sat on the end of the bed.

'What are your plans today?' he asked.

'Well, after my head feels better, I was thinking about catching the ferry over to Manly again. The beach there reminds me of home.' Joseph sat for a moment, twiddling his thumbs. 'When you return, I will have your things packed for you,' he said.

'Are we going somewhere?' Cinder asked, swallowing the pills.

'Just you,' Joseph said, standing and sliding his hands into his pocket. 'You will be leaving tonight, and you will no longer be working for me.'

'What?' Cinder said, putting down the mug of coffee. 'Are you firing me?'

'It's for the best, Miss Delacourt.'

'You can call me Cinder. You seemed to be fine with it last night.' Cinder crossed her arms and dropped her head to the side. 'You seemed to be fine with a lot of things last night.'

'Yes, it was very unprofessional of you to do that,' Joseph said, turning away from her.

'My memory is a bit foggy, but I'm fairly sure it was just a kiss, and from what I do remember, you didn't protest.'

'You know I'm not attracted to you in that way. You've taken advantage of my generosity, and things could have easily gone too far,' Joseph said.

'Taken advantage!' Cinder threw back the covers and got out of the bed.

'And now you're wearing my clothes, are you?' Joseph said, looking her up and down disapprovingly.

'Well, someone removed my clothes,' Cinder was yelling now. 'How professional was that: Stripping your employee down to her underwear while she was drunk?' Joseph stood next to the chair with Cinder's clothes draped over the back.

'I was concerned you might damage these like you did with the dress I gave you.'

'Damage them? Oh no,' Cinder said. 'Here, you had better have this shirt back too before I damage it.' She started to unbutton the shirt.

'Please put you freckled flesh away, Miss Delacourt, God knows I've seen enough of it already.' The look on his face made Cinder wish her legs were covered, too. She re-buttoned the shirt to the top.

'Are you really firing me?' she asked quietly.

'I believe it's for the best, Miss Delacourt. I'll give you two months' pay. Hopefully that will give you time to find something else.'

'How can I make this better?'

'Freci meta!' Joseph exclaimed. 'You've been taking advantage of me for months now. I've shown you everything and you still don't trust me. There is no making this better.'

'What do you mean *I don't trust you*, Joseph?' Cinder asked. 'I spent the night in your bed?'

'Who is Annabelle?' he asked.

'What?' Cinder took a step back.

'Who is Annabelle?' Joseph asked again. 'You have a daughter, and you've never said anything about her.'

'My daughter is my business, Joseph,' Cinder pushed past him, picked up her clothes from the chair and made for the door.

'Exactly,' Joseph said. 'Your business is your business. My business, my home, my bed, my clothes, my lips, they're all yours too. What's yours is yours and what's mine is also yours.'

Cinder turned to look at him. 'Do you want to meet my daughter, Joseph? Is that what you want?'

'I just want you to trust me like I trust you, Miss Delacourt.'

'It's Cinder,' Cinder said as she stormed from the room.

• • • •

Angus moved quietly through the dense undergrowth, his boots pressing softly against the damp earth. The towering pines cast long shadows under the silver moon, the whispering breeze through their needles masking the occasional crack of a branch underfoot. Alice walked beside him, her steps light, almost playful, her hand occasionally brushing against his as they navigated the tangled path.

'You're not leading me off in to the dark to take advantage of me, are you Angus MacAskill?' Alice asked, teasing in her voice. Angus smirked, keeping his gaze ahead.

'Maybe you're going to take advantage of me,' he said, ducking under a branch. Alice chuckled, nudging him with her elbow.

'You should be so lucky.' Alice didn't need to duck to follow him under the branch.

'I'd better be careful then.' Angus said, glancing at her with a grin. 'You could do anything with me out here with no one to stop you.'

'Would you stop me?' Alice asked, arching a brow. Angus opened his mouth to reply when a sharp rustling from behind made them both halt. In an instant, Alice had her knife drawn, and Angus's hand went instinctively to the hilt of his blade. A figure emerged from the brush, shoulders squared, expression stormy.

'Having fun, you two?' Torry's voice was flat, but her irritation was clear. Alice slid her knife back into its sheath, but didn't drop her stance.

'We're patrolling, Torry. You know, watching for wolves.'

'Sure, that's what it looked like,' Torry said, her gaze fixing on Angus. 'You want to tell me what's going on with you?' she asked. Angus frowned.

'What are you talking about?' he asked, looking back at Torry with confusion. Torry took a step closer. 'Cinder,' she said. Angus blinked.

'Who?' he asked. Torry's jaw tightened, her hands balling into fists at his sides.

'Why are you doing this, Black?' Torry asked, the hurt obvious in her voice. 'Don't stand there and act like you don't remember her.'

'We need to keep going,' Alice said, interrupting them and taking Angus by the hand. 'Come on.'

'You stay out of this!' Torry hissed. Alice backed away into the shadows. Angus shook his head, his brows knitting together.

'I'm not acting, Torry. I don't know what you're talking about,' he said. Torry let out a bitter laugh and turned away for a second, reining in her frustration. When she turned back, her expression was dark.

'I don't get what you're doing, Black, but I don't like it,' she said. 'I think I preferred you being sad and drunk over whatever this is.' She waved her hand in front of Angus. Angus opened his mouth to argue, but before he could, Dom's voice cut through the tension.

'If you two are done trying to out-brood each other, we've got a job to do.' He emerged from the trees, looking unimpressed. 'And I'd rather not have to explain to Duncan why we got distracted while the wolfies slipped past us.'

Torry shot Angus one last glare before stalking past him, her shoulder knocking hard against Angus as she went. Alice exhaled and shook her head.

'Well, that was rude,' she said. Angus watched Torry disappear into the trees, unease settling in his gut.

· · · ·

Cinder stood by the door of the hotel room that had been hers, but was now where Lulu was staying. She had her packed suitcase at her side, a bag over her shoulder, and her coat draped over one arm. She glanced at a notification on her phone. Her Uber was waiting. Lulu sat on the bed; her arms wrapped around her knees.

'You don't have'ta go like this,' she said. Cinder sighed, running a hand through her hair.

'Yeah, I do.'

Lulu shook her head.

'You're running.'

'I'm going home.' Cinder's voice was firm. 'To my sister and to my daughter. I need them now.'

'And what about Icky-man?' Lulu asked, using her nickname for Joseph Inkerman. Cinder let out a bitter laugh.

'What about him? I have a plan for Mr Joseph Inkerman, Lulu. I'll let you know more when I come back.' She slipped her coat onto one arm and swapped her bag so she could slide on the other sleeve. Lulu looked away, chewing her lip.

'You is comin' back?' she asked. Cinder softened. She pulled her hair out from under her coat and crossed the room, sitting beside Lulu and taking her hand.

'I'll be back in a few days, a week at the most.' She reassured her.

'I'll keep an ear out for what Icky-man's up to,' Lulu said. Cinder stood, adjusting the strap of her bag over her shoulder. She hesitated for just a second longer before heading for the door.

'Take care of yourself, Lulu,' she said.

'You too.' Cinder walked to the door and picked up her suitcase. With one last glance back, she stepped outside, letting the door close behind her.

Chapter 26
Who is Annabelle?

The gravel crunched underfoot as Angus and Dom walked side by side, their silence stretching taut between them. A cool breeze carried with it the faintest trace of salt, drifting up from the coastline below. The farmhouse loomed ahead, its windows catching the last of the evening light, glowing dimly against the deepening red of the sky. To their right, the land sloped gently down towards Heathcote, the small beach town nestled at the edge of the sea. From here, they could see the rooftops bathed in the soft amber glow of streetlights flickering to life. The harbor stretched beyond – a dark expanse. At the far end, boats in the marina bobbed lazily in the tide, their silhouettes swaying against the faint shimmer of reflected light. The farm was settling into twilight. Dark fields stretching wide and quiet, the grass moving in slow ripples under the evening breeze. The cattle in the lower paddocks stood still, heads lowered, their dark forms blending into the landscape. The last rays of daylight filtering through the gnarled branches of the majestic oak trees that surrounded the house and lined the long driveway.

The farmhouse was warm and bright when Angus and Dom stepped inside, shaking off the chill of the early evening. The scent of a freshly lit fire hung in the air, mixing with the faint aroma of coffee. They were there to check in on Gunn before they set out on patrol. Even though they expected an uneventful night, the tension between them still hung heavy. The sound of voices drifted from the sitting room. They had not expected that Gunn would have company. Gunn's deep timbre rumbled low, punctuated by the soft laughter of a woman. Angus glanced at Dom before entering the room. Marraine was perched comfortably in an armchair, her legs crossed, holding a mug of tea in one hand. Gunn sat adjacent to her, his ever-watchful eyes flicking toward the newcomers. The fire crackled in the hearth, casting long shadows along the walls. Marraine's gaze lifted as they entered, a smile already forming on her lips.

'Hello again,' Angus said, moving to sit beside her. He looked equal-parts confused and excited to see Marraine there.

'Hello, sweetie,' she replied smoothly. Dom lingered near the doorway, arms crossed, his expression unreadable as he observed the interaction.

'Hey, listen, I'm sorry about the other night. I didn't realise that you and Dom had a thing going,' Angus said, leaning back into the couch.

'Dom and I?' Marraine laughed. 'Dom and I do not have, nor ever will have, a thing.'

'Then what was everyone so upset about the other night at the surf club?' Angus asked.

'I think it's about the thing you have with my god-daughter, sweetie.' Marraine said.

'Who?' Angus asked. Marraine dropped her head to one side and rested a hand on her hip.

'My god-daughter. Your lover, the mother of your child,' she said. Everyone was watching Angus now. He looked at each of them in turn, his face twisted with confusion.

'What are you all going on about?' he asked.

'What's going on?' Marraine said, turning to Dom.

'Just ignore him. I told him that he needs to stop thinking about Cinder and now he's pretending that he doesn't know who she is.' Dom said. 'It's not funny anymore, mate.'

'Cinder who?' Angus asked.

'See!' Dom said, throwing up his arms. Gunn had been watching the exchange from his armchair. Pushing himself onto his feet, he limped over to Angus.

'Hey there, kiddo,' he said, resting his hand on Angus's shoulder. 'Do you want to come check in on Annabelle with me?'

'Who's Annabelle?' Angus asked, getting up.

'That's it!' Dom said, marching towards Angus. Marraine sat her cup down and stood to intercept him.

'Just settle down, boy,' Gunn said, placing a hand on his son's chest. Angus stood.

'But he's pissing me off now. Pretending about Cinder is one thing, but being a jerk about his daughter is going too far.' Dom said.

'Daughter?' Angus asked. Dom pushed past Marraine and Gunn and shoved Angus in the chest. Angus tripped on the sofa and slammed against the wall with a thud. Torry came running down the hall to see what had made the noise.

'Hey, hey!' Gunn said. 'You'll wake the baby.'

'Baby? What baby?' Angus asked. Dom slapped his face.

Chapter 27

Back For Blood

Angus stormed out of the farmhouse and slammed the heavy front door behind him. Crickets sung in the night but otherwise everything was still in quiet. His feet crunched on the gravel as he walked out through the towering oak trees that ran along the driveway. The stars twinkled in the clear, moonless sky above him. Far away to his left, he could just make out the dim glow of the streetlights of Heathcote. He kicked the dust and cursed under his breath. *What was everybody going on about?* He thought to himself. *Why would Dom tell him to have some fun and then get angry when he did?* He made his way past the stone fence that bordered the farm and stopped at the orange-gravel road. There were puddles on the opposite verge, leftover from the rain earlier in the week. Tall grass grew along both edges of the road, swaying gently. Angus turned and headed towards Heathcote. He had taken a few steps when he thought he could hear something moving on the other side of the road. Slowing, then stopping again, he tried to peer into the darkness. When he couldn't see anything, he trudged through the long grass and sat on the stone wall.

A breeze stirred in the oaks, carrying with it the faint scent of damp earth. Angus exhaled sharply and ran a hand through his hair, trying to shake off his uneasy feelings. The stone under him was cold, and the breeze was chilling his skin. He could just go back inside by the warmth of the fire, but then he would have to deal with everyone annoying him. His cheek still stung from Dom's slap. He reached up and felt the spot; at least one part of his body felt warm. The wind made rippling patterns in the grass at his feet; perhaps it was just that he had heard. Then he heard it again, a rustling in the grass. This time, it was behind him. He swivelled his head, eyes narrowing as he scanned the shadows. The wind whispered through the trees, but there was another sound. *A footstep?* His body tensed. *Did he imagine it?* Dom and he had seen no signs of Lycan tonight. Maybe there was something worse, or maybe it was just Dom playing a prank on him.

'Who's there?' he called out, his voice cutting through the quiet. Other than the usual sounds of the night, there was silence. His pulse quickened. He stood, his boots scraping against the stone wall, the sound unnervingly loud. The air felt charged, the hairs on the back of his neck standing on end.

Slowly, he stepped off the wall and turned in a slow circle, peering into the dark. He could see the faint glow of the farmhouse windows through the trees, but could not make out any movement. He let out a breath and chuckled at himself.

'Jumping at shadows,' he muttered. But as he turned back towards the road, he felt like the night itself had reached forward and run its dark tendrils down his spine. Something was watching him. He could feel it now. It was like some invisible weight pressing against his senses, a presence lurking just beyond his sight. The grass shifted again, and this time, it was closer. Angus swallowed hard. His fingers curled into fists. He took a slow step forward, then another. Whatever it was, it wasn't moving away. He turned back towards the house and hastened along the drive. From the corner of his eye, he saw a blur of movement. Angus's breath hitched. His heart slammed against his ribs as his eyes darted to where he had seen the movement. The grass swayed, the wind weaving through it like ghostly fingers. Just beyond the edge of the tree, a shadow shifted. He could stand and fight, but all of his weapons were inside. There was something else about the way whatever was out there was moving. He had never seen a Lycan move this quickly and quietly. He set off for the house again, his boots pounded against the gravel as he broke into a run. The darkness behind him thickened, pressing in. The farmhouse lights ahead of him suddenly feeling impossibly far away. He didn't dare look back. Every instinct screamed at him to keep moving, to get inside, to get to safety. The trees loomed on either side, their gnarled branches creaking as the wind picked up. The sound of his own footsteps was deafening, but beneath it, he could hear something heavy moving through the underbrush, following him. No, not following – chasing.

'Dom! Gunn!' he called out, coming to the end of the long driveway. A dark shape burst from between the trees, faster than his eyes could track. He barely had time to throw up his arms before it slammed into him, knocking him off his feet. A human-like creature was on his back. Angus grabbed his attacker and tried to shake them off, but it was strong, very strong. It wrapped its powerful arms and legs around him and sunk its fanged teeth into his neck. Angus called out in alarm as he felt the creature draining blood from his body. He pushed himself up and leapt into the air, crashing down on his attacker. For a moment, the teeth came free of his neck. Angus rolled over and pried himself free of the vice-like legs wrapped around him. The teeth sank back into his neck painfully. He screamed in anger. Feeling a rush of adrenaline, he took hold of his attacker, peeled it off and hurl it into the trees. The unknown creature crashed through the branches then fell to the ground with a moan. Angus backed away towards the farmhouse. His attacker had fallen down behind the stone wall where he couldn't see it. He listened carefully for any movement. Still moving backwards and keeping his eye on the place where the creature had fallen, he quickened his pace. Warm trickles of blood ran from the puncture wounds in his neck onto his collar. He put his hand to his neck and it came away wet and glistening in the low light coming from the porch.

'Dom, Gunn! Get out here,' he yelled as he reached the porch. He stumbled in the gravel and went down on one knee. As he did, he glimpsed something moving impossibly quick across the field to his left. 'Dom!' he yelled out again. A footstep behind him. He turned too late. The creature was on him again. It pulled him away from the house, back up the driveway. Pain shot down his neck again as the fangs pierced his flesh for a third time. But this time there was another feeling, one of extreme relaxation. If it hadn't been so concerning, it may have been exhilarating. Angus struggled, but the longer the creature fed on him, the less he wanted to. Flashes of coloured light danced across his vision as he tried to crawl forward. He felt the creature's hand groping at his hip pocket. He looked down and saw a hand, human-like but twisted with long claws. Angus reached out and took hold of the creature's wrist. As he did, a lock of red hair fell across his face. 'Cinder! Is that you?'

* * * *

'Great holy mother father!'

Dom stood in the doorway of the farmhouse with one arm in the sleeve of his long leather coat. After walking Marraine to the edge of the forest, he had returned to say goodnight to Torry and Gunn. He was heading out the door when he spotted something in the driveway. His brain needed a moment to register what he was looking at. At first, it looked like one of the cows had broken through the fences and was wobbling half-lame down the driveway. As the strange object moved into the porch light, he saw Angus crawling along the gravel, a red-haired woman on his back with her face buried in his neck.

'Get her off me!' Angus yelled. Dom launched himself from the porch. His coat flapped around behind him until he could shake his arm free. A clawed hand shot forward just as Dom's boot was about to connect with the woman's head. Dom's leg came to an abrupt stop, but his momentum kept his body moving forward. He toppled over Angus and the mystery attacker. All three of them went rolling across the gravel. Dom rolled over and onto his knees. A young woman's face appeared in front of him. She hissed at him through sharp fangs. Although her features were twisted and animal-like, Dom recognised her.

'It's you, you're back!' he said, trying to regain his bearings. 'Get off him!' he yelled and took hold of her shoulders. The woman pushed him away with one hand and he flew backwards, rolling in the dirt. Angus lay on the ground, groggy. He turned his head to look at the young woman. It took a moment for his eyes to focus and for his brain to process who he was looking at. The young woman crouched in the shadows a few metres away from him. Her face becoming more human each second.

'Katie? Why did you bite me?' Angus asked as he held his hand to the blood that was leaking from the small puncture marks on his neck. The young woman was Sase, the vampire that now lived in the body of his little sister. Sase lurched at him again. Angus managed to push her away, but as he did, Sase ripped away the pocket at his hip. The stone object that Alice had given Angus at the surf club fell to the ground. Sase snatched it away before Angus could pick it up, and she backed away from him.

'What the hell's going on, Katie?' he asked, holding one hand to his neck and pulling at the remains of his pocket with the other.

'I am sorry, brother,' Sase said. 'It was necessary for me to draw out the magic.'

Dom got to his feet and dusted himself off.

'It's nice to see you again, Katie,' he said, inspecting a gravel scrape on his elbow. 'You know you can just knock on the door, like other family do when they come to visit.'

'I will next time, Dominic, I promise. But as I said, this was necessary.'

'I think you need to explain,' Angus said, then put his head in his hands. 'My head is pounding.'

The commotion had attracted the attention of the others. Duncan and Torry spilled out of the front door, followed by Uncle Gunn, with his shotgun resting on his shoulder. The twins, Rory and Tavish, appeared at the side of the house. Alice, who was still in bed, ran around the corner a moment later. She was barefoot, wearing shorts and a singlet with pink and white kittens patterned across them. When Sase saw her, she held up the stone that had fallen from Angus's pocket.

'Are you Alice?' she asked. Alice didn't answer. She gave a small nod and started backing away. 'I think she's the one that needs to do some explaining,' Sase said. Alice turned to run, but in a flash, Sase moved to block her exit. To everyone's surprise, Angus moved almost as quickly and stood between the two women.

'Great holy mother father!' Dom exclaimed for the second time that evening. Angus stood with his eyes closed, swaying from side to side. He had the clammy complexion of someone who might be about to lose the contents of their stomach. His eyes shot open, and he turned on Sase.

'What did you do to me?' he demanded.

'It's okay,' Sase said, holding her palms towards him. 'It will wear off soon. I needed to do it to fix what she did to you.' She motioned to Alice.

'What's she talking about?' Angus asked, looking over his shoulder at Alice.

'I don't know what she's talking about,' Alice said. 'She's crazy, and she's the one that's done something to you.'

'Liar!' Sase yelled and flashed her fanged teeth. 'You gave him this.' She held up the stone again. The smooth surface glistened in the light coming from the farmhouse and Angus could see the rune carved into it.

'What is that?' he asked.

'It's nothing,' Alice said. 'Just a lucky charm.'

'Stop lying child or I swear I will force the truth from you,' Sase said, stepping towards Alice. Alice made to run again, but this time Angus caught her by the wrist and pulled her back.

'Ow! You're hurting me, Black,' Alice complained. Angus loosened his grip but did not let go.

'Tell me what's really going on,' he said. Alice was shaking, either from the cold or fear, or both. She was looking into Angus's eyes, but she dropped her gaze to her bare feet.

'I just wanted to help,' she whispered.

'Speak up, girl.' Uncle Gunn called from beside the doorway. 'I think we all have the right to know what's going on.'

'I just wanted to help Black be happy again,' Alice called out, throwing her head back and looking up at the sky. She looked at Angus and sat her free hand on his face. 'I just wanted you to forget.'

'Forget what?' Angus asked, pulling away from her.

'To forget about her. The one that broke your heart.'

'That's a load of bull!' Torry yelled. 'You just wanted to get into Black's pants.'

'I'm sorry, Black,' Alice said, reaching for him again. Angus pushed her away and turned to Sase.

'She did it, didn't she?' he said, running his hand through his thick, dark hair. 'She made me forget about Cinder. But not just her, everything about her. I even forgot Annabelle. I forgot my own daughter.' His head shot up like he had suddenly woken from a dream. 'Where is Annabelle? Is she safe?'

'She's sleeping mate.' Duncan reassured him. Angus watched as Duncan went inside, then turned back to Sase.

'What? How?' he asked.

'With this pretty little thing,' Sase held up the stone. 'And a little bit of magic,' she said, then took the stone in her fist and crushed it. 'It appears that this little Nephilim girl has some powerful friends.'

She dropped the remains of the stone on the ground and dusted the powder from her palm. Angus turned back to Alice.

'Is this true?' he asked, with a wounded tone in his voice. Alice, now shaking more, wrapped her arms across her chest.

'One of my exes is a witch. I convinced her to give me a memory spell. I thought it would just take away your bad memories.'

'You made him forget everything, you dumb bitch!' Torry called out. 'Sorry for cursing, Dad,' she said, turning to Gunn.

'I think that's an appropriate use of the word,' Gunn said, resting a hand on Torry's shoulder. 'Best you go back to bed, lass,' he said in Alice's direction. 'You'll be catching the early bus home in the morning.'

'We'll walk you back,' Tavish said and prodded his twin with his elbow. The brothers walked her sheepishly through the mire of glares from angry onlookers. Rory draped an arm over Alice's shoulder and Tavish placed a firm hand on the small of her back, pushing her forward. As they were about to move into the shadow of the farmhouse, Alice turned to look at Torry.

'By the way Torry, this was the only magic I needed to get into Blacks' pants,' she said as she slapped her backside. Sase lurched forward with her teeth bared and fangs glowing in the light from the doorway. Angus held her back.

'Come on, don't push your luck,' Rory said, moving Alice away with quickened pace.

'Let's go inside, everyone,' Angus called out and turned Sase towards the farmhouse.

'I'll put the kettle on,' Gunn said. As he moved inside, he unloaded the shotgun and slipped the cartridges into his breast pocket. Angus walked beside Sase, smearing away the blood that was still seeping from his neck.

'I still think you have some explaining to do,' he said.

'She's not the only one with some explaining to do,' Dom said as he pushed in front of them just as they got to the doorway. 'I think there is something you need to tell me, naughty boy.' Dom slapped his backside, mimicking Alice. Angus pushed him through the doorway.

'I'd like to know more about that too,' Torry said, following them in.

If it weren't for all the excitement of the evening, someone might have noticed the car lights on the hill on the opposite side of Heathcote.

Chapter 28
Who is Gemminae?

The aftermath of the fire had transformed the once-familiar gym space into a scene of devastation. Charred remnants of the wooden structure littered the floor, intermingled with twisted metal from the collapsed ceiling. The heavy timber door, once a barrier to the outside world, lay broken and blackened, leaning against a scorched wall. The patchy and worn boxing bag, once a focal point for Cinder's training sessions, hung limply from a charred joist, its fabric shredded and its surface singed. The smell of smoke lingered heavily in the air, mixing with the acrid scent of burnt wood and melted plastic. A bench where Cinder used to dump her clothes sat amidst the wreckage, its surface warped and stained with soot. The fire's destructive force had obliterated any trace of familiarity or comfort that once existed in this space, leaving behind only a haunting reminder of what once was. Even amongst this devastation, Cinder was surprised to feel more at home here than she had felt anywhere since her new life begun. She cautiously navigated a path through the debris, her heart heavy with the weight of loss and uncertainty. She had come down here hoping to find her lost notebook. It contained her poetry, a cherished collection of her thoughts and emotions, now potentially lost amidst the wreckage. Carefully stepping over charred beams and scattered debris, she scanned the room with determined eyes. The light from the headlight of her hire car filtering through gaps in the ceiling cast eerie shadows on the burnt walls, adding to the surreal atmosphere to the destruction.

Cinder knelt beside a pile of rubble, gingerly sifting through the ashes and remnants of what once was. Each piece of burnt wood she picked up, held the possibility of her precious notebook being nestled within. Her hands trembled with a mixture of fear and hope as she continued her search. Discouraged, she sat on the arm of her father's charred leather sofa, looking around and remembering what once was. Deciding to give up her search, she leaned forward to stand up once again, but stopped. There was the distinct sound of footsteps on the ground above. Cinder tilted her ear towards the sound and listened as more than one person, perhaps a whole group of people, walked past where she was sitting and moved towards the steps that led down to the cellar. Then the lights from the car went out, and the cellar fell into darkness. For several tense seconds, the sounds from above ceased. Cinder strained her ears. There was shuffling of feet but no footsteps. Cinder sat as still and as quiet as she could. Perhaps the new arrivals didn't know she was down here. They might not even know that there was a cellar under the rubble. If she kept quiet, they might go away and leave her alone. The footsteps started again, but just one set. They walked to the end of the cellar and paused at the top of the steps. Then they slowly descended into the darkness. Their footsteps on the ash covered stone reverberating through the large empty space.

'Hello, Miss Delacourt,' came a call in a boyish voice.

* * * *

Angus sat warming his hands. Flames flickered and frolicked in front of him. He spread his fingers to watch the glow between them change from red to orange. It was a calm night. The smoke from the fire rose gently up into the canopy of trees above, disappearing amongst the clear, star-filled sky. Next to him, Dom and Torry were arguing about Alice. They had decided she would leave for home on tomorrow's bus. Until then, Gunn had confined her to her room. Dom thought they should let her help patrol, as planned. Torry wanted her gone sooner and thought she should have been driven to Tallo's Bluff for the night and made to catch the bus from there. Angus stood up to warm his back, but remained quiet. He still had mixed feelings about Alice and thought it best to stay out of the conversation. He was happy to have some space from the events earlier in the evening and smiled as he looked around the fire at his close friends. His sister was here tonight, too. Katie sat next to Torry, a wide grin on her face, apparently very entertained by the siblings arguing. As if sensing Angus's eyes on her, she turned her head towards him, looked up then came to stand with him at the fire. Standing side by side, she stood at his shoulder height. She bumped him with her hip and asked.

'Can we speak, big brother?'

'Yes, I'd like that,' Angus said.

'Come.' Katie took hold of his hand. She led him away from the group.

'We'll be back soon,' Angus said. Torry and Dom acknowledged him with nods, but continued their argument.

Leaving the warmth of the fire, Angus and Katie ducked under the nearest branch into the darkness of the forest. Angus buttoned his jacket against the cold, but the change in temperature appeared to have no effect on Katie, who was wearing a thin cotton shirt with short sleeves. Angus needed to remind himself that his little sister was also a centuries-old vampire named Sase.

'You know your way around here better than I do,' she said, letting Angus lead the way. They walked in silence for a short time. Katie looked around with great interest. Beyond the few metres of starlit forest around him, Angus could only see the outlines of shapes in the darkness. He wondered what his sister's vampire eyes could see and what she could hear in the night.

When the firelight had died away to a distant orange glow and he could no longer make out the exchange of angry words between Dom and Torry, Angus took Katie's hand in his.

'I'm glad you're here,' he said, giving it a squeeze.

'I am glad also to be with you again.' Katie placed her free hand on his arm and rested her head against his shoulder. 'I wish that I could have returned under better circumstances.'

'Yes,' Angus agreed, placing his hand over the bite mark on his neck. 'Next time you drop by for a drink, can we make it a beer or a coffee?' he said, pulling his hand away to see that there was not fresh blood. Katie laughed.

Angus smiled at his sister's laughter, though there was an underlying weariness to it. They continued walking, the trees thinning as they reached the crest of the hill. Heathcote spread out below them. Katie let go of his hand and stepped ahead, standing at the very edge of the rise. Her silhouette was outlined against the sky, her loose hair catching in the wind. Angus watched her for a moment, knowing that despite her slight frame and youthful appearance, she carried an ageless weight within her.

'It looks different than I remember,' she said, her voice barely audible over the breeze.

'You've been gone a while,' Angus replied, stepping up beside her. He crossed his arms, gazing out over the town. 'But not much has changed.' Katie tilted her head.

'I've been gone just a blink of the eye,' she said. 'But here I am again. And a great deal has changed,' she added. Angus glanced at her, hearing the unspoken meaning in her words.

'You regret coming back?' he asked. Katie hesitated before shaking her head.

'No. But I do regret the circumstances,' she said.

'Alice will be gone tomorrow. Maybe things will settle down then and we can spend some time together,' Angus said hopefully. Katie turned to him.

'I will also be gone tomorrow,' she said, taking his hand again. 'I'm sorry.'

'You're not staying with me?' Angus asked, looking out across Heathcote towards the hill where Cinder's home once stood. Katie turned him towards her and placed her cold hands on either side of his warm face.

'I have to go away again. Even now I can feel Cinder's presence in this place. And you've never needed me or anyone else. You have all the strength you need in here.' She touched a finger to his temple, 'and here,' she placed one hand over his heart. Angus took hold of her hand and held it in place.

'You can feel Cinder's presence? Do you think she will ever come home?' he asked.

'I think she will have to. The pull of this place is too strong for her to resist forever. And listen...' She fell silent.

At first, all Angus could hear was the rumble of the ocean and the rustling on the gentle breeze in the trees. But then he heard it far off in the distance, a chorus of howls.

'You're not alone in your pining for her. She is more important than she realises.'

'The Lycan are out of control at the moment. Even with no moon, they're out,' Angus said.

'That's another reason we need your help.'

'I feel sorry for them,' Katie said.

'Sorry for them? They're monsters. They've killed people. If it wasn't for us, there would be piles of bodies all over the district.' Angus pulled away from Katie.

'I was a midwife once, in a past life,' she said. 'I know the sound of a child that needs their mother.' Katie took Angus by the shoulders and turned him towards the valley. 'Listen,' she said. For about half a minute, there was nothing but the breeze and crashing of the distant waves. Then the same breeze carried a mournful howl over the valley. 'They need their mother,' Katie said, closing her eyes and holding her hand to her heart.

'I need her,' Angus said. 'And I need you,' he added. Katie took a deep breath before opening her eyes.

'I told you once that your name meant 'One-Choice',' she said. 'It can also mean 'One-Strength'. You already have all you need. Find it in yourself and in the ones you love.'

'You're all about telling me what my name means, but what does your name mean?' Angus asked.

'Catherine was our mother's middle name, you know that,' Katie said. 'Don't tell me you've forgotten our mother, too.' she joked. Angus laughed.

'I mean your other name. What does Sase mean?' he asked. Suddenly, the young woman that was his sister seemed to disappear, replaced by the vampire, Sase.

'The title Sase was bestowed upon me by my father because he never cared to give my brothers nor I, a real name. I could have changed it for myself at any time, but I have held onto it.' Sase stopped to think for a moment. 'I believe I have kept the name as an act of defiance. The title that was never intended to be a name has now been my name for centuries.' She smiled defiantly.

'Yes, but what does it mean?' Angus asked, crossing his arms and kicking at the dirt.

'It means 'six'. For I was the sixth of my mother's offspring,' Sase said.

'And Patru, what number was he?' Angus asked, remembering the vampire that had tried to take Annabelle away from him. Sase held up her hand. Her fingers pointed to the sky, but she held her thumb to her palm.

'Four,' she said. Patru was the fourth born.'

Angus mulled this over in his mind for a moment then said. 'I still don't get why you bit me tonight,' he said, changing the subject. He held his hand to his neck. 'How did you know what Alice had done?'

'Gunn contacted me. He was concerned about you.'

'Gunn?' Angus asked, frowning. Sase nodded.

'He knows more than he lets on. You know he does.'

'But how did you know I was under a spell?' Angus asked.

'I heard whispers of a memory enchantment being prepared, one meant for the Nephilim. The witches aren't exactly known for keeping each other's secrets.' Sase laughed to herself. Angus tensed, remembering the feeling of her surprising him and sinking her fangs into his neck.

'Why didn't you just tell me instead of ambushing me in the dark?' he said. Sase hesitated before answering.

'I didn't know if you'd forgotten me, too. Or if you'd believe me. What if you had forgotten that I was back? If your dead sister showed up out of nowhere asking to bite you, how would you have reacted?' she said, resting her head on Angus's shoulder. Angus ran a hand through his hair.

'Probably not well,' he admitted.

'Exactly,' Sase said, taking hold of his hand again. 'But I had to do something. Memory spells don't just erase memories; they can replace them with new ones. Alice could have rewritten your mind, Angus. I thought that if I got to you first, I could draw your happy memories up. I could bring Cinder back to the surface before she buried her completely.' Angus narrowed his eyes.

'But you didn't even know if it would work.' Sase shook her head.

'No. It was a gamble. But I had to take it,' she said. Angus studied her carefully, trying to reconcile the sister he had lost with the ancient being before him. Despite the centuries, she was still Katie. Still reckless. Still desperate to protect him. He reached up, fingers brushing against the puncture marks on his neck.

'Well, it did work. I remember her now,' he said. Sase smiled faintly, though there was sadness in her eyes.

'Good. Then it was worth it.' Angus looked out over the valley again, his thoughts swirling like the wind through the trees.

'So now what?' he asked. Sase exhaled slowly.

'Alice will be gone by tomorrow. But the damage she's done isn't so easily erased.' She turned back to Angus, her expression grim. 'You have some hard work ahead of you, big brother.'

'Are you sure you can't stay and help?' Angus asked. As if on cue, another howl rang out from the hills above Heathcote. Angus sensed Katie was back now. With tears in her eyes, she turned to him.

'I fear I might already have been here too long. One day I hope that Cinder will forgive me, but until then I need to stay away from her and away from her pack. I'll only cause more harm.'

· · · ·

It was hard to tell how many of Gemminae's followers had come with him. Even with her vampire eyes, it was hard for Cinder to see them in the starlight that filtered through the charred ceiling. They were constantly moving and fidgeting, pushing up against the soot-streaked stone walls. But Gemminae stood still, watching Cinder, poised like a predator ready to strike. Cinder had remained seated on the arm of her father's armchair. She had watched as they clambered down the steps to the cellar. Gemminae's band of street kids had come armed to the teeth, but evidently, they were just there to stop Cinder from escaping. They swarmed around the entrance as their master had approached Cinder.

'Are you sure you want to do this?' she asked, waving one arm in the air provocatively. 'You underestimated me when we last met.' Her voice was low and steady, a smirk tugging at her lips. Gemminae stood opposite her, his face half-hidden in the shadows. The right arm sleeve of his shirt arm hung motionless at his side. His left hand clutched a jagged blade that gleamed faintly in the dim light.

'I don't need to use both hands to deal with you,' he spat, his voice laced with venom.

'It's sad how much you believe that,' Cinder scoffed. She stood, then darted left, aiming a quick strike toward Gemminae's exposed side. Gemminae pivoted, parrying with his blade in a sharp motion. Cinder ducked away. The blade sparked against the stone wall. Gemminae spun back, his weapon slicing the air just centimetres from Cinder's face. Cinder moved with him, fluid and relentless, striking again and again, each blow calculated; skills honed in this very room from years of training. She kept her focus on his movements, her strikes aimed at exploiting the weakness of his immobile right arm.

Gemminae was faster than she expected. He matched her speed, blocking and countering with precision. His jagged blade lashed out, nicking her shoulder.

'You're slow and clumsy,' he taunted, his eyes gleaming with malice. Cinder darted in again, aiming for his right side. Her fist shot forward, but this time, Gemminae didn't step away or deflect. Instead, a hand ripped through his shirt, snapped upward, catching her wrist in an iron grip. Cinder's eyes widened in shock as the tattered cloth fell away, revealing a fully functional arm.

'Surprise,' Gemminae said, twisting her arm and forcing her to drop to one knee. Cinder pulled herself free and stumbled backwards, barely catching herself before she fell. Her eyes darted to his right arm; disbelief etched across her face.

'Your...' she began, but her words were cut short as Gemminae lunged forward, slashing at her with his blade. Cinder dodged, but the tip of the blade grazed her side, drawing a line of crimson against her dark clothing. She hissed in pain, her movements slowing just enough for Gemminae to close the gap.

'You thought I was weak,' he snarled, his voice triumphant. 'You thought you'd already won before this fight even started.' He swung again, his attacks relentless now, forcing Cinder to retreat. She stumbled over a loose brick, her back hitting the wall. Gemminae's blade was at her throat before she could recover. She grabbed his wrist and held the blade back with all her strength.

'Your arm is back! How did you do that?' she asked through gritted teeth. 'Can vampires grow back limbs?'

'You know nothing. You're like a stupid little child.' Gemminae said, inching the blade closer to Cinder's flesh. Cinder raised one eyebrow. 'Well, this is new,' she said. 'If I cut off one of my arms, will it grow back?'

'Let's try it and see,' Gemminae said, shrugging. 'Better still, let's try it with your ugly head.'

'Ugly head?' Cinder asked. 'I just dyed my hair and got my eyebrows done.'

'You are so disappointing,' Gemminae said, looking her up and down. 'We were promised something amazing. The new mother was meant to be beautiful and powerful. It must have been right above where we are now that I first saw you. My old friend, Louvelle, loved to show you off. The plans my father had for you.' Gemminae looked at Cinder out of the tops of his eyes and licked his lips. 'All that power in such a young, succulent body. Maybe I should have turned you into a vampire, then.' He ran his hand up her thigh. Cinder kicked him in the groin, hard. He fell to his knees, and she darted away.

'It was unwise of you to come after me here, Gemminae. Although, that's not your real name, is it?' Cinder asked as she walked behind her old punching bag. Gemminae moved his head to the side to keep his eyes on her.

'There's no one here to save you now, Mother,' he said, becoming frustrated as Cinder moved out of his line of sight again. His followers moved towards her, but Gemminae held them back with a wave of his hand.

'Oh, yes,' Cinder said, doubling back towards the far end of the cellar. 'You had many names for me, didn't you? And I don't know your true name.' She strolled casually down the centre of the cellar, her heels tapping on the stone floor. 'You're one of the five sons. Not Unu, the firstborn, of course. He died before he ever made a postea. And not Patru, I know what happened to him.' She mimicked pulling off her head. Then, with her eyes closed, dropped her head to the side and poked out her tongue. 'Speaking of names, that reminds me, there's one name you forgot.' She opened one eye.

'And what's that?' Gemminae growled.

'Queen,' Cinder said, turning to look at him. 'This is my home, my domicile, my throne.' She held her arms out and slowly rotated around a full 360 degrees until she was looking at him again.

'Not much of a home. You burnt it to the ground,' Gemminae said, laughing. His followers laughed too.

'A home is not just a building; it's the people.' Cinder said.

'Not many of them either, you burnt them too. Like I said, you're all alone.' Gemminae's followers laughed again at his cruel taunt.

'But Gemminae,' Cinder dropped her arms and held her hands in front. 'Like I said, this is my home you're in and I'm the queen. The Red Queen.'

'So what?' Gemminae said.

'So, what makes you think I'm alone?' She bowed her head and closed her eyes, like someone about to say a prayer. Outside, a distant howl rang out. Gemminae's followers shifted apprehensively.

'What was that, Lord Gemminae?' the follower that Cinder knew was called Rach asked. She and several of the others took a step backwards towards the door. A second howl followed – this time closer. Then a third and fourth together, so loud they sounded like they were just outside the door. Rach changed her mind and moved towards Gemminae.

'It appears as though I'm not as alone as you thought, Gemminae,' Cinder said.

• • • •

Across the valley, Angus and Katie listened to the howling. 'I think that's my cue to leave,' Katie said. 'I love you, big brother. Try not to accept gifts from strange girls.'

'I love you, too.' Angus said and lifted Katie off the ground in a great bear-hug. 'Don't be a stranger,' he whispered in her ear.

Chapter 29

Queen's Gambit

The door to the basement shuddered violently, and a deafening snarl followed. Dust fell from the beams above as a guttural growl echoed through the cellar. The uneasy laughter of Gemminae's followers faded into tense silence. Rach turned her head sharply toward the door, backing away.

'Stand your ground,' Gemminae commanded, though his tone carried an edge of unease. His eyes flicked toward the door, then back to Cinder. She remained perfectly still; her head still bowed as though in quiet communion with the darkness. The door burst inward with a splintering crash. A dozen hulking figures charged in, their forms barely human, twisted with thick fur, clawed hands, and glowing amber eyes. Lycan. Their breath steamed in the cool air of the cellar, and their low growls harmonized into a terrifying chorus. Gemminae's followers scattered to the shadows.

'Stay back!' Rach hissed, drawing her blade. The steel trembled slightly in her grip. Cinder lifted her head at last, a wicked smile curling her lips.

'I told you I was the queen,' she said, her voice calm, almost maternal. 'And now my people have come home.'

'Deal with them!' Gemminae snarled to his followers. Some of them ran forward to confront the Lycan, but many of them were frozen with fear. They had never seen such terrifying creatures. Rach lunged at the nearest Lycan, her blade slicing through the air. It met fur and muscle, but the beast barely flinched, swiping her aside with a backhand blow that sent her crashing into the cellar wall. Another follower raised a crossbow and fired, the bolt burying itself in the shoulder of a second Lycan. The creature roared, its claws raking through the air as it advanced. The cellar erupted into chaos. Gemminae's followers scrambled to defend themselves. Snarls, screams, and the clang of steel filled the air.

Cinder stepped gracefully back, letting the battle unfold before her. She watched with cool detachment as her enemies faltered under the Lycans' ferocity. Her eyes locked with Gemminae's. Gemminae clenched his fists, his frustration boiling over. He darted at Cinder, but she side-stepped him with ease. The largest Lycan, a great beast with silver streaks in its dark fur, lunged through the pack of street kids. With a single swipe, he sent Gemminae sprawling. Cinder tilted her head, her smile widening.

'You should have stayed at home, Gemminae,' she said, her voice soft but cutting. 'You forgot whose throne you were trespassing on.' Gemminae staggered to his feet, his followers dwindling around him. Bloodied and desperate, he locked eyes with Cinder one last time.

'This isn't over,' he spat, his voice shaking with fury.

'I'm sorry Gemminae, but yes, it is,' Cinder said, stepping closer, her eyes glowing faintly in the dim light. With a snap of her fingers, the Lycan pack surged forward, their howls deafening as they closed in on their prey. Gemminae lashed out at them furiously, but their numbers were overwhelming. He managed to knock two of the Lycan to the floor and made a run for the door. As he got to the bottom step, one of the Lycan slashed at his neck with its claws. Gemminae stopped and turned back to look at Cinder with disbelief on his boyish face. His head hung to one side. A large chunk of his neck was missing. Without hesitation, Cinder launched a punch directly at Gemminae's nose, shattering bone and sinew with a sickening crunch. The gash in his neck widened and spread on both sides. Gemminae's head fell from his body. For a moment, his body remained upright, then collapsed sideways to the ground.

Silence followed Gemminae's death. The scent of blood and sweat thickened the air, but no one dared to move. The fight was over. One by one, the Lycans began to shift back into human form. Bones cracked and realigned, fur receded, and the monstrous figures melted away to reveal the warriors beneath. Some of them were young, barely older than the street kids they had just defeated, their eyes sharp with hunger and triumph. Others bore the weight of years and battles in the scars across their skin. But all of them turned to Cinder, waiting.

Gemminae's street kids huddled in small clusters, bruised, breathless, their spirits shattered but their bodies still alive. Their leader was gone, and with him, whatever fragile sense of defiance that kept them standing. Cinder stepped forward. Her gaze swept across the room, assessing the damage, weighing what remained. Rach pushed herself up from where she had been thrown, one hand braced against the wall for support. Her ribs ached, her head spun, but she forced herself to stay standing. She met Cinder's gaze. Slowly, deliberately, she stepped forward.

'I'll follow you, my queen,' she said, voice steady despite the exhaustion dragging at her limbs. A murmur rippled through the remaining street kids, but none of them moved to stop her. Some lowered their eyes, unwilling to watch. Rach walked to Cinder and knelt before her. She lifted her wrist, turning it toward Cinder. The gesture was unmistakable. The Lycans tensed, their sharp gazes flicking between the two women. Some of them looked expectant, others wary. But Cinder only tilted her head, studying Rach. The hunger still burned in her veins, deep and insatiable. The scent of blood lingering in the air was intoxicating. She could take what was offered. She could drink from someone offering their blood freely.

'Why are you doing this?' Cinder asked.

'Because that's how it works,' Rach said. 'If you kill the master, you become the master.'

Cinder took Rach's hand. She could see bruising and puncture wounds in various stages of healing along her arm. They reminded her of track marks on the arms of an addict. Probably a reasonable comparison, Cinder thought. Pity for Rach and her friends stirred inside her. They were just kids after all, seduced by the charms of an experienced predator, and maybe they just wanted to belong to something. Part of her felt repulsed by the idea of drinking from them. Would she just be the next one to take advantage of them? Cinder remembered how it felt to be taken advantage of by someone who was meant to be your provider and protector. She turned over Rach's outstretched hand. The words "*No*" and "*Get up*" hung in her mouth, but she couldn't seem to force them out.

She ran her thumb over the blue veins on Rach's wrist and could feel them pulsing just below her skin. Her stomach rumbled. She was hungry – so hungry. She couldn't remember when she last ate something. Her mouth watered. She ran her tongue along her teeth and could feel that her canines had grown long and sharp. "*Go ahead dear,*" Louvelle's voice filled her mind. She could almost see her step-mother standing by the door, nodding her head approvingly as Cinder lifted Rach's wrist towards her mouth. "*They are below us dear, take what you need.*"

Chapter 30

Alice? Alice? Who the #@*! is Alice?

Torry held her hand to her forehead, shielding her eyes from the bright spring sunshine. It was a cool morning, but the cloudless blue sky had attracted several visitors to the shoreline. Many were surfing, but there were some who had braved the cool water for a refreshing morning swim. Torry watched as a grey-haired man in very small bathers dived under a wave and climbed unsteadily back to his feet. To her left, she could see rolling white waves and the tiny figures in dark wetsuits as they glided across the turbulent green-blue surface.

'It looks like there's some good waves out there today, little Belle,' she said, leaning down to look into the stroller in front of her. Annabelle, wrapped safe and cosy in a lime-green blanket, cooed in agreement. It was a Saturday, so most of the shops along the Heathcote esplanade were open. Torry had never liked the smell of the butcher. She wasn't vegetarian. The smell of meat cooking was fine, but all that raw meat all together was too much. She hurried past, so quickly that she bumped Annabelle's stroller into a middle-aged woman who was looking at the offerings of fresh fish in trays of ice displayed in the front window. Torry offered an apology.

'That's fine, dear,' the woman said with a kind smile. People are always more forgiving when you have a cute baby with you.

Torry continued past the pharmacy and the Op-shop, as Annabelle chirped away happily. The next shop offered up a far more appealing aroma than the butcher. Freshly cooked waffles, intermingled with chocolate, vanilla, and coffee undertones. Torry took it all in, breathing deeply through her nose and letting the breath out with a sigh.

'How good's that, little Belle?' she said as they stopped in front of the ice-cream store. Long strips of rainbow coloured plastic had been hung from the door to keep out flies. They also offered people exiting a chance to practise their balance and fine-motor skills as they tried to get through without leaving some of their ice-cream on the strips. Some tell-tale creamy smears showed that not everyone was successful. After years of enjoying watching people attempt the manoeuvre, Torry had decided that it had to do with holding your tongue in just-the-right-way.

Even though it was a cool morning, there were still a handful of people in the store ordering cones, cups, and shakes. In the summer vacation season, there would be a line out of the door and a team of five kids behind the counter earning some summer money. Today, Mr Barlow, the owner, was the only one serving. Torry knelt next to Annabelle and adjusted her blanket.

'What should I get today?' she asked. Annabelle looked at her with wide, dark eyes. In the window's reflection, Torry could see a tall woman come and stand next to her.

'Excuse me,' the woman said. 'Are you Gopher Kinnard of the Surf Coast Banshees?'

'Sorry, what?' Torry asked, turning to look at the woman. She was tall, slim, and pale, with long black hair and piercing green eyes. 'Do I kno... oh my god! Cinder!'

'Hey there, sis,'

'Oh my god!' Torry called out again and threw her arms around Cinder. Cinder stumbled back and almost fell into the gutter. Just managing to keep her footing, she wrapped her arms around Torry. Torry began to bob up and down. They stumbled around the foot-path like they were locked in some kind of drunken tango. Torry moved her hands up to Cinder's face and moved her head from side to side.

'Is it really you?'

'It's really me,' Cinder said with laughter in her voice.

'You look so different. Your hair,' Torry said, taking hold of a strand of Cinder's black hair. 'You're so thin. Have you been eating? What have you been eating?' she asked, pulling away. Cinder could see the concern on her face.

'I can eat normal food; I just don't need to,' she said, reaching out and taking Torry's hand in hers. Torry took her hand, noticing how skeleton-like her fingers had become. She looked up at her face. Bones protruded from Cinder's cheeks and at her collar in a way they never had before she left.

'I think you do need to,' Torry said. 'I think you need an ice-cream.'

'Yes, I think you're right. Even vampires need a double scoop waffle cone from time to time,' Cinder said.

'They've got blood-orange. That might be your kind of thing,' Torry said with a grin. Cinder laughed and pulled her friend in close again.

'I've missed you,' she said into Torry's ear and kissed the top of her head.

'We've missed you, too. All of us.'

'How is he?' Cinder asked. 'How's Black?'

'He's not great. The whole thing messed him up good.' Torry said. Cinder turned her head towards the hill where The Big-house once stood. There were no longer any signs of buildings above the tree line.

'It messed me up good, too.'

'Have you, you know...sucked someone's blood?' Torry asked, shrugging her shoulders up around her neck.

'No, I've been waiting for just the right young woman,' Cinder said, trying to emulate the Transylvanian accent of a fictional vampire she had seen in a movie once. Torry jumped back, wriggling like someone had just slipped an ice-cube down the back of her shirt. Cinder winked at her.

'I think I'd be a bit tough,' Torry said. 'There's a few girls from my school I could recommend. But seriously, have you been tempted?'

'Yes, all the time. Mostly by animals though, I don't think I could bring myself to drink from a person.' Cinder said, remembering just how close she had come to drinking from Rach and her friends last night. In the end, she had resisted and sent them away.

'Animals?' Torry asked

'Yes! I can smell the meat in the butcher from here, and it's intoxicating. I think I'd like to try a pig.'

'Why a pig?' Torry asked.

'Their blood smells the closest to human blood. And I love bacon. I think it would taste a bit like bacon. That sounds horrible, I know,' Cinder said, seeing the look on Torry's face.

'As long as you're not drinking from me or anyone I love, then I'm okay with that. Speaking of loved ones, there is someone else that has missed you too,' Torry said as she let go of Cinder and took hold of the handles of Annabelle's stroller. Cinder took a step back.

'Is she...'

'She's great,' Torry said, turning the stroller to face Cinder. 'She's beautiful.'

An elderly couple exited the ice-cream shop. The man's wisps of grey hair flicked about in the breeze. His attention was solely focused on the spearmint choc chip that was already beginning to melt its way down the sides of his waffle cone. His wife held a spoon in one hand and a cup of lemon sorbet in the other. At first, Cinder thought that the look on the elderly woman's face as she looked her up and down was because of the sour treat. Then Cinder noticed that she was yet to taste her sorbet. Cinder glared at her. The woman turned, took hold of her husband's arm and hurried him away. Cinder turned back to look at her daughter.

'What's she like?' Cinder asked, clenching her hands.

'She's amazing,' Torry replied. 'She's eating well and sleeping through the night. She's very strong.' Torry could see Cinder's jaw tighten. Annabelle's small hand came up from under her blanket. Her fingernail scraped against her chubby cheek, leaving a thin, red scratch mark. Almost as quickly as it formed, the scratch faded away and her skin was smooth and clear again. Cinder took another step back.

'Has she hurt anyone?' she asked. Torry could see the fear in her eyes.

'No!' she exclaimed, shaking her head and bending down to pick up Annabelle. 'She's smashed through a few of her cribs, but Dad welded her up a steel one now, so that's fine.' As Torry lifted Annabelle into her arms, she could see Cinder folding into herself and continuing to back away.

'I don't know if I....'

'You'll be fine,' Torry said, bringing Annabelle close. 'Just hold her. In fact, I'll kick your arse if you don't.' She handed the bundled up little girl to her mother. 'Here's mummy, little Belle. Say hello.' Cinder's hands shook as she took Annabelle. For a moment, she held her at arm's length. Then baby Annabelle smiled, and warm tears clouded Cinder's vision.

'Hello there, Little Red,' she said in a stifled, crackly voice. Then coughed to clear her throat. 'Annabelle.'

'She looks like you,' Torry said, standing back, her hands resting over her heart. 'She has your smile.'

'She has Black's eyes.' Cinder held Annabelle to her chest and folded back her blanket. A small hand emerged and wrapped its tiny chubby fingers around Cinder's long bony one. Cinder tried to swallow back the tears, but one escaped down her left cheek. She smeared it away with her shoulder. 'I'm sorry I left you. I've missed so much,' she said, looking up at Torry. Torry stepped forward and stood next to Cinder, resting a hand on Annabelle. Annabelle smiled as she looked up into the faces of the two young women.

'You're here now,' Torry said 'I hope you're staying.'

'I'm not sure,' Cinder said. 'I have something I need to take care of first and I need to work out who I am. That's why I'm back. I have a plan, and I need your help.'

'Sure thing,' Torry said, 'but before we make any plans, I need ice-cream and I need to tell you about my cousin Alice.

Chapter 31
An Unwelcome Solution

Long drooping branches of three sprawling willow trees danced lazily in the spring breeze. On one side, their leafy limbs fell like green tendrils into a slow-moving stream. Shading the waters from the mid-afternoon sun. Tufts of grass laid flat from the movement of water after the recent rain sprouted from the muddy banks. The stream fell gradually down towards the south over moss-covered rocks and the glistening remains of a waterlogged and blackened tree. Ten metres or so from the willow trees, the water ran through a large concrete pipe to continue its journey under a blue-stone gravel road. Some of the local youths had left their tags in black paint inside the pipe and on the concrete structure built around it.

Sunlight reflecting from the water's surface played across the grey wall, and flickered off the chrome-work of a vintage motorcycle. The beautiful machine stood parked on the shoulder of the road that spanned the creek. Detective Peter Morgan stood next to the motorcycle. The tips of his worn-leather boots sat over the edge of the bridge. He looked down into the water as he pulled his notebook from the inside pocket of his jacket. Flicking to a page toward the end of his notes, he studied them for a moment before looking around. As he checked his watch, the sound of tyres on the gravel road announced the arrival of a car. He slid his notebook back into his pocket and stepped down from the verge of the bridge, and made his way onto the grassy edge of the creek. Shortly, Blair's 1971 Volkswagen rounded a bend further upstream and slowly came to a stop near the bridge. The rumbling engine and warn tyres disturbing the tranquillity.

Dom was the first to exit the vehicle, followed by Marraine.

'Hello, Mr Kinnard,' Detective Morgan said, raising his hand in welcome. 'Thank you for joining me,'

'I brought Marraine with me, like you asked,' Dom said, closing his door with a creak of old hinges.

'Yes, I see,' Peter Morgan said, walking towards them. 'Thank you both for coming.' He offered Dom his hand and Dom shook it. When he moved to offer Marraine his hand, she slammed the passenger door closed and crossed her arms over her chest.

'What's this all about?' she asked, looking around at the trees but not making eye contact with the detective.

'You didn't tell her?' Detective Morgan said, looking back at Dom and raising his eyebrows.

'This is your idea, mate. You can tell her.' Dom walked away from the Volkswagen to admire Detective Morgan's vintage motorcycle. 'You're brave, bringing your ride out on these gravel tracks.'

'Yes, I didn't realise that we would be quite so off the main roads,' Detective Morgan said, looking with concern at his vehicle. Marraine coughed.

'It's a lovely motorcycle,' she said, sitting on the bonnet of the car, 'but I'm sure we didn't come all this way to admire Detective Morgan's ride.'

'Yes, of course,' Detective Morgan said. 'As I said, thank you both for coming here today. I'm sure you both know about the damage that took place in Heathcote the week before last and you will no doubt have heard that one of my officers ended up in hospital.'

'Yeah,' Dom said, kicking the gravel under his foot. 'How is Henry going?'

'He is in good spirits, but it will be some time before he is fully recovered.'

'I am sorry about what happened to your colleague,' Marraine said. 'But I still don't understand why we are here today.'

'We are here because the town is terrified of this happening again and they want answers. This has gone beyond simple rumours and a war between your two groups. Innocent victims are getting involved. Where here to gather up the Lycan and put them somewhere safe at night until we can find a way to control their behaviour.'

'Somewhere safe?' Marraine looked from Detective Morgan to Dom and back again. 'You mean lock them up like criminals?'

'It will only be at night and when the moon is out,' Detective Morgan said.

'You must be joking!' Marraine said. 'Over my dead body.' She glowered at Dom.

Detective Morgan pulled his notebook from his pocket.

'It was not just my officer. There were two members of the public attacked. A young man died. It's only a matter of time before the story gets out and we have reporters flooding our town. You're lucky that I'm not arresting you too, Miss...' Detective Morgan paused, flicking through his notebook. 'You know, I'm not sure I know what your surname is.'

Marraine sprung from the car. In less time than one of Detective Morgan's quickening heartbeats, she had launched herself at him. She took hold of his jacket front and forced him to the edge of the creek. As the heels of his riding boots sunk into the damp soil, Detective Morgan pulled his Glock from a holster under his jacket and held it to Marraine's stomach.

'That's right,' Marraine said, ignoring the weapon and leaning her face in close to the detective. 'And it's going to stay that way. You're lucky I'm not ripping your throat out.' Dom ran forward and force himself between them.

'Hey! We're all friends here,' he said as he pushed the detective's handgun to the side. Marraine let go of his jacket and he almost fell backwards into the water. Dom took hold of his arm to steady him.

'You see why I didn't want to tell her?' he said into the detective's ear.

'I heard that,' Marraine said, pushing Dom in the back. Both men had to stumble sideways to avoid falling into the creek. Dom's foot slipped in the wet grass, toppled a mossy rock to the side, and splashed down in the cold water.

'Oh, great!' he said, lifting his foot out onto the bank, feeling water slosh around inside his boot and between his toes. Marraine turned, marched back to the road, and sat on the car again.

'Why aren't you taking me in with the others if you know what I am?' she asked. Detective Morgan slid his weapon back into his holster and straightened his jacket.

'Mr Kinnard,' he gestured towards Dom, who was unlacing his wet boot, 'tells me that the females are in control of their own thoughts when the transformation takes place. And he also explained about the moon pendant that you wear.'

'Fantastic, Dominic!' Marraine said, glaring at Dom. 'Did you tell him all of our secrets?'

'Hey! I did this for you. For all of you, actually,' Dom said as he pulled off his sock and began wringing it out. 'They were talking about hunting you all down, lynch-mob style. This is to keep all your kind safe as much as it is to keep the town safe.'

'My *kind*?' Marraine snapped, 'What do you mean by that?' She rose from the car again and started towards them.

'I'm not the enemy here,' Dom said, raising his hands submissively, muddy water running down his arms. 'Eighteen months ago, I would have been cheering the town on to hunt down the wolves. Heck, I would have been first in line to lead the mob.'

'So, what changed?' Marraine asked, taking his sock from him.

'I met you. You, and Cinder, and Bob.'

'Bob? You hated Bob.' Marraine said, holding the sock balled-up over the creek and squeezing a trickle from it. Dom mumbled something to himself. 'What?' Marraine asked.

'I said,' Dom paused and dried his hands on his thighs, 'I said Bob was a good guy.'

'Be careful, Dominic,' Marraine said, smiling at Dom and handing back his sock. 'I might start thinking you're a good guy.'

'Yeah, yeah,' Dom said, balancing on one foot, forcing his wet foot into a damp sock, each of his toe hairs feeling like they would be pulled out. 'Don't get carried away. I'm about to help put all your friends in lock-up for the next few nights.' He slid his foot back into his boot and looked up at Marraine. 'Are you going to help us or not? Because this will go better for everyone if you do.'

'Okay, I'll help,' Marraine agreed. 'But it's under protest. And you owe me a dinner, Dominic Kinnard. Somewhere nice – expensive. I'm talking fine dining with Michelin Stars.' She bent down with her head next to Dom's, drying her hands on his thighs.

'It's for their own good,' Detective Morgan said. Marraine looked at him out of her corner of her eye.

'As I recall, your people had their children stolen from them and they were told it was "for their own good." How did that work out for everyone?' she asked, standing up straight. Detective Morgan's eyes dropped to his boots.

'I appreciate that it's not ideal, but I think it's the best plan we have.'

'Far from ideal,' Marraine said, placing her hand on Dom's shoulder as he tied his laces. 'Well, let's get on with it then. I have better things to do with my time. What's the plan?'

'There have been reports of a group of men camping out along this creek, east of the river.' Detective Morgan said, walking up a grassy embankment to the road. 'The terrain that way gets too rocky,' he pointed along the creek on the opposite side of the bridge, 'so I'm assuming that we are more likely to find them in that direction.' He looked beyond the three willow trees.'

'And what makes you think these men are the ones we are looking for?' Marraine asked, following him to the top of the embankment. Dom followed behind, grimacing at the discomfort of his still-moist boot. Detective Morgan slid his notebook back into his pocket and clipped his Glock into its holster.

'There have been three reports of animal attacks out this way in the last few months. One just north of here and two more closer to town.'

'So, are we just going to walk through the bush until we find someone?' Marraine asked?'

'That's the plan,' Dom said.

'You could have told me we were walking, Dominic,' Marraine said, looking down at her heeled boots and tight pants. 'I'm not exactly dressed for a hike.'

'You look great,' Dom said, flashing her a cheesy grin. Marraine unzipped her boots.

'I know I do. That goes without saying,' she said, pulling off her boot.

'I would have offered to lend you my boots, but someone got one of them all wet,' Dom said. Marraine pulled off her second boot and stood barefoot in the gravel.

'Your shoes are fifteen sizes too large for me. I would look like a clown, Dominic.' Marraine walked to the car and placed her boots on the passenger seat. Dom shivered.

'I hate clowns,' he said. Detective Morgan coughed.

'Can we get moving, please?' he said. 'I'm not sure about you two, but I don't want to be out here after dark. I made that mistake once before.'

'Yes, but you can give the Glock to Dom,' Marraine said, approaching the detective.

'I can't give a loaded weapon to a civilian,' he said.

'Fine then, unload it. You can keep the ammunition. I would prefer it that way.' She held out her hand. 'It's that or I don't come. We're going to ask them to do this, not force them.'

'You trust me with a gun?' Dom asked, coming to stand beside her. Marraine placed her hand on his chest.

'Don't get excited, sweetie,' she said. 'I just know that the detective is a better shot than you.'

Reluctantly, Detective Morgan removed the clip from his weapon, checked that there were no rounds in the chamber, and handed it to Dom.

'Good,' Marraine said, intertwining her arms with both men. 'Tin-man and scarecrow, let's get on down the yellow-brick road.'

'Hey!' Dom said. 'Which one of us is the brainless one?'

'I think you both have straw in your head if you think this is a good idea,' Marraine said.

• • • •

Angus sat on the edge of the old bridge, his feet dangling above the water. He was back again in this place that had become his refuge. In his hand, he cradled a full beer bottle, absently swirling the amber liquid inside. Below, the river moved steadily, its gentle current carrying everything away toward the vast ocean beyond. With a slow exhale, he widened his legs and poured out the contents of the bottle, watching as it shimmered in the air before vanishing into the dark water below. He lifted the bottle, ready to let it fall, to let it drift away like everything else, but decided against it. Instead, he set the bottle down beside him on the worn wooden planks. As he pulled his knees up to stand, movement caught his eye. He hesitated. At the far end of the bridge, Alice was walking toward him. He exhaled again, his shoulders sinking slightly. Then, instead of rising, he sat back down and waited.

'I thought you caught the early bus,' he said as Alice sat next to him.

'I convinced Uncle Gunn to let me take the afternoon bus.' She picked up a pebble and flicked it. 'I wanted a chance to say sorry. I know I said I was trying to help, but that was a lie, too.' The pebble hit the water with a plop. Alice paused and looked at Angus. Angus kept his focus on the flowing water. 'I've imagined being with you so much that I had convinced myself that it was going to happen, and I didn't want to let anything get in the way,' Alice continued. 'When I heard that you had become a father, I thought I had lost my chance. But then I heard Tavish and Rory talking about how the mother had run away and left you heart broken. I tricked my friend into making the spell for me. I thought it would just stop the hurtful memories, not all of them. I should have known to not go messing with magic.' She crossed her legs and fingered a hole in the knee of her black jeans. Angus looked to see if she had finished, then turned back to the water.

'You do know that the point isn't if the spell worked or not?' he said. 'You shouldn't have used a spell on me at all. I liked you fine and you just being here helped me not think about the hurt. I mean, just think about what we did down there.' He pointed to the pool below. 'Was that another spell, or was that real?'

'No spell,' Alice said, resting her head in her hands. 'Unless you count the naked flesh and alcohol as magic.'

'It is a powerful combination,' Angus admitted. Alice let out a soft, breathy laugh, but there was no joy in it – just exhaustion. Angus sighed, rubbing his hands over his face before letting them fall heavily onto his knees.

'Look,' he said, his voice softer now. 'You made me realise something. That I can fight for love again. That I'm not just... stuck in the past, drowning in everything I lost.' Alice turned to him, her eyes searching his face.

'Angus...' The kiss caught Angus off guard. One second, Alice was speaking, the next, she was leaning in, her lips brushing against his. He didn't stop her. She pressed closer, and he let her, let himself feel the warmth of her. He kissed her back. Not out of passion, not out of longing, but because she was there. But the moment stretched, and something in him pulled away, even as his lips remained against hers. Alice must have felt it too. She hesitated, then drew back, her breath uneven. Angus met her eyes, and the realisation was already there, sinking into her like a weight.

'You didn't mean me,' she said, her voice barely above a whisper. Angus swallowed, guilt settling heavily in his stomach. He could lie. He could try to soften it. But what was the point?

'No,' he admitted. 'I didn't.'

Alice stared at him for a second longer, then turned away, her fingers gripping at the frayed hole in her jeans. She gave a small nod, like she had expected this all along, but had needed to hear it anyway.

'Guess I had that coming,' she murmured. 'Can you ever forgive me?' she asked. Angus picked up a stone and dropped it over the edge of the bridge. He watched as the ripples from the splash radiated out to the shore before he answered.

'You're my family, Alice. I always forgive family.'

'Ouch!' Alice said and stabbed an imaginary knife into her chest.

'What was that for?' Angus asked, raising an eyebrow.

'I think I've been sister-zoned.' Alice slumped her shoulders forward. Angus laughed.

'What's sister-zoned?' he asked. Alice let out a long breath and closed her eyes.

'It's like being friend-zoned but worse,' she said and rested her head on Angus's shoulder.

'Black, what are you doing here?'

'I told you before, this is where I come to think.'

'I don't mean here at the bridge. I mean, why are you *here*? Why aren't you out looking for Cinder?'

'I tried and now I'm just waiting for Marraine to let me know where she is.'

'Ha! Marraine,' Alice scoffed.

'What?' Angus asked.

'You are Nephilim, not Lycan. You should be calling the shots, not listening to those animals. And you, Angus MacAskill – we don't have leader anymore, not like we did in the past – but if the Nephilim were going to follow anyone, it would be you.'

'I don't think that's true,' Angus said, dropping another stone over the edge.

'Well, it is true, and it's about time that you realised it. Speaking of time,' Alice placed her hand on Angus's shoulder and pushed herself up off the ground. 'It's time for me to go. So, what's it going to be, Black?' she asked, standing up. Angus shrugged and got to his feet. 'If you went missing, I would turn the world upside down to find you,' Alice said.

'Why?' Angus asked.

'Because, Black, that's what you do for the people you love.'

'Do I love her?' Angus asked. Alice turned and started walking away.

'Of course you do, Black,' she said, then turned back to him. Reaching out, she took hold of his arm and turned it so that his anchor tattoo was showing. 'Anchors are good to keep you from drifting, but sometimes you need to raise your anchor,' she said, looking into his face with sad eyes. Angus looked down at his arm.

'You think this place is my anchor?' he asked. 'It's not. Cinder was my anchor. I've been adrift since I lost her.'

'Then, for God's sake, go and get her back.' Alice dropped his arm, turned on her heel, and walked away.

'I'll come with you to the bus stop.' Angus said, following after her.

'Do you need to check up on me, Black?' Alice asked without turning and waiting for him. 'Don't you trust that I'll get on the bus?'

'No, I want to say goodbye. That's all.' Angus jogged up next to her and draped his arm over her shoulder.

Chapter 32
She's Back

The sunlight filtered through the canopy of trees, dappling the forest floor in a patchwork of gold and shadow. As Dom, Marraine, and Detective Morgan pushed through the thick underbrush, the dense bed of leaves and soft soil muffled the sound of their steps. Marraine dabbed perspiration from her neck and sent Dom a look of disapproval.

'Not far now,' Detective Morgan said quietly, noticing Marraine's annoyance.

Ahead, the trees thinned. They pushed through overhanging branches to find themselves in a clearing bathed in soft daylight. Three great willows stood on one side, their long, trailing branches swaying gently in the spring breeze. The ground underfoot was damp from the recent rains, and the stream beside the clearing glistened as it trickled over smooth rocks. But the beauty of the scene was overshadowed by the figures standing in the centre of the clearing.

A group of seven large, dishevelled men stood in a semi-circle directly in front of them. Their massive muscles twitched and tensed beneath their dirty and torn shirts. Seven sets of inhuman eyes glowed with a predatory wariness, scanning the intruders with sharp suspicion. The largest among them, possibly their leader, stood at the front. A scar across his left eye and streaks of silver in his beard and shoulder length hair gave him an otherworldly appearance.

Dom swallowed hard, gripping the Glock tighter, though he knew the weapon wouldn't do much good. Detective Morgan shifted beside him, his eyes darting nervously between the Lycan and Marraine, who had stepped forward ahead of them. She ran a discerning eye over the men then around the clearing. The makeshift campsite was rough but functional. Around the edges of the shadowy glade, scattered tents made of mismatched canvas and heavy tarps were pitched haphazardly, their weathered fabric straining against the tension of the ropes that anchored them to nearby trees. The tents were simple, more like temporary shelters hastily erected than permanent dwellings. Some had patches sewn onto them where the fabric had worn thin, others sagged slightly, their ropes tied to gnarled roots and branches. A fire pit, long burned down to embers, lay at the centre, surrounded by jagged rocks and charred bits of wood. The ground around the fire was well-trodden; the dirt packed down from pacing feet and long, restless nights. In some places, the damp earth still held the imprints of enormous paws.

Around the campfire were old crates and makeshift stools, carved out of felled tree trunks. Some were cracked and splintered, clearly fashioned from whatever could be scavenged in the forest. A few battered metal cups and plates were scattered about, along with remnants of a meal. A half-eaten loaf of bread, a hunk of cheese, and a small collection of bones, stripped clean of any meat. The air was thick with the smell of damp earth and wood smoke, tinged with the musky scent of the Lycan themselves. The surrounding trees loomed overhead, their branches like protective arms encircling the camp. Here and there, the glint of sunlight broke through the canopy, illuminating patches of the campsite in fleeting warmth.

Marraine took another cautious step forward. The sunlight danced across her skin as she moved out of the shadows. Several of the men growled low in their throats, their dark eyes narrowing as she drew closer. But she remained steady, her voice clear and firm as she spoke.

'We're not here to harm you.' she said, her tone calm but carrying authority. The man with the silver-streaked hair stepped forward, towering over her.

'Why should we believe you?' he demanded, his voice a deep growl that echoed through the clearing. Dom crept closer to Marraine. Marraine looked up, meeting the man's gaze with unwavering resolve. The sunlight framed her face as she spoke.

'Because we're not your enemies. We came to talk,' she said. For a long, tense moment, the man didn't move and didn't break his gaze from Marraine.

'And why would we listen to humans?' he asked in a harsh, gravelly tone. Marraine stood tall, the sunlight glinting off the pendant at her throat.

'Because if you don't listen to them, there will be casualties on both sides. Innocent lives are getting caught in the crossfire, too. Besides, you know very well we aren't all humans.' The leader of the Lycan studied her for a long moment, his dark eyes narrowing.

'That one is,' he said, nodding towards Detective Morgan. 'We smelled him a mile off.'

'Yep, he smells like bacon,' one of the other men added. The seven men laughed. Dom started to laugh too but realised that all the men were glaring at him.

'And this one,' the silver-streaked man spat. 'You dare bring this Nephilim filth with you? Why shouldn't we rip his throat out right now?'

'Because you would have to go through me,' Marraine said calmly. 'And we both know that's not going to happen.' She looked around the group of men, then snapped her gaze back at the leader. He took a step back.

'Cornell!' someone called out. 'Is that anyway to welcome guests?' A short, balding man exited one of the tents and walked towards them. At first, Marraine thought she was seeing a ghost. In the shadows, the man looked just like...

'He looks just like Bob,' Dom said in Marraine's ear, obviously thinking the same thing.

'We are sorry to intrude,' Marraine called out to the balding man.

'It's okay,' he said as he came and stood next to the silver-streaked man, who was apparently called Cornell. 'We were expecting someone to come look for us. We've been waking up closer and closer to town each morning, so we guessed it was only a matter of time before someone would hunt us down. We are glad to see that it is you, Madame Marraine.' The balding man extended his hand to Marraine.

'Do you know me?' Marraine asked in surprise. She could sense that all these men were Lycan like her, but she didn't recognise any of them.

'Yes,' the man said. My name is Stanley Dart. You were good to my brother Robert, and he always spoke fondly of you.'

'You're Bob's brother?' Marraine asked, shaking his outstretched hand.

'Yes, Bob was my brother.'

'I told you he looked familiar,' Dom interrupted. Marraine turned to glare at him.

'That's because you're a species-ist. You think we all look the same.'

'That doesn't even make sense,' Dom said. Marraine ignored his bewildered look and turned back to Stanley.

'Bob was a good man, and he's sorely missed,' she offered. Dom nodded in agreement.

'We were already on our way here when I heard of his passing. My queen had also just died. Robert told me good things about his new queen, and many of us were already feeling the pull of her power. We here are all bonded to her now.' He gestured around the campsite with an open hand.

'But she's not here. Why haven't you all left?' Dom asked.

'It doesn't work like that Dominic,' Marraine said as she looked around the camp and acknowledge each of the Lycan in turn. 'They are bound to the place that their queen calls home or the place that their queen is thinking about most.'

'So why not get far away from that place so that you can never get there?' Detective Morgan asked. Stanley, Cornell, and the others exchanged glances.

'That would be worse,' Stanley said. 'We would run all night crazy to get back here and we would destroy anything and anyone that got in our way.'

'Besides, it's painful for us to get too far away, even in the day,' Cornell said. The rest mumbled their agreements.

'They are bound to this place.' Marraine said, turning back to look at Dom and Detective Morgan. 'None of this is their fault.'

'Fault or not, something needs to be done,' Detective Morgan said.

'But locking them up?' Marraine's voice was raising in volume. Dom had never seen this side of her. She was usually so cool and collected.

'We've had multiple properties damaged and people have died. It's only because of Mr Kinnard and his family that there have not been more deaths,' the detective said. Dom stood up straight with his shoulders back.

'Well, praise the lord for Mr Kinnard – the protector and saviour of Heathcote,' Marraine teased.

'My dad nearly died,' Dom said. Marraine looked around at her fellow Lycan, then placed her hands on her hips.

'Yes, I know,' she said, looking down at the ground. 'Your father is a lovely man, and I would hate anything to happen to him.'

'It's okay,' Stanley said. 'We are happy to do whatever needs to be done to keep people safe. 'As much as you might think of us as monsters, Mr Kinnard, we are not, nor do we want to be.'

'I don't think you're monsters,' Dom said quietly. He thought he saw a flicker of a smile on Marraine's down-turned face.

'I'm sorry, my brothers,' Marraine said, still looking down. 'It's only until we can bring home your queen and sort things out.' There was a murmur amongst the men.

'She is back,' Stanley said.

'What?' Marraine's head sprung up.

'She's back. We saw her last night at the burnt mansion.'

'Who did you see?' Dom and Marraine asked in unison.

'Our queen. The queen of hearts. Queen Cinder.'

Chapter 33

She's Gone!

Angus strolled along in the shadows of the great oak trees that lined the driveway to the farmhouse. With his hands in his pockets, he whistled a tune that his father had sung to him and his sister Katie when they were children. He had forgotten some of the words, but the melody was as familiar as a close friend. Before he could reach the front step, Marraine emerged from the front door and rushed to him. She took hold of his shirtfront and almost bowled him over.

'Where have you been? We've been trying to find you,' she said, shaking him.

'I was just...' Angus started reply, but Marraine cut him off.

'She's here. She's come back!' she said.

'She can't be here I just saw her get on the bus,' Angus said, pulling himself free of Marraine's grip.

'You saw her on the bus? When? Where?'

'Just then. She just caught the late bus. I said goodbye.' Angus stepped up on to the front porch.

'You saw Cinder and didn't tell me?' Marraine yelled and took hold of him again

'Cinder? No, I'm talking about Alice. Hang on. Have you seen Cinder? Is she here?' Angus asked, stepping back down from the porch and taking Marraine by her shoulders.

'I haven't seen her, but we got word that she was back. She was at The Big House last night,' she said.

'Last night!' Angus cried. He interlaced his fingers behind his head as a smile of happiness and relief flooded his face. 'Do you know where she is now?' he asked. Marraine shook her head and opened her mouth to answer, but there was a disturbance inside the house. Gunn exploded from the front door.

'She's gone!' he yelled, stumbling down the front step towards them. His face was pale and clammy.

'Gone? What do you mean? Was she here? Was Cinder here?' Angus asked.

'Not Cinder,' Gunn said, resting his trembling hands on his thighs and catching his breath. 'Annabelle. The baby's gone. You hear me, boy? Someone's taken the baby.'

Chapter 34
The Riddle of Three

Detective Morgan sat at his desk in the Heathcote Police station. A desk top fan swept from side to side next to him, threatening to blow stacks of paperwork from his inbox on each pass but dropping them back into place. On the desk in front of him lay a single sheet of paper. A coffee mug that stated he was the best boss ever weighed one corner down. The mug was a gift from the two members of O'Burket. He held his notebook open with one hand as he studied the sheet of paper. His other hand was occupied with spinning a ballpoint pen around the tip of his thumb. It had taken many hours of practise in his youth to acquire this skill, and now it was all muscle memory. He could hear the murmur of his guests in the cells.

Cornell, the Lycan with the silver streak in his hair, had protested but eventually the others had convinced him it was for the best that they spend moon-lit nights in the cells to keep themselves and others safe. Detective Morgan's pen came to rest in his hand and he added a note to his notebook. The murmur from the cells grew louder and he could hear someone calling out his name. He rose from his desk and made his way around the corner to where the holding cells were. The holding cells were three rooms that would usually be empty except for a slab to use as a bed and seat and a toilet in one corner. Because the Lycan had agreed to come freely and weren't actually being held for a crime, Detective Morgan had supplied them with some chairs, tables, blankets and a variety of books and games to keep them occupied. They had covered the small windows with thick cardboard to block out any moonlight, but just in case, they would lock the Lycan in the cells. As there were still a few hours of daylight remaining, the Lycan men were allowed to roam freely from room to room as long as they agreed not to leave the police station.

The balding man, Stanley, was leaning against the doorjamb of the first cell with a book hanging from his hand at one side.

'You've got some company coming,' he said as Detective Morgan appeared around the corner. 'Lady Marraine is approaching with two of the Nephilim.' He sniffed the air. 'And something's not right.'

'What do you mean, not right?' Detective Morgan said, looking back over his shoulder out through the front windows of the station. Stanley threw his book onto the cells bed.

'I'm sensing a lot of anger and anxiety,' he said. Detective Morgan's mouth twisted. He nodded to Stanley and moved briskly back to his desk. He pulled a key from his pocket and unlocked the bottom drawer of his desk. Reaching under a pile of papers, he pulled out his sidearm. He slid the weapon into the holster on his belt and was just locking it in placed when Angus burst through the door.

'She's taken Annabelle!' he blurted out, striding towards the bench that separated the front of the police station from the desks and cells. Dom and Marraine followed him in.

'You need to go after her and you need to go now,' Dom added. Detective Morgan approached the bench, looking at each of the new arrivals.

'Please, gentlemen, you need to calm down,' he said, noticing their agitation as the two men slammed into the bench like waves on the shore.

'Calm down?' Dom said. 'She took his daughter, Peter. She's got Annabelle and Torry too.' He slapped his hand down on the bench. Angus pushed himself away and paced the room. Detective Morgan looked to Marraine, who was standing near the entrance.

'What are they talking about?' he asked. Marraine approached the bench.

'While I was out searching for Cinder, Torry apparently packed her things and the baby's things and left,' Marraine explained. She clasped her fingers together and rested her hands on the bench before going on. 'These two think that Cinder has taken Annabelle.'

'We don't think, we know!' Dom interrupted. 'What other explanation is there?' His voice was growing louder and starting to crack. Marraine held her palm up to him and spoke calmly.

'You don't need to yell at me, Dominic. I'm here to help.'

'I'll yell at whoever I need to!' Dom said louder still.

'Dom,' Angus said quietly but firmly, shaking his head as he continued to pace. Cornell appeared around the corner behind Detective Morgan, shuffling a deck of cards and chewing gum.

'Everything alright, Lady Marraine?' he asked, eyeballing Dom with fierce intensity.

'Yes, fine. Thank you, sweetie. Please go back to your game,' Marraine said. Cornell held his gaze with Dom for a moment longer, then turned and strolled back to the cells.

'We're here if you need,' he called behind him, as his heavy footsteps reverberated off the smooth floor and walls.

'Yep, we're fine thanks, sweetie,' Dom jeered.

A low growl rumbled down the hallway.

'Dom!' Angus said again, more forcibly. Detective Morgan looked at each of the visitors in the foyer of this station.

'I can see that you're all obviously very upset by the situation. But I'm not sure what you're expecting me to do about it,' he said.

'Your job,' Dom spat. 'Go after them and arrest them.'

'On what charges?' Detective Morgan asked, turning and walking back to his desk. 'Was anything stolen? Did anyone get hurt?'

'What about kidnapping?' Dom said. Angus laughed and shook his head, but otherwise remained silent. Detective Morgan collected a sheet of paper from his desk and looked it over before looking back at Dom.

'From what you've said, it appears that the little girl, Annabelle, is in the care of her mother and Torry,' he said. 'And as I understand it, Torry has been one of the main caregivers to the child since her birth. Legally speaking, there's nothing I can do.'

'What?' Dom said, throwing his hands in the air before slapping them down on the bench.

'I told you he wouldn't be able to help us,' Angus said. 'This was a waste of time.'

'Is there anything you can do, Peter?' Marraine asked. 'As a friend?' Detective Peter Morgan studied the piece of paper in his hands. He looked like he was trying to decide something.

'There is one thing,' he said, walking back to the others. 'It's a letter, and it actually has nothing to do with any of you, but it's weird.' He sat the letter down and tapped his fingers on the bench. 'And I guess well... When anything weird comes across my desk, it usually does end up having something to do with you all.'

'Can I see it?' Marraine asked, stepping up to the bench next to Dom.

'Please,' Detective Morgan said and gestured for her to take the letter 'It arrived here two days ago addressed to P. Morgan. There was no return address, and all there was...was this, and a business card.'

Angus stopped his pacing and looked up. 'Can I see the business card?' he asked.

'Yes, I have it here,' Detective Morgan said, walking back to his desk and moving some other pieces of paper.

'That's odd,' Marraine said, looking at the letter in her hands.

'What?' Dom asked, looking over her shoulder.

'It looks like my handwriting.' Marraine said.

'What's it say?' Angus asked. Marraine looked at him and frowned.

'It's just a story, sweetie. I don't think it's any help.'

'Read it to me,' Angus said.

Detective Morgan returned to the bench and handed him the business card. Marraine read the story out loud.

Once upon a time, in a quaint village nestled by the sea, there lived a storyteller named Emilia. My tale is short, for I once was caught in a storm, she would often say, recounting the tale of how a fierce tempest had once taken her by surprise. One cloudy afternoon, as the clock struck three, Emilia found herself by the shore, gazing at the relentless waves crashing against the rocks. The sea was furious, and the sky was a dark canvas that had no sun in sight. She had ventured out to collect seashells for her collection, but now she could not see beyond the turbulent waters.

Suddenly, a thought struck her like lightning. She remembered an old legend passed down through generations. It spoke of a way to build with bricks to withstand the breeze, not with straw or limbs of trees. Emilia knew that this legend held the key to facing the storm. Determined and resolute, she rushed back to the village and gathered the townsfolk. 'One for all and all for one,' she declared, invoking unity and strength. Together, they gathered bricks from their homes and began constructing a protective wall along the shoreline.

As they toiled through the night, the wind howled, and the rain poured down relentlessly. But the villagers, inspired by their unity and determination, pressed on. They built a sturdy barricade that stood tall and strong. Just as dawn broke, the storm began to weaken. The relentless wind turned into a gentle breeze, and the rain transformed into a refreshing drizzle. Emilia and the villagers had succeeded in withstanding the fury of the tempest, thanks to their wise choice of building materials.

The villagers rejoiced, and their bonds grew stronger. Emilia's words, 'One for all and all for one,' echoed through the village, reminding them of the power of unity. As the sun emerged from behind the clouds, D'Artagnan, the village blacksmith, arrived, ready to join in the festivities. With a smile, he declared, 'D'Artagnan's along for some fun!' The village celebrated their victory over the storm, their hearts filled with gratitude for Emilia's wisdom and the strength of their community. From that day forward, they lived by the motto, 'One for all and all for one,' and together, they faced any challenge that came their way.

'Well, that's some bullshit.' Dom said, pushing himself away from the bench. 'It's not even a good story.'

'That was my thinking too when I first read it, Mr Kinnard,' Detective Morgan said. 'But then I noticed that some of the words and phrases were written in a different hand, almost like someone else had written them.'

'So?' Dom asked.

'So that's when things got interesting.' Detective Morgan pulled his notebook from his pocket. 'That's when this letter revealed a hidden message,' he said, flicking excitedly through the pages to the one he was looking for.

'What's the secret message?' Angus asked. Detective Morgan smiled, cleared his throat, and read:

My tale is short, for I once was caught.
The clock struck three that could not see.
Build with bricks to withstand the breeze.
Not with straw or limbs of trees.
One for all and all for one.
D'artagnan's along for some fun.

Angus held the business card in both hands. His brow folding low over his dark eyes as his large thumb ran across the embossed writing.

'Yes, but what the hell does all that mean?' Dom asked.

'It's elementary, my dear Watson,' Detective Morgan said.

'I don't know what's more of a mystery, this letter or that you have developed a personality.' Dom said.

'It's all to do with the number three.' Angus interrupted.

'Well done, Mr MacAskill.' Detective Morgan said. 'Yes. Three blind mice, three little pigs, and the three musketeers.'

'Come-on Dom, we're going.' Angus said, pushing Dom towards the door, leaving Marraine holding the letter. Marraine made to follow them.

'Hold on a moment,' Detective Morgan said to her. He collected something from his desk and sat it on the bench. Marraine stepped forward to inspect it.

'What is this?' she asked, looking at the large envelope that the detective had placed on the bench.

'It's the information you asked for... About Lady Gevaudan.'

'Where are we going?' Dom asked, as they exited the station. Angus squinted as he stepped into the dying afternoon light.

'We're going to Sydney,' he said as the door swung shut behind them.

'Why are we going to Sydney?' Dom asked. Angus turned and walked to the edge of the road.

'To kill a vampire and get my daughter back,' he said without turning back to look at Dom.

Marraine hurried out after them, still holding the letter and the envelope.

'What's the fastest way you can get us to Sydney?' Angus asked her as he stopped to wait for a passing car.

'I can organise Cinder's jet. Why are you going to Sydney now that Cinder's back?' Marraine asked, trying to make sense of what just happened.

'Because Cinder's going back there and taking Annabelle with her.' Angus paced up the footpath as another car passed. 'How long will it take to get organised?'

'Not long,' Marraine said, following him with her eyes. 'I've had it on standby for the past few weeks, just waiting for you to ask.'

'Alright then, I'll meet you at the air-strip in an hour,' Angus said, marching across the street to where he had parked. 'Are you coming, Dom?' he yelled, getting into Blaire's VW.

'Okay, just hold up a second,' Dom said. Marraine pulled her phone from inside her shirt, but Dom took hold of her hand. 'I think you should come too,' he said.

'Of course, Dominic. I was planning on coming. I already have a bag packed. But why did you say it like that?' Marraine asked, seeing the concern on his face.

'Because,' Dom said, taking hold of her shoulders. 'I think Black's going to kill Cinder.'

Chapter 35
Asses and Swine

Torry stepped out of the back door of a silver Toyota hatch back. She stretched and looked around as Cinder made arrangements for the driver to wait for them. They had parked on the gravel shoulder of a narrow street. Torry swatted away a fly and turned to look out onto a large paddock of canola. A breeze sent a ripple through the plants, like a wave on an ocean of yellow.

'When you said you were bringing me to Sydney, I thought I was going to see the opera house and the bridge. Some tall buildings, at least,' she said to Cinder as she collected Annabelle from her car-seat. 'I can see farms at home.' She slumped her shoulders and looked around.

'We will go into the city soon,' Cinder said. She took Annabelle and sat her on her hip. 'There is just something I need to pick up first.' She took hold of Torry's hand.

On the opposite side of the road, there was a white house with flaking paint. A veranda of rusty, corrugated-metal wrapped its way around three sides. The house sat quietly behind a chain-link fence. It was small, almost unnoticeable from the road, with its weathered white siding and a slanted roof that had clearly seen better days. A wide porch stretched across the front, complete with faded metal chairs. A layer of dust made it appear as though no one had sat out here for years. The windows, though clean, seemed to look out onto the world with a kind of resigned acceptance, like they knew their view hadn't changed in ages. The yard, overgrown in places, was a burst of unexpected colour. Along the fence, lavender grew wild amongst the unruly grass. Although the house wasn't abandoned, it felt as if time stood still there.

They crossed the road and Cinder lifted a latch on a small gate in the wonky chain-link fence. A rusty sign hung from the gate and rattled as the gate creaked open. Torry read the hand-painted words "Asses and Swine."

'What is this place?' Torry asked, ducking under the branch of a large palm tree on the front lawn.

'These people breed donkeys and pigs. You get it? Asses and Swine,' Cinder said.

'But why did you bring me here?' Torry asked, swatting away another fly. Annabelle giggled.

'These people are going to sell me a pig,' Cinder said. 'A piglet, actually.'

'Why do you need a...' Torry started to ask but then she remembered the conversation they had about pigs' blood. 'Oh, no. Poor piggy,' she said.

'It's important,' Cinder said, opening a squeaky screen door at the entrance to the house.

'Does it have to be a baby pig?' Torry asked.

'Yes, it has to be a baby pig.' Cinder knocked on the front door. Torry crossed her arms.

'I'm not okay with this part of the plan.'

Chapter 36
Sleeper

Cinder stood at the bottom of the staircase that snaked its way up to the second floor. She still had a key to the rear entrance to Mr Inkerman's home. So far, she had made her way through the guest-wing, past the pool and into the main building without being noticed. She could hear the murmur of conversation from the second floor and assumed that Mr Inkerman was in his office. It was reasonable to also assume that there would be at least two of his security team with him, haunting the hallways with their emotionless faces hidden behind dark glasses. She took in a deep breath and placed her hand on the banister. The carved, dark timber was cold under touch and worn smooth by the years of hands following the same journey as her own. Her inner-child wanted to run to the top and slide back down to the bottom. A memory of her doing this exact thing at her home as a child flashed across her mind. It was hard to know if it was her own memory or one that she had acquired from Marraine, but it filled her with joyful nostalgia all the same. Smiling, she continued up, stepping as quietly as the timber steps would allow in the great chamber of a space.

Reaching the top, Cinder thought that her prediction of two members of the security team was going to be proven wrong. A short, stocky man was standing by Mr Inkerman's office door with the dim hallway light glistening on his bald head. He held his hands in front, his head and shaded eyes were turned towards Cinder. *Not quiet enough,* she thought to herself. Cinder took a step towards the office, but the man held up a hand, indicating for her to stop. Cinder paused and someone appeared in the doorway. There's the second one. The second, a woman slightly taller than the man, with dark shoulder-length hair, looked Cinder up and down, then retreated into the office.

'Let her in.' Cinder recognised Mr Inkerman's voice. Confident and arrogant, but with the rehearsed warmth of a seasoned salesman. The bald man stepped to one side of the doorway and motioned with a sweep of his hand for Cinder to continue. Setting her shoulders back and adjusting her shirt, Cinder marched into the office.

Joseph Inkerman sat on the corner of his desk; an imposing and solid piece of furniture, hand-crafted, dark mahogany with brass corners and fittings. A stack of papers and an empty whisky glass sat on the green-leather surface, along with an antique gold and uranium-glass lamp. Joseph had his legs crossed and stretched out in front. He twirled a gold-plated pen between his fingers as he admired the shine of his shoes.

'I was not expecting you back,' he said, looking up.

'Ever?' Cinder asked. Joseph shrugged. Standing next to him, with her back to Cinder, was, as always, the very slim and very business-like Ms Chase.

'I hoped you would return. I suppose I thought it might take you longer. I was rather rude to you after all,' Joseph said, tapping his knee with the pen. Ms Chase huffed. Cinder could not see her face, but she assumed the huff was accompanied by one of her well-practiced eye rolls. 'I've kept your room set up for you,' Joseph added. Cinder walked forward and sat on the opposite corner of the desk. Joseph swivelled to face her. Behind him, three cathedral-like arched windows lined the wall. Of a night, these windows looked out over the lights of the city, but today a thick crimson drape was pulled across them. A thin slither of light escaping around the edge fell on Cinder's hand with tingles of warmth.

'I saw that when I arrived. Thank you,' she said. Joseph stopped tapping.

'Oh, yes. I had forgotten that you still have the key. Should I trust you with it?' He looked into her eyes. A studying look that went beyond the surface and tried to explore her thoughts. Cinder resisted the urge to look away and returned his gaze.

'It's funny that you said you didn't know I was coming, because I'm sure that one of your men was following me for the last part of my trip,' she said, getting up and walking to look through the gap in the curtain. She pulled the gap open a few more inches, the slither of light widened. Ms Chase glared at her. Joseph pushed himself away from the desk and stood.

'You noticed my shadow then? I'm impressed,' he said, motioning for Ms Chase to leave. Sour-faced, Ms Chase sauntered away. Joseph leaned with both hands on the desk and watched her go. 'Yes, I am impressed,' he said once she had left the room. 'But I'll ask again; can I trust you?'

'You can trust me,' Cinder said, walking towards him with an outstretched hand. 'That's why I'm here today, to prove that to you. Come, I have someone I would like you to meet.'

• • • •

Dom stood looking out over tiled roofs and tree-lined streets. Below, the city spread out before him like a challenge, daring him to take it on. The Harbour Bridge stood tall and unyielding, its steel frame gleaming in the sunlight. Beneath it, the harbour stretched wide and alive, the water catching the light like shards of shattered glass. Sailboats bobbed lazily on the surface, as if they had all the time in the world. Their white sails stark against the blue. The skyline loomed in the distance, jagged towers of glass and concrete punching into the sky. Closer to him, the scene softened. Rows of townhouses stood tucked among the trees, their rooftops glowing warm under the afternoon sun. A narrow street carved its way through the green, shaded by the arching branches of old trees.

'It's a beautiful part of the world isn't it,' Marraine said, coming to stand next to him. Dom shrugged, his lips twisting.

'It's okay, I guess.' He turned to look at Marraine. 'I hope we're going to go to Bondi after this. I've heard that's worth looking at.'

'The beach, or the girls on the beach?' Marraine asked.

'I can appreciate beauty in all its forms.' Dom turned away from the view of the harbour to look at the house behind him. Marraine had discovered that it belonged to a man named Inkerman. The business card that Detective Morgan had given them was for some kind of antique shop he owned. Angus seemed to think that Cinder had shacked-up with him.

'I can't see the beauty in this place,' Dom said.

'No. It's ugly,' Marraine agreed.

'When is your friend getting here?' Angus called out from the opposite side of the road. He had been pacing up and down in front of Mr Inkerman's house for the past five minutes.

'He'll be here at the time we agreed,' Marraine said, giving way to a cyclist before crossing the road to stand with Angus.

'We're here early, mate.' Dom called across the road. 'You kept telling the Uber driver to hurry up, so now we have to wait around.'

'My daughter's in there with a monster!' Angus yelled.

'We don't know that yet,' Marraine said, reaching out an assuring hand. Angus pushed her hand aside, glowering and continuing to pace.

'I know it,' he said, more to himself than the others. Dom crossed the road.

'Annabelle's going to be alright,' he said, stopping next to Marraine. Angus stopped and slammed the side of his fist against the wall around Joseph Inkerman's house. A fist-sized shard of stone cracked away from the wall and fell to the ground in pieces.

'The next time one of you says, "*Annabelle's going to be alright*," I'm going in there alone,' he said, kicking the wall for good measure.

Dom and Marraine looked at each other. Dom pulled an imaginary zipper across his lips.

With a squeak of its large tyres, a black Land Rover turned into the street. A man in dark glasses could just be seen through the tinted windows as it drove slowly past them and came to a stop 20 metres away on the opposite side of the road.

'That's him,' Marraine said. The three of them crossed the road together and approached the vehicle.

The Land Rover's door swung open with a smooth, deliberate motion and Marraine's friend, Carmichael, unfolded himself from the driver's seat like a panther stepping out of shadow. The sunlight poured a warm, golden glow over him, illuminating every inch of his striking frame. His broad shoulders filled out his leather jacket to perfection, while the tailored fit of his dark jeans hinted at legs built for endurance and strength. Every movement was a study in control, his body honed by years of discipline and relentless training. His skin, a rich, warm mahogany, gleamed in the light, the smooth planes of his face accentuated by the sharp angles of his cheekbones and the strong chin that gave him an air of authority. A closely cropped beard framed his jawline, its neat lines suggesting a man who valued precision in all things. He turned and smiled at Marraine and slid off his sunglasses. His smiling eyes, dark and intense, seemed to hold the weight of all he'd seen and endured. A faint, nearly imperceptible scar ran just above his left eyebrow, a reminder of battles fought and survived. His hair was cropped close to his head, the tight waves giving him a polished, confident look that suited his commanding presence. Next to Dom, Marraine made a noise that sounded like a purr.

'Are you okay?' Dom asked.

'Oh, yes, sweetie,' she replied.

'I still don't know why we need this guy,' Dom grumped, folding his arms over his puffed-up chest.

'Because we couldn't bring any weapons with us. Carmichael has contacts here in Sydney. Be nice – he's helping us.' Marraine tapped Dom with the back of her hand but kept her eyes focused on Carmichael.

Carmichael stepped away from the Land Rover, a black duffel bag slung casually over one powerful shoulder. The faintest hint of cologne followed him – woody, with a touch of spice.

'Hello again, Marraine,' he said in a deep, resonant voice.

'Hello, sweetie. You're right on time.'

'When you call, I come.'

'Yes, you do,' Marraine said. 'And sometimes the other way around,' she added. Carmichael gazed penetratingly into her eyes. Marraine held his gaze. Dom turned to Angus and mimicked their look. Angus ignored all of them.

'It looks like you have some friends this time. What have you got these kids into?' Carmichael asked, looking at the two men. Dom said something under his breath. Angus shifted his feet impatiently.

'What have you got for us?' he asked.

'Everything I was asked to bring,' Carmichael said, popping the hatch of his Land Rover, 'and some extras.'

'Is Carmichael your first name or your last name?' Dom asked. Carmichael pushed past him.

'Does it matter? If you met Madonna, would you ask her if that was her first or last name?'

'If I met Madonna, I'd ask her to go for a drink with me,' Dom said, looking Carmichael up and down.

'Isn't she a bit old for you, kid?' Carmichael asked, pulling open the rear door of his vehicle and flicking back a blanket.

'Aren't you a bit old?' Dom asked.

'This conversation is getting old,' Marraine interrupted them. 'As much fun as it is to watch, you two boys will have to compare the sizes of your weapons later. In fact, I will quite happily be the judge.

For now, though, we have a job to do.' She stood between them. Carmichael placed his hand on her shoulder.

'Are you sure you don't need my help in there?' he asked.

'You are helping,' she said, placing her hand on his. 'But I can't ask you to come in here. Remember Seattle? This is going to make Seattle look like a walk in the park.'

'Hell yeah, I remember Seattle. My jaw still clicks,' Carmichael said, opening his mouth wide. Marraine leaned in and kissed his jaw.

'Oh, mine too, sweetie,' she said with a wink.

'Are we doing this or what?' Dom interrupted. Carmichael looked him over again.

'Are you sure this kid is up to task?' he asked Marraine, loud enough for Dom to hear. Dom took a step towards him.

'Would you like *this kid* to show you *just* what he *is up to*, old man?' he said, jutting his chin forward. Marraine pushed herself between them again.

'Dom!' Angus said. 'Let's get on with it.'

They huddled around the rear of the vehicle and perused the assortment of weapons Carmichael had laid out for them. Dom found two tomahawks that he assumed were for him. He tucked the tomahawks into his belt, then continued to sort through some other bladed weapons. He slid four sheathed throwing knives into his boots, two for each foot, then picked up a large machete. Trying the machete out for balance, he began swinging it in a figure-eight motion. Angus pushed past him and collected a long pole with blades at both ends.

'Hurry up and stop messing around,' he said before turning and walking back towards Inkerman's house.

'Okay, okay. I'm coming,' Dom said, tossing the machete back into the car. 'Are you picking anything?' he asked Marraine.

'I have these.' She held up her hands. A second later, her fingernails formed into long claws.

'Come on, then. We'd better go before he goes in there by himself,' Dom said, securing the tomahawks in this belt.

'Just wait,' Carmichael said, placing his hand on Marraine's arm. 'I have these too.' He lowered the duffle bag from his shoulder and lay it across the weapons. He unzipped it to reveal a collection of handguns and a cut-down shotgun.

'Great holy mother father,' Dom exclaimed. 'Now we're talking! I'm hating you less by the second,' he said to Carmichael as he reached for the duffle bag. Marraine slapped his hand away.

'No!' she said firmly. 'You'll end up shooting yourself or one of us.' She zipped the bag shut.

'Thank you, Carmichael.' She rested her hand on his arm. 'We will see you back at the hotel tonight.'

'Good luck,' Carmichael said and kissed the top of her head.

As they hastened away to catch up to Angus, Dom called. 'Wait!'

'What now?' Marraine asked.

'I decided I do want the machete.' Dom turned and ran back to Carmichael's car.

· · · ·

Cinder stood in the hallway. Joseph had gone to change out of his work-shirt into something more comfortable. When he returned, he appeared very excited. Cinder linked her arm through his and rested her hand on his elbow. They stepped out together through the large glass door that led to the gardens. The house glowed white in the warm morning light, its illuminated arches casting golden reflections on the neatly manicured lawn below. Above, the second-storey balcony stretched the length of the home, its wrought-iron railings curling into delicate patterns. The scent of freshly cut grass mingled with the faintest trace of the ocean, carried on a breeze that rustled the leaves of a giant fig tree. Cinder had laid a white blanket with yellow trimmings on the shadowed lawn beneath the sprawling branches of the great tree. At the centre of the blanket, nestled between two pillows and draped over with a muslin sheet, was a small lump.

'She fell asleep in the car ride over here,' Cinder said, 'and I didn't want to wake her. Your house is always so noisy and it's a beautiful day; I thought I would just let her sleep out here in the shade.'

'Is that her?' Joseph asked excitedly. 'Is that Annabelle? Can I see her?' Joseph moved towards the blanket, but Cinder held him back.

'Just let her sleep. We should talk first.' Cinder led Joseph across the lawn. Joseph kept his eyes focus on the bundle under the sheet, his eyes widening at every minute movement. One of the sprawling branches of the fig tree stretched out over the stone wall that ran around the boundary of Joseph's property. Against the wall, in the shade of the majestic branch, was a stone bench. Cinder sat first and motioned for Joseph to sit next to her. His eyes flicked to the seat long enough to sit, then back to the sleeping child.

'How old is she?' he asked in a hushed tone.

'Almost eight months,' Cinder said, stretching and yawning.

'How long will she sleep?'

'Long enough, I think,' Cinder said.

'Long enough for what?' Joseph asked. Cinder placed her hand on his chest and moved her face close to his.

'Long enough for us to really get to know each other, Joseph.'

Chapter 37

Unwelcome

The home of Joseph Inkerman rose majestically above the quiet street. As Angus, Dom, and Marraine approached, their gaze was drawn upwards to the intricate detailing across the building's facade. Pointed arches stretching to the sky, crowned with delicate tracery. Stone-carved gargoyles, perched along the eaves, ever watchful in their silent vigil. A tower rose like a sentinel from deep within the property. Its sloping roof rising to a pointed apex high above the roofline of the other buildings. Lush greenery surrounded the house; large trees and neatly trimmed bushes, which partially concealed the facade. Palm trees added a tropical touch to the otherwise European architectural influence. A sandstone wall enclosed the property on three sides. Stones of white, ochre, and pale browns had been cut into blocks of different sizes and skilfully laid. Ivy grew lush and green along the tops of the walls, falling in thick clumps towards the ground like giant drips of green molasses.

'Who does this guy think he is, Batman?' Dom asked. Angus ignored him and pushed against the wrought-iron gate. He had expected it to be locked, but it swung open freely. The front yard inclined up towards the house. They scaled four large stone steps to a broad landing. The entrance to Joseph Inkerman's home looked more like an entrance to a church than a house. The double doors towered twice as tall as Angus, a striking portal of deep red oak. They were carved with intricate patterns, their symmetry as sharp as a blade. Above, a gothic arch of leaded glass framed the entrance, catching the light and refracting it into ghostly shapes that danced across the stone steps below. Once again, to Angus's surprise, the doors opened as he pushed against them.

'Hold on Black,' Marraine said, taking hold of his wrist and looking around. 'This all seems a bit too convenient. I think someone knows we're coming.'

'Yeah, I think you're right.' Angus shifted the grip on his weapon and pushed the door open slowly. 'Let's just be ready,' he said, looking back at Dom. Dom pulled one of the tomahawks from his belt and he and Marraine followed Angus silently into the house.

A dozen men stood in the large open foyer of the house. Their eyes were set deep in dark rings as if being pulled back into their skulls, just thin ovals of bloodshot white haloing all pupils at the centre, black and glistening.

'I guess they know we're here.' Dom said, no longer bothering to stay quiet. 'What's up with these guys?' he asked. Marraine looked apprehensively at the man closest to her. Sickly-grey skin sat tightly against his cheekbones. Cracked and blistered lips twitched agitatedly on his tightly pulled mouth.

'I think I've seen these before,' Marraine said. 'They drink a vampire's blood so that they can gain some of his strength. It makes them feel amazing, but it slowly eats away at their soul. It's like a drug. The more they get, the more they need and the less of them remains.'

'Are they Cinder's?' Dom asked. 'Is it her blood they've been drinking?' The other two glared at him. 'What?' he asked.

'I don't have time for this,' Angus said, continuing to walk towards an archway that led to a passage away from the foyer. One of the zombie-like men stepped into his path. Angus threw his weapon past the man into the passage. He grabbed the man by the neck and the crotch. Lifting him from the floor, he smashed the surprised man's head against the top of the arch. The plasterboard above the arch cracked, the man went limp, and Angus dropped him to the floor. Blood ran from a large crack in the back of the man's head, staining Joseph Inkerman's expensive tiled floor. Angus stepped over the limp body, collected his weapon from the floor, and continued up the passage.

Dom and Marraine watched him go.

'So, you and me, against a room full of jacked up zombies, hey? Hmmm,' Dom said, watching as two of the men circled around to their right. Marraine kicked off one of her ankle boots.

'What are you thinking, Dominic?' she asked, reaching down and removing the remaining boot.

'I'm thinking I should have been nicer to your boyfriend with the guns. We could use his help now.'

'Are you afraid, Dominic?'

'No, I'm not afraid, but contrary to popular opinion, I ain't stupid either,' Dom said, as Marraine threw her boot behind her. 'Should I take my shoes off?' he asked. Marraine looked at the thick soles of Dom's large military style boots.

'No, they look perfect for some arse-kicking. Leave them on.' She ran her eyes up to Dom's arms. The sleeves of his black shirt clung tightly to his tensed biceps. 'Your shirt is optional,' she added. A flicker of a smile flashed across Dom's face.

'Maybe later,' he said. Two of the zombified men leaped at him with tremendous speed. Dom's smile retreated.

Chapter 38
Who is Inkerman?

Angus stormed down a bright hallway, his large boots tapping heavily on the slate tiled floor. At the end of the hall, he came to a set of double doors with glass arches set in a heavy timber frame. The hinges squeaked and reverberated down the hallway as he opened onto a small landing. To his left, the slate continued until it met an open section of immaculately kept lawn. Above him, a walkway that ran from one end of the main building to the other shadowed him from the warm morning sun. Directly in front, a black metal fence circled a pool of clear blue water. The sun reflected off the surface, sending a shimmering pattern of light dancing across the stone wall beside him. Angus continued outside and down some steps. A stone retaining-wall that sat just above Angus's waist height ran along the boundary of the lawn, creating an upper level for the pool. He stopped to listen for voices. From inside the wall beside him, he could hear the hum of what he suspected was the cleaning pump of the pool. The water rippled and splashed, and he could hear as it ran down inside the wall where it was recycled and pumped back into the pool.

Turning back towards the house, he could see a large fig tree at the bottom of the lawn. Sitting on a bench in its shade was a woman with long dark hair and a very wealthy looking man. It took Angus a moment to register who the woman was. It was not just the hair colour. She looked far paler and far skinnier than when he last saw her. But those green eyes. They were unmistakable, the way they seemed to almost glow through the dark curtains around her face. He would recognise those eyes anywhere. Angus knelt low against the wall and watched as Cinder and the man that he guessed was Inkerman, stood together and walked across the lawn. The large fig tree stretched high above, its branches stretching halfway across Inkerman's vast yard. At the base of its enormous trunk, there was an object laid out on a blanket. With a sinking feeling, Angus realised that the small, bundled-up object must be Annabelle.

Cinder and Joseph stopped at the edge of the outstretch branches, just at the boundary of light and shade. When they turned to look at Annabelle, Angus got up and stormed towards them, weapon in hand.

'Get away from her,' he said as he approached them. Both Joseph and Cinder turned to look at him. Neither of them looked surprised by his appearance.

'Hello, Black,' Cinder said pleasantly.

'It appears I am having many unannounced guests today.' Joseph said, 'I really should look into my security, it seems.'

'Joseph,' Cinder said, 'this is Angus MacAskill. He's Annabelle's father.'

'Oh yes, the father and the one-time lover,' Joseph said, placing his arm around Cinder. 'I'm sorry to say, but Miss Delacourt and I have developed something more than just a professional relationship. Isn't that right?'

'I didn't mean her; I was talking about my daughter.' Angus said, walking towards the tree. 'I've come to take her home.'

'But she's come all this way, and I so wanted to meet her.' Joseph pulled Cinder forward so that they were both in Angus's path. All three stood face to face under the great shadowy canopy of the old tree. Angus lent forward and put his face close to Cinder's ear.

'Someone sent us a message,' he whispered 'He's not what you think he is. Annabelle isn't safe here.'

'It's okay, Black. She'll be fine.' Cinder said. The speckled sunlight played across her face as the green canopy above danced and ruffled in the breeze. Angus thought he saw Cinder wink, but he couldn't be sure. Joseph looked Angus up and down with an arrogant grin. He let go of Cinder and turned to walk towards the crib. Angus moved forward, but Cinder stepped in his path and placed her hand on his chest.

'Just don't get too close. She's just gone to sleep, and I'd like to keep it that way,' she said, looking up at Angus. This time, it was unmistakable. She winked at him again. Joseph paced out a semicircular path a few metres from the sleeping child. There was a movement of blankets and some quiet squeaks, but the child remained sleeping.

'I don't care if she's sleeping. Annabelle's coming with me now. I'm taking her home,' Angus said, pushing past Cinder.

'Home?' Joseph laughed. 'Her home is here now,' he said, walking towards Cinder. 'Here with me and her mother. Isn't that right, Cinder?'

As he got to the edge of the shadow, he reached out to touch Cinder's face. Cinder took a step back and Angus reached out to push Joseph's hand away. Before he could, Joseph pulled his hand back. After a moment's contemplation, he slowly stretched his hand out again. As the sun fell on his fingers, smoke begun to rise from them. Small areas of black formed on his skin, blistering. When the first tongue of flame appeared, Joseph pulled his hand back in to the shade and stepped back. With his unburnt hand, he unbuttoned his shirt, revealing a blue-stoned moon pendant.

'What have you done, Miss Delacourt?' he asked, pulling the pendant from his neck and analysing it.

'I've borrowed your pendant. That one's a fake my friend gave me. Don't worry, yours is safe.' Cinder turned and smiled at Angus.

'So, you know who he is?' Angus asked.

'Yes, of course I know who he is.' Cinder put her hands on her hips. 'Who do you think sent Peter the messages? More importantly,' she said, looking at Joseph's burnt hand. 'I know what he is.'

Joseph threw the fake pendant across the yard and it splashed down in the pool behind Angus and Cinder. 'I suggest you return my pendant to me immediately while I'm still in a civilised mood,' he said.

'I'm sorry, Joseph, I can't do that. I just gave it to my little sister. She'll be half-way to Circular Quay by now.' Cinder said. Joseph cracked his neck to one side then the other. He slipped his phone from his back pocket, pressed it once with his thumb and held it to his ear.

'She has something of mine and I would like it back... Yes, the little Nephilim girl... Apparently you weren't watching her well enough... Here at the house... Yes, immediately. And notify Ms Chase.' He hung up and slipped his phone back into his pocket. 'My men will have her shortly,' he said. Cinder smiled a devious smile.

'They will never catch her,' she said. Angus turned to look at her. She was beginning to look like the girl he remembered.

'Gopher Kinnard?' Angus asked. Cinder's smile widened. Her green eyes sparkled as she looked back at him.

'GO-PHER KINN-ARD!'

Chapter 39

GO FAR KIN ARD

Torry glided along the sidewalk on Minogue Crescent. She had noted the name of the street because her father had a huge crush on someone called Danni Minogue. According to Gunn, she was less famous but more talented and a "better looker" than her older sister. Torry passed a young girl walking hand in hand with her mother. The girl watched, wide-eyed and open-mouthed. When Cinder had explained her plan to Torry, she had asked Torry to pack lightly. Torry had argued, "If I'm going to do this, I'm going to do it right." Now, as Torry turned back to wave at the little girl, she was decked-out in her roller derby uniform. Black leather skates, helmet, knee and elbow pads. But most importantly, she was wearing her blue and yellow, Surf Coast Banshees number 7 singlet. Her Derby-name, Gopher Kinnard, proudly embroidered on the back. As she rumbled along past a white building shrouded by green native trees, she held her hand to her chest.

Moments ago, she had been sitting with her back against the stone wall of Joseph Inkerman's raucously audacious house. She had positioned herself under the overhanging branch as Cinder had instructed. She heard Cinder's voice, then an object fell from above and almost hit her. It was all part of the plan. Cinder had snuck into Inkerman's room and swapped the moon pendant for a fake. On the car ride over, Torry had held the fake pendant. It was still beautiful with its ring of gold and twisted silver branches that held a blue moon-stone, but it had no magical power. It was just a simple item of jewellery. Now, as she placed one foot in front of the other, she could feel the cold metal of the real pendant against her warm skin. There was something about it, something that made the hairs on her arms stand on end. She felt the pendant as almost weightless, like it had attached itself to her flesh – no, it was even stranger than that. It felt like it was sinking into her, becoming part of her chest. She felt the need to keep checking it was there. Each time she held her hand above it, it sent a tingle up her arm.

Torry picked up speed as she coasted down the slight incline of Minogue Crescent, the wind tugging at the edges of her helmet. She leaned into the movement, weaving smoothly between bins and parked cars, her wheels humming against the concrete. She had her reservations about Cinder's plan but now she could see that she might actually get away clean. No alarms, no shouts, no shadowy figures behind her. Just the city and her skates. She rounded a corner near a sandstone church and glanced over her shoulder. Nothing. A smile tugged at her lips. *Maybe I'm good at this sneaky stuff after all.* She paused to pull up her kneepads, but as she straightened up, a flash of crimson caught her eye.

A sleek red motorcycle eased into view from the opposite end of the street. Two riders, both wearing black helmets with dark visors. They didn't rev the engine or accelerate, they just stopped and watched her. Torry's stomach dropped. She'd seen that bike before. Parked out front of Joseph Inkerman's mansion. She remembered the chrome flame decals on the tank.

'No way,' she said. Torry pushed off hard and ducked into the next street. Her skates clattered over a rough patch of road as she picked up speed. Cars honked, and a man shouted something obscene as she wove through the traffic. Her eyes darted to shop windows, to reflective glass, anything to get a glimpse of what was behind her. The motorcycle was still there. Still following. She veered off the main road and down a tight lane lined with overflowing bins. The stench of rotting fruit and diesel hit her hard. She skated fast, her breath loud in her ears. The lane twisted, narrowed, then spat her out onto a graffiti-covered back street. She ducked into a delivery alley behind an old pub, barely missing a stack of milk crates. At last, when she dared glance back – nothing. No bike and no riders. She stopped beside a chain-link fence, chest heaving, sweat dripping from under her helmet.

'I lost them,' she said, bending over with her hands on her knees, laughing breathlessly in relief. She reached for the pendant under her singlet. It was still there. Still humming with energy.

A milk crate sat upturned against a brick wall. After checking again that she had lost the motorcycle, Torry sat on the crate. Removing her helmet, she wiped the sweat from her brow and leaned back against the cool bricks. She adjusted her knee and elbow pads and, once she had caught her breath, she rolled back out to the streets.

Cinder had told her that if she lost her bearings that she should head towards the water. She could just see a thin line of blue through a gap between two houses. She paused to put her helmet back on. Across the street, a sleek black BMW pulled up. It moved like a shark. Slow, silent, and unmistakably predatory. The car had tinted windows, nearly opaque. The passenger window rolled down. Four men in dark suits sat inside. One with tattoos crawling up his neck. Another adjusting an earpiece. The driver turned in Torry's direction and smiled. Torry didn't wait. She launched off again, wheels thumping against bitumen, heart in her throat. The BMW surged after her.

'You've gotta be kidding me,' she said.

Torry felt the vibrations of the road beneath her wheels as she sped away. For every street, Sydney had two or more back streets and laneways. Torry took advantage of this. She ducked into a narrow lane. Graffiti-covered walls whizzed by in an explosion of colour and urban art. The lane opened onto a street where outdoor cafes spilled onto the sidewalk. Torry thought she had lost her pursuers, but the BMW swerved around the corner a second later, tyres squealing. Diners looked up in shock as Torry zipped past, her roller-skates a blur of motion. She narrowly avoided a collision with a server carrying a tray of coffee, the porcelain clinking dangerously close to disaster.

The driver of the BMW showed no such restraint. He ploughed through the outdoor seating area, scattering tables and chairs like a hurricane, his pursuit unwavering. Torry's heart pounded in her chest, the adrenaline surging through her veins as she left the chaos of the cafe behind. The BMW pursued her relentlessly, its engine growling like an angry beast. The driver's piercing eyes fixed on Torry with an intensity that sent shivers down her spine. He was determined to catch her.

She manoeuvred through the narrow streets with the grace of a dancer, expertly weaving between parked cars and darting past pedestrians. The scent of fresh flowers from a nearby garden mingled with the exhaust fumes of passing vehicles, creating a sensory whirlwind. As they raced downhill, Torry narrowly avoided a collision with a delivery truck, her heart skipping a beat as she swerved around the massive vehicle. The man in the BMW wasn't so lucky; he cursed loudly as he narrowly missed the truck's bumper, his car screaming to a stop. With one last burst of speed, Torry made a daring move, swerving into a narrow alley that led to the waterfront. She leaped down a set of stairs and landed safely, but exhausted at the bottom. The waters of Blackwattle Bay stretched out in front of her.

Torry's roller skates glided along the picturesque waterside promenade. Across the water, Anzac Bridge rose into the skyline. Her breath came in sharp bursts, but she was grinning now. The wind on her face, the salt tang in the air. She skated past couples walking hand-in-hand, joggers, kids with melting ice creams. No one was chasing her. No one was shouting. She was just another figure gliding along the gleaming edge of the bay. Her legs were burning, her lungs tight, but she felt invincible. She reached up and touched the pendant again. It pulsed faintly against her skin, like a second heartbeat. She pushed on, weaving between picnic-goers and cyclists. The mid-afternoon sun was warm on her back. The water shimmered beside her, and for a moment, everything was still. When this was all over, she would love to come back here for a picnic. *I wonder how Cinder is going?* She thought. Seabirds were squawking in the distance. It reminded Torry of home. The squawking grew louder. Torry realised it wasn't just birds, someone was screaming.

Not just someone, lots of someones.

An engine revved.

The BMW clipped her from behind.

Metal slammed into bone and flesh.

Torry flew through the air.

Chapter 40

Inkerman, Inkerman, and Inkerman

'You've a date with the Devil,' the man closest to Marraine said with a sneer.

'The Devil?' Marraine feigned surprise. 'A date with Lucifer himself! That sounds hot! What ever should I wear Dominic?' she asked. Dom looked sideways at her with an amused grin.

'Something red, I would think,' he replied.

The man closest to them grunted angrily, then lunged at Dom. A second man followed close behind his companion, their movements unnaturally quick and jerky. Dom faced off against the approaching duo, brandishing his tomahawks with a lethal confidence. The men, driven by the unnatural thirst for their master's blood, also possessed unnatural strength. Their movements lacked finesse but compensated with an unsettling ferocity.

Marraine, having discarded her boots, moved gracefully. She circled the remaining men. Her eyes focused on their every move as she gauged the best moment to strike. She lunged at the closest zombie; her claws extended. The creature attempted to block her attack, but her strength easily overwhelmed him. Her claws sliced through his defences, leaving deep gashes on his sickly-grey skin. The wounded zombie stumbled backwards, momentarily disoriented. As Marraine dispatched the wounded zombie, she turned her attention to Dom. One of the remaining attackers landed a glancing blow on Dom's shoulder, but the injury seemed to only fuel his determination. With a powerful kick, Dom sent the zombie sprawling to the ground. He sidestepped another attacker. With a swift and calculated motion, he swung his tomahawk, aiming for the neck of a second assailant. The blade connected, severing the head cleanly from its shoulders. The lifeless body crumpled to the floor. Dom's arm was slick with blood and sweat. Another snarling figure lunged from the corner of the room, and he barely had time to swing again. Marraine was a blur beside him, her claws slashing at the horde.

'They just keep coming!' Dom shouted, as the zombie-men forced him back against a wall. Marraine didn't answer. Her eyes flicked around the room. They were penned in. Two of the zombie-men grabbed at Dom. One latched onto his arm. He yelled and drove an elbow into their temple, but a third was already on him.

'Dom!' Marraine shouted, her voice raw. She stepped between him and the swarm, her hands curling into fists. Her shoulders rolled back. Her spine straightened. And then the change began. Bones cracked. Skin rippled like water. Her back arched as muscle tore and re-knit beneath her flesh. Fur erupted from her arms, her jaw elongated, and her fingers stretched. Her growl reverberated around the foyer. Dom fell back against the wall, eyes wide as her transformation finished. Marraine stood there, towering and monstrous, with power coiled in every limb. Her fur bristled, dark and silky. Her eyes glowed like blue embers.

• • • •

'Well, Miss Delacourt – no, Cinder, we are on a first name basis now,' Joseph said, standing at the edge of the shadow of his fig tree. 'We apparently have nothing to hide from each other now, so it only seems proper to lose the formalities.' He waved his hand through the sunlight and a wisp of smoke formed on his skin. 'This is an unforeseen turn of events, but not unfortunate. In fact, I welcome it.' He paced slowly along the boundary of the shadow. 'You obviously know who I am.'

'You're the vampire, Trei,' Angus spat angrily. Joseph laughed and clapped.

'You even know my true name.' he said, nodding encouragingly. 'Well done, boy.'

'You almost had me fooled,' Cinder said. 'You have a heartbeat and everything. That is a neat trick.'

Joseph lifted his shirt and tapped his chest. 'I had a pacemaker implanted so that it would make my blood pump again.'

'Did you want to be more human, Joseph?' Cinder teased. Joseph pulled his shirt down.

'Don't be ridiculous. It was purely for camouflage. It has had another interesting side effect of helping me age more like a human, too. Maybe there is something about it ticking away that has made my body more aware of the passing time.' Joseph turned towards the sleeping child. She wriggled beneath her protective cloth.

Angus stepped forward. 'What do you want with our daughter? If you hurt her, I swear...' he yelled. Joseph stopped and turned back to Cinder and Angus.

'Hurt her?' he asked. 'What on God's forsaken earth makes you think I want to hurt her? I mean her no harm. On the contrary, she is just as precious to me as she is to you. She is the most important creature ever formed. Your daughter is the light at the end of my abyss –, my future. It's true what I told you, Miss Delacourt, I do hate the vampire. I hate what we have become. With every new body we take on, we lose a little. I am now just a diluted version of what I once was, a poor excuse for what I should be.' He looked down at the burn marks on his hand.

'My brothers always had such close minded and small ideas about the prophesy of the New-Mother. They all thought it would be someone like you, Miss Delacourt. Someone who would give birth to a new vampire. I, on the other hand, saw a greater opportunity. Why stop at one? Could not the New-Mother be the mother of an entire new generation of vampire, a nation of vampires?'

He pulled his phone from his pocket and grinned his crooked grin.

'Your daughter is the key to the future. A powerful new race of pure blood vampires. I will take the child, and I will love her as an obedient daughter, then groom myself a wife. No, a queen of a new empire. Finally, I will be able to create real children of my own, not these disgusting watered down, recycled flesh, carbon copies of what I once was but real offspring.'

He looked down at his body in disgust.

'If she gives me daughters, I will create a harem. And when my days are at an end, I will finally be able to leave this God-forsaken place with the knowledge that my dynasty will continue.'

'The hell you will,' Angus said, his fists clenched and the veins in his neck large, blue, and throbbing. He stepped into the shadow of the tree, but something fast moving and solid crashed into his back. A small but powerful arm wrapped around his neck, cutting off his air.

'Hello, father,' said the one-armed boy hanging from Angus's back.

Chapter 41
Broken

Torry lay on the side of the path, rolling from side to side, moaning. She rolled on to her back and watched as a fluffy cloud glided slowly across the blue sky. It looked a little like a teddy bear. The car that had struck her had turned around now. It pulled up alongside her. The driver's side window slid slowly down. The tint was too dark for Torry to see the driver until the window was halfway down. Sunlight fell on the face of a bald man with pale skin and dark sunglasses. He stared at Torry for a moment, then spoke in a voice that was much higher pitched than Torry was expecting.

'Give us the pendant, child, and we don't need to take this any further,' he said, reaching his hand out of the window.

'And why would I do that?' Torry asked, sitting up.

'Because you're hurt, and because my patience is running thin.' The man made a hurry-up gesture with his outstretched hand. Torry laugh, hurting her ribs.

'Hurt?' she said, brushing the dirt from her uniform and standing up. 'There is a player for The Cranberry Hill Crushers call Tiny Dancer and she's anything but Tiny. I swear her hips are made from solid concrete. When Tiny Dancer knocks you down, you know about it.' Torry stretched her arms across her chest and cracked her head from side to side. 'That little nudge with your car was nothin'. A love-tap, my dad would call it.'

The man retracted his hand and turned to say something to the other unseen occupants of the vehicle. All four doors of the car opened together, and four large men all dressed in the same black suits emerged. Each man was holding something long, black, and cylindrical in their hands. The man who exited from the driver's seat spoke again.

'This is your last chance. Hand it over or we will take it from you.'

'This is *your* last chance,' Torry responded. She set her shoulders back and widened her stance. Her face was set in a confident smile. 'Leave while you can still walk upright and don't need to be carried away.'

One of the men on the opposite side of the car took the cylindrical item in both hands. Sliding his hands apart, he revealed something metallic. Squinting, Torry could see the sun reflecting off the sharp edge of a katana. The remaining three men drew their katanas and lay their sayas on the hood of the vehicle.

In the distance, a motorcycle engine revved. The men turned to see a bright red Kawasaki approaching slowly, carrying two riders. The riders wore dark clothes, thick leather boots and matching black helmets with mirrored visors covering their faces.

'More of your friends?' Torry asked. 'Good. I was starting to think this wasn't going to be a fair fight.' Outwardly, she looked confident and stoic, but inwardly, concern was growing. Yes, she had laughed off being hit by the car, but in truth, her right hip throbbed with pain and her leg was numb from the knee down. She had to put all her weight on her left leg to cope with the pain. Facing four men with weapons was going to be hard enough. She had no weapon of her own and she wasn't sure how well her wrist and elbow guards would stand up against katanas. Now there were six of them. The odds were tipping further out of her favour.

· · · ·

Cinder pulled Gemminae from Angus's back. His lack of a second arm allowed him to come away easily. She spun and threw the boy vampire across the yard. He slammed into the wall with a grunt. The sun, now sitting high in the sky, flickered off the blue stone pendant hanging from his neck.

'Like I told you, Miss Delacourt, always have a spare.' Joseph called from the shadows. Angus dropped to his knees, trying to catch his breath. Cinder reached out a hand and helped him up. Together they watched as Gemminae crawled towards his father.

'I had figured out that you had made yourself two sons, but I have to admit, the second pendant is a surprise. Well played Joseph,' Cinder said. Joseph bowed.

'Good my son,' he said, walking to where Gemminae was lifting himself up from the ground.

'Now give me the pendant and get the child.'

'No,' Gemminae said, slapping away Joseph's outstretched hand and stepping quickly into the sunlight. 'If you were too weak and stupid to hold on to yours, why should I give you this one?' He backed away, holding the moon pendant firmly in his one remaining hand.

'You insolent child,' Joseph said, glaring out at him from under a twisted brow. 'I knew I should never have created two of you. You only ever had half a brain each.'

Behind Cinder and Angus, the doors to the house swung open. Ms Chase hurried out to the lawn, her long, black hair flowing behind her.

'I apologise, sir,' she said. 'I was collecting your pendant, but all the commotion woke your son and I'm afraid he took it from me.'

'Never mind that now, Ms Chase. I will deal with my son. You can deal with my guests. These two were just leaving.' Calming herself and straightening her shirt, Ms Chase set her shoulders back and walked across the lawn to where Cinder and Angus were standing.

'If you and your friend would be so kind as to follow me now, Miss Delacourt,' she said, motioning with her arm for Angus and Cinder to walk ahead of her.

'I'm not going anywhere without my daughter,' Angus growled. He took a step forward, but Ms Chase sent her fist into his chest. The force and speed of her blow was so unexpected that Angus fell backwards onto the ground. Ms Chase sent her next punch in Cinder's direction, but Cinder managed to catch her wrist before she could make contact. Cinder pushed her arm away but screamed in pain. Ms Chase had stabbed the pointed heel of her shoe into Cinder's thigh. Cinder ripped the shoe from her leg and slammed her fist into Ms Chase's bony face. Blood exploded from Ms Chase's nose as she flew back towards the house.

Once again, Angus was struggling to catch his breath. The punch to his ribs had knocked the air from his lungs and possibly broken a rib or two. He lay on the ground, holding his side. Joseph sprung to the patch of shadow closest to him, creeping forward like a cat stalking its prey.

'Not what you were expecting, boy?' he whispered. 'Ms Chase has been micro-dosing small amounts of my blood for years now. Not only does it keep her looking just the way I like, it has some other fringe benefits, too.' Angus punched him in the left eye and rolled away. Joseph stumbled back, laughing and blinking.

'Not bad, Mr MacAskill, not bad at all.'

'How dare you touch my father!' Gemminae yelled and leaped on top of Angus. Angus took hold of Gemminae's neck as he pushed his twisted face and fang-filled mouth towards Angus's neck. Cinder ran to them and kicked the one-armed vampire off Angus. Gemminae shrieked as he rolled across the lawn. Angus rolled onto his feet. He sprinted the short distance between Joseph and himself and spear-tackled Joseph into the sunlight. Joseph let out a surprised and painful scream. Flames burst from hands and face – the parts unprotected by his clothing. He took hold of Angus's hair and slammed his smouldering forehead into Angus's face. Angus stumbled but kept hold. Joseph, with Angus still holding tight around his waist, leaped back into the shade. As they landed, Joseph slapped Angus across the left cheek. The sound echoed off the wall of the house. This time, Angus couldn't hold on. He fell to his knees, his ear ringing and black spots forming across his vision. From somewhere inside the house, gunshots rang out.

'Is that a gun in my house, Miss Delacourt?' Joseph yelled in anger. 'What did I tell you about guns?' In his distraction, Angus grabbed his wrist and pulled his arm behind him. Before Joseph could pull it away, Angus brought his elbow down. Joseph's forearm bent, and with a crack, snapped up, facing the wrong way. He lashed out at Angus, screaming and cursing in a multitude of languages. Angus ducked away and rolled for the sunlight.

• • • •

Marraine had lost sight of Dom. In the fighting, they had become separated. When she heard the gun shots, she feared the worst.

'Dom, where are you?' she yelled. Her voice was deep and harsh. She was still in her full Lycan form – tall, muscular, and covered in a glossy layer of black hair. She slashed her claws across the breast of one of the zombie-like men. Four bloody gashes opened up in his shirt. The man stumbled back but slashed at her with his razor-sharp katana. Marraine jumped back, but not quick enough. The blade sliced through her hairy leg. She growled through her sharp teeth. Leaping forward, she took the man's face in her large beast-like hands and slammed his head into the floor, cracking one of Joseph's slate tiles.

'Dom!' she called to him again.

'Up here,' Dom yelled from somewhere upstairs. Marraine leaped up the stairs and ran towards Dom's voice. Ducking to fit under the doorway as she entered a room.

In the room that appeared to be Joseph Inkerman's office, Dom was standing over the body of one of the zombie-like men. He was running his hand over a sheet of cracked glass in the wall. Marraine was slowly transitioning back into her human form. She stood next to him and looked at the glass. There were three bullets lodged in the panel. Directly behind the bullets was a large vase.

'It's just as well the glass is so thick. That looks expensive,' Marraine said. 'Did you get hit?' she asked, turning with concern and looking around Dom's body.

'Why would I?' Dom asked, watching with interest as the hairs on her face retreated under her caramel skin.

'Weren't they shooting at you?' she asked.

'Oh no,' Dom said with a grin. 'That was me.' He pulled a hand-gun from his back pocket.

'Where did that come from?' Marraine asked. She had now returned to her normal height, but there was still a layer of fur over her body.

'Your boyfriend with the Land Rover gave it to me. He's not as bad as I first thought,' Dom said.

'I said *no guns*,' Marraine said, taking the weapon from him. The last remaining of Joseph's zombified guards ran into the room. Before Marraine could turn around, he crashed into her and sent her sprawling across the floor. The man then came for Dom.

Dom stepped to the side and pulled his tomahawk from his belt. He swung the heavy blade down. The man's arm dropped to the floor, severed off at the shoulder. The fingers twitched, nails tapping against the floor. With disbelief, the dazed man watched blood gush from the area where his arm had recently been attached. In grief and rage, he lunged at Dom. Dom lifted him from the ground and threw him into the glass display cabinet. With a pop and a smash, the glass gave way, and the man slammed into the vase. The man fell to the floor. The vase rocked forward.

Marraine slid across the floor as the vase toppled off the shelf and fell. She reached out, getting her fingertips to the vase just in time. The vase hit the ground, but she slowed it just enough to stop it from breaking. She breathed a sigh of relief. Carefully, she lifted the vase and sat it back inside the cabinet. When she was sure it was secure, she stepped back. Dom picked up the gun that she had dropped and made to slip it into his pocket.

'Hey,' Marraine said, 'no guns.'

'It's okay,' Dom said. 'It's out of rounds now, anyway.' He pulled the trigger. A shot rang out. The centuries-old antique vase exploded into a thousand pieces.

• • • •

'This is the problem with these bodies. They take forever to repair themselves and it gets worse with each incarnation,' Joseph said, looking down at his bent arm. He gritted his fanged teeth and forced his arm back into position with a click. 'My first body repaired injuries almost as quickly as they were inflicted. Your child will be like that. You'll see,' he said, looking lustfully towards the child still sleeping on her blanket. Darkened strips of scorched clothing hung from the left side of his body. Red blisters covered one side of his face and hand. He touched the burns that were still smouldering and fell to his knees in exhaustion. 'It was like this the night your father died, Miss Delacourt,' he said, ripping off his burnt and tattered sleeve. 'Do you remember? I do. I wasn't stupid enough to be in the room with your father. I knew he was no ordinary Lycan, and I still had the body of a child. No, I left that up to my brother.' He was talking to Cinder, but she was too occupied with the one-armed Gemminae and the surprisingly strong and fast Ms Chase. Each time she dodged a blow from one, the other would land a hit or a kick. Angus, bruised and bloody, lay prostrate on his back.

'I'm coming Annabelle. Daddy's here, baby girl,' he murmured to himself. Ms Chase kicked out at Cinder again. Cinder grabbed hold of her leg. She took her by the neck with her other hand and lifted her off the ground. She threw Ms Chase in Gemminae's direction. With a loud crack, Ms Chase's head collided with Gemminae's face. They both went down. Joseph was still kneeling in the shadows, watching his hand. The skin was slowly turning to its usual shape and colour.

'I remained outside and had an interesting chat with your step-mother,' he said, continuing with his line of thought. 'Our plan didn't quite work how we thought, but we have arrived at the same point now.' He turned and crawled towards Annabelle's blanket. Grunting, Angus rolled over onto all fours. He crawled to where Gemminae was laying, groping with his remaining hand at a large crack in his forehead. Before Gemminae could register that he was there, Angus stood, took him by the ankle, lifted him, tossed him at Joseph, and fell to his knees. Joseph caught Gemminae, and they tumbled together on the green grass of Joseph's lawn. 'Give it to me,' Joseph yelled, reaching for Gemminae's chest.

'No!' the boy vampire squealed and clawed at his father's face. He rolled away. Joseph took hold of his ankle and dragged him back. Gemminae clawed at the lawn with his single hand.

Cinder, holding her side, limped over to Angus.

'I'm sorry,' she said. 'I wasn't expecting there to be three of them. I had no idea she was so strong.' She motioned towards Ms Chase, who was lying motionless a few metres away. 'How are you going?' she asked, kneeling beside Angus. Blood was flowing from his nose and a split above his right eye. The eye itself was red and swollen shut.

'Bite me,' Angus said, smearing blood away from his nose and spitting it from his mouth.

'What?' Cinder asked, taken aback.

'Bite me,' Angus repeated. 'Take some of my blood. You need your full strength.'

'No,' Cinder said, shaking her head and moving back from him. 'I'm not going to do that. Not ever.'

'You have to,' Angus said, shuffling his broken body towards her. 'It's the only way we're going to get out of this. You need to do it for Annabelle.'

'No!' Cinder insisted again. 'Annabelle will be fine. If I start drinking, I don't know if I'll be able to stop.' Angus took her hand.

'I trust you. It's okay.'

Gemminae kicked his father's face and scurried out of the shadows. He turned to run at Cinder and Angus, but Joseph yelled.

'Wait!'

Angus let go of Cinder's hand and raised his wrist to her face, rubbing his warm skin gently against her lips.

'Drink,' he said.

Chapter 42
Girl Power

Revving, the motorcycle turned and came to a stop. The driver of the BMW turned to one of the other men and said something that Torry couldn't hear. A second man, taller than the driver, with greasy dark hair and a goatee beard, turned and walked towards the new arrivals. The remaining three men watched Torry in silence. Torry tightened the straps on her wrist guards.

'We gonna do this or what?' she said. 'I've got somewhere I need to be. Let's move this along.'

With a graceful movement, the rider swung a leg over the motorcycle and dismounted, as the passenger steadied the bike. Torry's breath caught in her throat as she realised the rider was a woman. Though her features remained hidden behind the visor, there was an undeniable magnetism to her presence, a potent blend of strength and sensuality that sent a shiver down Torry's spine. In that moment, amidst the looming threat of violence, Torry couldn't help but feel a surge of unexpected admiration for the mysterious woman who had entered the fray.

The man with the goatee held up his hands to warn her to stay back, but the rider quickened her pace. She pulled off her helmet, but the tall man blocked Torry's view of her face. With the katana gripped in both hands, he called out for the rider to stop. Before the man had time to react, the woman leaped towards him, swinging her helmet in an arc up over her head and forward, collecting him right in his goatee. Torry heard the crack of his teeth crunching together. The katana dropped from his limp hands, clattering on the road. As the goateed man fell backwards like a tall tree lopped for its timber, the rider swooped down and picked it up. She continued forward.

Placing the katana in her left hand with her helmet, she ruffled out her shoulder-length brown hair.

'Alice!' Torry said.

'Hi cuz. I bet you didn't think you would be happy to see me again so soon.'

'I don't know if I hate you or love you right now,' Torry said.

'As long as I'm stirring up strong emotions, I'm happy,' Alice said, swapping the katana back to her right hand.

The remaining man on the far side of the car ran towards Alice. Alice blocked his swinging katana with the one she had collected. She swung her helmet at his head, but he ducked down and backwards, avoiding it. Seeing him shift all his weight to his back foot, Alice swept low and kicked out his front leg. The man stumbled backwards and fell to the road.

Meanwhile, the two remaining men ran at Torry. Inspired by Alice, Torry pulled off her helmet to use as a shield. The driver was the first to take a swing at her, but Torry move quickly to her left to avoid his katana. Pain shot through her hip, and she fell to her knee. She gritted her teeth to stop from calling out. The second man's sword came down at her head. Torry deflected his blow with the helmet. The blade was strong and sharp. It sliced into the helmet. Torry pushed the katana aside, forcing its owner to move between her and the driver, who was readying to make another strike. As the man was still struggling to free his blade, Torry punched him hard in the groin. With a cry of surprise and agony, the man crumpled to the ground. Torry rolled away, taking her helmet and the stuck weapon with it. She took hold of the katana's handle just in time to deflect the next blow from the driver. Torry pushed the man back. She kicked at the helmet to dislodge it from the blade. The helmet struck the driver in the face. He stumbled backwards and over his accomplice.

Torry turned to see where Alice was. She was still holding her own well enough. Behind her, Torry noticed her passenger had removed her helmet and was walking towards the fight. She was a young woman, maybe around the same age as Torry. Her violet hair framed and shadowed her pale face. A fierce intensity burned in her smoky, kohl-rimmed eyes, as if she were about to unleash a storm. Torry couldn't help but stare. The purple-haired girl's dark lips curved in a smirk. She held out both hands, palms up. Tracing her thumbs in circles around her fingers, she began chanting words that Torry didn't understand.

The two men in front of Torry were on their feet again. Struggling to draw her attention back from the purple-haired girl, Torry prepared to face them.

'Somnius!' the girl yelled and clicked her fingers. Red sparks shot from her fingers. The men in front of Torry fell to the ground, as did the ones fighting Alice. Torry hobbled backwards in surprise.

'You're a witch!' she said. She knew witches existed, but she had never met one, not a real one, anyway. There were people on her roller derby team that claimed to be witches, but this was the first time Torry had seen anyone perform a spell right in front of her. 'Are you the one responsible for the spell that made Angus forget?' she asked, eyeing the girl hesitantly as she came closer.

'Yes,' the girl said, stopping to glare in Alice's direction.

'This is my friend, Eloise,' Alice said.

'We are not friends,' Eloise said, crossing her arms. 'Friends don't lie to each other. Friends don't use each other.'

'I'm sorry,' Alice said. Eloise turned back to Torry.

'It's nice to meet you, Torry, but we need to go. These men are only sleeping, and they will wake very shortly. And before you ask,' she said, seeing the look on Torry's face, 'that trick only works once.'

Chapter 43
Dying for a Drink

Nothing could possibly be this delicious, but it was. Cinder's mouth knew what to do. It was instinct, like a baby suckling at its mother's teat. Her teeth grew and found their mark as simply as a key slipping into a lock. Such warmth and ecstasy flowed over her tongue and down her throat. Cinder had never experienced a drug-induced high. She had never been to those kinds of parties. She had never been to any parties. Cinder wondered if this was a bit like how it felt, but she decided that even to most expensive designer party-drug couldn't possibly feel this good. She knew she should stop, but then again, why? She was more than him now, a dominant, evolved creature, and what was he? He was the one that made her this way. He was the one that had betrayed her and turned her into this monster. Joseph crept closer.

'Drink, Miss Delacourt. Drink! Take it all.' Joseph whispered in her ear, in her mind, deep down in her very being. 'He made you like this. Taking the life of my creator was the greatest joy of my life.'

Then the memories started flowing: Angus's happiest moments. They rushed over Cinder like a crashing wave of joy and nostalgia. Visions of playing with his sister under a garden hose on a hot summer day. His parents were there, they were all happy. Next, she was sitting on a wave on a moonlit ocean, looking out through Angus's eyes at his friends around him. Leafy green trees, their laden branches hanging into calm dark waters. A girl with blue eyes and braces on her teeth. Smiling as the wind rustled the leaves and birds called. Kelly was her name. Her cheeks rosy as they kissed. Then Cinder's own face appeared, the lights of Rome twinkling behind her. "I love you." ...Annabelle crying; she stops when lifted. Her chubby face twisting and her eyes twinkling with recognition.

'Just a few more mouthfuls, Miss Delacourt.' Joseph's voice said, distant, like a radio left on in another room.

It's just like he is falling asleep, Cinder thought as Angus grew limp in her arms. In her minds-eye, they were back on the beach of Heathcote, watching each other across a fire. But she was falling, no – not falling – she was fallen. Cinder was looking down on her lifeless body laying broken on the ground next to the rose bushes of The Big House. But wait, she's not dead! She's alive! Cinder's alive! A maelstrom of conflicting emotions erupted through Cinder's mind. How could this one event be so joyful and so repulsive at one time? Her own anger and misery wrapped around Angus's happy memory like dark tentacles of suffocating smoke. Her eyes shot open, and she sat up.

'Black! I'm sorry, are you alright?' She slapped his face. Angus didn't move. His body lay limp and pale. Cinder slapped him again. Slowly, Angus lifted a hand and flopped it against her face.

'I'll be okay when you stop slapping me,' he said.

'Why did you stop, Miss Delacourt?' Joseph called out. 'You are ever the disappointment.'

'Sorry to disappoint you, boss,' Cinder said. She could feel renewed strength and vitally coursing through her body. 'I needed to keep him alive to find out who Kelly is.'

'Kelly?' Angus asked, his voice raspy. 'Who's Kelly?'

'You tell me. Was she your first kiss or something?'

'Oh, yeah, Kelly. She was on holidays with her family,' Angus said.

'So, summer-fling girl was one of your happiest memories?' Cinder asked, laying him on the ground. Angus sat up. The colour returning to his face.

'She was my first kiss alright, and she had cute braces.'

Seeing that Cinder would not keep draining Angus like they had hoped, Gemminae sprung at him with alarming speed. Cinder's reaction was quicker still. Alive with the energy from Angus's blood, she caught Gemminae by the throat and slammed him into the ground. Still weak from blood-loss, Angus tried to crawl away. He only moved a short distance before his arms gave way under him. Gemminae slashed at Cinder's face with his one hand. Cinder recoiled. Deep scratches marred her cheek.

Angus lay with his face in the grass. Through the blades of green, he could see Cinder and the child-like vampire exchanging blows. His heart, which had stopped for a moment while Cinder was drinking, was thumping in his chest. A high-pitched hum was ringing in his ears and a warming sensation, like water, was flowing through his limbs. He raised his head to see Gemminae kick Cinder across the lawn. Then Gemminae leaped at him again. Gemminae was fast, but Angus moved quicker still, surprising everyone, himself included. He had sprung from the ground and launched himself forward like a frog. He paused for a moment to regain his bearings, then sprinted for the weapon that he had dropped earlier. His legs moved him too quickly, and he overshot his target, needing to turn back. Gemminae was on him as he lifted the double-bladed weapon from the ground. Angus swung desperately, but Gemminae struck the staff with a powerful blow, snapping the weapon in two. One half remained in Angus's hand, but the other half flew out of his grip. Angus stepped back, but Gemminae came on him again. They locked together in a violent embrace. The child-like vampire clung to Angus like a giant parasite, trapping his arms to his sides with his small but powerful legs. Unable to shake off his attacker, Angus launch himself into the air. Man and vampire crashed through the fence around the pool and landed in the water with a great thumping splash.

Cinder got to her feet and turned for the pool. Something caught her leg. She fell forward. Ms Chase had her by her ankle.

'Let me go, you stupid bitch!' Cinder yelled, and kicked out at Ms Chase's not-so-perfect-now face. Ms Chase dodged the barrage and held tight.

Gemminae rose from the water, laughing manically. He held Angus's head under the water with his child-like hand. His eyes burned with malice and glee. The sun reflected off the rippling water, the light warped and cavorting across his twisted vampire face. The half-healed gash across his forehead adding to his grotesque appearance. One half of Angus's broken weapon lay on the grass a few metres to Cinder's right. Her face, like Gemminae's, was also now deformed and ugly. Sharp, black, talon-like claws had formed at the ends of her fingers. She dug them into the ground and pulled herself towards the weapon.

'Black!' she cried out, inching her way forward, dragging Ms Chase with her. 'Black, are you alright?' Reaching out, she snagged the shaft of the weapon with her claw. Ms Chase dug her knees into the dirt and yanked Cinder back.

Cinder could see that Angus had not emerged. She dug her claws into the lawn again and pulled up a clump of dirt and grass. A fat worm wriggled between her fingers as she threw the clump into Ms Chase's face. Ms Chase squealed and let go of Cinder's ankle. She was still trying to spit the dirt from between her teeth when the blade slashed through her throat. Blood dripped from between Ms Chase's fingers as she clutched desperately at the wound. She stumbled to her feet and ran for the house. Cinder watched her go as she got to her knees, then turned for the pool again.

Gemminae looked relaxed now – smug satisfaction on his ugly face. He cracked his neck from side to side.

'You're too late, Miss Delacourt,' he said, wading across the pool. He had just placed his small hand on the edge when Angus rose from the water, like Poseidon rising from the ocean. Water dripped from his powerful arms and thick, dark hair. His wet shirt clung to his muscular torso.

'Black!' Cinder yelled with relief and a flicker of unexpected arousal. Gemminae turned, Angus lunged. The small body of the boy vampire shot up out of the water, pierced by the blade at the end of Angus's weapon. The remaining twin of the pair sired by Trei, the third-born brother, the vampire that now called himself Inkerman, yelled and cursed at them in his native tongue. He screamed, waving his legs and one-remaining arm, like a fish flailing at the end of a fisherman's spear. Angus thrust again. The end of the blade popped out just under Gemminae's left shoulder.

'I'll kill you, you filthy maggots!' he yelled. With his sharp teeth bared, he gripped the staff of the weapon and pulled himself towards Angus. Cinder still held the other half of the weapon. With a running leap, she flew towards Gemminae. With one great swing, she decapitated the small vampire. His head splashed down in the water as she landed on the opposite edge of the pool. The moon pendant that had been hanging from Gemminae's neck slid out from the bottom of his shirt and fell to the water with a plop. Angus snatched it up before it sunk to the bottom. He let Gemminae's lifeless body drop into the water.

'Give it to me or I'll take Annabelle with me into the sunlight.' It was Joseph. He was standing at the edge of the tree's shadow. As the breeze moved through the leaves, small speckles of light flickered across his exposed skin, sending tiny wisps of smoke into the air. He was holding a wriggling bundle in his arms. 'I'll step out of the shadows. You know how that turns out, don't you, Miss Delacourt?'

'The hell you will!' Angus shouted, splashing his way out of the water. Cinder ran around the outside of the pool and stopped him with an outstretched arm.

'Do you trust me, Black?' she asked, looking into his eyes.

'I'm not sure I know you anymore,' he said, pushing her hand aside. Cinder took hold of his hand and pulled him to her. Her lips pressed to his. Initially surprised, he yielded as she cradled his face in her hands.

'It's going to be alright,' she said as she pulled away. Angus wrapped his arms around her. He had waited months to hold her like this again, but now it was as much to hold himself up as it was an offering of affection. He was exhausted. Cinder turned to look at Joseph, his trembling arms wrapped tightly around the small bundle. 'We're leaving now, Joseph, and we're taking the baby with us,' she said.

'She stays here, or she dies now,' Joseph said, leaning forward.

The rage ignited in Angus once more. The edges of his vision were growing dark and cloudy, but he could see his daughter in the arms of a monster. He pulled himself free of Cinder and forced himself forward. He vaulted the pool fence and ran towards Joseph with lightning speed. Joseph and the baby were forced back into the shadow. Joseph stumbled backwards but slashed at Angus's face. Talon-like nails opened four bloody scratches on his cheek. Angus winced with the pain, but he was ready for the next slash. He took hold of Joseph's wrist and slammed his fist into the Joseph's large nose. Joseph twisted around and the bundled baby slipped in his grip.

'Black! Stop!' Cinder yelled. Angus, too deep in his rage, ignored her plea. He struck out at Joseph again, connecting with his ear. Joseph called out in pain, and he lost hold of the bundle for a moment. Something fell to the ground with a thud. A cry rang out. *Not a cry*, Angus thought. *A squeal, something unnatural, unhuman. What have I done?* Angus thought. *Annabelle has never made that sound before. What have I done to my daughter?*

'What's wrong?' Marraine asked, seeing the look on Dom's face 'Are you hurt?'

'No, I'm fine.' Dom kicked away the broken pieces of vase and looked all around the room. Anywhere but at Marraine's exposed body parts. Marraine had returned to her human form now, but her clothes hung off her in torn shreds. She pulled off the last remnants of her shirt and dropped them to the floor. Her jeans had fallen away during the fighting.

'What are you looking at?' Marraine asked as she looked over her shoulder, stepping closer to Dom.

'I'm just checking that there aren't more of them.' Dom's eyes paused on Marraine for a moment before bouncing off again. Marraine put her hands on her hips and stepped closer still.

'You seem a bit uncomfortable, Dominic. Don't tell me you don't like the sight of blood?' She stepped within arms-reach. Lycans didn't heal as quickly as vampires but faster than humans. Marraine's many cuts and scrapes were closing, but she still had blood running from a wound on her shoulder. Dom swallowed before answering.

'It's not the blood. It's just that... um...' He waved his hands in circles in front of his chest and looked down at his feet. 'It's just that you are all...um... exposed.'

'So I am,' Marraine said, looking down at herself. 'Does that make you uncomfortable?' she asked as she reach forward and unbuttoned Dom's shirt.

'What are you doing?' Dom asked, finally looking straight at Marraine.

'I was just thinking you might be more comfortable if we both had our bodies showing.'

'I'm not sure if that's helping,' Dom said, blushing. Marraine undid the last button and pushed herself against Dom. Skin to skin.

'Dom,' she said, looking up into his eyes. Dom placed his hands on her hips.

'Yes, Marraine?' he asked, returning her gaze. Marraine pulled his shirt off one of his broad shoulders. She could feel his heart pounding in his chest. Standing on the tips of her toes so she could place her mouth next to his ear, she whispered.

'Do you think you should give me your shirt?'

'What?' Dom asked, his voice cracking.

'Your shirt Dominic, can I wear it?'

'Oh yes, yes, my shirt. Good idea,' Dom said, stepping back and pulling the shirt off his other shoulder. He gave his shirt to Marraine and watched her put it on.

'Oh shit,' he said, suddenly remembering why they were here. 'We need to find Cinder before Black does.'

'I really don't think he is going to kill her,' Marraine said, buttoning the shirt. Outside, someone was yelling, a woman. Cinder was yelling.

'No, Black! Stop!'

Dom and Marraine ran towards the sound. There was a trail of blood that led down the hallway and out to the garden.

$$\bullet\ \bullet\ \bullet\ \bullet$$

Joseph, still holding the bundle of material, was blocking Angus's view of Annabelle. He pushed Joseph to the side and realised that he was laughing. His daughter was badly hurt, and this monster was laughing! He had never hated a person or creature more than he hated Joseph Inkerman in that moment. He wrapped his hands around Joseph's neck and looked down at his daughter.

'Help her, Cinder!' he yelled, but Cinder was standing beside him.

'She's fine. Annabelle is fine,' she said, resting a reassuring hand on his shoulder.

Angus looked down at where the horrible noise was coming from. A strange creature was on its back, squirming in the grass, four legs in the air. A wriggling curly tail protruding from its spotted backside.

Chapter 45
Girls in the Park

Lulu sat on a bench under the shade of a large eucalypt, listening to a magpie above her singing. She pulled the collar of her shirt to her nose for the third time in the past five minutes. Cinder had given her some new clothes, but for today's mission, she was wearing her old clothes. They still looked used, thread bare and sun bleached but they smelled much better than they had in a long time. Lulu sniffed again.

The bench was at the top of a grassy embankment. A concrete path snaked away in both directions, disappearing behind raised garden beds. Lulu watched as a group of teenage girls heading home from school walked up the hill towards her, weighed down by their large backpacks full of schoolbooks. Behind them, an athletic young man in small running shorts and a tight singlet was running at a steady pace. Lulu's eyes tracked him as he ran past the girls and up the hill. She craned her neck to watch him round the corner then lost him amongst the gardens. One of the schoolgirls laughed when she saw Lulu's exaggerated look of disappointment. Lulu smiled and waved. The girls giggled, waved back, and hurried up the hill. Lulu turned her attention back to the path. Two women dressed in black were approaching. An uneasy feeling flowed over her. Lulu reached down to a cardboard box that was sitting next to her and pulled it onto her lap with a grunt. It was heavier than it appeared.

The two women were coming closer. Lulu could see their eyes now and could tell they were looking at her. Most people tried to avoid looking directly at her. She took hold of the box and made ready to leave, but spotted a third person. It was another woman, a young woman. Unlike the other two, she was not in black; she, in contrast, was wearing bright yellow and purple. Lulu recognised the young woman as Cinder's friend Torry. Torry was being pulled behind a purple-haired girl, rolling along on her skates. As they approached, Lulu saw that Torry was injured. Dirt-smeared scratches ran across the exposed skin of her arms and legs. She grimaced and groped at her leg with each bump in the path. Lulu sat the box back on the bench and stood to greet them.

'Hey, hey!' she called with a wave. 'I was starting to worry you weren't coming.'

'I got held up, sorry,' Torry said.

'Who's ya friends?' Lulu asked, eyeing the others. Torry let go of her escort and rolled onto the grass at the edge of the path.

'This is my new friend, Eloise' she said, sitting down painfully and unlacing her skates. 'The other one is Alice. She's not a friend, she's family,' she added, pulling off one skate and tossing it on the grass next to her before starting on the other. 'They helped me out with my little hiccup. How did you find me, anyway?' she asked, tossing the second skate next to the first. Alice sat on the grass further up the hill, away from Torry.

'When Eloise found out what I did with the memory stone, she told me I needed to help Angus to make up for what I'd done,' she said, trying to avoid Eloise's disapproving glares. 'We did a tracking spell to find Cinder. We tracked her to that giant house and that's when we saw you skating away. We thought we would follow you for a bit. We assumed you were with Cinder. Then we saw those nut-bags following you.'

'How'd ya track Cinder?' Lulu asked. 'Don't ya need some'n of hers?'

'Yes, we did.' Eloise said, surprised by Lulu's insight.

'Sorry, Eloise, I didn't introduce Lulu,' Torry said. 'She's our Sydney expert.'

'Nice to meet you, Lulu.' Eloise said, 'and yes, you are correct. The spell required something of Cinder's. Alice had a page of one of Cinder's journals.'

'You are a piece of work, aren't you?' Torry said, shaking her head incredulously. 'And you helped her with this?' she asked, turning to Eloise, who was now standing in the shade of a tree on the opposite side of the path.

'I didn't know that was what she was going to do with it,' Eloise said. 'A memory stone can also be used to help you remember things. Alice told me that her uncle was starting to forget his late wife, and that she wanted to help him remember her. I didn't realise that Alice had been reading my spell books. I didn't even know you knew how to read them.' She glared at Alice. Torry turned on Alice, too.

'You used my mum and dad as part of your sick plan too?' she said with such force that pain shot through her hip again. Alice shrank under their accusatory glares.

'I didn't mean... I just thought I could help Angus,' she stammered, but Torry had already looked away, shaking her head in disgust.

'Help yourself to him more like it,' she said. Eloise folded her arms.

'Intent doesn't erase the damage, Alice. You have to understand that.' she said. Alice opened her mouth to reply but was cut off by Lulu, who let out a deep sigh and slumped back onto the bench, placing a protective hand on the cardboard box in her lap.

'Well, ain't this a mess,' she muttered, half to herself. She shifted the box slightly, and a soft rustling came from within. 'Not that I ain't enjoyin' the drama, but we got more important things to worry about.' Alice looked up, frowning.

'Like what?'

Lulu gently lowered the cardboard box to the ground before carefully peeling back the flaps of the box. Inside, nestled in a tangle of old blankets, was a sleeping baby. The group fell silent.

'Is that Annabelle?' Alice asked, getting to her feet. 'What's she doing here?'

'She's having a nice day out with her Aunt Lulu.'

'Cinder thought she would be safer with Lulu today than with either of us,' Torry said, nursing her sore shoulder as she reached for her skates. 'But Lulu's right, we need to work out where we're going next.' Eloise stepped forward. She hesitated for a moment, then crouched beside Torry.

'We will go now, but can I give you something first?' she asked.

'Give me something?' Torry asked. Eloise nodded.

'Yes, a gift.' Eloise said, lifting her eyes to meet Torry's. Torry rolled her shoulders, wincing as her bruises protested.

'I guess that's okay,' she said, a little embarrassed. Eloise reached into the pocket of her jacket and pulled out a small braid of hair, glinting in the dappled sunlight. It shimmered faintly. Strands of purple woven with a thread of something that caught the light unnaturally.

'I made this for Angus, but I'd like you to have it,' Eloise said, offering Torry the braid. 'As an apology. For what I did.'

Torry eyed it warily. 'Is this another spell?'

'Yes, but not the bad kind,' Eloise assured her. 'It's protective. My hair is braided with a Motus spell. If you wear it around your wrist, and you think of me, I will feel your emotion. If you're in danger and you need help, I will know and I will help if I can.' Torry hesitated before reaching for it. She turned it over in her hands, tracing the delicate weave with her fingers.

'Why would you do this?' she asked.

'Because I was part of what happened to Angus. And because I want to make things right. I know this doesn't change what happened, but it can help your family in the future.'

'I think we will be okay without your help, but thank you,' Torry said. Eloise's shoulders relaxed, and she gave a small smile as Torry tied the braid around her wrist. As soon as she secured the knot, a faint warmth spread from the braid, like the ghost of a comforting hand on her skin.

'It was nice to meet you, Torry. I hope one day you might need some magic in your life,' Eloise said and rested her hand on the braid. Torry blushed and turned away, busying herself with tying the laces of her skates together.

'So, are we okay now?' Alice asked. Torry slung her skates over her shoulder and stood, resting her weight on her good leg.

'Let's see if I'm okay with my cousin, shall we?' Torry placed her hand over the braid. 'Tell me Eloise, what emotion am I feeling when I think of Alice?'

'Oh, my,' Eloise said, holding back a giggle.

'Oh, yeah, and before we go,' Torry said, looking from Alice to Eloise. 'I'll have that page of Cinder's journal back too.'

Chapter 46

This Little Piggy

'That's a pig!' Angus said as the small creature rolled onto its feet and ran off around the yard. Angus let go of Joseph's neck and fell to the ground. Joseph crawled away, coughing but still laughing.

'I had two mothers,' Cinder said, smiling and watching the piglet run circles around Joseph's lawn. 'One of them I never knew and one that was indeed a terrible, terrible woman. But for all her failings as a mother, Louvelle did teach me how to play the long game. She also taught me how to manipulate arrogant men.' She ran after the pig, and after rounding it into a corner, she picked it up. 'Both of you were convinced that I was so naïve to bring Annabelle here.' The piglet wriggled and squealed in her arms.

'Well played, Miss Delacourt,' Joseph cried, laying down on the grass and clapping his hands. He sprung at Angus, but Angus rolled away into the sunlight. He pulled the moon pendant from his pocket and tossed it to Cinder.

'This was all for a pig?' he asked, leaning forward with his hand on his knees.

Marraine and Dom burst through the doors into the gardens. Marraine ran and embraced Cinder. The piglet protested about being squashed between them. Dom walked up beside Angus.

'Who's the douche?' he asked, looking at Joseph pacing his way along the edge of the shadow.

'That's Inkerman,' Angus said, nursing what he suspected were several cracked ribs.

'Is he the vampire?' Dom asked, suddenly fitting the puzzle pieces together.

'Of course he's the vampire,' Angus said. 'Who did you think I meant when I said we were coming to kill a vampire?' Dom pulled his tomahawks from his belt. He looked from Cinder to Joseph.

'I thought you meant Cinder.'

'You came here to kill me, Dom?' Cinder asked, looking up in concern.

'Not me,' Dom said, stopping next to Angus. 'I thought he was.' He motioned to Angus. Angus looked back at him incredulously.

'The whole plane ride here and you didn't say anything.'

'You were angry,' Dom offered with a shrug.

'Is that right, Black? Did you come here to kill me?' Cinder asked, stroking the nose of the piglet that was now becoming more comfortable with the situation.

'No!' Angus yelled, holding his ribs again. 'I came here to kill Inkerman, or Trei, or whatever he's calling himself. You sent us that message to let us know that he was here.'

'Well, let's get on with it then,' Dom said.

'Yes, let's,' Joseph jeered. 'Come get me, boy. I'm right here.'

'Leave him,' Cinder said. Marraine, who was still holding her, took a step back.

'Are you sure?' she asked.

'Yes, leave him,' Cinder said louder.

'Leave him?' Angus said, limping towards Cinder. 'Did you hear what he wants to do to our little girl? He wants to use her and manipulate her. He needs to die.'

'Black, if we start killing every man that wants to use or manipulate our daughter, the bodies will stack up to the moon,' Cinder said. 'You're the father of a daughter. You need to realise that most of the men she meets will want to take advantage of her.'

'But he's a vampire – a monster.' As soon as the words left Angus's mouth, he wished he could take them back. Behind him, Dom cringed. Even he knew Angus had made a mistake. Cinder stroked the piglet's head.

'Am I a monster? Is your daughter?' she asked, not looking up.

'That's not what I meant,' Angus said apologetically. Cinder looked up at Marraine and said,

'Let's go.'

Marraine put her arm around Cinder, and they headed towards the house. 'I liked the story you sent us, sweetie. Dom thought it was silly, but I thought it was very clever.'

'Was that you?' Dom asked.

'Yes,' Cinder said, 'the silly story was mine.'

'It was only the story that I didn't like,' Dom said, looking embarrassed. 'I thought the hidden message was cool.'

'So that's it, we're just going to leave him alive?' Angus asked, looking back at Joseph. Joseph smirked back at him. Cinder turned back to look at the man that now looked very small under the branches of the giant fig tree. More than ever, she could see his resemblance to the small boy she had seen in the newspaper clippings.

'He is a powerful man who values precious things,' she said, 'and while I don't agree with his intentions, he values our daughter most of all.' She looked at Angus with his bruised and swollen face. 'Our daughter is going to need all the help she can get. Maybe it's not a bad idea to have some more people in her corner.'

'She's got her family. Family is enough.' Angus said, still glaring at Joseph as he paced the edge of the shadow. 'We should deal with him now while we can.'

'Black,' Cinder said. when Angus didn't look at her, she said it again, louder. 'Black!'

Angus turned to her.

'I know I'm a vampire. I've accepted that now,' she said. 'But I'm not like them.' Rach's words played in her head. *"If you kill the master, you become the master."* She studied Angus's face. 'Don't make me like them. Please come away.' She kissed the piglet's head and kept walking. Dom came and stood next to Angus.

'So, are we killing him when they go inside?' he whispered. Angus thought for a moment.

'No, not today anyway,' he said. He gave Joseph one last glare, then turned to follow the girls inside.

'I'll come after you and I'll take her, Miss Delacourt,' Joseph called. 'I'll take Annabelle.'

'Thank you for the lessons, Joseph. I'm taking your sword,' Cinder said without looking up. 'The one under your bed. If you come anywhere near my family, I'll cut your big ugly head off.'

'Not if I get to you first,' Dom said. 'I'll cut your *little* ugly head off,' he added, walking backwards, spinning the tomahawks on his fingers.

'Give back my pendant!' Joseph yelled, as they left him in the garden and walked back into his house. 'Miss Delacourt!' he was still yelling as Dom closed the door.

'Hey Cinder,' Dom said. 'You are still called Cinder, aren't you?'

'Yes, Dom. I'm me. I'm Cinder,' she said. 'Hey Dom,' she went on, 'not that I'm complaining, but how is it that you always end up with your shirt off?'

'Just luck, I guess.' Dom shrugged.

'How is taking your top off lucky?' Angus asked. Marraine and Cinder shot each other a look.

'I don't know, Black,' Cinder said. 'I feel lucky to get to see it.'

'Where is she? Where did you stash Annabelle?' Angus asked, suddenly very serious.

'I didn't stash her anywhere,' Cinder said, stepping over the body of one of Joseph's men. 'I left her with my friend Lulu.'

'You left her with some stranger, a homeless woman?' Angus asked.

'Would you have preferred me to bring her here?' Cinder said, looking back at him. 'Besides, Lulu isn't a stranger. I've hired her to be my nanny. She was the perfect person for the job. To the people in Joseph's world, Lulu is less than human. They don't see her. They don't even acknowledge her existence. To them, Lulu is practically invisible. She might not be educated, but she has street smarts. She knows how to disappear into her surroundings.'

'What I would have preferred was for you to leave her at home,' Angus said.

'Well, I think it was a brilliant plan,' Marraine said, touching the piglet's nose. 'Are we keeping this little baby?'

'Yes, of course,' Cinder said, kissing the piglet's head again. 'I couldn't get rid of her now.'

'What are we going to call her?' Marraine asked. Cinder Looked over at Dom.

'I was thinking of calling her Alice,' she said. 'What do you think, Dom?'

'Perfect!' Dom yelled and clapped his hands together. 'Ha, ha!'

'Of course,' Cinder said, looking back at Angus. 'I will need to find a farm for her to live on. Do you know a place, Black?'

'I think our place has had its fill of Alices for the moment,' he said, blushing.

'So, I hear,' Cinder said. 'There is one thing I need to get before we leave,' she added.

'We'll get it. You two go ahead,' Marraine said. 'Dom and I will have a look around here and see if there are any other hidden gems like your boss's pendant.'

'Ex-boss,' Cinder said. 'I don't plan on going back to work on Monday.'

'No?' Dom asked. 'Why's that?' he asked sarcastically.

'Let's just say I found it to be a hostile work environment,' Cinder said. 'Oh, and that reminds me.' She balanced Alice-the-pig on one arm as she fished in her pocket. 'Here.' She handed Dom the moon pendant.

'What's this for?' Dom asked, taking it from her.

'The rest of us already have one,' Cinder said. 'It only seems fair that you have this one.'

'Thanks,' Dom said, looking pleased.

'What was with the gunshots?' Angus asked. Dom looked at Marraine.

'One of Inkerman's guys had a handgun,' he said.

'That's odd,' Cinder said. 'He's very much against guns around his things.'

'I guess it's hard to get good zombie-henchman help these days,' Dom said.

'Did anything get damaged?' Cinder asked, looking around at the bodies on the floor, the cracked plaster above the entrance to the hallway and the ripped and blood-stained tapestries hanging from the walls. Dom and Marraine looked at each other.

'No,' they both said, shaking their heads.

Angus opened the double doors of the entrance for Cinder. As she exited into the bright afternoon sun, she turned back to Dom and Marraine.

'Don't be too long,' she said, 'there are only a few hours before the shadow from the house meets up with Joseph's garden and he'll be able to get back into the house.'

'We'll be quick,' Marraine assured her. 'It's very good to see you again, sweetie.'

'It's good to be seen,' Cinder said, then she and Angus left.

'I bet there are a few bedrooms in this place,' Dom said, looking around then stopping on the exposed skin of Marraine's legs.

'What's wrong, Dominic? Do you need a rest?' she asked.

'That's not what I meant,'

'I know,' Marraine said, taking his hand. 'Come on. Who knows what treasures we might uncover?'

Chapter 47

Love me to life

. . . .

Beneath a sullen, overcast sky, the sand dunes stretched out like a forgotten expanse, their soft, undulating slopes dusted with tufts of resilient grasses. The air was thick with the scent of salt and the faint rustle of the sea breeze weaving through the coarse vegetation. Above, the clouds churned in shades of grey, promising rain that hung in suspense over the horizon. In the distance, a line of pine trees stood as silent sentinels, their dark silhouettes contrasting sharply against the muted tones of sand and sky. Their needles swayed ever so slightly, a subtle motion against the stillness of the landscape. Cinder sat on a sandy peak of the dunes, her hair flicking wildly in the swirling breeze. She slipped off her shoes and socks. She pulled anxiously at the socks before sliding them inside her shoes. Sitting the shoes behind a tuft of grass, she stepped down on to cold sand, her bare feet sinking below the surface. She no longer felt the cold like she once did. Her blood provided no warmth, no life for that matter, yet she still shivered.

Death and rebirth took many things from her. But now, as she looked out at the ocean, a rumbling terror of white foam churning at the edge of an endless nightmare of blues and greens, she realised that she still carried her fears with her. Pushing her shoulders back, she trudged forward. Turning her head, she looked along the long stretch of beach. Behind her, the green shrubs and gently swaying tuffs of grass called, inviting her to retreat into the dunes.

At the far end, the beach curved out into the ocean. A hill, rocky at the base, then lined with trees at the top, rose into the greying blue sky. There was nothing visible now above the tree line, but in Cinder's minds-eye she could still see every detail. Berkley's Manor. Louvelle had reminded people of the proper name when anyone had the indecency to call her home, The Big House. When Cinder thought about it now, she realised that big was not a strong enough word. She stopped at the edge of the wet sand and turned her body towards the now empty hilltop. The Big House was big, it was huge. For her, it had been her world. It had been a home, a school, a prison. She had been born there and died there.

'Poetic,' she said to herself. Still, as she looked to where it had once stood, she was not sure why she had set fire to her home. It was hers again. She had won it back from Louvelle. Perhaps it was because that was the home of Cinder the Lycan and that was not her anymore. Maybe it was simply that now she wanted to destroy things. Perhaps that is what vampires did.

She turned back to the ocean, remembering why she was here. She wanted to prove that she didn't just destroy, that she could heal, repair, grow. The afternoon would soon turn to evening, and the sun would sink below the hills far behind her. She had been sitting out here for hours. It needed to be now, or she would lose the light. Biting her lip, she stepped forward. The cold water rushed to meet her, lapping at her toes. She clenched her hands into fists and continued. As the waves splashed up on her cotton shorts, she wished she had taken the time to buy herself a bathing suit, but it was a spur-of-the-moment decision to come here. When her hooded top moved below the waves and became floppy, wet, and heavy, she cursed her thoughtless wardrobe choice. The sea breeze chilled at her fingers as she groped at the bottom of her top and pushed forward, her tiptoed feet sinking in the churning sand of the ocean floor. To find her bearings, she turned back towards the beach. The sleepy little town of Heathcote sat nestled at the top of the dunes, peaceful as it was when the summer crowds had left. The small collection of shops and townsfolk went about their lives. As always, they were blissfully ignorant of the hidden world in their midst. There had been times when Cinder had held their lives in her hands, but to them, now she was just some crazy girl going for a swim in her clothes, in the cold.

A wave crashed over Cinder's back, pushing her forward and snapping her attention back to the task at hand. She screamed through gritted teeth as she peeled wet strands of hair from her face. Deciding that this was the right spot, she took a deep breath and forced her face below the surface. She assumed a vampire might not need to hold their breath underwater, but she still didn't want to see what it felt like to have lungs full of salty water. Her eyes were closed at first, but she forced them open, and the salt stung. Every instinct told her to pull her head from the water, but she fought against them. Her existence was painful now. What was a bit more?

She could just see her feet on the ocean floor. The sand was smooth and white out here, scattered with small rocks and shells. She was startled the first time a fish swam past her feet but soon realised there were dozens of them, small, translucent-brown, and fast. They were beautiful and soon Cinder felt at peace with them. In fact, she was thankful for the company. A small voice at the back of her mind was screaming for her to lift her head from the water and take a breath, but she found her body didn't need it. She had moved out past the breaking waves now and after several minutes of forcing her head under the surface; she was growing accustomed to the feeling. The salty water was also no longer stinging her eyes. She stretched out her arms and let her feet float up behind her. Soon, she was lying face down on the surface of the water. The fight between her heavy clothing and the buoyancy of her air-filled lungs kept her bobbing up and down with the movement of the water.

Unknown time passed and as much as Cinder appreciated that she was overcoming her fear of the ocean, she had come out here for a reason. There was something out here that she wanted to find. It was a long shot to begin with, but now that she was out here in the swirling current and dying light, the futility of the endeavour was dawning on her. She searched the ocean floor, but all that was out here was rocks, sand, seaweed, and the occasional piece of floating rubbish. Turning around, she paddled back against the current that had carried her down the beach towards her former home.

A school of the small brown fish, startled by her movement, shot away towards the shore, sending a cloud of sand behind them. As Cinder watched the sand settle, the shimmering beams of light falling through the water glinted off something to her left. In the excitement, her mouth came open and a small amount of stinging water went down her throat. She tried to ignore the urge to cough and dropped her feet to the ocean floor. For a moment, she lost sight of the shiny object, then found it again. She sent a desperate hand out towards it, but as she did, she felt something wrap around her body and start pulling her away. *NO! Not now*, she thought. She pulled herself free and forced her hand out, her fingertips almost touching the object. Something pulled her back harder this time. Two arms were around her waist, lifting her out of the ocean.

She was facing the beach, dripping with water. Cinder looked down at the arms around her. They were large and muscular, and she could see one side of a familiar anchor tattoo on one forearm.

'Angus!' she yelled, coughing and spluttering. 'What are you doing?'

'Saving you,' Angus said. His face was close to her ear, and he was puffing hard, His large chest heaving behind her. Cinder squirmed free from his arms and pushed him away. She dove back under the water. Angus lifted her up again. 'Cinder. What are you doing?' he asked, holding her face.

'You don't need to save me all the time. I can look after myself. You need to stop,' she said, pushing him away and smearing the water from her face.

'No,' Angus replied.

'No?' Cinder lost her footing as a wave crashed over her. 'What do you mean no?' she shouted over the rumble as the current pulled her towards the beach.

'I mean, no. I'm never going to choose not to save you,' Angus said.

'But why?' Cinder asked, regaining her footing and moving back to Angus. She looked into his eyes and could see the beginning of tears pooling.

'You know why!' Angus bit back, his voice growing to a shout. Cinder took a step back and watched him for a moment before offering a response.

'No, I don't. I don't know why.'

'Because you are part of me,' he said, staring back at her. 'Asking me to not save you is like asking me to not try to protect my own hand, or my own eyes, or my heart.' He placed his hand over his chest.

'But I don't need you,' Cinder said, almost too quiet for Angus to hear over the crashing waves. The dam in his eyes broke, and a tear rolled down his left cheek.

'I don't need you either,' he said, smearing it away with the heel of his palm. 'In fact, my life would be a whole lot easier without you. But I'm not going to choose easy. I'm choosing love.'

Cinder waded her way towards him and placed an icy hand on his wet face.

'I...,' she dropped her hand to her side and looked into the water. Something glittered on the ocean floor. 'I found it!' she yelled excitedly, pushing Angus away.

Angus stepped back and watched her disappear under the water again. A moment later, she emerged holding something in her hand. Wet, dark hair framed her face. It hung in strands like paint running down her freckled cheeks. In the palm of her outstretched hand was something round and metallic. Angus picked up the object and held it up to the last pink and purple light of the evening.

'You were out here drowning yourself for a ring-pull?' he asked. Cinder's shoulders slumped and her legs gave way under her. The current took her again for a moment and she drifted away from Angus. It's gone, she thought to herself. It's gone and I can never get it back. Cinder screamed up at the sky and splashed her arms in the water. Forcing her legs to move again, she trudged back towards the shore.

'Cin, wait. What's going on?' Angus asked.

'This is pointless,' Cinder said, almost falling over as a wave crashed against the back of her legs. 'I'm so sorry Black.'

'Sorry for what?' Angus said, following her. His black jeans had stiffened in the water and squeaked as he walked. His black t-shirt clung to the curves of his chest and torso.

Great, Cinder thought. *How is it fair that he looks all sexy and I'm a mess?*

'I thought you were drowning.' Angus said. Cinder flopped down on the wet sand and pulled the hair from her face.

'I can't drown. I'M A VAMPIRE!' she called out to the sky. Angus ruffled the water from his shaggy hair and sat down next to her.

'What's going on Cin? You hate the water.'

'I had to go in. I thought I could find it.'

'Find what? This?' Angus was still holding the soda-can ring-pull. He held it up in front of them.

'No, the ring,' Cinder said, resting her head on her knees. 'I'm sorry, Black. I thought I could find it.'

'What ring?' Angus asked.

'Your mother's ring,' she said, turning her sad eyes towards him. Angus started to laugh. Cinder blinked the salty water out of her long eyelashes.

'Why is that funny?'

'Why would my mother's ring be in the ocean?' Angus asked, pushing the wet hair from her face. Cinder pulled his hand away and held it.

'I saw you throw it in,' she said.

'Where?' Angus asked

'In there.' Cinder dropped his hand and gestured out to the ocean. 'The night that I burnt the Big House down.'

'So, it was you that lit the fire,' Angus said.

'Yes, of course it was me. I was waiting in the dunes to talk to you, and I saw you throw your mother's ring into the ocean. I thought I could find it,' Cinder said. Angus took her hand again and held it to his chest.

'Why would I throw away something so precious?' he asked.

'Because you were angry. I don't know, you tell me, you did it.'

'So let me get this straight,' Angus said, reaching his free hand inside his wet T-shirt. 'You think I got so angry that I threw this into the ocean?' he said, pulling a silver chain out from under his shirt. Cinder sat up straight, her eyes wide; unblinking. Angus's mother's ring dangled from the end of the chain.

'But I saw you,' Cinder said, 'You were right there in the water. I could see the sparkle of the ring and then you threw it.'

'I threw away the box,' Angus said, smiling. Cinder reached out and carefully held the ring between her thumb and index finger.

'Oh, Black, I'm so happy, so happy you still have it. I thought it was out there, lost forever.' It was Cinder's turn to laugh. She threw herself back in the sand and rested her hands on her chest. Angus Lifted the chain over his neck and carefully removed the ring.

'Walk with me,' he said. He stood and offered his free hand to Cinder. She took it and he lifted her to her feet.

They walked together in silence for several minutes. Cinder looked up into the now darkening silhouette of the hills above Heathcote. She was happy to once again have that familiar backdrop, no towering buildings here. Out of the corner of her eye, she watched Angus as he walked. His wet t-shirt clinging to his body. *I miss that body*, she thought to herself. *Those powerful arms around me.* The last light of the day glistened off his arms and twinkled in his dark brown eyes.

'What are you thinking about?' Angus asked, turning to look at her.

'I was just thinking about how much I missed it here,' she said, swivelling her head away. 'I'd forgotten how beautiful it is.' She looked around. Everywhere but back at Angus.

'Yes, beautiful,' he said, his eyes fixed on her.

'Where is Annabelle?' Cinder asked, changing the subject.

'She's with Torry. She offered to watch her tonight.'

'We owe Torry a lot, don't we?' Cinder said, turning to look in the direction of the farm.

'She's been a better parent than I have. That's for sure,' Angus said, continuing to walk up the beach.

'I've missed so much,' Cinder said, following him. *Lust, hatred, warmth, anger, love? How can I feel all these things at once for this man?* She thought as they walked on, leaving two sets of prints in the soft sand. What Angus said next made her question if he had read her mind.

'Uncle Gunn told me something about love, when Torry was in the hospital. It was the first night we...'

'The night we kissed?' Cinder asked.

'Yes.' Angus said, blushing. 'You remember that?'

'I do,' Cinder said, holding her fingers to her lips. 'I don't know if it's my memory or yours. Maybe it's a mix of both. Whichever, it's a good memory.'

'It feels like a lifetime ago,' Angus said.

'It was for me.' Cinder turned to look out to the horizon. Even with her vampire eyes, it was difficult to tell where the ocean ended, and sky begun. 'What did Gunn tell you about love?' she asked, turning back to Angus.

'Basically, he said that love hurts and that it's hard work and that's the point of it,' Angus said.

'Then why would anyone want to be in love?' Cinder asked, moving closer to him.

'Because it's better than the alternative.' Angus reached out his hand and Cinder took it in hers. She turned back to look at the beach, their two sets of prints drifting together to become one.

'I guess you will want me to change my hair back to red,' she said, running the fingers of her free hand through her damp locks. Angus looked at her.

'I liked it red, and I liked it blonde. Now we match,' he said, running his hands through his own black hair. 'It's unlikely that I will get to see your hair grey,' there was a touch of sadness in his voice, 'but I would love it then too.' Cinder squeezed his hand and rested her head on his shoulder.

Together, they strolled along the moonlit beach, the soft caress of the ocean breeze tousling their hair. The waves whispered their rhythmic serenade. They ascended the sand dunes, the shifting grains beneath their feet. Moonlight bathed the dunes in a silvery glow, casting elongated shadows. At the top of the dunes, they stopped to look back out over the ocean.

'I'm glad that you have the ring. I wish now I could find my journal too,' Cinder said.

'I have it,' Angus said.

'Where did you find it?' Cinder asked. 'I searched the basement of The Big House. I thought it must have burned.'

'You left it under my bed,' Angus said, resting his arm over her shoulder.

'Where is it now?'

'In my room. Do you want to come and get it?'

'Why, Angus MacAskill,' Cinder said, batting her eyelids, 'did you just invite me back to your room?'

'It's your room, too, if you want. The ring too.' Angus said. Cinder slipped out from under his arm.

'I'm not sure about the ring yet,' she said, turning away from the ocean to look at the town. 'I need to get to know who I am again as myself before I can decide if I can be with someone.'

'I understand.' Angus said, turning to look at Heathcote too.

'Will you run with me, Black?' Cinder asked.

'Why do you want to run? You just got back?'

'Not run away. Just run. Together.' Cinder clarified.

'There's no way I can keep up with you.' Angus said.

'There is one way.'

Chapter 48

The Queen Returns

Flashes of colourful light danced across Angus's vision. He held Cinder's wet clothes bunched in his fists as tingling electricity coursed along his fingers. 'I wasn't sure if you were going to stop,' he said, as his body vibrated with energy. Cinder pulled back from him and grinned, baring her sharp, blood-soaked teeth in the night, then turned on her heel and sprinted away. Her bare feet kicked up sand as she darted up the dunes, her soaked clothes clinging to her as she moved. Angus took off after her, his heart pounding in his ears, but his legs felt light, his strides longer and faster than they had ever been. He shouldn't have been able to keep up with her, not with what she was now, but somehow, he did. Cinder leapt effortlessly over a fallen tree branch, her body fluid and powerful. Angus followed, his muscles straining but responsive. He could feel it now, the remnants of her bite, the way her power still pulsed faintly within him. It wasn't just adrenaline. It was fire in his veins, supercharging his muscles.

They cut through the hills of Heathcote, weaving between the towering pines and the dry shrubs that littered the landscape. The town quickly disappeared behind them. Ahead lay the winding path back to the farm. The scent of rain still clung to the air, though the clouds held off, hovering over them like a silent audience. Cinder let out a breathless laugh, the sound carried away by the wind.

'Not bad, Black,' she called over her shoulder.

'Not bad yourself,' Angus shot back, pushing himself harder.

He surged forward, closing the gap between them until they ran side by side, their feet barely touching the ground as they sped through the night. It felt like flying.

For a moment, Cinder forgot everything, forgot what she had lost, what she had become. Here, in the open wild, with Angus running beside her, she was nothing but movement and speed. She was the wind itself. Soon, the farm came into view. The dark outline of the milking shed stood against the backdrop of the hills, the dim glow of the farmhouse windows casting warm rectangles of light onto the grass. It was home, and yet, it was also not. Cinder slowed first, her steps becoming deliberate, controlled. Angus pulled up beside her, panting, hands on his hips as he caught his breath. They stood there for a moment, staring at the place where they shared so many memories.

'Are you coming in?' Angus asked between laboured breaths. Cinder hesitated. She glanced sideways at Angus, his face still damp from the ocean, his dark curls sticking to his forehead. She reached out, slipping her hand into his.

'Yes,' she said. 'I am.' Together, they stepped forward, crossing the threshold back into the place that had been their home.

The guest house smelled more like Angus now than it did when they were staying there together. Angus pushed the door open, stepping into the space they had once shared. Some of the furniture had changed, but the air still held something familiar, something that made Cinder's chest ache. Angus ran a hand through his damp hair.

'I'm going to get changed,' he said and disappeared into the ensuite.

Cinder moved toward the bed, trailing her fingers along the bedside table. Her old journal sat there, worn at the edges, just as she had left it. She picked it up and sat on the bed. The ensuite door was slightly ajar. Cinder glanced towards the gap and froze. She could see Angus in the reflection from the mirror, peeling off his wet shirt. His back was to her, but something about him seemed... different. The lean lines of his body were sharper, the shadows of his muscles more defined. Cinder inhaled sharply and dropped her eyes to the journal.

Angus emerged in a dry t-shirt and jeans, shaking out his damp hair.

'You found it,' he said, nodding towards the journal. Cinder smirked, flipping through the pages.

'It was just sitting there. Have you been reading it?'

'I might have given it a quick look from time to time,' Angus said. Cinder rolled her eyes but said nothing. Instead, she pulled at her wet clothes. Angus sat on the corner of the bed. It was his bed now, but it had been the one that they had shared before Cinder went away.

'There's a bag of your clothes in the wardrobe,' he said. Cinder sat the journal back on the table, stood and walked to the wardrobe. She quickly found the bag and began searching, pulling out clothes and sitting them in a pile on the floor. When she was happy with her selection, she pulled off her wet top. Angus turned and looked the other way. Seeing what he did out of the corner of her eye, Cinder smiled to herself.

'You don't need to look away. It's nothing you haven't seen before. I know for a fact watching me undress is one of your happy memories,' she said, peeling her shorts off her legs. Angus blushed but didn't turn around.

'That was different,' he said. 'We were together then.'

'Even if we're not together, there is always going to be a bond between us,' Cinder said, searching through the collection of her clothes. Angus glanced her way. 'Besides,' Cinder continued. 'I took a look at you in the mirror while you got changed.' Angus looked through the open door of the ensuite. He could just see Cinder's legs in the reflection.

'Seriously?' he asked.

'Yes. Sorry, I have a bit of Marraine in me now, remember?'

'Well, I hope you enjoyed the show.' Angus said, rubbing his hand over the back of his neck

'I didn't not like it,' Cinder teased. Angus turned side on to her and glanced in her direction.

'You've gotten skinny,' he said. Cinder held a t-shirt up to her chest.

'Yes, some of these things are too big for me. Do you think I look better like this, Black?' she asked, seeing Angus's sideways glances.

'I like you however you come, but this...' he trailed off and looked away again.

'But what?' Cinder asked.

'I worry that you're not eating. No, that's not it,' Angus corrected himself. 'I worry about what you need to eat and you're choosing to not eat it.'

Something cold and damp landed on his shoulder. With embarrassed realisation, he pulled Cinder's bra from his shoulder and sat it quickly on the bed next to him. He turned to see where Cinder had been standing, but surprisingly, she was sitting right behind him. She was wearing her t-shirt and, as predicted, it was a size or two too large for her now. She placed her hands on Angus's shoulders and sat her mouth close to his neck.

'Now, now, Mr Angus MacAskill, are you afraid that I want to eat you up?' she whispered as her lips brushed his ear. A shiver ran down his spine. It was painfully exciting to have her this close to him again, sharing the same space, breathing the same air. He reached up and took hold of one of her hands on his shoulder.

'I'm not worried about that,' he said. In truth, some part of him was excited by the idea. Her lips on him as they shared each other's emotions. Not to mention the thrill of that brief rush of sharing her power. 'I'm worried that you're not eating at all.' He turned and looked into her eyes, her face just a breath away from his. Cinder Kissed the top of his head then stood.

'You don't have to worry,' she said. 'Torry introduced me to blood-orange ice-cream. I had two today and I plan on having three tomorrow. Come on.' She pulled him up off the bed. 'Time to run again.'

'Don't you think you should put some pants on first?' Angus asked looking down at her bare legs.'

'Oh, yes.' Cinder ran back to the pile of clothes and hurriedly jumped into some track pants and pushed her feet into her runners. 'Come on, come on,' she said, taking his hand again and pulling him toward the door. She grabbed her journal from the side-table, and they headed for the door.

'Where are we going now?' Angus called, stumbling behind her and struggling to keep up.

'You'll see. Come on.' Cinder flung open the door and set off across the darkened paddock, her hair streaming behind her in the moonlight.

• • • •

The wind rushed over Angus's face, roaring in his ears. He was alive on a whole new level of existence. They ran like shadows through the night. It was hard to catch his breath as they went on, faster and faster. A wire fence on the northern boundary of the farm stood sentry at the top of a gradual rise. Cinder ploughed on. Was she going to turn or run straight through it? Angus tried to slow their approach by taking hold of her hand, but Cinder pulled him forward again. The fence grew larger in front of them. Ten metres away from the fence, Cinder leaped into the sky. Angus called out in exhilaration as Cinder pulled him upwards, their hands clasped tightly. He saw the lights of Heathcote come into view over his shoulder and the shimmering ocean beyond. They cleared the fence and fell with a thud on a grassy verge on the other side. They rolled together, wrapped in a protective embrace before being flung apart by their momentum. Angus skidded to a stop in the moist grass. He thought he heard

Cinder call out in pain, but soon realised that she was laughing, laughing hysterically. He had forgotten how good that sound was.

'Are you alright, Black?' she called out between her laughter.

'I'm fine,' he said, as he lay back looking up at the stars; his chest rapidly rising and falling. 'I'm amazing. How are you?' he asked, turning to see Cinder smearing joyous tears from her eyes.

'I'm happy to be home,' she said after a moment's pause.

'I'm happy you're home, too.' Angus said, getting to his knees.

Cinder sprung to her feet and playfully pushed him to the ground again. 'Hey!' he called out and tried to grab Cinder, but she ran off into the forest.

Angus groaned as he pushed himself up from the damp grass, shaking his head with a wry grin. Cinder's shared power and the thrill of their flight still buzzed through him. Cinder's laughter echoed through the trees, teasing him, daring him to follow. With a quick breath, he sprang to his feet and charged after her, weaving through the towering pines. The scent of resin and damp earth filled his lungs as his boots pounded against the forest floor. Ahead, the flickering shadow of Cinder danced between the trunks like a ghost in the moonlight.

'You can't outrun me forever!' Angus called, half-laughing, half-breathless.

'Watch me!' Cinder said, her voice teasing and full of excitement. She darted up a steep incline, her movements effortless, barely making a sound as she climbed. Angus followed, his legs burning with the effort, but he refused to let her slip away. They crested the rise together; the trees thinning until they stood on the very edge of Vivien's Ridge. Below them, Heathcote sprawled lazily, its streets glowing with golden lights, the ocean beyond shimmering beneath the moon. The wind howled across the ridge, tangling Cinder's hair, making her look even more untamed and free. Angus came to a halt beside her, breathing hard, his hands on his hips.

'I think your power is starting to wear off,' he said between breaths. Cinder smirked, her eyes glinting as she turned to face him.

'You did well to keep up,' she said.

'I'm not letting you out of my sight again.' Silence settled between them, but it wasn't uncomfortable. It was the kind of silence filled with understanding. Angus followed Cinder's gaze as she looked down at Heathcote.

'Did you miss this?' he asked softly. He watched her carefully. There was something in her expression, a depth of emotion he wasn't sure he had seen before. He wanted to say something – to tell her how much he'd missed her, how different everything had been without her – but the words caught in his throat. She turned to look at him.

'Why didn't you come and find me earlier?' she asked. Angus's clenched jaw moved slowly from side to side, as if struggling to hold back a torrent of unspoken words.

'The night you set The Big House ablaze, I got there as soon as I could. There were already giant flames shooting into the sky and exploding windows. I ran into find you but couldn't see or breathe in the smoke. I got second-degree burns to my shoulder trying to get to your room, but there was nothing left of it except heat and flames. Dom and Duncan had to pull me out and hold me back as I watched your home crumble in front of me. I spent three weeks, from sunrise to sun-set, searching the rubble to prove you weren't dead, coming home each night with my hands black and bleeding, soot in my mouth and eyes, clogging my ears and nose. When I didn't find you there, I searched everywhere we had been together. I even went back to Europe, back to Rome. I chased after every red-headed woman on the street like a crazy person. I was gone for months, then Gunn needed me to come back for Annabelle.'

Cinder turned away, gazing out to the horizon, the silver shimmer where the ocean met the sky.

'I'm not sure I was there to find anyway,' she said, ruffling her hair and letting the breeze from the valley roll over her. 'My mind was a churning storm. It wasn't until I was focused on hunting down Gemminae that I started to get back some control.' She turned back to Angus, her lips quirking into a half-smile. Then, without warning, she grabbed his hand and yanked him sideways. 'Do you remember laying on this log?' She pulled him towards a fallen tree trunk at the end of the ridge. 'I'm not sure if my memories of this place are yours or mine, but they're good memories.' She stopped, her smile fading away.

'What's wrong?' Angus asked, continuing forward. A low growl cut through the wind, stopping him in his tracks. He spun, his muscles tensing as figures emerged from the darkness. Many sets of eyes glowed among the trees, and the scent of wild beasts filled the air. Cinder stepped forward.

'Stay,' she commanded, her voice firm. The figures hesitated, their forms sharpening under the moonlight. A pack of Lycans – Cinder's pack. Their lean, powerful bodies stood poised on the edge of the forest, their eyes flicking between Cinder and Angus. Angus clenched his fists, his body taut.

'Friends of yours?' he muttered.

'Don't worry, they won't hurt you. They're mine.' Cinder said, walking towards the pack.

'They are just here to see their queen.' Cinder placed her hand on the head of the closest Lycan. It twisted its head and pushed back against her hand affectionately.

'They are supposed to be locked up.' Angus said, eyeing them suspiciously.

'You've been locking them up?' Cinder turned on Angus and the Lycan closest to him growled. Angus pulled his fists up defensively and glared at the Lycan.

'It was Detective Morgan's idea,' he said. 'Without you here, they were causing all kinds of issues. They kept getting closer to town,' he said as he circled around behind Cinder. Cinder looked around at the gathered Lycan, her shoulders slumped.

'It's my fault,' she said. 'All the time I was away, as much as I tried to ignore it, I just wanted to come home. They were just acting on my desires. I'm sorry.' She looked at each of the gathered pack in turn.

'So, they get an apology, but I don't?' Angus asked. Cinder turned on him.

'An apology for what?' she asked. All the Lycan growled in unison. Angus's eyes darted around them.

'You left me. You left us,' he said.

'Left!' Cinder yelled, walking away from him to the edge of the ridge. 'Oh my god, Black. I died! Remember that?'

'I was there. I could never forget that,' Angus said.

'And you turned me into this.' Cinder's face twisted, and her fangs emerged from her mouth. 'Where is my apology for this?' she demanded.

'I'm sorry,' Angus said. 'But I would do it again to save you.'

'What of me did you save? I don't even know what is really me or not. I've known loneliness in my life, Black, but there is nothing as lonely as being a stranger in your own mind.'

'I was lonely too,' Angus said.

'Oh no. Don't you even go there,' she said, waving her hand at him and walking away. 'Was it terribly lonely between Alice's ample thighs, was it?' she said sarcastically. 'You poor thing.' She stood dangerously close to the edge of the ridge. Angus stepped towards her, but she stopped him with a glare. 'I could survive that fall unscathed. Thanks to you. Like I said before, I don't need you to save me.'

Angus looked down at the forest and the town beyond. 'You weren't here. I didn't know if you were ever coming back.'

'So you just jumped into bed with the next girl that came along?' Cinder said.

'It wasn't like that. It was nice to feel something other than the pain.'

'Well, from what I've heard about her, she had plenty of bits to feel.'

'I was hurting,' Angus said, stepping towards Cinder again, but with each step, the Lycan became more agitated.

'I think you should go, Black,' Cinder said without looking at him. 'I need to spend some time with my pack.'

Angus turned away and moved towards the forest. He stopped at the tree-line and turned back.

'I forgot you and I forgot, Annabelle,' he said, his eyes downcast. 'When I got those memories back, I realised how much I wanted you back, how much I cherished those memories and how I want to spend a lifetime making more of those memories.' He looked to Cinder. Cinder looked up. Their eyes met. Cinder took a step to close the gap between them, but stopped. her eyes dropped to her feet.

'I don't know which memories are my own. I'm not sure I'm ready to create new ones yet.'

Chapter 49

Give My Love to Angus

Cinder sat alone on the fallen tree at the edge of Vivien's Ridge, the wind whispering through the pines. The town of Heathcote lay below, its golden lights twinkling like distant stars. Her pack was running free in the deep, dark areas of the forest, far away from people. She could hear their distant howls and she could feel their joy.

Angus had invited her to return with him to the farm, but she had declined and sent him away. It was good to be alone. She needed this space to collect her thoughts. She held her journal in her lap; the leather worn and softened from years of use. Flipping through the pages, she let the familiar scrawl of her own writing wash over her. Memories, fragments of thoughts, the echo of a life that felt both hers and not hers. Then she found it: a loose sheet tucked between the pages, edges curled, the ink slightly smudged. A poem in someone else's handwriting – Angus's handwriting. Her eyes warmed as she traced the lines with her fingertips. She hadn't seen this before. He must have written it while she was away. The words spilled across the page, raw and unguarded, filled with longing and grief. Her jaw clenched as she read:

The fire took you,
left me ash and ember,
burned the world we built together.
I searched the ruins,
the shadows, the sky,
but you were gone,
just smoke, a lie.
Memories replay
in a cruel dance,

your laughter echoes in empty halls.
I wander through our past,
a phantom grasping
at love that never stalls.
Your touch, a whisper now,
fades like mist
at dawn's reluctant light,
I search for you
in every sunrise,
but find only
a long, lonely night.
When I lost you,
I lost my heart
and

I'm afraid my mind is not far behind

Cinder exhaled, steadying herself. A salty smell permeated the paper, and at first, she thought Angus must have written the poem while wet from the ocean. But as she turned the page under the moonlight, she realised the stains weren't from the sea. They were tears. Angus had cried over this page. A lump formed in her throat. He had mourned her, searched for her, suffered in ways she hadn't fully understood. She clenched the journal to her chest, her mind swirling. She had spent so long burying her emotions, pushing forward, surviving. But this — this was something else. It was far from great writing, but it was a piece of him laid bare, a wound still open. The wind howled over the ridge as she stared down at the town below. She slid the page back inside her journal. Holding the precious book of her memories tight in her fist, she stepped back into the shadows of the forest.

Cinder walked through the farm under the cover of night, her senses heightened by the quiet hum of the world around her. The farmhouse loomed in the moonlight, its windows dark and still. She could smell the remnants of smoke from the fire that had now died to embers. She took her time, letting the sounds of the night wash over her. The distant squawk of a bird, the rustling of unseen creatures in the grass, the soft creak of gates moving in the breeze. Each noise was familiar, grounding her in the place she had once called home. And yet, it felt different now. The land, the buildings, even the air itself. Everything had changed in the time she had been gone. Or perhaps she was the one who had changed.

Her boots crunched lightly against the dirt path as she made her way towards the guesthouse. She hesitated at the porch steps, her fingers ghosting over the wooden railing before she pushed the door open. The inside was dark and quiet, save for the faint sound of breathing. She slipped through the shadows; her steps deliberate. The floorboards squeaked in the stillness as she made her way towards the bed. In the darkness, she could make out the shape of Angus's body under the sheets. His breathing was peaceful and rhythmic. As Cinder moved closer, she could see his exposed shoulders rising and falling to the same rhythm. She watched him for a moment, studying him. The tops of his scars on his back that sat above the line of his sheets. The way his thick hair curved around his ear. His shoulders and arms, with their thick, rope-like muscles. Eventually, her eyes fell on the two small puncture wounds on his neck. The memory of his blood in her mouth stirred deep inside her, and her body tingled with feelings of hunger, excitement, and arousal. She closed her eyes and swallowed the feeling down.

'Black,' she whispered, opening her eyes. 'Are you awake?' she reached out and placed her hand on his shoulder. His skin felt warm against her cold skin. Angus stirred, mumbling something incoherent before blinking groggily. He shifted under the sheets, stretching, then attempted to sit up. In his sleep-drunken state, his legs tangled in the sheets. As he tried to swing them off the bed, he lost his balance. With a startled grunt, he tipped forward. Cinder reacted instantly, her reflexes sharp. She darted forward and caught him before he could crash to the floor. His weight pressed against her as she steadied him, her arms firm around his torso. His skin was hot against hers, and she felt the slow thump of his heartbeat beneath her fingertips.

'Smooth, Black,' she teased, her voice laced with amusement.

'Were you going to bite me?' Angus asked. In the thin sliver of moonlight coming through the curtains, he glimpsed Cinder's retreating fangs. Cinder pulled her lips closed and thought for a moment.

'No. I wanted to, but no. I don't think I should do that again,' she said.

'Well, thanks for not biting me in my sleep, and thanks for saving me from falling on my face,' Angus said, getting to his feet.

'I will always try to save you.' Cinder repeated his words from earlier in the evening. She looked into his sleepy eyes.

'Why?' Angus asked, placing a hand on her hip. Cinder moved in and pushed her body to his.

'You know why,' she said as she took hold of the sheet wrapped around his waist. With a tug, she pulled the sheet free and let it drop to the floor. Angus stood naked, illuminated by the creeping moonlight. With her vampire eyes, Cinder could see every inviting twist and lump, every smooth and warm inch of his body.

'Are you going to stay?' Angus asked. Cinder pushed her lips to his then moved her mouth to his ear.

'Yes,' she said, 'If you'll have me.'

The Heathcote cemetery was quiet in the late afternoon, the golden light of the setting sun filtering through the branches of the old cypress trees. The air carried the salty tang of the ocean, mingling with the scent of drying flowers and aging stone. Cinder knelt before a simple headstone, her fingers brushing against the cool granite as she placed a bouquet of roses at its base. The elegant script on the stone displayed the name, but offered no warmth. No softness. Just a mark of a life that had ended. Behind Cinder, Marraine stood with her arms crossed, watching in silence. Angus and Dom lingered a few paces away, looking out over the ocean to the horizon. Torry had wandered off with Annabelle to visit her mother's grave.

Cinder sat back on her heels. Marraine took a step forward, tilted her head, studying Cinder with a mix of curiosity and disbelief. As she turned to face the headstone, the fading sunlight glinted off her blue eyes.

'She destroyed so many lives,' she said.

'I agree she was a horrible woman,' Cinder admitted, getting to her feet. 'But she saved me in her own way, and she saved Annabelle.'

'She was personally responsible for the death of three out of four of Annabelle's grandparents. Even in death, she doesn't deserve beautiful things,' Marraine said, nudging the bouquet with the toe of her boot.

'These are supermarket roses,' Cinder said. 'Louvelle hated roses, and she'd be rolling over in her grave that I bought her cheap ones.'

'Petty. I like it.' Dom let out a low chuckle. Angus shook his head with a bemused smile. Cinder shrugged.

'She did teach me a lot, most of it awful, but some of it useful. Like how to hold a grudge.'

The four of them stood in quiet reflection for a moment, the sounds of distant waves crashing against the cliffs carrying through the stillness. The town of Heathcote stretched beyond the cemetery, life going on as it always had. After a moment, Cinder exhaled and turned to Marraine.

'There's something I need to talk to you about,' she said. 'Ever since... since I came back... as this, I've been having memories that aren't mine. They're yours.' She turned her back to Dom and Angus. Marraine raised an eyebrow.

'Interesting. And what exactly do you remember?' she asked. Cinder hesitated before answering, then leaned in closer to Marraine.

'I remember... things with you and my mother, and you and my father, and all three of you... together. Things I don't want to remember. Things about you and my parents. Intimate things.' Marraine's lips curled into a wicked grin.

'What can I tell you? We were young, and hot and happy to experiment,' she said. Cinder groaned and rubbed her temples.

'I really, really don't want to think about it,' she said. Dom, who had been listening with increasing interest, grinned broadly.

'Well, I do,' he interjected. 'I want to know everything.'

'Dom!' Cinder exclaimed, turning to glare at him. Angus slapped his shoulder, but he was grinning, too.

'I'll tell you later, sweetie,' Marraine mouthed to Dom.

'I saw that!' Cinder said, turning back to Marraine. 'No-one is going to say anything more about my parents and Marraine. Does everyone understand?' She swept her eyes over the other three. They all nodded in turn.

'What about Marraine and Black?' Dom asked with a mischievous grin. 'Can we talk about that?'

'Seriously?' Angus said, pushing a grinning Dom away from him. 'I've apologised a dozen times for that. And it wasn't even my fault. I couldn't remember Cinder because of the spell, and because of that

I didn't even know who you were.' He motioned towards Marraine. Marraine walked to him and placed her hand on his chest.

'I know, sweetie. It's okay,' she said, pulling something from her pocket. 'Here, have this.' She handed him a card.

'What's this?' Angus asked.

'It's my business card, you know, for the next time you get cursed with a "Forgetting spell" you will have my address,' Marraine said, running her fingernail down his torso. Cinder marched towards them and snatched the card from Marraine's hand.

'I'll take that,' she said, slipping the card into her pocket.

Torry returned, and Angus took Annabelle from her. 'Hey there, Little Red,' he said, kissing her hand. 'Did you go for a walk with Auntie Tor-Tor?' he asked. Annabelle grinned and talked back to him in baby babble.

'We all done here?' Torry asked, keen to move away from Louvelle's grave. Dom sighed, shoved his hands into his pockets, and sat down on Louvelle's headstone.

'Alright, since we're all here,' he said, slapping a beat on the cold stone between his legs. 'I might as well ask. What do we think about what Detective Morgan said? Do we all think the dragon lady is rising from the dead?'

'I'm tempted to dig up her grave and see if she's really down there,' Angus said, staring at the bouquet of roses.

'She's down there,' Marraine said. 'I made sure her body was in the coffin, and I watched them lower her in.'

'Yeah, but Peter said her body disappeared for hours and showed up again drained of blood?' Dom said. Marraine turned to Cinder.

'What do you think about it, sweetie?' she asked. Cinder glanced at her; her expression unreadable.

'I think it's unsettling,' she said. Dom grunted.

'Hell yeah, it's unsettling. Bodies don't just go missing and then come back like that. Someone had to have taken it.'

'But why?' Angus muttered. Marraine strolled past Louvelle's grave, looking down at the ground. She half-leaned, half-sat herself down on Dom's lap.

'If anyone could figure out a way to return from the dead, it'd be Louvelle,' she said. Her words sent a chill down Cinder's spine, though she didn't show it. Instead, she crossed her arms.

'Maybe. But she didn't, did she?' she said. 'If she did, we'd know about it, wouldn't we? She wouldn't just be lurking in the shadows. She'd want us to see her. She'd want us to know she was back.' Marraine hummed thoughtfully.

'Unless she's waiting for something.' A heavy silence followed. The wind picked up, rustling the dry grass and making the branches overhead creak. The cemetery suddenly felt colder, the sun dipping low above the hills. Cinder turned on her heel.

'Let's go,' she said, walking away from the grave. 'I'm done giving her my time.' The others hesitated before following.

As they walked together past the rows of headstones, towards the cemetery gates, Cinder took a deep breath and let it out slowly. 'I thought that coming back here... that it would never feel like home again,' she admitted. 'That I'd never belong anywhere. But I do.' She turned to Angus, her voice softer. 'With you. With all of you.'

As they left the graves behind and walked along the stone path, Marraine placed her arm over Torry's shoulder. Dom pulled Marraine and Torry in next to him, and Marraine rested her head on his shoulder. They walked together in a line; the stones crunching under their feet. Cinder smiled and looked at the others as they made their way past the last row of headstones. The past would always linger, like the ghosts in this graveyard, but she would no longer let it hold any power over her.

'But what if Louvelle does come back?' Dom asked, as he swiped a white tulip from a grave and presented it to Marraine. Marraine glared at him and pointed for him to put it back.

'There's also a bunch of vampires after this little one,' Angus said, hugging Annabelle. 'We know where one of them is, but what if the other's come?'

'Then we handle that like we handle everything,' Cinder said, sliding her arm under Dom's and linking their elbows. Dom quickly dropped the tulip back on the grave.

'And how is that?' Angus asked, walking up beside Cinder. Cinder took his hand in hers. As she did, the last rays of sunlight glinted off the ring on her finger, Angus's mother's ring.

'We do it together,' she said.

Acknowledgments

To my readers, thank you for joining me in this fun, mysterious, and sometimes heartbreaking world that has been floating around in my head for nearly twenty years. I've loved sharing Cinder, Angus, and their friends with you, and though this trilogy brings their central journey to an end, the people of Heathcote still have many stories to tell. Characters like Dom, Torry, and Marraine are clamouring for their own adventures. I also suspect Angus, Cinder, and baby Annabelle will return from time to time. I hope you'll help me keep them alive by sharing these books with others.

A friend of mine likes to say, "You can polish a turd." So here they are, Mark—my polished turds. To my editors: Jenn, who guided me from amateur scribbler to author, and Stef, who has been my chief polisher over the years; I'm deeply grateful. To my beta readers, who helped shape the conclusion of this trilogy, especially my indie author buddy Lindsey Kinsella and my super-fan Megan, thank you. Special mention also to another amazing indie author Liv Evans for the local knowledge you brought to Cinder and Torry running around Sydney. Your insights were invaluable.

We all judge a book by its cover, no matter how the saying goes. I had a vision for this trilogy long before book one was done, and Paul Mah brought that vision to life beautifully. Holding these books in print for the first time was and continues to be surreal. Paul, your work is everything I hoped for.

From the very beginning, I've had a core group cheering me on. Ben and Troy, my alpha-readers and support crew, you helped me silence imposter syndrome and believe I could finish this. To Sarah, Lana, the Fenkins crew, the lunchtime writing club, and my students—you've given me endless encouragement and inspiration.

The indie author community lives by the phrase "A rising tide raises all boats." Publishing independently is rewarding but often overwhelming. The support I have had from others in the community has been invaluable. I owe so much to so many, but I need to mention those that have been there from the start: Renee Conoulty, Michelle Ham, Sarah Cole, and Kristine Fitzgerald. Not only are these four amazing, generous and supportive people, but they're also talented authors. I encourage you to find their books and read them.

Music has been a constant companion on this journey. Bands like Pearl Jam, Foo Fighters, REM, Passenger, and Dermot Kennedy helped me channel my emotions into writing. And while I've never been a young woman, many of my characters are, so I've leaned on the voices of Vera Blue, A Fine Frenzy, London Grammar, Gretta Ray, Gabrielle Aplin, Danielle Durack, Maisie Peters, and Nina Nesbitt to help me find my feminine side. If you'd like a soundtrack for Heathcote, here's one of my Spotify playlists. Perhaps listen while revisiting the trilogy.

Finally, to my family: none of this would have been possible without you. Despite the learning disorder that made reading and writing difficult in childhood, my parents, sisters, and brother helped me discover a love for stories. My boys, Alex and Harvey, were my first audience and urged me to share these tales with the world. And Amanda, my wife; thank you for holding our life together while I lose myself in these fictional worlds, and for still loving me when I return.

It's often said that it takes a village to raise a child. These books are my paper-babies, and many people have been part of raising them. Even if I haven't named you, please know I'm grateful to you all.

Merci - Mulţumesc - Thank you